Allon

Book 8

Divided

Shawn Lamb

Allon Books

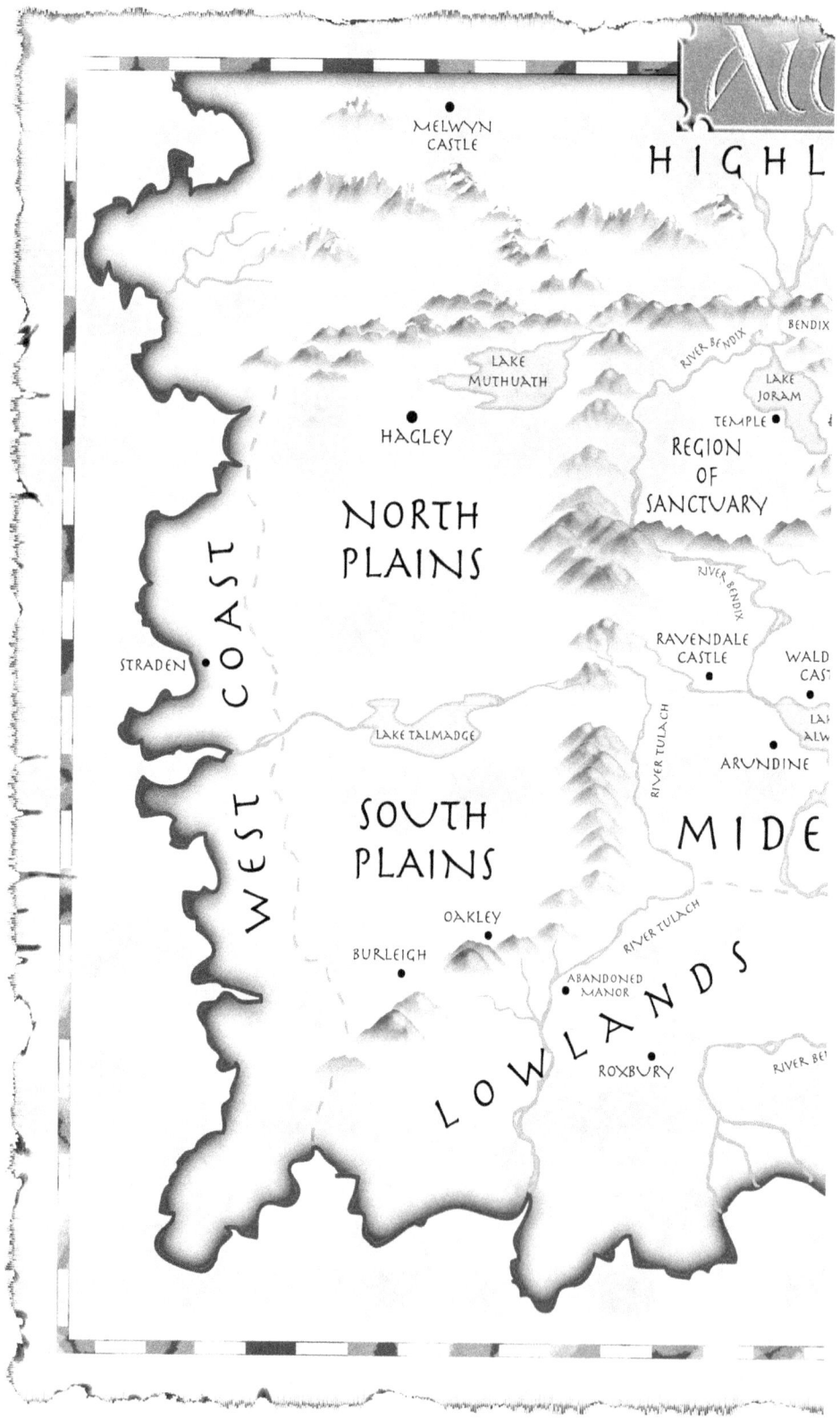

ALLON ~ BOOK 8 ~ DIVIDED by Shawn Lamb
Published by Allon Books
209 Hickory Way Court
Antioch, Tennessee 37013
www.allonbooks.com

Cover design by Robert Lamb

International Standard Book Number: 978-0-9891029-3-3

Other Books by Shawn Lamb

Young Adult Fantasy Fiction
ALLON ~ BOOK 1
Published by Creation House, a division of Charisma Media

Published by Allon Books

ALLON ~ BOOK 2 ~ INSURRECTION
ALLON ~ BOOK 3 ~ HEIR APPARENT
ALLON ~ BOOK 4 ~ A QUESTION OF SOVEREIGNTY
ALLON ~ BOOK 5 ~ GAUNTLET
ALLON ~ BOOK 6 ~ DILEMMA
ALLON ~ BOOK 7 ~ DANGEROUS DECEPTION
PARENT STUDY GUIDE FOR ALLON ~ BOOKS 1-4
THE ACTIVITY BOOK OF ALLON

For Young Readers – ages 8-10
Allon ~ The King's Children series
NECIE AND THE APPLES
TRISTINE'S DORGIRITH ADVENTURE
NIGEL'S BROKEN PROMISE

Historical Fiction
GLENCOE
THE HUGUENOT SWORD

Coming from Allon Books
ALLON ~ BOOK 9 ~ IN PLAIN SIGHT

ALLIES

THE ROYAL FAMILY

King Tyrone
Queen Tristine
Prince Nigel, Tristine's brother, the King's Champion
Princess Mirit, wife of Prince Nigel, the Queen's Champion
Princess Necie, Tristine's younger sister, wife of Lord Angus
Prince Titus, son of Tyrone and Tristine – age 17
Prince Fraser, son of Tyrone and Tristine – age 15
Prince Eli, son of Tyrone and Tristine – age 13
Princess Mikaela, daughter of Tyrone and Tristine – age 10

COUNCIL OF TWELVE – DIVIDED

Vicar Uriah	Region of Sanctuary
Lord Angus, Duke of Allon	Southern Forest
Lord Fagan	Highlands
Baron Mathias	West Coast
Sir Hayden	Lowlands

Captain Chad
General Wess
Valery, daughter of Lord Braden – age 18
Florie, wife of Lord Braden
Ellis, son of Lord Fagan, brother of Jillian – age 18
Jillian, daughter of Lord Fagan, sister of Ellis – age 16
Eric, son of Baron Erasmus
Karly, daughter of General Wess, wife of Eric
Magan, wife of Chad
Lieutenant Dylan, son of Lord Bosley, nephew of General Wess

ALLIES

GUARDIANS

Captain Kell – Commander of the Guardians of Jor'el
Armus – Guardian of Allon
Avatar, Commander of the Elite Jor'ellian Guards
Vidar, an archer
Virgil, a warrior
Egan, Overseer of Prince Titus
Kendrick, Overseer of Prince Nigel
Jade, Overseer of Princess Mikaela
Skylar, Overseer of Prince Eli
Ridge, a ranger
Mahon, a warrior
Gulliver, a Sea Guardian
Eldric, Guardian Physician

TRIO LEADERS

Gresham	Midessex
Priscilla	East Coast
Chase	West Coast
Callie	Northern Forest
Wren	Southern Forest
Alrick	Delta
Zadok	Region of Sanctuary
Nixie	Meadowlands
Barnum	Highlands
Derwin	Lowlands
Mona	North Plains
Elwood	South Plains

OPPOSING FORCES

COUNCIL OF TWELVE – DIVIDED

Sir Gareth	South Plains
Lord Malcolm	North Plains
Baron Erasmus	Delta
Baron Ned	Northern Forest
Baron Hollis	East Coast
Lord Braden	Meadowlands
Lord Bosley	Midessex

Lord Zebulon, former Council Member, Sir Gareth's older brother
Ellan, Princess Tristine's older sister
Garrick, eldest son of Lord Bosley

IMMORTALS

Locan
Mannix
Hueil
Phelan, a Shadow Warrior
Fitch, a shape-shifter

Chapter 1

Suspended between time and space, between the physical world and the heavenlies, lay the Fringe. The grayish expanse was capped by a bright white ceiling obscuring a view of the heavenlies. A semi-glass floor revealed the world below in blurry shapes of muted colors.

From a dim flash of light a lone Guardian appeared, cloaked and hooded. By his height and broad shoulders, he appeared to be a warrior. The hood fell back to reveal his auburn hair and thin beard. Bright yellow eyes darted about and he pulled the hood back up. He no sooner replaced the hood then another dim flash of light appeared. He started to draw his sword but stopped at seeing the one who arrived: another warrior. Only he wore no cloak over his uniform, leaving his red hair and bright green eyes clearly visible for anyone who happened to be nearby.

"A little dangerous coming uncovered, don't you think?" he chided.

"Relax, Locan. Who would be here but the select few?" the newcomer calmly said.

"Which could happen anytime. Especially Vidar," Locan continued his argument and slammed his half-drawn sword back in the scabbard for emphasis.

"You summoned me, remember? What's the problem? She is safe."

Locan drew closer and spoke in a low, husky voice. "I can't keep Vidar and Kell from discovering her escape much longer. When will we leave our posts?"

"Soon," came the nonchalant answer.

"Mannix! No more evasive answers. When?"

Mannix gripped Locan's shoulder. "Take heart. At this moment they are meeting with the first recruits. Once the agreement is established, the discovery will be too late, and we can shed this pretense and join them." He sneered up into bright white ceiling.

"Don't speak so loud. Kell and Vidar have not yet discovered our treachery, but what makes you think Jor'el doesn't already know?"

Mannix sardonically snorted and heaved a careless shrug. "So why hasn't he struck us down while we're standing here?"

"I don't know. But we can't keep this up much longer before paying the ultimate price."

Suspicious, Mannix glared at Locan. "Are you backing out? Afraid of taking that final step?"

"I'm not afraid, just cautious."

Mannix chuckled. "Soon. Now return. When next you see me, it will be time."

Once the light from Locan's departure faded, Mannix again glanced up and snarled before vanishing.

***

In the late autumn night, Sir Gareth, Lord of the South Plains and member of Allon's Council of Twelve, arrived with his elderly brother Lord Zebulon at a remote and abandoned manor house deep in the forest. At seventy-seven Gareth was ten years younger than Zebulon and still a robust figure. His salt and pepper hair receded and his beard and mustache neatly trimmed. Most Allonians aged well and didn't begin to slow down or show signs of age until ninety. Zebulon drew near that age and needed help dismounting, though moved steady once on his feet. Unlike Gareth, he remained clean-shaven and almost bald.

With his usual disdain, Zebulon regarded the manor. "Why pick this place to hold a meeting?"

"When you see who is here and learn why, you will understand."

They proceeded inside. Only a few candles lit the room, and no fire to chase away the night's chill. Several men already assembled at a rough-hewn table. Two bolted to their feet ready to draw when Gareth and Zebulon entered.

"Be at ease, gentlemen," said Gareth.

"Zebulon?" began Erasmus, lord of the Delta province and fellow member of the Council. At age sixty-five his curly white hair was close-cropped and mustache trimmed. The ruddy complexion darkened to the color of an aging rose. The bright blue eyes never dulled, and at present shown with vexation. "How did you get him here?" he asked Gareth.

"I can ask you the same question," chided Zebulon. He waved Erasmus aside to make his way to a chair. His critical eye passed to the others in the room, all fellow members of the Council. Bosley of Midessex, who rose with Erasmus, ready to draw; Hollis of the East Coast was second-in-command of the royal navy, Malcolm of the North Plains, and Braden of the Meadowlands. Zebulon questioned Gareth. "Is this a Council meeting the king is not aware of?"

"Ay, and for a reason that will be made clear very soon."

"I hope so," Malcolm painfully groused. "Night activity and travel is taxing." He squirmed to get comfortable in his chair. Years of illness made him look older than sixty-two, his hair all white and deep lines about the mouth and forehead. His eyes were dulled by constant pain.

Braden sat beside Malcolm and gave the ill lord a supportive squeeze on his arm. "When this is over, I will take you home."

Malcolm patted Braden's hand. "You are as good a friend as your father." He made a plaintive sigh. "I still miss Allard."

"Thank you. I'm trying. Heaven knows I could use his wisdom at home."

"Trouble with Florie?"

"No," he said with a rueful smile. "My wife is well. Valery is the issue. Teenage daughters are vexing."

"I wouldn't know, since I have no children."

"Interesting you should bring up the topic of family," began Gareth with a deliberate tone. He never took a seat, rather stood at the head of the table. "The matter for which I have called you all here concerns the *royal* family."

"Then shouldn't the others be here also?" asked Erasmus.

"Ay. What about Angus, Mathias, Ned, Fagan and Uriah?" added Hollis.

"Don't forget Hayden," said Bosley.

Zebulon growled in anger. "That popping jay should be drawn and quartered. Of all the men to take my place in the Lowlands—"

"Easy, brother," said Gareth. "Once our guest is revealed, we will find a way to deal with Hayden and the others."

"You say that rather ominously, why?" asked Erasmus, now guarded.

Gareth squared his shoulders, as his gaze swept over his fellow Council members. "I called you here because of a past featly we once swore. The one who sits on the throne is not of legitimate birth to hold such honor."

"Tyrone is Jor'el's chosen to be king, same as Ellis was," said Erasmus, his guardedness turning to anger.

Zebulon's lips curled in annoyance. "That half-breed—"

"Take care, you are speaking of the king!"

"*I* am speaking of the queen," rebuffed Gareth. "The half-breed has no royal blood. Only by way of marriage is he even to be considered. But, gentlemen, what of Tristine?"

"What about her? She is of royal blood," said Bosley.

"But not in the order of birth to hold her title of queen."

Erasmus gave a frustrated wave. "Nigel gave up his claim in favor of her and Tyrone."

Gareth smiled in cunning triumph. "Nigel was never crowned but another was."

The surprise apprehension registered in a moment of silence until Hollis spoke. "You mean Ellan?"

"Ay. Ellan. Rightful *crowned* queen of Allon, to whom we all swore fidelity."

"Not I," said Braden.

"Your father did. Would you dishonor his word?"

Braden recoiled at the rebuff. "No, my lord."

Gareth nodded and proceeded. "By right of birth and succession, Ellan is the true queen of Allon, not Tristine, who is third born."

"Ellis made the succession official and Ellan banished for her coup," argued Erasmus. "How can that be changed—?" He stopped when Gareth laughed, and watched him cross the room and open a door.

"My lords, the *rightful* queen of Allon."

Two cloaked and hooded figures entered; one smaller and slender, while the other unusually tall. Upon reaching the table the two paused and the smaller figure removed the hood. Eighteen years had passed since any of them laid eyes on Ellan. Her brown hair pulled back to reveal time had sharpened her features from a twenty-year-old young woman into a mature woman of thirty-eight. The candlelight reflecting in her blue eyes showed she retained the proud and unbending pride she did when crowned. In open challenge, she gazed at each of them. None moved or spoke.

The individual with her stepped forward and scolded them. "Do you not bow to you queen, mortals?" He tossed back his cloak. A Guardian with icy blue eyes and yellow hair sneered at them. He was not a warrior according to his dark suit and armed only with a large dagger.

"A Shadow Warrior," murmured Malcolm.

The Guardian laughed. "I'm better than that. Better than Dagar himself. I am Hueil," he announced. "Now, bow to your queen, insolent worms!"

Hueil, Erasmus more mouthed the name with anxiety than spoke it.

Only a brief pause followed the command before Zebulon stood and bowed at the waist to Ellan. The others did likewise.

"That's better, gentlemen," she said. "My lord Gareth, is this all you were able to assemble?"

"All who could be reasoned with, Your Majesty."

She sent a wry glance to Hueil. "We shall see." She sat in the chair at the head of the table. "Gentlemen, I summoned you here to hold you to your vows. You will help me take back my throne from my upstart sister and her half-breed husband."

"That is a bold request, Madam," said Erasmus.

"It is a just request, my lord."

"In the eyes of some that may well be. However, your father, the king, made a decree absolving you of all claims to the throne."

"How so, my lord? With or without my consent?"

"Without, of course. Ellis was king."

Ellan laughed with ridicule. "You are obviously not familiar with royal law or else you would know that is not possible." Her eyes looked about the room. "What of Lord Allard? He knows the law."

"If it pleases you, Madam, my father is dead five years. I stand in his place among the Council."

"Your name?"

"Braden, Madam."

"I recall your name. How did he die?"

"On a diplomatic mission that turned tragic."

She nodded and proceeded. "Then be informed, gentlemen, royal law stipulates that any renouncement of claim must be made with the person's consent, else it is void."

"The exception is death," said Erasmus. "I know more than you think."

Her smile grew caustic. "I'm hardly dead, my lord."

"You were imprisoned by Jor'el, which could be viewed as good as dead."

"A loophole," she said in annoyance.

"How did you escape?" asked Hollis.

She used a graceful hand to indicate Hueil. "With the help of one who wishes to right an injustice."

"Injustice?" echoed Erasmus, rage mounting. "He claimed to be the god of Tunlund and kidnapped your nephew Prince Titus to start a war!"

She put up a hand to stop the argument. "I am fully aware of everything."

"Then, Madam—"

"Then, Madam, nothing!" she snapped and bolted to her feet. "I am *rightful* queen of Allon and I hold you, Lords of the Council of Twelve, to your vows. If any one of you fails me, I will have all here executed for treason, along with their families! Then confiscate all holdings and take the throne back with whatever means necessary!" She stared at Erasmus. "Do you understand, my lord?"

For a brief moment he regarded her; the implication of her threat unmistakable. He turned aside and gave a feeble nod of acknowledgement.

In great concern, Malcolm seized Erasmus' hand. Erasmus could not look him in the eye as he said, "We have no choice."

"Indeed," said Hollis. He nudged a grim Bosley. "What say you?"

Bosley's voice sounded nervous. "My brother is the king's general. I don't know how I can fight against Wess."

"The king is illegitimate!" declared Ellan, yet her tone softened toward Bosley. "Perhaps you can persuade him. I know Wess is an honorable man, and once he hears the true facts he may be convinced."

Bosley sluggishly nodded.

Ellan addressed Malcolm, Braden and Zebulon. "And you three, gentlemen?"

"You don't need to ask me twice," replied Zebulon. "That cursed half-breed has caused my family enough trouble and heartache. Only I have no means to give you support since he forced me to retire."

Ellan smiled. "At present, some of my loyal followers are convincing Sir Hayden to abandon his post in favor of one more willing."

"Then the Lowlands are mine once again?"

"Indeed, my lord."

He grinned and bowed his head. "Consider the province in your service, Majesty."

Her focus went to Braden and Malcolm, who sat side-by-side.

Braden spoke first. "As you have said, my father was well versed in royal law. His past friendship to your father notwithstanding, he would uphold the law with all he possessed. Count the Meadowlands among your supporters."

"Thank you. Lord Malcolm?"

Malcolm appeared fragile and uncertain and again looked to Erasmus. He couldn't look at Malcolm, but nodded an affirmative.

"Well, my lord?" she repeated her question.

"Ay," came Malcolm's weak reply.

"What of the others, Majesty? If we can convince them, it could be a bloodless coup," said Bosley.

"Ay, Tyrone and Tristine would be forced to abdicate," said Braden.

She flashed a toothy grin of tolerance. "Of course we shall try. Meanwhile, it is prudent to be ready for the alternative." She stood. "Gentlemen, return to your provinces and begin preparations. I'll send word *if* the time comes." She replaced her hood. She and Hueil moved to leave the way they came.

Gareth followed her to the door. "I shall join you shortly, Majesty."

"A peaceful coup isn't what she wants," said Hollis after the door closed.

"Indeed not," said Zebulon with a caustic laugh. "By driving Hayden off and putting me back, the half-breed will have something to say about it, and it won't be without arms."

With dreadful expression and voice, Erasmus spoke. "With one swift, well-placed stroke she is forcing Tyrone to make the first move by holding us to our former pledge and dividing the Council from him."

Braden began to smile with admiration but quelled it. "She is clever."

Hollis shook his head. "Not just clever. Her threats made it clear that with Hueil's help, she will use deadly force against any who oppose her."

Irate, Erasmus sat forward. "So will the king when he learns of this!"

"That half-breed—" began Zebulon in rebuke but interrupted when Erasmus bolted to his feet and spoke.

"He is the king! To uphold one vow we must break another. I do not do so lightly, and tell you, our actions this night have set Allon on the road to civil war!" He knocked the chair over in his effort to depart.

"Gentlemen, we must proceed with all diligence and caution." Gareth took Zebulon's arm to depart. "See everything is put back in place," he said to Braden. The latter nodded and Gareth and Zebulon withdrew.

"Well, I'm impressed," said Zebulon upon exiting the house. "You acted on your accord without help or prodding from me. Well done."

"Did you think I would allow my son's death to go unanswered or your disgrace to be unavenged?"

Zebulon studied Gareth. "To be honest, I wasn't sure. Although his betrayal dealt a severe blow, his execution was unnecessary. I thought forfeiting the Lowlands would spare Loren's life. Alas it did not!"

"This will bring justice to our family." He helped Zebulon to mount.

Inside Braden waited for Bosley and Hollis to depart. Malcolm shifted in his seat with a low groan. "Can you make it to the inn or should we stay here for the night?" he asked Malcolm.

"Staying here is not an option." Malcolm began to stand when a commotion outside the room made him stop.

The door burst open. One of Braden's men entered with a struggling hooded and cloaked person in tow. "I found this spy listening at the window, my lord." He motioned to the window behind Malcolm.

"Who is he?"

"Let go!" The person spoke in an attempted manner to disguise a voice while trying to jerk away.

Braden pulled off the hood, taking the cap beneath it also. A girl of eighteen with a long braid of bright strawberry blond hair glared with defiance in her green eyes. "Valery! What are you doing here?"

"I followed you, what do you think?"

"What?" stammered Malcolm. "Oh, we are undone!"

"We are not!" Braden turned his attention back to his daughter. "You've gone too far this time, girl."

"Me? Who is talking about raising arms against the king?"

Braden's backhand slap sent her staggering sideways, stunned and injured. The violence split her lower lip.

"We are if she talks!" insisted Malcolm.

"She won't talk." Braden seized Valery, which made her cry out in fear. "Afton, take Lord Malcolm home." He pulled her from the room. She tried to resist, but he wouldn't yield and forced her from the house.

Outside he slammed her against the house and pinned her between him and the wall. "One word of this and it will be your last, do you understand?"

She gaped in fearful disbelief. "You would kill me? Your own daughter?"

"I will find a way to keep you silent. For all our sakes. You have no idea of where this can lead."

"Civil war."

Braden didn't reply as he saw Afton help Malcolm to mount. He drew Valery further from the house. "Where is your horse?"

"Behind that tree."

Still keeping a grip on her, he snatched his horse's reins from the bush then went to where she indicated her horse waited. He draped his horse's reins over a low branch before disarming Valery of her sword. He then took off her belt to use as a binding for her hands. "Mount."

"I can't ride like this," she protested.

"I'll lead the horse so you won't escape." He took the reins of her horse and held her arm so she could mount. Once she was astride, he mounted and began leading her horse from the vicinity.

"You treat me cruelly because you believe I will betray you, but what about betraying the king? Or better yet, Grandfather? How do you think he would feel about this?"

"Don't speak to me of my father! What do you know of him? You were a child when he died."

She straightened in the saddle. "I was thirteen and remember him very well. He often spoke of his love for King Ellis and his family."

He snorted in annoyance. "You speak foolishly of love. You know nothing of politics and how the fortunes of power can turn on a royal whim."

"I know Grandfather would not be so easily swayed into taking arms against Tristine, whom he loved like a daughter. Unlike a natural father."

Braden pulled his horse to a stop. "He didn't have a daughter as stubborn, pigheaded and rebellious as you!"

"Rebellious? It's not I who agreed to treason!"

This time when he went to strike, she ducked and he missed. Angered, he snapped the reins and hurried from the forest, forcing her to hold on for dear life.

***

With the abandoned manor located in the Meadowlands, Braden and Valery didn't have far to travel to Mylton. In fact, they arrived home by sunrise. The grand manor stood open and sprawling upon a plain in the heart of the Meadowlands. Defense could be made, but Mylton more reflected the wealth and vast openness of the province.

Braden didn't wait for the grooms before yanking her off the horse and into the house. He continued on his course with complete disinterest to her protests. Even when she stumbled, he pulled her up the stairs.

In the hall of the family quarters they met Florie, an early riser.

"Mama!" cried Valery.

"Braden? What are you doing?" demanded Florie.

He ignored her and continued dragging Valery to her chamber. He went to slam the door closed when Florie entered.

"What is going on? Why are you treating Valery in such a harsh manner?"

"Because she has gone too far in defying me!"

"You're the one who met in secret to plot treason," rebuffed Valery.

This time Braden anticipated Valery's dodge of his assault and caught her under the chin. The blow sent her off her feet and falling hard against the foot of her bed. The impact knocked the wind from her and she gulped to catch her breath.

"Keep your tongue, or I will kill you!"

"Braden!" Florie rushed to Valery. "What has happened?"

His eyes narrowed in threat at his wife. "I advise you to keep your daughter under lock and key, madam. Our very survival depends on it." He left, slamming the door.

Valery couldn't hold back tears and wept.

"What have you done?"

"Not I, Mama. Him! It's worse than we feared." She lifted her hands for Florie to undo the belt. She continued speak in a low, hurried tone. "I followed him like we agreed and surprised to find him and others talking treason. Then *she* arrived."

"She, who?" Florie now held the belt, Valery's hands free.

Valery leaned closer to whisper. "Ellan."

Florie eyes went wide with horror. "The queen's sister?"

Valery nodded. "She wants them to help her take back—" An urgent hand covered her mouth to stop further speech.

"You were discovered and he is furious," she said and Valery nodded. "Do others know about you?"

"Only Lord Malcolm, but he looks so weak. Oh, and Afton."

"I must get you out of here." She helped Valery to stand.

"What of you, Mama? He's already been violent with me."

Florie lead Valery to a back corner of the room. "He wouldn't dare lay a finger on me." She took Valery by the shoulders to look directly at her. "I never told you this because to speak of it is dangerous, but your father knows, so did your grandfather and Vicar Archimedes. I am of royal blood of the house of Tristan, through one of Ellis' uncles, though an illegitimate line." Valery gasped and Florie stopped her from speaking by continuing. "To harm me would be foolish on his part, but you have always taxed him, especially being favored by your grandfather over him. Now he has reason to strike out." She began to search the corner shelves.

Being momentarily speechless, Valery forced the words from her mouth. "I didn't know he is jealous of me."

"Ay," said Florie while still searching. "Being the eldest grandchild, you were naturally favored, but Allard found your shrewd intelligence refreshing, thus he favored you even more. Ah, here it is." She removed the books to uncover a panel. Opening the panel revealed a compartment containing a lever and a small box. She removed the box. "This is the signet ring of my great grandsire Delwin." She opened the box and held out the ring to Valery. "Hide it, and only produce it if your life is at stake. Now put on your belt and take an extra sword from the closet."

Valery followed instructions. Florie put the box back in the compartment and waited for Valery to be armed. She flipped the lever. The corner bookshelf separated by sliding apart, amazing Valery.

"I never knew that was there."

"Nor does your father. Allard's ancestor built it for secret escape during the uncertain time of Grand Master Zared. I know because Allard told me when I first arrived. A moment of pride to share with the descendant of one his family helped." She lit a lantern and gave it to Valery. "Quickly! Follow it to the end."

"Where does it lead?"

"To the forest. Once you are away, find a place of safety and stay there until this over." She embraced and kissed Valery on the forehead. "Jor'el protect you."

"And you, Mama."

"Now, go." She shoved Valery into the passageway. She waited until the light faded then used the lever to close the panel. Once everything was put right, she left the room.

At the end of the hall, Braden spoke to his lieutenant, a coarse man by the name of Oakes. Florie tried to appear nonchalant when turning a different course. Braden's call stopped her departure.

"Did you make her see reason or did you excuse her behavior?"

"I made certain she understands the gravity of the situation."

Braden huffed and stared down at her. "I hope so because I just learned we have visitors. Sir Gareth and Lord Zebulon."

The name stunned her. "Zebulon? But he retired."

"He still visits his brother on occasion. They must have been traveling all night and sought shelter." He noticed her agitation. "Why are you nervous? I thought you said you helped Valery to see reason."

"I did. I'm just surprised. I'll prepare the guest rooms." She left.

In the drawing room, Braden discovered Ellan and Hueil with Zebulon and Gareth. "Majesty. This is an honor," he said with a slight stammer.

"You seem nervous, my lord," said Ellan.

"Surprised. I was only informed of Sir Gareth and Lord Zebulon."

"By my instructions. I wish to keep my presence from being discovered prematurely."

"Of course." Braden caught Hueil's steady stare and turned back to Ellan. "Can I offer Your Majesty food or drink perhaps?"

Ellan hid a smile at Braden's disturbance of Hueil. "No, just a bed." She faked a yawn. "I am fatigued."

"I'll take you to the guest room myself." He bowed and motioned for Ellan to accompany him. The others followed.

Upstairs, Florie emerged from a guest room. Shocked recognition appeared at sight Ellan. She glanced to Braden for clarification.

"My dear, we have more guests than I anticipated," he said.

Florie curtsied. "Welcome. The room is prepared, but I was only told of two guests."

"We will consent to share a room," said Gareth, indicating Zebulon.

"Thank you, my lord," said Florie with a nod. "This way, Madam." Once across the hall, she opened the door. "I hope you will find the accommodations acceptable."

Ellan smiled. "Any bed is more preferable to where I have been lodging these many years."

Before following Ellan, Hueil stared at Florie. She shied away from the Guardian's intense eyes, to speak to Gareth and Zebulon.

"The other room is across the hall, my lords."

At the door to their room, Gareth spoke to Braden and Florie. "You realize silence is expected along with full support?"

"I understand, my lord. You can depend upon me," said Braden.

"If not, we will know where the fault lies." His shut the door.

Florie leaned against a table in the hall to regain her composure. Braden moved beside her, his voice low and thick. "Now you see why she must be dealt with severely?"

She barely managed a whisper. "I must go." She hurried away.

Hueil peeked out of the room. The Guardian's eyes compelling when he waved for Braden. "Where is your wife going?"

"Her prayer room. She always does so when overcome or troubled."

"She is a devout follower of Jor'el?"

"Ay. Sometimes too much," he groused.

"I heard your father was also a man for Jor'el and Allon."

"Ay, but not as zealous as my wife. To Jor'el I mean. Allon was another matter." Braden practically spoke the last sentence to himself.

Hueil surveyed the mortal at hearing the sobriety. "You find fault with his devotion?"

He tried to be noncommittal. "It was sometimes irritating."

"I sense that is an understatement."

Flustered, Braden lashed out, "Take it for what you will." Hueil stopped his departure. Braden found himself staring up into the Guardian's icy blue penetrating stare. It chilled him to the core. He winced and lowered his eyes. Hueil released Braden to leave.

Inside the guest room, Ellan removed her cloak and inspected the bed before sitting on the mattress. She smiled. "Feels very comfortable."

"Like your bed at Waldron?" asked Hueil.

"No, but it will serve. What about Braden? Can he be used?"

Hueil flashed a cunning smile. "He harbors deep-seated resentment I believe can be utilized. However," he continued speaking while investigating the room, "tomorrow you will continue with Gareth and Zebulon. I sense something here that requires further investigation." He paused to look out a window.

"Is that why you changed our plans to come here instead of the Lowlands?"

"Ay. It started with Braden, but being here, I sense a familiarity I've not felt in centuries. Especially from the wife."

"What?"

He shook his head. "Vague, but I will find out."

"While you're here how shall I proceed?"

"You already sent a powerful message. Now, wait for their response. In the meantime, I'll deal with the Guardians and the half-breed."

She flashed a smug smile. "I saw your anger when Gareth spoke of Avatar's promotion. You have some history? In Tunlund, perhaps?"

He stared down at her. "As do you with him from what I hear."

She scowled. "For years I endured his insufferable presence as my Overseer. I hope whatever you plan for him is as devastating as I have for my sister."

"I will come at him in a way he won't suspect and his end will be delightfully ironic." He laughed, full throated and menacing. "Get some rest. Our plan is launched and victory close at hand."

She went and opened the wardrobe. Only a few garments hung in the closet. "Well, I suppose something in here will have to do for the night."

Chapter 2

IN THE REGION OF SANCTUARY, ATOP A GENTLY RISING PLATEAU surrounded by four hills, stood the Temple of Providence. This was only building in Allon that rivaled the splendor and majesty of Waldron Castle. The entire facade of the Temple gleamed in white marble with gold accents. The arch-shaped windows of colored glass were blown and assembled in Midessex. At certain peeks of the day, the Temple reflected the sun's rays in a brilliance of white with a kaleidoscope of gold and rainbow effects dazzling the eyes.

The Fortress of Jor'el was adjacent to the Temple, and built on a grand scale with towering battlements of gleaming marble decorated with symbols of Allon's past. Completely self-contained, The Fortress housed two thousand Jor'ellian Knights and one hundred priests.

Inside a room overlooking the training yard sat the Guardian warrior, Avatar. He stood an imposing seven and a half feet tall, handsome with bronze hair, silver eyes and a small goatee framing his lips. His Guardian uniform altered from the normal tan with beige trimmed to white with gold and purple trim to signify his position as Commander of the Elite

Jor'ellian Guards. He wore a new sword and dagger, both finely crafted with gold, as another sign of his new position.

He read the daily roster. A rap on the door caught his attention. The person entering appeared mortal by his height and build, around twenty-six years of age with red hair and green eyes. He wore a winsome smile.

"Morning, Commander."

"Captain Chad," Avatar returned the greeting.

Chad's smile widened. "I like the title."

"And Magan? What does she say about your promotion?"

Chad took a seat in front of Avatar's desk. "The extra pay will help feed the growing boys." He marveled and shook his head. "I can't believe they're so big for being only two years old, especially Ephraim."

"He is the stronger of the two. He tried to pull off my beard when Magan brought them for a visit the other day."

Chad chuckled. "Ay, he can be a handful." He grew a bit thoughtful. "I must confess, Chandler's quietness concerns me." He leaned forward, his brow leveled. "Do you think something could be wrong with him?"

Avatar set the roster aside and took a deep thoughtful breath before answering. "I didn't sense anything unusual when they were born or since. With Ephraim so dominant, it could be a normal reaction. What does Magan say about Chandler's behavior?"

"She doesn't believe there is anything wrong. But I'd hate to think we were missing something that may cause him trouble later."

"Have you spoken to Uriah?"

"No. He takes such pride in his great-grandsons, I don't want to dampen his spirits with a feeling and nothing confirmed."

Avatar looked baffled. "I thought you and he were getting along well since you married Magan."

"Oh, we are. I mean out of respect for him, not anything amiss in our relationship. I've learned much from him." Chad smiled, which faded slightly. "The birth of the twins was bittersweet with Leslie dying only a few weeks prior. Magan still misses her father. It is our hope the boys will become Jor'ellians and keep the family tradition."

"There are different ways to serve Jor'el than becoming a knight, but," he added at seeing Chad's concern, "I can send for Eldric or Phoebe and get a more certain opinion."

"I appreciate that—" A bright surge of light in room interrupted them. Chad bolted to his feet to draw his sword.

Vidar appeared from the light. The renowned Guardian archer stood a few inches shorter than Avatar with auburn hair and bright copper eyes. He wore the uniform of his leadership station and function, a forest green jerkin, brown cowl, green breeches and brown leather boots.

Avatar snickered and waved for Chad to put up his sword. "Be easy, Captain. He likes to make an entrance."

"I don't think he—or you—will be at ease with what I have to report," chided Vidar. "I don't know how, but when I arrived for daily inspection I discovered Ambrose seriously wounded. He told me the attack came sudden, from behind. Falkner was vanquished during *her* escape."

Indeed, Avatar became troubled about the fate of fellow Guardians, and the implications. "Could he tell you who attacked them?"

"No."

"Who escaped?" asked Chad, curious.

Vidar looked directly at the mortal and replied, "Ellan."

Chad paled with astonishment. "She was imprisoned in a nether dimension with you as her jailer. How is that possible?"

"As I said, I don't know yet! A mortal cannot escape the nether dimension so she had Guardian help." He gave a low sigh of lament. "Falkner was a fine warrior."

"What of Ambrose?" asked Avatar.

"I took him to Melwynn. He will survive."

"Have you told Kell?"

Vidar nodded. "I came here while he went to Waldron to inform the king—" he stopped in mid-sentence with a sudden piqued look.

Avatar became wary of the archer's sudden distraction. "Vidar?"

"Something else is terribly wrong. I must return. Go to Waldron, I'll join you as soon as I can."

Chad shielded his eyes against the light of Vidar's departure.

Avatar's jowls tightened with determination and said, "Place the Guard on full alert. Dispatch a vassal to fetch Nigel and Mirit back from the coast. And have your company meet me at Waldron with all speed!" He vanished in dimension travel.

• ⚜ •

The massive size, strength, and breadth of Waldron Castle rose in stunning splendor in the middle of the plain. Two gatehouses flanked an elaborate oak and wrought iron gate. From the gatehouses stretched fifteen-foot high walls, ending in massive square corner turrets at each intersection. The Grand Courtyard was made of white marble cobblestone with a cascading fountain in the center. Across from the fountain stood the Great Hall, a carved stone structure of grand proportion to impress the visitor with the strength of Allon's King. To the right of the fountain was the Castle Chapel honoring Jor'el.

A two-story enclosure ran from the left front side of the Great Hall leading to a building on the west wall. This corridor served to divide the Guest Quarters from the Family's Private Quarters on the west and south walls. The lower level served as a galley way, while the second story housed Waldron's offices, the King's study, Captain of the Guard's office, and the private quarters of the King's Champion.

In the study, King Tyrone paced in long agitated strides. His half-Guardian heritage gave him the impressive height of six feet eight inches, strength beyond mortal men and stunning gray eyes in contrast to his black hair. It also helped to retard the normal mortal aging process. Now forty-three years of age, he appeared no older than at age twenty-five when he helped Ellis put down Ellan's first coup attempt.

Two individuals watched the king. Kell, the Captain of Jor'el's Guardians, stood seven and half feet in physical perfection with flawless features, golden eyes and black hair. The other, General Wess, a distinguished and virile looking man of fifty-five whose dark hair turned gray at the temples.

"You think she plans another coup?" asked Tyrone.

"I believe it is a possibility, Sire," said Kell.

Light appeared in the room. Wess drew his sword and stepped in front of Tyrone. He lowered his weapon when Avatar appeared from the fading light. The Guardian wore a grim expression.

Tyrone moved from behind Wess. "I take it, you've been told."

"Ay, Sire. I placed the Guards on full alert; had Chad dispatch a vassal to fetch Prince Nigel and to have his company join me here with all speed. Unfortunately, Vidar sensed more trouble and made a hasty return—"

Another flash of light appeared in the study and Vidar arrived.

"This gets annoying! Can't you send advance word or something?" Wess complained to Kell.

Kell didn't reply rather took note of Vidar's vexed and troubled state.

"There is worse news. Hueil has escaped," announced the archer.

Avatar stiffened in brief shock that turned to intense anger. "How?"

Vidar became defensive. "Again, I don't know! There were signs of conflict but I couldn't find Mannix to learn what happened. I assume whomever he assigned to guard Hueil suffered the same fate as Falkner and Ambrose."

The news distressed Kell. "Marshall and Banning were the others."

"Wren's Trio Mates?" asked Vidar in surprise. "You sent them to help Mannix with Hueil?"

Kell nodded, sobriety on his face. "She said Banning was growing lax and influencing Marshall, so I reassigned them."

"I take it she doesn't know of their demise yet."

"No. Nor have I given her new Trio Mates," he said in regret. "What of Locan?"

"I couldn't find him either. But, there is more," said Vidar, warily. "I discovered a breach in the Shadow Warrior nether prison. I sealed it, but not before two hundred escaped."

"How is that possible?" demanded Tyrone, making Vidar recoil with an uncertain shrug. "Captain?" he pressed Kell for an answer.

"Sire, Hueil is from the beginning. Like Armus, Vidar and myself, he is one of the Originals. He was created to function as Guardian Overseer of the scribes and priests directly detailing Jor'el's words and laws. Jor'el entrusted him with great secrets and knowledge, more so than even Dagar, who protected the Almighty's throne. While Dagar's hatred and lust for power made him powerful and evil, Hueil employed his intelligence and subtly, as you saw in Tunlund."

"You admit he can outthink you, Captain of Jor'el's Guardians?"

Although visibly irked by the accusation, Kell tempered his reply. "What I'm saying is we must anticipate his action differently than another foe. He is crafty, and with his knowledge of Ancient secrets, more dangerous than Dagar. Whatever he is planning may involve Ellan and we must keep our wits."

"Wonderful!" chided Avatar. "Hueil, Ellan, and Shadow Warriors."

"Tyrone!" Tristine rushed into the study. Whereas he didn't age, she looked like her thirty-six years would indicate, a pretty mature woman with golden hair and hazel eyes. She appeared greatly upset and indicated a piece of paper she carried.

Armus, her loyal Guardian since birth, followed her. He equaled Kell and Avatar in height, but brawny with brown hair and bright chestnut eyes. He sent his fellow Guardians a look of great warning.

"What's wrong?" asked Tyrone.

"Read it!" She gave him the paper and spoke to the others while he read. "It's from Ellan! She threatens to kill my husband and children and send me to the nether dimension!"

Armus placed a steadying hand on her shoulder.

Tyrone thrust the letter into Kell's hand. "She declares her intent to take back the throne by whatever means necessary."

"How did she escape?" Tristine demanded of Vidar.

Vidar shrugged, shameful of meeting her gaze.

After reading, Kell spoke in an almost apologetic tone. "Sire, her threats, or rather, her claim may be legitimate."

"No!" insisted Tristine. "Father renounced her and decreed her claim to the throne forfeited by her treason."

"She cites an ancient royal law that she did not renounce her claim."

Baffled, she stared at him. "I don't understand. How?"

"Hueil helped to write the laws. He may have found a loophole. To be certain, I suggest another course of action." Kell turned to Tyrone and continued to speak. "You and the royal family go to the Region of Sanctuary and the Fortress under Vicar Uriah's protection—"

"Give Ellan the upper hand? I don't think so, Captain!"

"To consult with the Vicar about the legality of her claim and then decide upon a course of action," he argued. At Tyrone's resistance, he waved the paper. "Will you risk your family?"

Tristine took hold of Tyrone's arm. She gazed imploringly at her husband. "I know Ellan's vindictive nature. I endured it for years and I won't see you or our children suffer at her hand!"

"She may just be posturing to see how we will react. To retreat will show weakness and embolden her." He held her hands. "I know it is a risk, but we can't back down when she first shows her head. So," he continued with resolve, "we leave this afternoon as planned for Garwood and the annual hunting festival. Naturally, we'll keep vigil on the situation. Should something else happen, I'll consider Kell's suggestion."

"Nigel said he and Mirit were going to leave Leith in time for the festival," said Avatar.

"I thought you sent a vassal to fetch them?"

"I did, but that can be altered."

"At least the family will be together if we need to act," said Armus.

"I suppose," she said in reluctant agreement.

Tyrone told Avatar, "Send a new message to Nigel," then to Wess, "Secure Waldron and admit only Chad's company. All else, I will decide."

Wess saluted and left the study. Avatar stepped back and vanished.

"Have you seen Titus this morning?" he asked Tristine.

"No, but he's usually up early for training exercises."

He escorted her to the door. "Continue as you would for departure, I'm going to speak to Titus."

"Shouldn't I be with you? News of Hueil will hit him hard."

"No. This is for he and I to discuss. Unfortunately, situations like this can occur when he is king and he needs to learn to handle them without motherly intervention."

She stiffened with insult. "Are you saying I'm too soft with him?"

"No, only he must learn to rely on his own resolve. Take advice, but not be influenced by emotions. He tends to do that where you and his siblings are concerned."

"And you don't, I suppose?" she chided.

He scowled with a snorted chuckle. "You know what I mean so why pursue an argument?"

"Overly sensitive since it involves her sibling," said Armus.

Tyrone cocked a smile at her. "Like mother, like son."

She huffed and left with Armus.

In the exercise hall of the armory, Titus participated in a wrestling match with another young man. At seventeen years old, Titus stood six feet four inches tall. Being part Guardian, he inherited his father's height, dark brown hair, but mortal colored blue eyes. He wore only breeches; no sock or shoes, and his bare chest muscular and shoulders broad. His opponent was a year older, four inches shorter with chestnut brown hair and teal blue eyes. Even mortal, he appeared strong and capable of matching Titus in muscle and sinew.

The bout took place under the watchful eye of the Guardian warrior Egan, Titus' Overseer. Each member of the royal family had a Guardian assigned at birth to protect them for life. Like all warriors, Egan stood seven and half feet tall, but slender in build with black hair and keen, vivid blue eyes. He watched the young men circle each other on the mat, looking for an opening to attack.

Titus chuckled. "Are you sure you want to go again, Ellis? It will only make it three out of three for me."

Ellis laughed with teasing ridicule. "Your overconfidence will prove your weakness this time."

"Weakness? I could take you down with one arm."

"Ah, relying on your Guardian strength again?"

"I'll do it blindfolded if you like."

"Ah!" Ellis dove at Titus and snatched him around the hips.

Titus grabbed Ellis from above and tried to lift him, but Ellis shifted his weight to one side. In doing so, he drew Titus off balance. Titus braced his feet to regain his stance and wouldn't release Ellis. Again Ellis shifted his weight and this time they broke off.

"I'm not so easy to take down," said Ellis.

"Who said I was trying?" Titus faked a lunge and Ellis jumped back.

"And who said I haven't let you win?"

"What? You wouldn't." He made a real lunge at Ellis, who barely escaped being ensnared.

Ellis grunted with a sardonic smile. "Part of my duties as retainer to the prince royal is to boost your ego."

"Insolent braggart!" This time when Titus lunged, he caught Ellis and they tumbled to the mat. "Now I have you!" His gloating proved short lived, as Ellis made a move in which he ended up on top.

Ellis pinned Titus' arms to the mat. "Insolent braggart, am I? Is that anyway to talk to your future brother-in-law?"

"Jillian will be pleased if I were to beat you to pulp." He kneed Ellis in the back near the kidney, sending him falling to one side.

Ellis cried out in pain and reached to grab his aching back. "Foul!"

"The foul is putting up with your taunting." He scrambled to his feet. Ellis only rose to his knees. "Get up. You're not hurt that bad."

"How do you know how bad a person is injured when you use your extra strength?"

He became concerned. "Did I really hurt you?"

"Ay," came the grunting reply.

Contrite, Titus knelt beside Ellis. "I'm sorry. I didn't mean to."

"I know. Help me up." He grabbed onto Titus' shoulder and gingerly stood. "Well, you can tell Jillian you beat me to a pulp."

"No. She would be cross with me if I hurt you. I feel bad enough."

Ellis made motion to sit on a nearby bench.

Egan came to help. "Should I fetch Eldric, my lord?"

"No. I'll be all right in a few moments."

"Are you done with morning exercises?"

Surprised at hearing Tyrone, Titus whirled about. "Sir! I think so. At least until Ellis recovers," he hastily replied.

"Are you hurt?" Tyrone moved to the bench to examine Ellis.

"It's nothing serious, Sire."

Titus grew sheepish. "I got a little carried away when I kicked him off me during our wrestling bout."

"That can happen if you and I aren't careful," said Tyrone.

"I try to be."

"I don't fault the prince, Sire." Ellis stood yet arched his back in pain. "I goaded him."

"Friendly teasing. We were both doing it," said Titus.

Tyrone chuckled. "I know how that goes." He patted Ellis' shoulder. "Find Eldric and have him apply a soothing balm."

"Really, Sire, I'll be fine."

He shook his head and smiled. "Nigel and Angus have said the same to me, only to be very sore later. Now, go see Eldric."

"Ay, Sire." He gathered his shirt, doublet, stocking and boots. He gave Titus a friendly smile before leaving the armory.

"I really didn't mean to hurt him. He's my best friend," said Titus.

"I know. And someday he'll be your brother-in-law." Tyrone nudged Titus towards his clothes. "Fetch your things and come with me."

Titus pulled on his socks, boots and shirt. He then gathered the rest in his arms to follow Tyrone from the armory. Egan kept a respectful distance as they crossed the compound. Soldiers, Guardians and servants bowed or saluted when they continued through the back yard, into the main building and up to the king's study.

Titus noticed Kell's presence. The Guardian captain acknowledged him with a somber nod. "Sir, is there a reason *you* came to fetch me rather than send a servant? Perhaps the reason Kell is here?" He spoke while putting on his doublet but didn't fasten it closed.

"Ay, and I needed some fresh air." He then spoke to Kell concerning Titus. "Give him the letter."

Titus began reading. His initial curiosity turned to concerned confusion. "I don't understand. I thought she was imprisoned by Jor'el."

"We all did."

Titus asked Kell, "How did she escape?"

"We're not sure, Highness. Vidar is investigating—"

"Investigating? She escaped and is making horrid threats!"

"Steady, Titus," said Tyrone. "The matter is far worse than Ellan; for us and the Guardians." He faced his son and said, "Hueil also escaped."

Titus paled, as every memory of his kidnapping, imprisonment and near sacrifice in Tunlund came crashing back. He had to sit.

Egan sat next to Titus in support of his charge and looked to Kell for confirmation. The captain nodded.

"I realize this is difficult, but we must be prepared for whatever Ellan and Hueil have planned," said Tyrone.

Befuddled, Titus struggled to comprehend. "They are working together?"

"That is a possibility. She had Guardian help since no mortal can escape the nether dimension."

"What are we going to do?"

"Leave for the hunting festival as planned—"

Titus practically leapt to his feet. "What? We can't!"

"Listen to me," insisted Tyrone, and firmly took Titus by the shoulders. "Ellan may be bluffing, so we must feel her out. That is why we'll continue as usual, but keep a close watch on what she does. If we must act to protect our family, it would best for all of us to be together. Remember, Nigel and Mirit will join us at Garwood."

"I suppose." He chewed on his lower lip in consideration. "What about Mother? This letter must have unsettled her."

"Your mother is a strong woman and she agrees with the plan."

"Hard to believe she's bluffing with such threats and Hueil's escape."

"Ay, but the alterative is civil war. Although I will take to the field if needed, I'm not ready to commit to it just yet."

"What about the Council?"

"They may not be aware of her escape yet. Act too hasty and I risk further anger of those harboring misgivings about me. I told Kell to alert the Trio Leaders and closely watch each member. Wisdom and discretion must be used before reacting with force that may not be necessary."

"I understand, sir."

"You must act as normal, and tell no one yet. At Garwood, we'll speak to Angus and Nigel, and wait to hear back from the Trio Leaders."

The young man made a sheepish frown. "That'll be hard with Ellis. I can never keep a secret from him."

Tyrone grinned. "For not being related by blood, he has the same uncanny ability as your grandfather to ferret out trouble."

"Perhaps there was more than one reason Lord Fagan named him in honor of his benefactor," said Kell.

"What makes you say so?"

He replied with a considering tilt to his brow. "Lord Fagan esteemed King Ellis, whom he once believed to be his blood cousin. He is also a man of great faith and insight. He may have foreseen something about his son's future when taking such a liberty to name him after the king."

Titus chuckled. "Don't say that when Ellis can hear you. He loves his father and admired Grandfather and sometimes feels the burden of bearing a king's name."

"Better the name than the responsibility, Highness." Kell looked directly at Titus. Guardian's eyes were not only unusual in color, but also keen in perception.

For a moment, Titus absorbed the implication. Egan's touch on his shoulder broke the intense scrutiny, and they left the study.

Titus wandered the compound, lost in thought and horrid memories he believed dealt with long ago. Although the kidnapping happened ten years ago, it felt like yesterday, as vivid images played across his mind's eye. He looked at his wrist almost seeing the chaffed bloody marks left from the tight bounds that held him during the voyage from Allon to Tunlund.

Mirit had been involved with the kidnap plot, but later discovered she was duped into participating. Due to an accident at sea, she recalled nothing about her Allonian past. Once she learned Titus' true identity, she helped Nigel find him. Unfortunately, she was captured during the rescue attempt, which is when he met her again. She swore to protect him no matter the cost. She made good on her pledge when intervening during the sacrificial ceremony to save his life. Titus flinched, for it cost Mirit her life, at least for a brief time.

To show the falsehood of Hueil's claim of being a god, Vicar Uriah performed the Breath of Life. Jor'el responded by restoring Mirit's life for the Tunlundians to experience the power of the real god. Upon reviving, her memory returned and she recalled being Baron Mathias' daughter and not Tunlundian.

Her unselfish act led to Hueil's defeat and imprisonment, Titus reunited with his family and Mirit with her father. A small smile appeared at the thought that eight months later she married Nigel and became his aunt. The smile faded, for what would happen now that Hueil was free? Surely he would remember and help Ellan take revenge upon his family. No! He was now old enough to act to prevent it.

"Titus?"

Hearing his name jolted him out of his dreadful pondering. He hadn't realized he made his way toward the armory. It took a moment to recognize the voice calling him was his brother Eli. In fact, Fraser accompanied Eli. The family resemblance between the three brothers was strong with each having various shades of brown hair. Fraser and Eli had brown eyes compared to Titus' blue. Fraser was fifteen years old and Eli, thirteen. Both had been sparring, as a told by being sweaty and carrying their doublets.

"You look like you've just been told something awful," said Eli.

"Maybe Jillian came to her senses and refused to have him as husband," teased Fraser. He poked Eli with his elbow and laughed.

Titus made a mocking snort of amusement at Fraser.

"Is he right?" asked Eli, curious at the reaction.

"No!" Titus headed for the family garden.

Eli hurried after him. "Then what's wrong?"

Titus tried to change his mood. "Nothing is wrong."

"I bet," snickered Fraser.

He stopped and confronted his brothers. Fraser possessed a more cynical nature while Eli sensitive. At present, he didn't want to talk to either of them. "Aren't you two supposed to be at morning training?"

"We're taking a break," replied Fraser.

"Well, take it someplace else!"

Behind his brothers came two Guardian warriors, Kendrick and Skylar. They were of the brawny sort, with Kendrick the larger of the two. He had silver gray hair and thin beard with bright copper eyes while Skylar, golden hair and clean-shaven with striking robin's egg blue eyes.

"Do your duty or something," he said to the warriors.

"The queen sent for the princes to prepare for departure," replied Skylar with a wry smile.

Titus demanded of Fraser, "Why did you lie?"

"I didn't lie. We were taking a break when word came."

"Go! Don't keep Mother waiting." He turned on his heels.

Irate, Fraser lashed out, "What about you?"

"I wasn't sent for!"

Eli pursued and caught Titus' arm. "Please. What troubles you?"

At Eli's genuine concern, Titus curbed his harshness. "There are simply more things I must think about than you or Fraser. Now go, I'll be fine." He gave his brother a partial smile.

Eli left with Skylar. Fraser and Kendrick already entered the building.

Titus drew near the rear entrance to the royal garden when his sister, ten-year old Mikaela, ran from the postern gate toward him. She was small for her age with doe-colored hair and large blue eyes. She appeared concerned and stumbled. He knelt to catch her. She labored to breathe.

"You're not supposed to be running." He cast a scolding glance to the female Guardian warrior following Mikaela. She resembled Kell with medium length black hair and often mistaken by mortals for his twin. The difference between them being her vivid jade eyes compared to his brilliant gold.

Mikaela took a deep breath to speak. "They won't let Jade and I go to the stream." She pointed back to the gate.

"I was speaking with the guards when the princess saw you and began running," said Jade. "They are under orders from General Wess not to allow passage in or out of Waldron without permission."

"We go to the stream everyday. It's one of my favorite places," complained Mikaela.

"Well, today you must be content with the fountain," he said.

"It's not the same." She began coughing, and had difficulty breathing.

"On second thought, enough of being outside." He picked her up.

"No," she protested with a pout. "At least sit with me by the fountain. I love the water."

He chuckled. "Very well. But if you don't calm down, I'll have Jade take you inside."

She smiled and eagerly nodded. "I will."

Ellis joined them on the walk to the rear terrace garden. He made a fake frown at Mikaela. "What is this? My little sweetheart cheating on me in the arms of another?" He tickled Mikaela, which made her giggle.

"Stop! I just calmed her down after a fit. She doesn't need another."

"Oh, I'm sorry."

"Don't listen to Titus, I think you're funny."

Ellis made an elaborate bow. "Thank you, Princess."

Being autumn, most flowers in the royal garden were past blooming; the lawn a dormant brown; the trees bare of leaves; and the fountain only running at half-strength. Titus carried Mikaela to one of the benches around the fountain. He and Ellis sat on either side of her.

"It doesn't look as good as the stream," she complained.

"Of course not. It's nearly time to turn off the water and prepare it for winter," said Titus.

"I don't understand why General Wess won't let the guards allow me to go to my stream."

"The general has his reasons."

"Really?" asked Ellis. Receiving a scowl of warning from Titus, he amended his speech. "Oh, he must," he said to Mikaela. "As soon as possible, I will escort you to the stream."

Mikaela smiled. "I'd like that."

He noticed Titus' continuing glare. "It's only fair. You claim my sister and I claim yours." Titus made a look of taking brotherly exception to the idea and Ellis laughed. "You're jealous!"

"Jealous of what?" asked Mikaela, which increased Ellis' laughter. "Titus?"

"Never mind." He summoned Jade, who waited a respectful distance behind the bench with Egan. "Take her inside."

"But I've calmed down," insisted Mikaela.

"It's too cool out here for you." At her disappointed frown, he added, "I'll come by later and we'll play your favorite game."

"Very well."

"Should I carry you, Princess?" asked Jade.

"No. I can walk." She took Jade's hand and they left the garden.

Ellis still laughed and Titus struck his arm.

"You can carry teasing a bit too far. She's very fragile."

"She's stronger than an overprotective brother gives her credit for."

"And you're not overprotective of Jillian?"

"Not like you with Mikaela."

"Ay, Jillian is stronger, but she didn't nearly die when coming into the world." He watched Mikaela and Jade enter the main building.

Ellis placed an arm around Titus' shoulder. "Jor'el has granted Mikaela a good life. Although physically weak, she has a great capacity for affection and loves you dearly."

"She told you?"

"Ay. On occasion she confides in me and calls me *her knight protector*," he said with a swaggering smile.

"You? What game where you playing when she said it?"

"Shadow Warrior slayer."

Titus laughed.

"That's beside the point. She does confide in me." He switched subjects. "So what is this about General Wess?"

Titus tried to act nonchalant. "He must have orders."

"And you're going tell me you don't know what those orders are?"

He wanted to deny it, but one look at Ellis and he couldn't. So, instead, he turned away and stared at the fountain.

Ellis pursed his lips. "You're not at liberty to speak."

Titus leaned forward on the bench, elbows on his knees and hands clenched. He tried to concentrate on the fountain as Ellis continued.

"I'll learn soon enough from the normal scuttlebutt. Or better yet, Fraser. He's always good for information."

Titus sighed and hung his head. "Why do you do this to me?"

"Do what?"

"You know very well, *what.*"

Ellis leaned forward to look Titus in the eye. "Because I care. Who else do you have to confide in? Your father has Prince Nigel and the duke. What of you? Fraser? As I said, he is loose-lipped, while Eli—" he stopped when Titus sat up straight, offended.

"You're speaking about my brothers and princes of Allon!"

"And I am speaking *to* the future king. Not to mention one I hold as dear as any blood brother." He continued when Titus scowled. "Will you deny their faults? Fraser can be indiscreet and Eli too sensitive to bear any heavy burden."

Titus bolted up and paced a few steps in annoyance.

"So, you do the same with them as Mikaela."

Titus whirled about, and the flush of insult on his face brought Ellis to his feet. For a long moment they stared at each other. Wounded royal pride clearly evident in Titus' expression.

In formal salute, Ellis clasped his sword and bowed. "Highness." He left the terrace garden by way of the rear entrance.

"You know he's right," said Egan.

"Don't you start!"

The Guardian shrugged. "Doesn't change the truth."

Titus pursed his lips, staring in the direction Ellis left. "We should see how preparations for departure are progressing." He went to the main building.

Chapter 3

ELLAN, GARETH AND ZEBULON DEPARTED MYLTON TWO DAYS ago. Hueil freely wandered about the manor. The mortal servants continued their chores unaware of his presence. To Braden and Floric, he made his activities known. In fact, he pressed Braden upon discovering Valery not in her room.

Furious, Braden paced his study. "She's a vexatious wench since birth!"

"From what I hear, your father favored her."

Braden stopped and shot a hot glare at Hueil, then admitted, "Ay."

Hueil slyly grinned. "Jealousy is a powerful emotion."

"I'm not jealous."

"Oh? To be usurped by your daughter in your father's eyes and affection?" He stared deep into the mortal's eyes. "I see anger and resentment, along with jealousy that belies Allard's good reputation."

Bitterness crept into Braden's voice. "The rest of the world thought of him as a good man. At home was a different story. He could be harsh and unyielding, touting devotion to the crown above everything."

"Including family."

"Ay!"

"Isn't that what you've done? Only you substituted one crown for another. You are not as different from your father as you pretend."

Thunderstruck by the comparison, Braden plopped in a nearby chair.

With a feigned sigh of concern, Hueil continued. "But are you of the same mettle to finish what you started like he did?"

Insulted, Braden sat forward in the chair. "You question my honor and courage?"

Hueil assumed an immediate attitude of submission. "Not I, my lord. By wavering to take action after what I told you concerning your daughter's disappearance, you seem to question yourself."

Braden pushed himself off the chair and boldly approached Hueil. The Guardian showed no inclination of retaliating to the aggressive move. Still, Braden stopped from reaching Hueil due to the icy blue eyes and clenched his fists. "Come! Florie will know about Valery." He marched from the study and headed to the private chapel. He paused at the door. "She may not be forthcoming in your presence."

Hueil grinned. "No problem. I shall use the same means to watch you confront her as I have exploring Mylton." From out of his doublet pocket, he pulled a gold chain with a square embossed medallion at the end. He placed the chain over his head and when the medallion fell against his chest, he vanished.

Braden blinked in astonishment. "Where are you?"

"Right beside you."

He jumped in surprise at hearing the voice.

"Hold the door a moment longer when you enter and I will follow."

The small intimate chapel was a quaint room of wood paneling containing a small altar, a padded bench for kneeling and a shelf of various books. A side table separated two cushioned chairs. Nervous, Florie paced and muttered prayers under her breath. She halted in anticipation of the door opening. Braden entered, and she sighed in relief.

"This is unbearable! I can't even pray without fear he will spy on me."

"My dear, your unusual nervous behavior is enough to arouse anyone's suspicion."

His benign tone made her wary. "You only say *my dear* when you want something."

His agreeability vanished. "I want your full *and* calm cooperation."

"Calm? How can you be calm with that creature lurking about?"

"He's a Guardian."

Florie rubbed her arms as if warding off a chill. "He's unlike any Guardian I've ever met."

Braden grinned. "Granted, he is intense." He took her arm and steered her to a chair. "Read the book of Verse to steady your nerves."

"If only it were that simple." She sat.

He handed her the book, only wouldn't release it to ask, "By the way, why hasn't Valery joined you in your daily reading and prayer?"

She balked in reply. "You confined her to her room."

He snorted an ironic laugh and released the book for her to take. "Since when does she obey me?"

"You can't blame her. You threatened her life!"

He sat in the other chair, eyes harsh upon her. "Where is she?"

"In her room."

"That's a lie," said a third voice.

Stunned, Florie looked around, but saw no one else. "Who said that? It didn't sound like you," she said to Braden.

"Are you lying, *my dear?*"

"No. You put her there—" She gasped in fright when Hueil appeared in front of her. No flash of light, he just appeared. "How?"

He held the chain of the medallion. "Simple." He placed the chain over his head and when the medallion touched his chest, he vanished. He then reappeared holding the chain. "It's called a shielding medal. Mortals can't see me, and Guardians can't sense me. Ingenious." He leaned down to Florie. "Where is Valery?"

She shrank back in the chair. "I don't know."

"How did she leave?"

She shook her head trying not to answer. Hueil's hard grip on her face stopped her. He stared at her. She tried to turn away from his menacing glare. He wouldn't let her so she screwed her eyes shut.

"Look at me," he said in a low, commanding voice.

As if against her will, Florie obeyed.

The icy gaze narrowed with inspection. "What I sense is about you. About your daughter." He snarled. "You helped her to leave."

"Ay," she stammered in a fearful whimper.

Braden rose. "Woman, what have you done? Where has she gone?"

Hueil continued to study Florie. "She doesn't know only that she helped her leave." He squeezed her face to get her attention when she glanced at Braden. "What did she tell you?"

"Everything!" She wept.

"If she tells what she knows we are undone!" chided Braden.

Hueil released her and motioned for Braden to leave with him.

Frantic, she stood. "Please, Braden, leave her alone!"

Hueil turned upon her, eyes flaring in brightness but not touching her. She struggled to breathe. Her eyes rolled back in her head and she collapsed to the floor, the book of Verse still in her hand.

Braden knelt and hesitated in feeling for a pulse.

"She's dead," said Hueil, in cold, callous voice. "It's what you wanted. Correct?" he asked when Braden looked up in alarm.

"I just wanted her quiet," he spoke in solemn regret.

"So she is. Now, we must quiet your daughter."

Braden's expression shifted between distress and resolution. "I'll issue the order for men to search for her." He paused in leaving. "Can you dispose—?" He couldn't finish and motioned at Florie.

"Consider it done." Hueil picked her up and vanished.

***

Deep in the forest surrounding Mylton, Mannix and Locan waited. Mannix sat on a boulder tossing pebbles into a fast flowing stream. Locan paced.

"You'll give yourself worry lines, or so the mortals believe," said Mannix. "Actually, this is relaxing." He continued tossing pebbles.

"Playing silly mortal games isn't going to help me relax! It's been three days. We're fortunate Vidar hasn't found us yet."

"Who says he's looking for you?" said a voice from behind.

In one fluid motion, Locan drew his sword and turned to face the intruder. Mannix dropped the pebbles, hoped off the boulder, drew his sword and stood shoulder-to-shoulder with Locan. To their annoyed surprise, Hueil appeared from nowhere, no light, he just appeared.

"How did you do that?" demanded Locan.

"This." Hueil held up the medallion.

"I thought all of those were destroyed after Owain's rebellion."

"Apparently not," groused Mannix and sheathed his sword. "Where did you get it?"

Hueil pocketed the medallion. "I have my ways of acquiring things. At the moment I have two assignments. The first, Braden's daughter is loose and must be found before she talks."

"About what?" asked Locan.

"The wench followed him and spied on the meeting."

"I don't see how a mortal girl can stop what is happening," said Mannix.

"The Son of Tristan was a mortal youth who stopped Dagar!"

"I thought you were better than Dagar."

Before Mannix could react, Hueil grabbed his throat, only not touching him, rather holding out his hand. Mannix floated off the ground, gasping for air.

"I am! I learned from Dagar about what to do and not to do when dealing with mortals. Have you forgotten, I ruled a nation as a god?" With Mannix on the verge of passing out, he released him. The warrior fell and gulped for air. "That is your last lesson in questioning me."

Mannix said in a raspy voice, "Ay, my lord."

"About ten miles north is a series of shallow caverns. There you will find a pack of *madah-dune*. Use them to track and dispose of the girl."

The warriors exchanged wary glances and Mannix asked, "How can we control them? We're not forest Guardians."

"Tell them in the Ancient, *The master commands your presence for a hunt.* They will listen to you until the task is complete."

"Ay, my lord. And the second assignment?"

Hueil grinned, wide and malicious. "You will capture a certain Guardian and bring him to me. I have a special task for him."

"Who?" asked Locan.

"I will not speak his name for fear of prying ears, so know him *anna a'inntinn.*" He stared at each of them with great concentration.

Both warriors stepped back as if struck hard, and momentarily mute. Finally, Mannix asked, "*Him?* After what we've done, how can we get close enough to capture him?"

"That's for you to decide. However, I will not accept failure of either assignment."

Mannix bowed. "Ay, my lord."

Locan also bowed. "It will be as you command, my lord."

This time Hueil vanished in flash of light.

Locan punched Mannix. "How did I ever let you talk me into this?"

Befuddled, Mannix shook his head. "I'm beginning to wonder that myself, but it's too late now."

"Why? We could—"

Mannix clamped his hand over Locan's mouth. "Mind your tongue! If he fears to be overheard, what about us? We have no choice now."

Locan pushed Mannix's hand away. "Ay. Let's take care of the girl first."

Chapter 4

B Y THE SECOND NIGHT OF HER FLIGHT, VALERY ONLY MANAGED to reach the border where the Meadowlands intersected Midessex and the Southern Forest. This was one of the few places in Allon where three provinces met. She made slow progress without a horse and trying to avoid her father's men. She dare not take a room at an inn or hire a horse since word of either could find way to her father. She wondered what would happen to her mother upon discovery of her absence. She couldn't think too long on it or become distracted by fear.

What little money she carried, she spent carefully on purchasing provisions in a town or at some farm. Food would have to last until she decided where to hide. She couldn't take refuge with any of the extended family and expose them to danger. Perhaps a Fortress would be best, but would any place be safe during civil war?

She settled down in a secluded and sheltered hollow off the main road just inside the Southern Forest side of the border. She built a small fire to warm up the piece of meat leftover from lunch. She had little water left in her flask, and the small loaf of stale bread. She would have to save some food for the morning until she could buy more.

Placing the meat on a stick, she held it over the low flames to reheat it. Something sprang out from behind a nearby tree. She jumped up in fear and let go of the stick. The meat fell into the fire. A nocturnal possum-like creature scampered away. Seeing the meat hissing and burning, she snatched the stick. Unfortunately, it was too hot to handle and the meat fell back into the fire.

"Oh, no!"

"It's beyond saving."

Valery bolted up at the voice. A stunningly beautiful, tall woman appeared on the other side of the fire. She had long auburn hair and bright green eyes that glowed in the firelight. She wore a forester green jerkin, brow cowl, and breeches of identical color to the jerkin tucked into knee-high leather boots. A brown leather belt gathered the jerkin about her waist. Instead of a sword she carried a golden crossbow over one shoulder, quiver of arrows on her back, a plain-sheathed dagger on her belt along with a pouch.

"Who are you? Where did you come from?" asked Valery.

The woman kindly smiled. "My name is Wren. I'm a Guardian and Trio Leader of the Southern Forest."

"Wren," Valery repeated, trying to calm down. "I heard my grandfather mention your name."

Wren's smile widened. "Lord Allard was a good man. You bear a strong resemblance to him with your color hair and eyes."

"I've been told that before." She sat down and grabbed the stick, only to discover the meat burnt beyond eating. "So much for my dinner."

"Will this do as replacement?" Wren displayed a small dressed fowl.

"How did you do that? It's already plucked and ready to cook."

She chuckled and took a seat beside Valery. She placed her bow on the ground by the log. "I'm a Guardian hunter. When I saw you enter the forest not carrying a bow or trap I knew you would need food. Watching your effort with the meat, I'm glad to be of help." She skewered the foul on another stick and placed it over the fire. She spoke in a language Valery couldn't understand.

"What did you say?"

"I asked Jor'el's blessing."

"Oh. Thank Him for me too, please."

"You can do that yourself."

Valery lowered her head and closed her eyes. Upon opening her eyes, she noticed Wren's regard and grew uncomfortable. "Sounds like you've been watching me. Why and for how long?"

"*We,* myself and Nixie, have been watching you. She is Trio Leader of the Meadowlands, and alerted me when you left Mylton heading in this direction. Has something happened with your father?"

Valery avoided Wren's probing gaze by turning to watch the fowl cook. "I don't know what you mean."

"Nixie tried to speak to Lord Braden only to be rudely dismissed. She asked me to try since he knows me, but he dismissed me also."

Valery became curious. "I didn't know you spoke to Father or Grandfather."

"Naturally. Guardians and mortals frequently talk to each other," she said with a wry smile.

"I meant I haven't seen you at Mylton before, or this Nixie. Is she a hunter too?"

"No, she's a warrior. We don't make a big display like mortals when dignitaries visit. It is part of our duty to keep vigil of our charges."

Valery nodded. "I remember Grandfather telling me about Guardians. I've seen them—I mean you—your kind at Court. Most are nice, yet quiet. Except for one called Armus. He's always with the king and queen."

Wren laughed at the comment, and tended to the fowl. "Armus is the Guardian of Allon. He serves as Jor'el's advisor to their majesties. He can be talkative at times. Many Guardians serve the royals at Waldron, but we generally keep a low profile outside of Court." She took the fowl off the fire. "I hope you're hungry."

"Done already?"

"Ay." Wren placed the fowl down on a rock and used her knife to cut off a leg to hand to Valery. "Be careful, it's hot."

Valery took the leg and tentatively began to eat. "Ay, it is a bit hot, but very good." She blew on it before taking another bite. She noticed Wren not eating. "Aren't you going to eat?"

"Food isn't necessary for Guardians."

"Are you sure? I can't eat it all."

"You'll need some for breakfast."

"True," she said with a mouthful.

For a moment, Wren watched Valery eat before speaking again. "In all honesty, my lady, Nixie and I are concerned. Something must be wrong for you to be out here like this."

Valery continued to eat and didn't answer.

"You can trust me. Your grandfather did."

Valery paused in eating, with a ripple of consideration on her face. She finished the meat and tossed the bone into the fire.

"More?" Wren cut off a piece of the white meat.

Valery accepted the meat and in doing so, caught Wren's steady, penetrating gaze. She sighed in resignation. "You truly knew my grandfather well?"

"I did."

She made a brief frown of consideration before continuing. "Something is wrong, but I'm not sure the extent. Only it has do to with the royal family and a person by the name of Ellan."

Wren immediately grew concerned. "Are you certain of that name?"

"Ay. They pledged to support her."

"Who?"

"The Council. I got caught watching, spying, as my father said."

Wren's urgent hand on Valery's arm stopped further words. "Are you heading to Waldron?"

The grip and question surprised Valery. "I don't know. I only thought of hiding someplace my father would not find me." Seeing Wren's continuous stare, she grew nervous and fretful. "If I go to

Waldron, he will know I betrayed him! And I hate to think what would happen to my mother. She helped me escape."

"Was all the Council there?"

Valery thought before replaying. "No. I heard a few names mentioned who didn't come."

"Who?"

"Hayden, Ned, Angus, Fagan and Mathias."

Wren pursed her lips in momentary thought. "Go to Garwood and the Duke of Allon. Say I sent you and tell him what you told me."

"How will that be better than going to Waldron?"

Wren took Valery by the shoulders to get her direct attention. "How well did you love your grandfather?"

She stiffened with offense. "I loved him dearly, but what does that have to do with this?" Her objection turned to understanding by the end of her own protest and she said, "It is what he would do, warn the king."

Wren took Valery's face in her hands. "Don't let fear stop you from doing what your heart knows is right."

Her eyes grew misty. "But my mother?"

"Nixie and I will do what we can to help her. Now," she handed Valery a cloth to use as a handkerchief, "I'll stay with you until the morning and set you on the road to Garwood."

She nodded, wiped her eyes and blew her nose.

Wren took the small loaf of bread. Again she spoke the unknown language and the handed the bread to Valery. "Eat some more."

Valery marveled at the warm softness of the loaf and ate.

"When you're done, get some sleep. I'll keep watch. Nothing will disturb you." Wren motioned to an area on the other side of the fire prepared like a sleeping pallet.

Valery finished the bread and lied down. "I don't think I can sleep."

Wren whispered something, and within a moment Valery slept.

Nixie emerged from the shadows. She stood six inches taller than Wren with shoulder-length blonde hair and bright violet eyes. "Did she tell you anything?"

"Rather disturbing news. Some of the Council met with Ellan."

"Did she mention Hueil?"

Wren shook her head, yet watched Valery. "No, and I didn't press her. She's upset and concerned for her mother's safety. It took prodding and urging to get her to agree to go to Garwood and speak to Angus. I promised that we would protect her mother."

"No, I will. You make certain she reaches Garwood."

Wren flashed a wry smile. "I hoped you'd say that. In all honesty, there is something odd about Braden I can't figure out. He was rude but nervous, like something ..."

"Acted like a repulse, keeping us at bay," said Nixie.

Wren became suspicious. "Being familiar wasn't the *real* reason you asked me, was it?"

"No, I wanted to make certain I didn't sense something wrongly. A shielding medal produces a similar affect to what we felt."

"A shielding medal is strong enough to hide—" Wren couldn't finish for realizing what she was about to say. "You think Hueil is at Mylton."

"It's a possibility, which makes it imperative the king is informed about what she heard and saw."

"Then I should take her there now, without delay."

Suddenly a low, eerie growling echoed all around and increased in volume. Nixie drew her sword and Wren armed her crossbow.

"What do you think it is?" asked Wren.

"I was about to ask you since it sounds like an animal."

"What's going on?" Valery began to rise.

"Stay down!" Wren moved to shield Valery.

The growling grew deafening loud and painful, making Valery cover her ears and grimace. Nixie and Wren tried to withstand the noise and keep a tight grip on their weapons.

From out of the trees, four wolf-man beasts charged. They stood nine feet tall on two legs with the body of a man but completely covered in fur. Their heads were wolves with snarling, drooling fangs, and large hands with sharp claws. They wielded large clubs with spikes on them.

Nixie dodged a club at her. She retaliated by swinging her sword at the creature. The blade sliced into its back making it howl in anger.

Wren only got off a shot. The dart pierced one beast in the right shoulder, but didn't stop its charge. "Run!" she shouted at Valery.

Valery scrambled to her feet only to be forced to dive to the ground to avoid a swinging club. She rolled away and came up to her knees. She drew her sword in time to cut off the large hand reaching down to seize her. The beast yowled in pain and momentarily retreated. Angry, it swung the club at her. She again dove away and the club smashed into the ground. When the beast yanked the club from the ground for another attack, an arrow stuck it between the eyes, killing it.

Wren pulled Valery to her feet. "Run. That way!" She shoved Valery in the direction she indicted. "And don't look back!" she shouted to the fleeing Valery. A spiked club sliced deep across Wren's back. The strength of the blow sent her sprawling to the ground in great pain. She heard the snarl and caught sight of the beast raising a club. She didn't have the strength to make defense.

Bright light filled the hollow. The beast growled in rage when forced back by the light. Two male Guardian warriors appeared, armed and ready. The beast about to strike Wren was killed. In short order, the male warriors and Nixie dispatched the remaining beasts.

"About time you two showed up. What kept you?" Nixie chided.

"Blame Ewert. He couldn't sense exactly where you went," said Bailey.

Wren lay face down on the ground. Hearing her groan, they hurried over. The club cut the quiver strap, ripped open her jerkin and left a serious, deep wound across her back under the shoulder blades.

"Bad," said Ewert.

"Take her to Eldric," said Nixie.

"No!" Wren grunted and pushed herself to her knees. She gritted back the pain to continue speaking. "Just put medicine and a bandage on it. I must find Valery."

"Not with that wound. I'll send one of them to find her." Nixie spoke of Ewert and Bailey.

"Not with Hueil here. You three need to stay close to Mylton."

"Hueil?" asked Bailey.

"Nixie will explain later, there isn't time now. The medical supplies are in my pouch."

Nixie took the pouch off Wren's belt. "Help her sit up and hold her."

They knelt on either side of Wren. Once sitting up, Bailey gingerly moved her hair out of the way so Nixie could work. Wren hissed and tightly held onto them when Nixie applied the salve. She didn't loosen her grip until Nixie finished and she fully relaxed against Ewert.

"Nixie's right about taking you to Eldric," he said.

Wren shook her head, took a steadying breath and put her arms up over Ewert and Bailey's shoulders for the bandaging. Nixie wrapped the bandage four times around Wren's torso, over her left shoulder for support, and a final time around Wren's torso before tying it off.

"Do you want something for the pain?"

"No." Wren attempted to stand, but faltered so Ewert and Bailey helped her. She grunted and flinched when fully standing on her own.

"Is the bandage too tight?" Nixie examined her work.

"No, moving is painful."

"You're being stubborn," groused Ewert.

"Look who's talking, mister cynic."

"Maybe next time I'll delay a little longer."

Nixie's hard punch to his midsection made Ewert flinch. "You never leave a Trio mate to face danger alone!"

"Fortunately, he's your Trio mate not mine," said Wren.

"Where are your Trio mates?" asked Bailey.

Her expression turned to grief. "Vanquished during Hueil's escape."

The news stunned the others. "We're sorry," said Nixie.

Wren nodded, trying to mask the pain and sorrow on her face. "Now, I've got to find Valery. Remember Lady Florie."

"We will."

She picked up her bow and quiver then hurried off into the darkness.

"I was only joking about delaying," Ewert called after her.

"I know! But you're still a cynic!" came her reply.

Still holding a bloody sword, Valery didn't know how long to run or exactly how to get to Garwood. Whatever those creatures were she had to get away. Breathing became difficult and her legs grew weak and unsteady. Finally she tripped over her own feet and fell to the ground, gulping for air. After taking a moment to recover, she tried to get her bearings, but difficult in the darkness. Partial moonlight filtered through the bare branches. Hearing a noise, she pushed herself to her knees and gripped her sword in anticipation. Not an expert with a blade, she possessed enough skill to keep attackers at bay. A snapping sound came from behind. She made ready to face danger.

"Easy! It's me." Wren threw up her hands. She still held her crossbow and quiver.

"Don't scare me like that!"

"I made noise so you would know someone was coming."

Exhausted, Valery sat on the ground. "What about the beasts?"

"Nixie and two others warriors arrived. We killed them, but not before one wounded me." Ginger in movement, Wren sat beside Valery.

"How bad?" She glanced to the bandage around Wren's torso.

"Bad enough. It won't stop me from taking you to Garwood."

"I thought you were going to help my mother."

"The others will. By that attack it's obvious someone doesn't want you to reach the king."

"Do you think it was the one called Ellan?"

Wren shook her head. "No. Hueil. He's a Guardian, Ellan is mortal."

"Why would a Guardian want to hurt me? I thought your kind protects us." She suddenly became fearful and quickly spoke before Wren could reply. "Unless he knows."

"Of course he knows."

"No, no!" She searched her pouch and doublet before sighing with relief. "Thank Jor'el."

"What?"

She grew cautious. "I'm not certain if I should tell you. Mother told me to keep it secret unless my life is at stake."

Wren snorted an ironic chuckle. "I think the attack qualifies your life is at stake. Lord Allard trusted me, and so can you."

After a brief hesitation, she took the ring from an inside pocket of her doublet to show Wren. "Mother gave me this before I left."

The Guardian's eyes grew wide in surprise. "The royal crest of the House of Tristan?"

"She said she is of royal blood through one of King Ellis' uncles, but not properly acknowledged, if you understand my meaning."

"I understand. Did she give a name?"

"Delwin."

Wren echoed the name under her breath. "No one knew if he survived the coup. This proves he did." She closed Valery's hand upon the ring. "Keep it hidden until we reach Garwood."

Valery put the ring back. "Are we continuing the journey tonight?"

"No, we both need rest." Wren closed her eyes. Her lips moved, but no words spoken. After a moment she swayed and would have fainted if Valery hadn't caught her. "Not good. I can't create a defensive shield, as the wound is hampering my energy."

"What does that mean?"

"Even with rest I won't be able to dimension travel you to Garwood."

"What kind of travel?"

"How Guardians go from place to place through time and space."

Valery's face screwed up with skepticism. "That sounds impossible.

"For mortals, ay. They usually faint."

"Then I don't think I'd want to do it."

"It is the quickest and safest way, but not now. It's too dangerous for me to use my power."

"So we do continue tonight."

"No, rest is important for both of us. I'll protect us another way." She spoke aloud, *"Creutairs de anoidche, uaireadair agus dion sinn."* She repeated, "Creatures of the night, watch and protect us."

Valery jumped in fright when a pack of eight wolves appeared from between the trees and surrounded them.

Wren stopped Valery from retreating. "No need to fear. These are dear friends of mine." She spoke to the two largest of the wolves. "Greetings, Auden and Saree."

The alpha male and female approached with their heads lowered in submission. Auden, the male replied in yelps and grunts.

"Indeed, it is a mean night."

Saree sniffed Wren's wound, licked the bandage and whimpered.

"Ay, a bad wound, but I will survive. I need your aid tonight to protect this one who serves the king and Jor'el."

Auden started howling. Saree and the rest of the pack joined in. A moment later, in the near and far distance, wolf howls came in reply. Valery flinched in surprised when something swooped passed her. Four owls arrived and perched on branches covering each direction. Auden ceased howling, so did Saree and the rest of the pack. Auden then spoke to Wren in grunts and yips.

The Guardian smiled at Valery. "The watch is set. Auden says Cody, the youngest male, will sleep beside you as guard and to keep you warm."

Auden barked at Cody. The young wolf came forward and bowed his head to Valery.

"He's awful big for being the youngest," she said, tentative of Cody's approach.

"You can touch him, he won't hurt you."

Cody made a low whimper and nudged Valery's hand. She smiled and petted his head and neck.

"I'm never petted a wolf before. He's so soft."

Cody licked Valery's hand then her face and wagged his tail. She laughed when he knocked her over in his exuberance.

Wren chuckled. "He likes you."

"I can tell. He doesn't seem much different than a dog."

"Oh, wolves are different. They are wild creatures, but once they give their affection and allegiance, it is a bond you can depend upon for life."

Auden made a short bark and Cody backed away from Valery. He still wagged his tail.

"Try to get some sleep."

Valery made herself comfortable. Cody lay down beside her with his head resting by her head. The pack took up position around them.

Valery turned her head toward Wren, the Guardian lying on her side facing her. "Why did you speak with certainty about my service to the king and Jor'el when I'm not certain of what to do?"

Wren softly smiled. "I told you I spoke to your grandfather. He was very proud of you and your devotion to Jor'el in daily study and attitude. Along with your intelligence and expressed loyalty to the king. He was certain you would do well at Court."

"How could he tell? I just turned thirteen when he died. In fact, my first introduction at Court was the ceremony in honor of his memory and service. Not my Coming of Age party, like it should have been."

"Some mortals have a heavenly gift of insight. He spoke with certainty about you, but not Braden." She grew thoughtful. "About him, he may also have been correct."

"Ay," droned Valery. "Even as I child I knew they didn't get along. When I was eleven they had a terrible argument that frightened me. I thought he would strike Grandfather. I rushed between them. Father barely stopped in time, and stormed from the room. Grandfather became cross with me, more for fear of my being injured. From that day on, I only saw him occasionally and usually alone, when he could arrange it." Her eyes grew misty and she sniffled. "I miss him terribly."

Cody rose, whimpered and licked Valery's cheek.

"He's upset to see you sad."

She grinned and petted Cody. "I'm sorry. I'll try not to be too sad." The wolf lied down and put his head on her abdomen.

"Indeed, you have a made friend."

"I like him too." She scratched Cody behind the right ear and he made a contented noise, closing his eyes.

Wren smiled. "Sleep. We need to be ready for the morning."

Locan and Mannix gathered in a small grove with twelve more *madah-dune*. The creatures lowly snarled and huddled together, eying the Guardians, who conversed a few feet away.

"That didn't go well," groused Locan.

"I don't think he counted on Wren or Nixie knowing about her," chided Mannix

"Bah! We could have sent more to finish them if Ewert and Bailey hadn't arrived." He motioned at the beasts and received a snapping growl from one of them. He spoke in a lower voice. "I thought you sent Ewert and Bailey on a wild goose chase?"

"Obviously not wild enough."

Locan scowled in annoyance. "Now the forest protects them."

"Come the morning, we set them loose again."

"Attack in board daylight?"

"No, for tracking."

Locan cocked a contrary expression to the beasts then to Mannix. "You're going to tell them to track and not attack? That I'd like to see."

Mannix squared his shoulder and gripped his sword before taking several steps toward the beasts. One beast, perhaps the alpha, bared its fangs and raised his club, halting Mannix's approach. "The master commands your presence for a hunt."

To their surprise, the alpha male replied. "You already said that."

"You can talk?"

"Talk and understand."

Locan rolled his eyes. "Great! Something else he neglected to tell us."

"Why should the master trust turncoats?" asked the alpha.

"We turned to help him!"

The alpha snarled viciously at Locan.

"Don't upset him! We're supposed to work together," said Mannix.

The alpha huffed and squared his shoulders. "We serve only the master."

"As do we! So let's continue to work together. Since you speak, do you have a name?"

"The master called me Tagi. He said it means *the day has come*."

Locan frowned in befuddlement. "Must be another language for it's not an Allonian or Ancient name."

"Some form of Tunlundian," said Mannix. "What of the others? Do they have names?"

"No, only me." Tagi thumped his chest. "I lead them."

"Very well. If you understand then you know we need to track the mortal female until there is an opportunity to destroy her."

Tagi stoutly nodded. "We will do so. Provided you can keep pace."

Insulted, Locan took a few steps toward Tagi. Mannix intercepted him when Tagi readied his club. The others were at his back snarling, fangs showing and looking anxious for a fight.

"Enough! We *will* work together!" scolded Mannix.

Locan scowled and took a step back. Tagi lowered his club.

"Good. We'll get in position before first light to track them."

***

Valery woke to the smell of cooking and felt something push against her shoulder. Cody nudged her. Recognizing the morning light, she sat up. At a fire, Wren warmed up what appeared to be a half-eaten fowl.

"Is that same bird from last night?" she asked.

"Ay. Auden brought it to me."

Valery moved to the fire. She broke off a piece to offer to Cody. Auden barked what sounded like short command and Cody didn't take the meat.

"He says the bird is for you, not Cody."

"As a reward for his kindness last night." Again Auden barked and Valery confronted him. "I insist," she said to Auden then held the piece of meat out to Cody. This time the younger wolf took it.

Wren leaned closer to speak. "You realize you and Cody just defied the pack leader?"

"Mama taught me one kindness deserves another." She turned to Auden. "You all were kind last night and I'd like to share this food."

Auden barked and yelped a few times. Wren translated. "He says thank you, and insists the meat is to strengthen you. They are capable of hunting for themselves." She took Valery's arm. "Your kindness is done, now eat. We must leave as soon as possible."

It took a few minutes for Valery to eat. Wren extinguished the fire, making certain no clue remained. Once ready to depart, the owls flew off and Auden lowly howled. The pack turned and headed into the trees.

"Where are they going?" asked Valery.

"The night watch is done. The day creatures will warn us." Wren pointed to the sky. Through the trees, two large hawks circled.

Valery watched Cody follow the others then stop at the tree behind which Auden moved. Cody lowly howled and barked. There was a response. Cody again barked, followed by a unified pack howl. When all was quiet, he returned to Valery.

"He has chosen to remain with you."

"And leave his family?"

"He is the youngest and lowest of the pack. Auden gave his permission. That's what the conversation was about."

Valery knelt down and looked Cody in eye. "Thank you." He licked her face and she hugged him. "You won't regret it."

"Come. We must go. An uneasiness stirs the wind." Wren slung her bow over her left shoulder then tied the severed quiver strap to her belt before leading the way.

After a mile from the hollow, Cody began snarling, his head moving from side to side.

"What's wrong?"

"He senses danger." Wren readied her bow, but kept walking. "Something is near, watching, maybe even following us."

"More of those beasts?"

"Let's pick up the pace."

Valery jogged after Wren. For three miles they traveled until Valery ran out of breath. She stopped in the middle of an open field and sat on an old hollow log to rest. Cody positioned himself in front of Valery. Now his hackles were up and he growled, baring his teeth.

Wren pulled Valery to her feet. "We can't stop."

"I don't know if I can continue."

"You must! If not running, at least fast walking. Just to the trees." She nudged Valery to move.

Valery was sluggish at first, and Cody came alongside to encourage her. After a few yards, her pace became steady. A hawk's cry made her stop and look up. Immediately the low, eerie growling echoed from all around. Feared gripped Valery at recognizing the sound.

Six wolf-men rushed them. Wren fired at the beasts. Cody leapt at another, only to be batted aside by a swipe of the beast's arm.

"Cody!" shouted Valery. Anger replaced fear and she drew her sword. She swung the blade at a charging wolf-man. The beast retaliated by using the club to bat her sword aside. The might of the blow threw her off balance and she tumbled to the ground, losing her sword upon impact. The beast bore down on her. Cody leapt and sunk his teeth into the beast's throat. Both fell with Cody ending on top and viciously ripping at the beast's throat and face with teeth and claws.

Valery scrambled to her feet and retrieved her sword. "Cody! Down!" The wolf obeyed. She plunged her sword through the beast's chest. A horrid gurgling sound emerged from the torn throat before going silent.

At Cody's warning bark, Valery saw Wren waylaid by two beasts. The Guardian tried to rise but couldn't. Just beyond Wren, she noticed a group of eight horsemen and two Guardian warriors on foot racing towards them. These weren't the same warriors from earlier rather one blond, the other bronze-haired with a goatee. With mighty swings of their swords, they made short work of dispatching the remaining wolf-men.

A man on a horse drew rein beside her. "Are you all right?"

"Ay, my lord."

He smiled. "Captain Chad, at your service, mistress."

"Thank you, Captain." Valery moved to where the blond Guardian helped Wren to her feet. "Wren, are you hurt again?"

"No. Just extremely sore," she groaned in reply.

"I take it this wasn't your first encounter with the *madah-dune,*" he said, motioning to her bandage.

"No," she hissed in discomfort. "And I don't think it'll be the last." Cody nudged her hand. She responded by patted his head.

The other Guardian joined them. "A friend?" he asked about Cody.

"Actually, he is a friend of Lady Valery."

He turned silver eyes friendly to her. "Lord Braden's daughter?"

"Ay, sir."

He smiled. "I am Commander Avatar. This is Mahon. I think you already met Captain Chad of the Jor'ellian Guard."

"Ay. And I thank you both as I did the captain."

"We shouldn't stay here any longer," said Wren, biting back pain.

"Do you sense more beasts?" asked Chad.

"No, but for safety."

"My lady, you may ride with me." Chad reached down to give Valery a hand up, only Avatar lifted her onto the back of Chad's saddle. "What about you, Wren? Do you need a horse?"

She shook her head. "If we walk, I can make it."

"To Garwood," he told his men and moved his horse at a walk.

"Are you sure you don't need help?" asked Mahon.

Wren rolled her eyes and started walking, slow and painful with Mahon beside her. This gave Avatar a clear view of her back. Fresh blood stained the bandage.

"Your wound is more serious than you're admitting," he said.

She grabbed onto Mahon just before swooning and he caught her.

"Take her to Eldric at Garwood," said Avatar.

Mahon lifted Wren in his arms and disappeared. Avatar paused to glance around the field, silver eyes narrow and careful in their scanning. He then ran to catch up to Chad and the Guards.

Concealed on nearby bluff overlooking the field, Mannix, Locan and Tagi watched the scene unfold.

"We told you to track them not attack!" scolded Locan. "Now we've lost them both. Not to mention, your attack placed him on alert."

"Fortunately, he didn't sense us as a result. We'll just have to find another way to get him alone," said Mannix.

"Like that should be simple," Locan sarcastically groused. "What is the Jor'ellian Guard doing here anyway?"

"Probably the same thing we are."

"Only they succeeded and have the girl!"

"I said, we'll think of something. For now let's not lose sight of them." Mannix carefully left the bluff, and the others followed.

Chapter 5

ARWOOD CASTLE STOOD PERCHED ON THE HIGHEST PEAK IN the Southern Forest, overlooking the town. The castle rose like a sentinel protecting the town and the road leading to Jor'el's Fortress. The ramparts offered a commanding view of the countryside. Over the last forty years Garwood underwent many improvements, expanding from its original enclosed six acres to ten acres.

Since assuming the title eighteen years earlier, Angus incorporated his own style to accommodate his expanding family. He, and his wife Necie, had six children in the span of eleven years. Ten-year-old Daria was named after her grandfather. Avery was the eldest son at age eight, followed by Galen age five, Spencer age three and infant twins, Mace and Maddie.

At age thirty-four Angus bore a strong resemblance to the grandfather for which he was named. He kept his naturally thick brown well trimmed and sported a thin beard. His physique filled out from a lanky youth to a hearty, healthy man of powerful build. Necie contrasted Angus, being shorter and gentle in features. Youthfulness still showed beneath the maturity of womanhood. Even after bearing six children she retained her girlish figure.

The family met in the private salon with Tyrone, Tristine, Titus, Nigel and Mirit, who arrived after dinner. Nearing the age of forty, Nigel stayed in peak physical condition. With the Allonian lifetime of one hundred to one hundred and ten years of age, Nigel was just entering the prime of life. Being the King's Champion and Knight of the Temple, he maintained a vigorous and strict training regiment. Mirit kept to his schedule since she bore the title, Queen's Champion. Whereas she wore gowns for state occasions, her daily uniform incorporated a cross between the feminine and masculine world she straddled.

Nigel stood at the window, his face fixed as he once again read Ellan's letter. The emotional battle could be seen in his tight features and brooding silence. Mirit approached and touched his arm to get his attention. He didn't acknowledge her and kept reading.

"I realize this is difficult," she said, her voice low and sympathetic.

"You see it for yourself," insisted Tristine with impatience.

"Ay," he droned in reply.

"Yet you still find it hard to believe."

He pursed his lips and shrugged his shoulders. "In part, I suppose."

Tristine didn't hold her passion in check. "Ellan means what she says! She is vindictive. I endured her torment for years, so did Necie."

He took a deep breath to control his temper at her outburst.

"Nigel doesn't know. He wandered for those years," said Tyrone.

"But why can't he believe me?"

"I do!" insisted Nigel.

"With reservations."

He fought to moderate his reply to her testiness. "What do you want? For me to take a troop and capture her?"

"Would be better than standing here watching your indecision."

"Tristine," said Tyrone in gentle warning. She moved away from them. He pursued her. "This difficult for all of us. True, this affects you and Necie more, but do you think Angus and I will stand by and let Ellan fulfill her threats?"

"Of course not. You weren't around during those years either, yet I can depend upon you. Sadly I can't do the same with my brother."

That stung! Nigel drew to his full height and his face flushed with anger. Mirit seized his arm in an attempt to curtail any harsh reply.

Angus spoke. "That's not fair, Tristine. Since returning, Nigel has been diligent in his attention to family and duty."

She winced at the rebuff and recanted. "I'm sorry."

Nigel's fury abated at the apology. He crossed to her, looked her straight in the eyes and spoke. "I acted wrongly back then, and I can't tell you how much I regret not being here for you, for Necie," he held up the letter, "and for Ellan." He put up a stiff hand to stop her beginning protest. "*If* I had, things might have been different for all of us."

"Maybe," she admitted with some reluctance. "Yet even as children she and I never got along. Call it jealousy, sibling rival, but you remember *that*. Many times you intervened and tried to make peace between us." She snatched the letter from him, her passion rising. "She made the severance permanent by aligning with Musetta and Sullivan. Or have you forgotten she poisoned Father in an attempt to kill him! Now she threatens to kill my husband and children!"

Nigel held her when passion made her upset to the point of being unable to stop the tears. "Tyrone is right, we won't let that happen."

Titus approached. "Mother. I wasn't there either, but I know Uncle Nigel will do what is necessary to help."

She wiped her eyes, then with compassion, regarded Titus. "I appreciate your confidence and I hope you never experience with your siblings the pain we have."

Titus grinned and clapped Nigel's shoulder. "Joy also. I hate to think what would have happened if Uncle had not returned. I owe he and Aunt Mirit my life."

Tristine took a deep, steadying breath. "I'm letting her threat rattle me more than I should. This brought back such painful memories."

Tyrone flashed a wry smile. "I suppose if you call needing the help of a certain blacksmith painful."

"No," she chuckled and reached to take his hand. "That part I would never change."

"We wouldn't have met without the pain of that time. Nor would Nigel's return have occurred."

"As I said, I let it get to me, but no more." She turned to Nigel. "I'm sorry for being cross."

He smiled. "I understand. Still, where you wouldn't change the past in regards to Tyrone, I wish I could change some things with Ellan."

"Then I guess you both need to come to terms about her," said Mirit.

Nigel's eyes went to the letter still in Tristine's hand.

At his interest, Tristine folded the letter and handed it to Tyrone. "Mirit's right. We must if we are to face the present."

Mirit took Nigel's arm. "We should retire. After a night's rest you may be able to think more clearly." They bade the others goodnight and left the salon.

In the hall, they met Fraser. He and Nigel embraced in greeting and Fraser kissed Mirit's cheek. "When did you arrive?"

"An hour and half ago."

"About the time I took Mikaela to bed."

"How is she?" asked Mirit.

"Better overall. She had a mild fit so I remained with her until Eldric's remedy put her to sleep."

"The journey must have been hard for her."

"Journeys usually are. This time she showed no sign of distress, so we thought she might avoid one. Have you spoken to Mother and Father yet?"

"Ay, along with Angus, Necie and Titus," replied Nigel.

"Then you've been told." Fraser frowned in dispute. "I'm not sure I agree with all the fuss. It's been so long what could she possibly do?"

"She has greatly upset your mother," rebuffed Nigel.

"Of course I'm concerned for Mother," he recanted to the scolding. "Yet without arms or aid, Ellan's practically powerless to do anything."

"Don't under estimate a determined female. Those words were filled with malice and intent," said Mirit.

Nigel looked askew at her. "That's a different attitude from earlier, or were you trying to placate me?"

"I was trying to keep you and Tristine from further angry words."

"You and Mother argued?" asked Fraser, astonished.

"We have our occasional disagreements." When Mirit grunted to the contrary, he grabbed her arm to draw her away. "Goodnight, Fraser."

"What was that about?" she asked.

"I could ask you the same."

She kept walking but pulled her arm away from his grasp. "You can't shield him. He's fifteen and quite intelligent."

"I wasn't shielding him. And I'm well aware of his intelligence."

With sudden insight, a caustic grin appeared and she said, "You want to maintain the façade of agreeability and the invincible uncle."

"No." At her skepticism, he continued. "Fraser tends to express himself rather freely."

She laughed in light ridicule. "That's a diplomatic way of saying he talks too much." At his disapproval she added, "I've been his aunt for ten years. I know him, just like I know Titus, Eli, Mikaela, Daria and the rest. You don't need to hid their faults from me."

"Then why say what you did in front of him?"

"Because *trust* is also an issue. How can he overcome his tendency if he's constantly treated with disregard? He is second born and it's about time you, Angus and Tyrone took him seriously."

Nigel's annoyance increased, however, they reached the corridor to their room. Virgil, a Guardian warrior, stood post at the door. Nigel ignored Virgil's greeting to enter the room and shut the door. He continued the discussion.

"We do take Fraser seriously, only with discretion."

"And that's part of the problem. It seems the same with Ellan."

"What?" he asked, a bit confused by her switch in names.

"Didn't you hear Tristine say how Ellan was treated with discretion in favor of you, the heir?

He shrugged with ignorance. "No. When was this?"

"While you were reading. I wondered if you heard. That's when I approached, to get your attention."

"I guess I didn't hear much."

"Tristine believes it is part of what caused Ellan's jealous resentment, which eventually grew into full-blown spite when she took your place."

For a moment he stared at her, digesting her words. "I hadn't thought about it in those terms." A bit baffled, he said, "I sensed no jealousy when we were children."

"She may not have given it voice until her whole world changed at your supposed death. Her bitterness spilled onto Tristine."

He took a seat on a nearby sofa, still pondering the concept.

She joined him. "You told me about Ellan's actions so why does this disturb you?"

"I told you what *I* was told. I never witnessed it. Father and Tristine were very adamant in describing her behavior while Avatar, Angus and Necie confirmed everything."

"Now you read it in her own hand."

His brows furrowed in disturbed consideration. "You think our treatment of Fraser may foster the same resentment?"

"I'm not certain, but do you want to take a chance?"

"No, of course not. What can I do about it other than alter my attitude towards him? That still leaves Tyrone and Angus."

"You can do more than you think. Angus is a good, honorable man, and I've grown to love him and Tyrone like brothers. However, to Titus, Fraser and Eli, you are special. Why? I don't know, but they respect you and look up to you."

"We dealt with Titus favoring me over his father in Natan."

"And he has done well these past five years. Now Fraser. We are at a critical time. We cannot afford to lose his trust and support."

He surveyed her and grinned at the assertiveness on her face. "I take it you have a suggestion."

"Speak to Tyrone about Fraser joining the Jor'ellian Guard. You, Chad and Avatar can oversee his training, not only in arms, but more important, in personal character, discretion and self discipline."

He sat back to consider the idea as she continued.

"Think of what it can do for his confidence and possibly allay any form of resentment from taking hold. You heard Tristine tell Titus she hopes he does not experience the same pain with his siblings she did. Now, *you* have the means and opportunity to do for Fraser what you couldn't do for Ellan."

He smiled, pleased and relieved. "Your suggestion is well founded. I'll speak to Tyrone in the morning."

After Nigel and Mirit left, Fraser wondered about the reason for his exclusion from an important family discussion. The answer was always the same: being second born. The serious responsibilities fell to Titus. He wondered if he should continue on his original course to bid his parents goodnight. Why? They didn't summon him to participate in the discussion. *Uncle didn't mention Eli being there. Mikaela needed me. At least someone did.*

"Fraser?"

Hearing his name startled him until he saw Ellis along with his sister Jillian, Titus' betrothed. She was sixteen years old with luxurious wavy brown hair, light brown eyes, slight of build and tall. She appeared small standing beside Titus. In temperament, she was agreeable and sweet. At the moment she appeared concerned while Ellis wore a partial smirk. Of course he would, being Titus' confidante and all.

"Is something wrong?" asked Jillian.

"Mikaela had another fit," he said in excuse to mask his annoyance.

"Is she all right?" asked Ellis with genuine concern.

"Ay. Eldric's remedy helped and she sleeps."

"I'm glad," said Jillian. "Have you seen Titus this evening?"

"He is in the family salon with Father and Uncle Angus."

"Anything important? I wanted to bid him goodnight."

Fraser heaved a shrug and grumbled, "Affairs of state probably, I wouldn't know. In fact, *Ellis* would know more than I."

"Not necessarily," said Ellis in mild dispute.

Fraser scoffed, turned on his heels and left.

"Highness," called Ellis.

"Don't provoke him," she said.

"I wasn't going to provoke him."

"You always do. You and Titus."

"That's not true. Tease, maybe."

Jillian huffed and headed for the salon.

Ellis followed, a mischievous expression on his face. "I thought you fancied Titus not Fraser. Is the truth coming out now?"

She stopped and gaped at him in outraged surprise. "How could you say that?" He laughed and she stormed off.

Again, he pursued her. "I'm teasing. I know you love Titus even though you defend Fraser." A thought struck him, and he took hold of her arm to stop her. "Unless it's the reverse and Fraser fancies you. Which would naturally make him jealous and take jabs at Titus."

"You're impossible! There are no feelings between Fraser and I."

"I should hope not," said Titus. He arrived unseen and startled her.

"No, Titus!" she clamored and tossed an angry glare at her brother. "Ellis is being ... Oh, you tell him!" she scolded.

"We encountered Fraser and I started teasing."

Titus smirked and took Jillian's arm. "Between your brother and mine it's a wonder we get a moment's peace together."

She gave Ellis a triumphant grin and left with Titus. "Truly, there are no feelings between Fraser and I."

"I don't doubt you. I sounded angry for Ellis' benefit."

She rolled her eyes. "You two are impossible! And often Fraser bears the brunt of it."

"Your compassion toward him is commendable, but he can take it."

"Are you sure? Fraser looked hurt just now."

"How so?"

"When I asked if he had seen you, he said you were with your father and the duke, probably discussing affairs of state. He accused Ellis of knowing more than he in such matters."

"I just happened to be paying my nightly respects when Nigel and Mirit arrived. We did discuss the situation."

"By Fraser's expression and words, I believe he felt excluded."

"Fraser isn't sensitive. That's Eli."

"Not sensitive, but easily provoked. Which you and Ellis tend to do."

He chuckled. "Ay." They reached the sheltered rear terrace. He took her hand and kissed it. "Enough about Fraser. I assume you were coming to bid me goodnight." He smiled.

"Of course." She giggled when he kissed her cheek, then took her in his arms and kissed her on the lips. A loud coughing interrupted them.

Egan stood in the threshold. He motioned to the figure of man briskly making his way toward them. Fagan, Jillian's father, and a comely looking man with salt and pepper brown hair and clean-shaven features. The family resemblance between them was noticeable; with Ellis, in height and shape of face, and with Jillian, in smile and brown eyes. At that moment Fagan wasn't smiling, rather wore a fatherly frown.

"My lord. I was bidding Lady Jillian goodnight."

"A rather ardent goodnight."

Titus blushed. "No more than a kiss, I assure you, my lord. I would not compromise my betrothed's honor."

Fagan smiled and the resemblance to Jillian returned. "I thought nothing of the kind, Highness. Still, prudence should be observed."

"Of course, my lord." Titus turned to Jillian and formally bowed. "Goodnight, my lady."

She smiled and curtsied. "Goodnight, Highness." She and Fagan left.

Egan cocked a grin. "I tried to warn you."

"Ellis probably sent him after us to have found us so fast."

Egan smiled. "You would do the same for Mikaela."

"If she was with Ellis I would not let her out of my sight."

"Oh, so you besmirch the honor of your fiancé's brother? Wonderful," said Ellis. He appeared from the other side of the terrace.

"You did send him!"

"No. I thought to give you both some time before stopping you myself. Father just beat me to it." He drew closer to Titus to speak confidential. "However, I did see Fraser leaving the adjacent hall."

"You think he told Fagan? That's taking your teasing too far."

"I'm not teasing. I'm serious. I saw him and he didn't look pleased."

"Why would he do that?"

Ellis shrugged, yet fought a smile. "Who knows? But you need to be watched around women."

Titus' return smile grew wide. "Better watched than made mute."

Ellis frowned at the retort. "I'm going to bed." He left.

Chapter 6

THE FOLLOWING MORNING, FRASER RECEIVED A SUMMONS FROM his father and hurried to the private study. Not unusual for Tyrone to send for him, but under the circumstances it may be important. The guards at the door saluted then one announced his arrival.

Upon entering, he saw that Armus, Nigel and Angus were with Tyrone; only Titus was absent. *Better and better.* Tyrone sat on the corner of the desk.

"You sent for me, sir?"

"Indeed," said Tyrone with a friendly smile. "Please, sit."

Fraser did so, grinning in anticipation. "Is there good news, sir?"

"I hope you will find it so. It is something that could be very beneficial for you."

"Beneficial?" he asked, growing guarded.

Tyrone chuckled. "I suppose that was not the best choice of words. I mean you should find it much to your liking."

"Really? How so?"

"Actually, your Uncle Nigel made the suggestion so he'll tell you."

Fraser's earlier anticipation returned as he gave Nigel his full attention. The latter grinned and spoke.

"How you like to join me in the Jor'ellian Guard?"

The question made Fraser momentarily speechless for excitement, and brought him to his feet. "The Jor'ellian Guard? Do you mean that, Uncle?"

"Ay. You're a fine figure of a young man. Broad in shoulder, firm in muscle, quick of mind and you can look me in eye."

He noticed Tyrone watching him. "Do you agree to this, Father?"

"Ay. That's why I called."

Fraser's smile stretched from ear to ear.

Angus chuckled at the enthusiasm. "I think he likes the idea."

"Indeed! It is much to my liking. When?"

"As soon as your father gives us leave to return to the Fortress," said Nigel.

There came a knock at the door, which Armus answered. He announced the arrival of Commander Avatar, Captain Chad and Mahon.

"Good timing," said Nigel to Tyrone.

The trio saluted Tyrone. "Sire, we've come to report a rather disturbing incident that occurred on patrol," began Avatar. "Near the border of the Meadowlands we rode upon an attack of *madah-dune*."

"*Madah-dune?*" asked Fraser.

"Creatures of the Dark Way, part wolf, part man."

"Who did they attack?" asked Tyrone.

"Wren and Lady Valery."

"Braden's daughter?"

"Ay. She is unhurt and being escorted to the guest quarters to rest. Wren was seriously wounded in a previous attack, and is in Eldric's care."

"Did Wren say why they were attacked?" asked Nigel.

"Unfortunately, her wound prevented her from saying much. She fainted and I brought her immediately to Eldric," said Mahon.

Chad spoke. "Lady Valery reported serious trouble with her father, but didn't elaborate. She is very upset."

Tyrone pursed his lips. His considering gaze shifted between Chad and Mahon, ending on Chad. "I'd like to speak to Lady Valery."

Chad saluted and left the study.

Meanwhile, Titus and Ellis made their way along the balcony of the great hall. Titus spied several of the duke's men escorting Valery through the hall to the back corridor. She wore soiled men's clothes indicating she just arrived. Titus seized Ellis and pulled him to hide behind an arch.

"Of all the places, the *man-crusher* is here!" He pointed downward.

Ellis caught a glimpse of her and the others exiting the room into the rear corridor. "You mean Valery?"

"She followed me to soothe her ego again."

"Whose ego took the bruising?" countered Ellis in correction.

"She's a tyrant."

"Just because she's better at intellectual games than you is no reason to degrade her with foul names."

Titus tossed an arm about Ellis' shoulder. "Ellis, my dearest friend and comrade, have pity on me and keep her away."

He balked in surprise. "You want *me* to keep *her* away from you?"

"Ay. What's so hard about that?" Titus scrutinized his reluctant friend. "Unless she intimidates you also."

"I never said that," stammered Ellis.

"No, just women in general. You get tongue-tied around them."

"I do not! I just haven't met one who captures my fancy, yet."

Titus laughed at the awkward answer. "As retainer to the prince royal, it is your duty to honor the request." He patted Ellis on the chest before continuing to make his way in the direction they originally headed.

"You mean to save your ego!" shouted Ellis. He received a wave and verbal affirmation from Titus, who didn't look back and kept walking.

Ellis took a deep breath of determination and took the nearest stairs down into the hall. He wasn't halfway across the room when Jillian called and rushed to intercept him. "Is something wrong?"

"Valery is here."

He rolled his eyes. "Ay. Titus and I just saw her."

She seized him, her eyes pleading. "Dear brother, you must do me a great favor and keep her away from Titus."

"Not you too," he grumbled under his breath.

"What?"

"Never mind." He waved the comment aside. "Why do you want me to do that? She means you no harm."

"She's overbearing. There is no telling how she would coerce or manipulate Titus."

Curious, he regarded her. "You sound jealous. Has Titus given you some reason to think he could even take the slightest interest in Valery? They can barely exchange civil words."

"No, of course not. He is most attentive. Only she is calculating and cunning." She became annoyed when he chuckled. "Will you refuse to help me? Your sister betrothed to the royal prince from being outdone by this man-crusher?"

He stopped chuckling at hearing *man-crusher*. He caught movement out of the corner of his eye. Titus ducked back into a doorway "He put you up to this didn't he?"

She grew sheepish. "Not exactly, though he told me he saw her." He moved to leave so she grabbed his arm. "I do have my own reservations. Please, dear brother, do me this favor."

He grunted in resignation and hung his head like a whipped puppy. "You and Titus take unfair advantage of me."

Jillian touched his cheek. "We don't mean to, but we depend so much upon your love and support."

"Very well. I was on my way to call upon her."

She smiled. "Courage, brother."

"Courage and an untied tongue." He cast a glowering glance at the doorway; only Titus wasn't there. Ellis continued on his way.

In the hall of guest quarters, various guards stood their posted, both the duke's men and royal soldiers. One of the duke's men met him.

"Can I help you, my lord?"

"I was told Lady Valery arrived. I wish to call upon her."

"This way, my lord." He led Ellis to a room in the middle of the wing and knocked. "My lady, you have a visitor."

"Enter."

The soldier opened the door to admit Ellis then quickly shut it. Immediately, Ellis came face-to-face with a wolf. He stepped back into the door. The wolf stared at him. His cautious glance shifted from the wolf to Valery. She stood at a side table with a pitcher and basin. She wore no cloak, her doublet opened to the shirt underneath and her hair tied back. She finished wiping her face with a towel.

"Oh, it's you," she said in a tone of disappointment.

"Sorry if my presence offends you," he managed to say. His eyes darted back to the wolf. "A friend of yours?" He carefully nodded to the wolf for he dared not move any further.

"Cody, meet Lord Ellis. He's harmless."

"He's a wolf!"

"I meant you."

Cody wagged his tail and approached Ellis.

"Let him greet you and smell that you are no threat."

Ellis flashed an uncertain smile when Cody sniffed him and then nudged his hand.

"Pet him. If you don't, he'll think you're afraid or more important, mean trouble."

He began to pet Cody, tentatively at first. Cody licked his hand then jumped up, placed paws on Ellis' shoulder and licked his face. He chuckled. "He doesn't act like a wolf. More like a dog"

"Oh, he's wolf, wild and untamed, but he must like you. He wasn't so friendly toward the guards. Cody."

The wolf obeyed and moved to lie down.

She tossed the towel over a rack on the side of table. "I suppose you calling on me means the prince is here."

"Ay."

She grinned, sly and challenging. "So, he sent you to ferret me out."

He struggled with a reply. "Not exactly."

She chuckled. "You never could lie very well, even for your master."

Ellis became offended. "He is my dear friend."

"Perhaps, but he also commands your attention."

He didn't reply since it wasn't a statement he could refute. She regarded him in a way he recognized as sizing him up, ready to make her next salvo when he spoke, *if* he spoke. Normally he made a polite exit, but Titus and Jillian depended upon him. *Oh, put a sword in my hand and I'd vanquish the enemy, but …*

"At a loss for words, my lord?"

He snapped out of his pondering and blurted out, "No, merely admiring your … manner of cleaning …" He stopped in annoyance at his fumbled words.

She heartily laughed. In fact, she laughed so hard she had to sit in a chair. "Oh, you are a wit! I see why Titus keeps you around."

Red-faced with anger and embarrassment he chided, "My lady, I do not take being ridiculed and laughed at lightly."

She struggled to bring her mirth under control. "I'm sorry. Your humor is unique." He turned to leave, and she quickly stood. "Wait!" She swallowed back a laugh. "You come here on behalf of your mast— friend—to test me no doubt. Yet you manage to make me laugh. It is a rare gift to place the test subject at ease."

"My lady, I wasn't meaning to be humorous or to test you."

She regarded him with some consideration, her combativeness gone. "Perhaps not, but you did make me laugh, and for that I am grateful. My journey here was far from easy."

He noted a catch of grief in her voice and a shift to awkwardness; both unusual for her. "I'm sorry to hear that. Can I be of some service?"

She balked at the offer. "I don't know. I—"

There came a knock at the door and a soldier saying, "My lady, Captain Chad to see you."

Her eyes grew wide in fear. Another unusual emotion he was unaccustomed to seeing from her. She always acted self-assured during the times she and Titus were in company, which grew frequent when her father took his place on the Council. The last time he recalled her so discomposed was at her grandfather's memorial service when they were children. Indeed something awful happened. His consideration lasted a brief moment before the guard spoke again.

"My lady?"

"Shall I admit him?" asked Ellis. She nodded, so he complied.

"Thank you, my lord." Chad bowed to Ellis and turned his attention to Valery. "My lady, the king wishes to speak to you."

"Oh," she said and paled. She fumbled in closing her doublet and fiddled with her hair. She looked to Ellis. "Would you do me the service of lending me your arm, my lord?"

"Willingly." He held out his arm for her, and surprised by the strength of her grip. He made no show or remark to cause further upset.

Cody started followed, when said, "Stay. I'll be back." Cody stopped and she and Ellis left with Chad.

When admitted to the duke's private study, Valery's grip on Ellis' arm tightened. In fact, she showed every sign of being very nervous. Those present with the king now included Titus and Fagan.

"Lord Ellis," said Tyrone.

"I was with Lady Valery when Captain Chad arrived and offered my services as escort, Sire. She is rather unnerved by her experience."

"No doubt." Tyrone kindly smiled at Valery. "Please, take a seat." He motioned to a nearby chair. Ellis helped her to the chair indicated. "You may stay if the lady is in need of further service."

Ellis glanced at Valery, who appeared uncertain and she said, "As Your Majesty wishes."

Tyrone grinned and said to Ellis, "Remain."

He bowed and stepped back to stand beside Titus and Fraser.

After a brief pause, Tyrone spoke. "I heard quite a tale of your experience since leaving Mylton, but not the reason why you left."

Her eyes shifted from Tyrone to the others in the room.

He again smiled, his grey eyes kind. "You have nothing to fear. You are among friends."

"Forgive me, Sire, but I don't know everyone here save by reputation or brief encounters. My reason is very personal and troubling."

Nigel stepped forward, and also kindly smiled. "That maybe so, but your grandfather was dear to all of us. By the love we bore him, we are concerned for you. You may speak freely."

She still appeared nervous as they stood about her.

Tyrone gave Nigel a private wink. "Let's all sit. Friends should be relaxed when talking. Titus." He indicated the chair beside Valery.

Titus balked, so, Ellis sat. "To continue my service to the lady, Sire."

Titus flashed a small, relieved smile at Ellis and sat on the sofa with Angus, Fraser and Fagan. Tyrone and Nigel sat in chairs opposite Valery. Avatar, Armus, Mahon and Chad sat on the window seats.

"Is that better? No one hovering over you?"

She wore a timid smiled. "I appreciate your consideration, Sire. I will try to speak what is difficult, as I do not fear for myself, but my mother."

"Is she is danger?"

"She could be if it is discovered she helped me escape."

"Escape? From Mylton?"

She nodded. "Because of what I learned, my father threatened me, and my mother thought best to take quick action."

"What did he threaten?" asked Nigel.

"To … kill me."

Ellis gripped her hand when her voice quivered and her eyes grew misty. He darted a glance at Titus, who sat on the edge of the sofa, stunned by the response.

Disturbed, Tyrone also moved in his seat. "Why would he do that?"

Fear made her hesitate. Ellis squeezed her hand. "Please, tell us."

Her reticent gaze turned from Ellis to Tyrone. "I overheard a secret meeting between several Council Members who swore to help support a coup against you, Sire."

Although he fought to contain his temper, his voice and face turned to resolution. "Who?"

"My father, Sir Gareth, Lord Zebulon I know for certain, and I heard other voices along with names of those not present."

"I know of no Council meeting," said Angus.

"Nor do I," said Fagan

Valery spoke to Fagan and Angus. "Your names were among those not present and for reason that you couldn't be made to swear allegiance to Ellan. Along with Mathias, Hayden and Ned. The rest agreed."

Upon hearing Ellan's name, Tyrone began to bolt up, yet managed to remain seated for Valery's sake. Whereas he remained seated, Armus, Avatar, Mahon and Chad did not. She flinched at their reaction.

"Are you certain of what you heard?" asked Nigel to draw her marked nervous attention from the others.

"Ay, Highness. She was there, along with a Guardian named Hueil."

At this news, Tyrone pushed himself out of the chair and chided to Nigel, "She's working faster than I anticipated."

"After your mother helped you escape, you met Wren?" asked Avatar.

"Ay. She, and one called Nixie, watched me since I left Mylton." Valery turned back to Tyrone. "All I wanted to do was hide from my father. Wren convinced me I should come to Garwood, tell my story and show something my mother gave me." She reached into her doublet and pulled out the ring. She held it for Tyrone to take. She spoke when he did so. "My mother said the ring belonged to her great-grandfather."

By his reaction, Tyrone recognized the ring and gave it to Nigel. Nigel rose to his feet in surprise. His glance shifted in apprehension between Tyrone, the ring and Valery.

"What name did she give?" he asked.

"Delwin."

He sighed in relief then motioned to Armus and gave him the ring.

"What is it?" Titus moved to look at the ring Armus held.

"The royal ring of the House of Tristan," said the Guardian.

"She's of royal blood?" Astonished, Titus took the ring to inspect it. "Then she could also lay claim to the throne."

"No!" Valery bolted to her feet to confront Titus. "Mother told me to show the ring only if my life was in danger. Wren convinced me to give it to the king. I make no claim! Hang you for even suggesting it!"

Ellis tried to calm her, only she shrugged him off, defiant of Titus.

"No one says you are," said Tyrone.

"With all due respect, Sire, he does. He bears me ill will."

"Valery, enough," warned Ellis with firm compassion. Some of her combativeness waned as he held her gaze. Finally she gave a faint nod, to which he spoke aloud, "Sire, she is distraught by the whole situation."

"Indeed. You experienced a horrible ordeal and perhaps I should have allowed you more time to recover before pressing you for answers. Lord Ellis will escort back to your chambers. When you are able, we shall discuss it further."

Forgetting all manner protocol, she left with Ellis.

"Truly, sir, I don't bear her ill will," insisted Titus.

Tyrone spoke to the contrary. "Oh? You think I don't know of the combative nature of your relationship? You two repel each other like equal magnets. One constantly bouncing off the other."

Titus pursed his lips in resignation. "Ay, but I would never wish her harm. I'm only concerned for my family."

"Of which she is a *direct* member," said Armus and indicated the ring.

Taken aback, Titus stared at Armus, so Fraser asked, "How so?"

"Delwin was Prince Akilles' youngest brother. We weren't certain if he survived Zared's coup since Niles only managed to save Akilles and two of his four brothers. The others died childless."

"As a descendant of Delwin, she is our cousin," said Nigel to his nephews.

"Wren was right in bringing her here for our protection," said Angus.

Visibly disturbed, Fagan spoke. "After he and others made a secret alliance with Ellan, he threatens to kill his own daughter to keep her quiet. I couldn't imagine harming my own child."

"It is more than a secret meeting he wanted to hide," began Armus. "Considering his wife's heritage, she and Valery are an unknown threat to Ellan. If she learns, she will not let any of them live."

"Only Braden would have been more merciful in killing her than if the *madah-dune*," said Avatar.

Titus and Fraser exchanged fearful glances.

"Maybe now you can be more kind towards her," said Tyrone.

"Ay, sir. I should start by apologizing." He handed Tyrone the ring.

Shouting and a blustery entrance halted Titus' departure. A road dusty nobleman of forty years of age arrived with Kell and Vidar.

"Sire!" he said breathlessly. He appeared on the verge of collapse.

"Chad. Wine for Sir Hayden."

Chad fetched the wine, which Hayden drank in one long gulp.

"Thank you." He gave the cup back to Chad before speaking to Tyrone. "Zebulon has retaken the Lowlands. I couldn't stop him. He was too heavily armed being aided by Shadow Warriors and Gareth's men. My family and I barely escaped to warn you."

"Sire, if Zebulon and Gareth are in league with Ellan and Hueil, the Council is divided," said Kell.

"They already are. Lady Valery told us how she witnessed a secret meeting where most of Council pledged their support to her."

A flash of light made all edgy. Gulliver, a silver haired sea Guardian, appeared. "Sire, I bring bad news. The East Coast fleet has left Leith."

Tyrone's eyes narrowed in wrath. "Hollis!"

"Were any ships commanded by Guardians?" asked Kell.

"No, all mortals."

Agitated, Angus chided, "How is she moving so fast?"

"Dagar communicated from his nether dimension, perhaps Hueil found a way to do the same from his imprisonment," replied Kell.

Tyrone picked up on the Guardian captain's line of thinking. "You mean to help Ellan move all the pieces into place beforehand?"

"Ay. However, Hueil had to use Guardians since he had no means to communicate with mortals like Dagar did with an altar and talisman."

"Locan and Mannix," groused Vidar. "I haven't been able to locate them nor have they been reported vanquished like the others."

Tyrone's eyes turned menacing. "Gulliver, fetch Chase, Seacrest and any other sea Guardian you can. Tell Mathias to mobilize the rest of the fleet to counter Hollis. Vidar, go to Waldron and inform Wess to notify all royal outposts and commanders to go on full alert."

Both vanished at the same time, filling the room with blinding light.

"How can you be certain Mathias will respond favorably?" asked Hayden after recovering from the double disappearance.

"Valery said he was among those not present because they couldn't be persuaded to join Ellan. I can only hope and pray nothing has happened since to change his mind."

"He won't," said Nigel with firm assurance about his father-in-law.

"Sire, with everything happening so fast, I believe now is the time to seek out Vicar Uriah," said Kell.

In visible fury and unwillingness, Tyrone stared at Kell.

Nigel gripped Tyrone's arm to get his attention. "We must find a place of safety to think and regroup." He nodded to Titus and Fraser.

Tyrone's regarded his sons, who stood side-by-side. He took a deep breath then spoke to Kell. "Prepare for immediate departure, Captain."

Kell saluted and left the study.

"Now, we must tell our families," he said to Nigel and Angus.

"With your permission, sir, I'd like to tell Valery," said Titus. He saw Fagan's curiosity so he added, "and Jillian, of course."

Tyrone fought a grin. "I was about to suggest to Lord Fagan that Jillian join us. If he can bear to part with her."

"I would be honored, Sire. After all, she is betrothed to His Highness."

Titus departed.

"Does this change me joining the Jor'ellians?" asked Fraser.

"No," said Nigel. "If anything it makes it more imperative in defense of our family and the kingdom."

"Ay. You are now under your uncle's command," declared Tyrone.

Features firm, Nigel approached Fraser. "Understand this, you will receive no special treatment, no favoritism. You are a cadet."

"I understand, Uncle."

He raised a hand of correction. "Champion—to a cadet. You are not to call me *Uncle* in public and only in private *if* I allow."

Fraser stiffened to attention. "Ay, Champion."

Keeping an eye on Fraser, he addressed others. "Commander Avatar, Captain Chad, have our new cadet properly installed among his peers and prepare the Guard to escort the royal family to The Fortress."

"Ay, Champion." They slapped their swords in salute.

Ellis and Valery reached the rear corridor of the guest rooms when a blonde female Guardian warrior met them.

"Lady Valery, my name is Nixie. I'm the Trio Leader of the Meadowlands."

"I recognize you. Wren said you went protect my mother."

Nixie grew somber. "I arrived at Mylton too late. I'm very sorry."

Valery swallowed back an outcry of sorrow.

Ellis took hold of her hand. "I'll take you to your room."

"No. A chapel, please." She barely kept from crying.

Ellis escorted Valery to the west wing of Garwood. She remained silent in desperate struggle against being overcome. They no sooner entered the chapel then she ran from him and fell before the altar sobbing. For a long awkward moment, he watched with uncertainty of what to do or say. This was one occasion his lack of words gnawed at him. He thought of something and quietly left.

He ran to the guest quarters and ignored the guard to enter Valery's room. His rushing entrance startled Cody and the wolf stood, growling.

"Easy, Cody. I came to fetch you and bring you Valery. She can use your help. Will you come with me?"

"*Fois, Cody,*" said a voice from the threshold.

"Wren. Are you well enough to be up?"

89

She leaned against the doorpost, pale and tired. "I've been better. When I heard about Florie I came to call upon Valery."

"She's in the chapel. I thought having Cody would help her."

"*E tu caraid de Valery. Rach comhla ri Ellis, Cody,*" she said. Cody barked and wagged his tail. "He'll go with you now."

"Cody." The wolf followed Ellis back to the chapel.

Once inside, Cody made his way to Valery. She lay on the altar step weeping. Cody whimpered in greeting and licked her face.

"Cody!" She hugged the wolf's neck. "How did you get here?"

"I thought you could use a friend," said Ellis.

"Thank you."

He gave her a modest smile then turned to leave. He reached for the door handle when Cody cut in front of him. The wolf circled him twice before taking hold of his sleeve and tugged for him to turn around.

"He doesn't want you to leave." She stood and wiped her eyes.

"I don't want to disturb you."

"I'd like you to stay."

Cody went behind Ellis and jumped up against his back, which made Ellis fall forward a few steps.

"Very well. Although I'm not certain what to say."

She sat on the front pew, once again trying to restrain her emotions. "Say something humorous to make me laugh."

He joined her. "If I do, it'll be by accident."

She flashed a teary smile. "The best kind of humor is spontaneous and unplanned."

"Planned or unplanned, I'm not good with words."

"You haven't seemed so at Court."

He snorted an ironic chuckle. "I'm usually with my comrades. We talk about war, training, athletics and hunting. Around women—I don't know what to say."

"You have a sister. Don't you talk to her?"

"It's not the same as making polite conversation or witty, flirtatious banter."

90

"Honestly, I don't like such conversation. All a façade."

"Ay, you've made that known."

She stiffened in anger. "I said humorous, not insulting."

"I'm sorry," he said, then balked at how to form his words. "What I meant is, you are not like most women at Court—you speak your mind, straightforward and honest."

"I didn't think those qualities were appreciated. At least in a woman."

"Being straightforward and honest are some of the better qualities, whether for a man or a woman."

"My mother thought so too," she sniffled. Cody placed his head on her lap.

Ellis touched her shoulder. "Then your mother was a fine woman."

She petted Cody as her voice wavered between emotional and scornful. "Father didn't think so. He always criticized her—both of us, especially after Grandfather died. Yet, recently he acted more agreeable, even friendly. His sudden change in attitude made Mother suspicious. She told me to follow him."

His became confused. "I thought he threatened your life?"

She took a breath to steady her nerves. "After I was discovered."

Cody moved away and snarled toward the back of the chapel.

Titus entered. "Where did the wolf come from?" He made a waving gesture at Cody, to which the wolf moved to confront him.

Egan stepped in front of Titus and drew his sword.

"Cody, no!" said Valery.

The wolf stopped a few feet from Egan. She hastened to Cody and spoke a hurried explanation to Egan. "His name is Cody. Wren called for him and his pack to protect us on our journey here."

"Wren?" Egan lowered his sword.

"Ay. We needed their help when some wolf-men creatures attacked us and she became badly wounded."

"Where is she?" he asked with concern.

"Mahon took her to someone called Eldric."

He relaxed in featured and posture. "Then she's here."

"Cody chose to stay with me." She patted Cody's head as the wolf stood beside her in a non-threatening manner.

Ellis spoke to Titus. "He is harmless, if he can determine whether you are friend or foe."

"How does he do that?"

"Let him sniff you. If he likes you, you'll know."

Titus waved Egan aside, and the Guardian sheathed his sword.

On a hand signal from Ellis, Cody moved forward and sniffed Titus. He nudged Titus' hand, but Titus withdrew his hand. Cody did a snort-like sneeze and returned to standing between Valery and Ellis. Ellis laughed. Valery smiled and patted Cody's head.

"What's so funny?" demanded Titus.

"He wanted you to pet him. When you didn't, he snorted at you in annoyance," she explained.

"When I petted him, he wagged his tail, got up on my shoulders and licked my face in greeting like a loyal dog." As if to emphasis the difference, Cody licked Ellis' hand while wagging his tail. "See?"

"Well, I guess you're better with wolves than women," groused Titus.

Seeing the sting on Ellis' face to the remark, Valery took hold of his arm. "Lord Ellis has been most helpful in my distress. He's even made me laugh with his spontaneous humor."

Surprised, he pointed at Ellis. "Him?"

"Now who's taking teasing too far?" scolded Ellis.

"Is there a reason you're here, Highness?" she asked.

Titus was slow to take his curious focus off a piqued Ellis. "I came to offer my sympathies, and regret for any past tension between us."

"Is this genuine or are you still afraid I may bear a claim against you? Or rather the throne."

"No!" he snapped. At her offense, Ellis' frown and Cody's growl, he changed his tone. "I mean it in all sincerity." She wasn't convinced and he continued. "You may not be aware of this but I am very concerned for my family and jealously guard them."

"True," said Ellis in confirmation, briefly interrupting Titus' speech.

"By this revelation, you are no longer one among many nobles ladies at Court, you are my cousin."

"Cousin?"

"Delwin was Akilles' youngest brother. That makes us cousins."

"I hadn't thought about it. Mother only told me before …" New emotions stopped her speech.

"I didn't mean to upset you," said Titus in quick apology.

"Everything is happening so fast, I'm not certain what to think or feel." She shyly glanced at Ellis, who held her about the shoulders in support.

"Unfortunately, you won't have time for consideration, my lady," said Chad. He arrived unnoticed and stood in the threshold. "The royal family is making ready for immediate departure to the Region of Sanctuary."

"Why?"

"The threat has grown greater and faster than anyone expected. Please, come with me. I'll help you prepare."

Valery hesitated by looking to Ellis.

"I'm afraid Lord Ellis has duties elsewhere. Please, my lady, we must hurry." Chad held out his arm to her.

"I'll call upon you when all is settled," said Ellis.

Titus watched Valery leave with Chad and Cody. "Have you taken a fancy to her?"

"No, I did what you and Jillian asked. When word came of the king's summons, I acted as an honorable gentleman and offered my services. Have you taken back what you said in regard to your new *cousin?*"

"No, just surprised to learn you made a woman laugh. *And* one who seemed genuinely to enjoy your company."

"I'm not totally hopeless in that area!"

"I didn't mean to offend you."

"Maybe not. Your reference to *cousin* joined with what I heard earlier, there is a distinct possibly my uncle is involved."

Titus nodded. "I thought of that. However, Bosley wasn't mentioned among those involved."

"Nor among those who couldn't be persuaded. I love my uncle, but he doesn't have the courage of Wess or the resolute mind of my mother." His expression changed to remorseful. "This is one time I'm glad she isn't alive to learn her brother may have betrayed the king."

Titus tried to comfort and encourage Ellis. "Don't dwell on it until we know for certain. In the meantime, we must get my family to safety or should I say, our family. Some day soon, you will be my brother-in-law."

Garwood buzzed with activity for departure. Kell met with Avatar by the armory. Someone called to him. Wren tried to make her way across the compound in awkward steps. Eldric protested her even being out of bed. He grabbed her arm. In her weakened condition she couldn't pull away and again shouted.

"Kell! Tell this overgrown babysitter to let me go!"

The captain grinned at the terse humor and shook his head. "I don't know if I'm willing to do so with your wound being so bad."

She stopped struggling against Eldric's hold to confront Kell. "You can't leave without me. This is my province and I'm responsible for the safety of all who travel here."

"You're in no condition—" began Eldric.

"Then heal me!" she snapped. When Eldric clamped his mouth shut, she turned to Kell. "As captain, order him to use his power and heal me."

He met the request with reluctance. "You know what a healing requires. What it would do to Eldric to expend such energy."

Despite the pain, she stood straight to continue her confrontation. "*You* ordered my Trio Mates to aid in guarding Hueil, leaving me alone until *you* assigned replacements. That hasn't happened. Now they are vanquished and I am incapacitated. To whom will *you* turn for help in protecting the royal family in *my* province, Captain?"

Kell's jowls flexed with anger and regret at her bold, public rebuff.

"She has a point," said Avatar.

Kell closed his eyes. For a moment they waited and watched the captain. A flash of light appeared. It faded to reveal Ridge, a ranger. He reached the height of Kell but with red hair, thin beard and light golden eyes. He wore the black and brown clothes of forester with a dagger at his hip and quarterstaff across his back.

Wren lashed out. "You want *him* to replace me in my province?"

"No. I called him to help once Eldric has healed you." Kell put up a hand to stop Eldric's protest. "The task is too important and time too critical. Take her and do what you must. Ridge, go with Wren, she'll explain the situation."

Chapter 7

ELTORIA, HOME OF BARON ERASMUS, LORD OF THE DELTA, contained splendid, spacious and open rooms. The numerous courtyards, sparkling pools and fountains contained the Delta's famed healing waters. All still flowed since autumn was mild in the province. However, the flowerbeds were bare and trees had shed their leaves.

Erasmus and Bosley met in the private drawing room with Erasmus' eldest son Eric and his wife Karly. Eric was almost the spitting image of Erasmus when younger. As an only child, Karly favored her father, Wess, in the shape of her face, brown hair, blue eyes and winning smile. Only now she wore no smile, rather frowned at her uncle in distress.

"Please, Karly, understand I don't do this lightly!" urged Bosley.

"Neither of us do," added Erasmus.

Eric placed a hand on Karly's shoulder. His face and voice stern toward his father and Bosley. "This is difficult for us to believe. Especially considering how well you know the royal family."

Erasmus winced and droned, "I know."

"And you, Uncle? What will my father say when he learns you betrayed him?" she chided.

"I haven't betrayed Wess!"

High passion brought her to her feet. "You have!"

He seized her by the arms. "No! I am standing by an oath I made years ago. An oath I am bound to uphold. Wess would understand."

Protective of his wife, Eric drew her from Bosley to confront him. "What of the oath you swore to Tyrone and Tristine? Does it mean nothing?"

Erasmus stepped between Bosley and Eric. "Of course it does! But by royal and Jor'ellian law, the oath we swore to Ellan precedes the one to Tyrone and Tristine. Can't you see our quandary?"

Eric shook his head in stout refusal. "No. We don't."

Bosley sighed with great anxiety and began to pace.

Erasmus drew closer to Eric and spoke in a hushed voice so only his son could hear. "She made threats more compelling than any oath." His gaze darted toward Karly then back to Eric.

"You mean—?"

"Ay. We have no choice to protect those we love."

His argument thwarted, he asked, "What can I do to help?"

"Eric?" said Karly in surprise.

Bosley stopped pace. "No! They must not become involved."

Erasmus waved Bosley silent and answered Eric. "You and your family leave Deltoria immediately and take shelter with Wess."

"And leave you to face this alone?"

Erasmus gripped Eric's arm as he struggled for words. "I must save something of my family!" He took off his signet ring and shoved it in Eric's hand. "The province is yours. Pledge allegiance to Tyrone and all will be well."

"Father—"

"No, Eric, it must be this way! You are not bound by a prior oath. I'll do what I can to keep up the façade so they don't suspect anything."

"What about your other sons and their families?" asked Karly, now moved to compassion.

"Living away from Deltoria may help to spare them. But Eric is my heir and Bryson will follow him. By sending you to him, and making the pledge, Wess will see the truth of what we are forced to do."

Bosley took Karly's hand and fought his emotions. "Tell Wess, I wish to heaven it didn't have to be this way. Give him this." He held out his signet ring. "Tell him to pass it to whichever one of my sons survives. I can't wear it any more."

She clenched the ring and embraced him. "I will."

"Leave now. Don't even pack." Erasmus ushered them to the door.

A flash of light filled the room. Erasmus, Bosley and Eric reached for their swords. Karly moved to stand behind Eric. All watched the light fade. A Guardian warrior appeared. He was more mature in feature with white hair and striking light eyes with only a hint of emerald green.

"Alrick," said Erasmus in relief.

"I sent Cort and Kent to start a delaying action, but I don't know much longer we can repel Hueil."

"Is there nothing you can do to stop him?" asked Eric.

"We're doing everything we can. I sent word to Kell, but even he is stymied at their quickness. Hueil's power seems equal to Dagar."

There was only a brief moment of digesting the news when Erasmus spoke to the Guardian. "Take Eric, Karly and Bryson to General Wess."

"That leaves you and the Delta vulnerable."

"The Delta is lost! I wish to save something."

"Ay, my lord."

"Now, no more argument or delay, you must leave at once."

"Dimension travel," said Bosley.

"I can't with three, my lord. Two mortals is a Guardian's limit. Unless I leave one and return—"

"No! We can't risk any delay," snapped Erasmus with impatience. "They must go together, because of what they carry and must explain."

Eric agreed. "We'll fetch Bryson and leave immediately." Alrick followed them out.

"Jor'el be with you!" said Bosley and closed the door. "I pray we're doing the right thing."

"At least we're saving them. Return to Midessex and see what can be done to spare some of your family before Hueil's grip spreads further."

Bosley shook his head. "You know my wife died last year, Dylan serves in the army with Wess and Garrick has taken to the sea with Hollis." He sighed in heavy lament. "My sons are also divided by this."

"Then begin doing as we discussed."

A servant entered carrying a small silver plate with a letter on it. "My lord, this just arrived."

The letter bore the royal seal stamped on the sealing wax. Erasmus took it and waved the servant to leave.

"Tyrone or *her?*" asked Bosley with trepidation.

Erasmus didn't answer, broke the seal and read. "Ellan commands us to Roxbury in the Lowlands to report our progress of readiness."

"Readiness? It's only been a week. What does she expect?"

"Who knows? Stay the night, and we'll leave at first light."

The heavily fortified manor house of Roxbury sat on a plateau in stark contrast to the flowing wheat fields of the surrounding countryside. The late fall harvest drew near. Small settlements of farmers scattered about the plain. Between the settlements, military camps assembled.

Bosley and Erasmus observed the rising tents, backlit by the twilight sun. Twenty-five of Erasmus' men accompanied them on their journey.

"She didn't mention bringing troops, did she?" asked Bosley.

"No. By the banners those are Gareth and Zebulon's men."

"The Meadowlands is over there." Bosley pointed to a red, green and white banner.

A quarter mile from the manor, Erasmus stopped and summoned his captain. "Make camp by the stream while Lord Bosley and I continue."

Arriving in the courtyard of the manor house, grooms scrambled to take the reins of their horses.

"My lords. Lord Zebulon instructs all Council Members to gather in the hall," said a groom.

A swarm of activity buzzed throughout the manor. Once inside, servants offered refreshment and took hats and cloaks, but they did not yield their gloves. Across the hall, Braden and Malcolm sat on a bench. They joined them.

"Malcolm? Have you been home yet?" asked Erasmus.

"No. I was three days out when word reached me of the summons. I turned around and came here."

"You look tired."

"I am," he groused. "I'm not certain how I'll do on a campaign."

"We'll see that you remain behind to help with coordination while we do the actual fighting," said Erasmus.

"Let's hope it doesn't come to that," chided Bosley.

"Do you really believe it can be avoided?" asked Braden.

Bosley's jowls tightened in anger at Braden. Erasmus spoke, in effort to prevent a confrontation. "What one believes and what one hopes are often different. Take this morning, for example. I woke hoping it wouldn't rain, but my aching joints told me different and we rode thought a cloudburst. I keep my gloves on to warm my aching joints."

Malcolm laughed, but stopped when Braden scowled. Bosley wasn't so accommodating to Braden's annoyance and continued to laugh.

Braden forced a smile. "Sounds like something my father would say."

Erasmus bowed his head to the compliment. "Thank you. Allard often tried to engage me in a sporting exchange of wit, much to my embarrassment. At last now, I succeeded."

"My lords, welcome!" Gareth's voice boomed. He, Zebulon, Ellan and Hueil entered.

"Gentlemen, it is good see you are prompt in replying to my summons," said Ellan. They bowed to her.

"We would be remiss to do otherwise, Madam," said Braden.

She smiled. "Indeed, my lord." She proceeded to the front of the hall where several chairs were arranged. One stood elevated, two other chairs faced the elevated chair. She mounted the small platform to sit in the elevated chair. "Please be seated, Lord Zebulon, Lord Malcolm."

The rest remained standing since only Zebulon and Malcolm were permitted to sit in the royal presence.

"The time is growing near to mobilize. Words of warning were sent to the half-breed. Including informing him of Lord Zebulon's success in retaking the Lowlands, Baron Hollis launching the East Coast fleet, and names those of the Council Members in allegiance with me. In short, his reign is crumbling around him and he is powerless to stop it."

In a moment of stunned silence Erasmus, Bosley, Malcolm and Braden absorbed the news. Finally, Erasmus spoke in a grim voice.

"You have doomed us to war! Tyrone won't give up without a fight. He'll order Wess to muster the royal troops."

"Hence the reason for the gathering of our troops." Her features fixed. "Only I am disappointed you didn't bring more men, baron."

"Your summons didn't mention troops. I brought a detachment of men to ensure safe travel. The rest are assembling at Deltoria."

Her gaze passed to Bosley. "And you, my lord?"

"I've not returned home yet, Madam. Baron Erasmus and I concluded the trade business interrupted by the first summons. We thought we had more time than a few days for all to be accomplished."

"The journey alone for Lord Bosley is four days," said Erasmus.

"Add at least five days to assemble my men, four more days to travel back for be a total of about two weeks," said Bosley.

"And Malcolm, up to three weeks, correct?" said Erasmus.

"Indeed. Though pressing upon my health I would do it, Madam."

Ellan glanced to Hueil. The Guardian gave a barely discernable nod and she assumed a relaxed posture.

"Those are reasonable explanations. However, speed is requires from this day forth, gentlemen. I will accept no more excuses. You will have your forces assembled here in twelve days."

Malcolm paled even more so than his normal hallowed complexion. "As you wish, Madam."

Showing great impatience, Ellan stood. "Go!" She waved hands at them before she stormed from the room with Hueil at her heels.

She grumbled complaints all the way back to her chamber. When Hueil closed the door she gave voice to her frustration. "Delays, delays!"

"Patience."

"Easy for you to say since Guardians are immortal. I spent eighteen years rotting in isolation." She looked at him, cold and calculating. "Launch the trap."

"Move too soon and the half-breed may gain an advantage. Let us proceed according to the original timetable. If more drastic measures are needed, I will take care of it."

"How?"

A devious smile appeared. "In Tunlund I gave him much to think about by bringing to his mind's eye visions of events before they occurred—or rather what I intended to do. I can use the same method to cause mistrust and derision."

She regarded him in challenging skepticism. "He defeated you."

Icy blue eyes narrowed in remembrance. "Only by the act of an interfering mortal female. If not for her, the boy would be dead, the half-breed defeated and I the supreme god of two countries."

"And I still captive," she chided. He heaved a careless shrug and she lashed out. "Who is this mortal female? I should thank her, since your defeat offered me this opportunity." At his icy stare, she gripped her hands together in an effort to keep from retreating.

"Her name is Mirit. She married your brother." He flashed a taut sardonic smile. "Do you still wish to thank her?"

"No." Frustrated, she sat. "What about the other part of the plan?"

He snapped his fingers and a small metal hooked device appeared in his hand. "With this, he won't be able to resist. Careful. It's very sharp and painful," he warned when she examined it.

At one end was a pin sharp tip. She gave it back to him. "What is it?"

"One of Dagar's ingenious reconditioning devices. While the Guardian is rendered unconscious by an inducing potion and ready to take subconscious suggestion, this is placed behind the ear with the pin inserted near a pain nerve. As long as the Guardian does what is required, the device is harmless. If orders are not carried out, intense pain punishes disobedience."

She was not convinced. "His will is very strong. It won't bend easy."

He pocketed the device and spoke with indifference. "Then the pain will grow so intense as to kill him. So he is dead, either by killing himself due resisting or others kill him for betrayal."

"Have you thought of how to capture him? He's not going to just let you use that thing on him," she said with impatience.

"I ordered Locan and Mannix to do so, along with disposing of Braden's daughter."

Irritated, she paced again. "If the girl talks!"

"Why trouble yourself about her? You already sent word."

"Not exactly. I sent the letter before knowing whom Gareth managed to convince. I only hinted at a divide." She groaned, weary and frustrated. "I don't want to argue anymore. I just want this over quickly."

He held her hands "No need to argue when there is the alternative, my dear one." He tenderly touched her cheek.

She flashed a caustic smile. "A Guardian flirting with a mortal? Since when?"

He held her chin to gaze into her eyes. "Since I found a mortal female whose unbridled ambition is equal to my own."

She stared back at him, a slight ripple of annoyance on her brow. "A moment ago you scolded me, now I'm to believe you care for me?"

He grinned. "My scorn is for the female, Mirit, not you." He leaned close to her face; his lips near her lips and whispered, "If you doubt me, feel my passion." He kissed her.

Upon separating, Ellan had to recover her breath. "I didn't know a Guardian could be so passionate."

He smiled. "We can do everything mortals can, only far better." He moved to kiss her again and when she became receptive, he backed off. "However, if you are unwilling to fully commit to the coup."

"Commit? I put the poison in my father's wine."

"True, but your allies were mortal."

"Morrell was involved."

Hueil laughed in ridicule. "Tell me, did you willing yield to him?"

"We collaborated and very often I took his advice."

He grinned, his fingers tracing the curve of her face. "Not the same."

She snatched his hand away. "By trying to woo me like a love-starved female, I'm supposed to believe you are different than Morrell?"

A brief look of wounded pride crossed his face. When she scoffed, he resumed the suitor's façade. "I am from the beginning. One of the Originals, like Kell and Dagar. I can do things Morrell could not, but to what extent are you willing to go?"

She leaned closer as if to kiss him and lowly said, "Willing to kill my entire family if necessary." She pushed away from him with a smirk.

"What then? You would have the throne by making a statement in blood, but what about real power? How will you keep the people in line? And what about an heir?"

She looked sideways at him. "Or dealing with an ambitious rival."

He shook his head, a longing smile appearing as he turned her face towards him. "Not if joined together. Between us we can create a kingdom like no other and secure it with our progeny and heir." He took her head between his hands and gazed into her eyes. "I give you my word as a Guardian, you will be queen again."

Outside in the main courtyard, Bosley and Erasmus passed close to Malcolm and Braden on their way to their horses. They overheard Malcolm ask Braden, "What happened to Valery? Were you able to convince her to keep silent?" They waited to hear Braden's answer since they had not been seen.

"She's taken care of, but this is not the place for discussion."

Piqued by the reply, they approached. "Here now, what is going on? What is this about Valery?" demanded Erasmus.

"You can be an interfering cur!" Braden stormed off.

"What was that about?" Bosley asked Malcolm only he appeared too weak to answer.

Erasmus helped Malcolm sit on a nearby crate. "Take a moment to compose and gain your strength, then tell us."

After a couple of moments, Malcolm spoke. "I don't know if I should tell you, but it can't be kept secret either."

"Try, and with as little emotion as possible," said Erasmus.

"We were the last to leave the meeting when one of his men arrived with a spy in tow. The person spoke in an obvious attempt to disguise the voice so Braden removed the cowl and hat to reveal Valery."

"What did he do to her?" asked Bosley.

"I don't know! He dragged her from the room …" Overwhelmed by emotion, he collapsed back against the building. "How I wish I could have done something. Curse my weak body!"

Erasmus sat in an effort to calm Malcolm. "Easy, my friend."

He shook his head. "I fear by his reaction, he has done her injury. Though if she speaks, we are undone!"

"It would be pointless. Ellan made our names known, so Valery telling of the meeting is of minor consequence."

"You really believe that?"

"Ay. Other than Braden's manly pride and anger at her actions, she can't place us in any more danger than we have placed ourselves."

"Your reasoning is sound, but doesn't ease my concern for her."

"I understand." Erasmus gave Malcolm an encouraging pat on the leg. "Now, let us help you to your horse." He and Bosley each took Malcolm by the arm and help him mount the horse.

Servants rode with Malcolm when departing the manor.

In tone and expression of skepticism, Bosley asked, "Do you truly mean to leave this business with Valery alone?"

"No."

Instead of leaving the manor, they rode to where Braden and his men were camped. Braden spoke with two officers.

"I would have a word with you," said Erasmus.

"Can it wait? I have business," replied Braden in tone decidedly unwilling.

"No." When Braden appeared reluctant, even hostile, Erasmus added, "Need I remind you of our differences in rank and station to command your attention?"

Braden stiffened. "No, my lord *baron*." He waved his men to leave. "We are fellow Council Members and respect should be both ways."

Erasmus and Bosley dismounted. "As a fellow Member, you were remiss to withhold such information as the possibility of a spy and breach in Council security."

Annoyed, yet cornered, Braden's clashing emotions became manifested. He clenched the hilt of his sword and his wary glance shifted from Erasmus, to Bosley, then back to Erasmus. "I have made it clear to her that she is to be silent or suffer severe consequences."

"It sounds like her actions are serious enough to inform the others, *and* Ellan," said Erasmus to Bosley.

"And bring Valery into our custody for security's sake."

Braden paled. "Is that necessary?"

"Of course, unless you can assure us of her silence and safety."

"She is safe, isn't she?" asked Erasmus in a tone of insistence.

Braden balked, yet at their skepticism blurted out, "Ay."

"Doesn't sound very convincing," said Bosley.

"We should go to Mylton and speak to her ourselves," said Erasmus.

"No! You can't," said Braden.

"Oh? And why not?"

Braden stammered for words to form of a flimsy excuse. "We have only twelve days to bring our troops here."

Erasmus looked around at the encampment. "Your troops are here, and we can spare a few hours delay before returning home."

"Ay," agreed Bosley. "Besides, Florie always offers tasty treats to guests." Braden grew paler and his breath quickened, which made Bosley concerned. "Is something wrong with Florie?"

Braden swallowed back his discomposure. "I'm afraid this whole situation proved too much for her. She collapsed … her heart gave way."

Stunned, Bosley asked, "Florie is dead?"

Unable to look at them, Braden just nodded.

"Poor Valery," said Erasmus. "Indeed, we shall call upon her to pay our respects and offer condolences."

"No!" snapped Braden, now completely unsettled. "She doesn't know. At least, I haven't told her."

"How could you not tell her?"

"She's gone!"

Erasmus seized Braden. "Get a hold of yourself, man!"

Braden drew them into a nearby tent, and made a hasty explanation. "I wanted her to be quiet so I threatened her."

"Florie?

"Valery! When we arrived home I locked her in her room. At least I thought I did. Then they arrived, Gareth, Zebulon, Ellan and *him*. They wanted to make sure all was well with me. They left the next day, but *he* stayed behind, spying. It made Florie nervous. I wasn't too happy, but what could I do? Anyway, a few days later he discovered Valery wasn't in her room. He accused me of allowing her to escape, which I denied."

"How did she leave?" asked Bosley.

"I don't know! I told him Florie would know and he confronted her. She confessed to helping Valery escape and … it happened so fast, Florie lying on the floor, vacant eyes staring up at me," he muttered with disconcertion. "I'll never forget her eyes as long as I live."

"Hueil killed Florie," said Erasmus.

Braden nodded. Emotions suddenly drained away and he fell into a chair. "For years we didn't get along and I wanted her quiet, but not dead!"

"You threatened Valery," accused Bosley.

"That's different."

"How? She is your daughter and Florie was your wife. Did you value their lives so cheaply?"

Irate, Braden stood. "How I treat my family is my business."

"And a fine job you've done. One is dead and the other missing!"

Braden launched at Bosley and tried to wrap his hands around Bosley's throat. Being younger and faster, Bosley avoided him. Braden turned to attack again but found Erasmus' sword pointed at him. The deadly look and intent were undeniable.

"You made it our business by not informing us of the situation. We will agree not to tell the others, if you keep your wits. Be warned," Erasmus pressed his blade to Braden's throat, "one false move towards Bosley or myself, and we talk. Understand?"

Braden flashed a sneering glare at the blade then to Bosley. He also drew his sword. Braden had no choice. "Ay."

Erasmus sheathed his sword. Bosley didn't sheath his sword until they left the tent and mounted for departure.

"Now what?" he asked.

"We go about our business. I think we contained Braden. He doesn't have Allard's courage or intelligence."

"He is more volatile and unpredictable."

"It doesn't change what we must do."

A full moon and stars shone brightly in a cloudless sky. "I hate night travel," said Bosley.

<hr />

Hueil entered the anteroom from the bedroom. Mannix waited and became curious at catching sight of Ellan before Hueil shut the door.

"You and the female?" he questioned, to Hueil annoyance.

"All part of the plan. Remember Dagar's progeny?"

"Ay. I fought his offspring."

"Then you know the power they commanded. Not to mention the half-breed! Enough of my actions, I hope you're here to report success."

"No, my lord," he hastily continued at Hueil's displeasure, "We fetched the *madah-dune* as instructed and attacked them twice."

"Them?"

"Wren and Nixie found her when we launched the first attack. Wren became badly wounded and split off from Nixie to take the girl to Garwood. We tracked them and made a second attack, but *he* arrived with some of the Jor'ellian Guard—"

Hueil seized Mannix, drawing dangerously close to the warrior's face. "You had both of them in your grasp and they escaped?"

Mannix swallowed back his trepidation to reply. "Ay, my lord."

He tossed Mannix across the room. "Incompetent fools!" With a loud menacing growl, he moved toward Mannix,

The warrior put up his arms in defense. "There is more, my lord! The half-breed in on the run—!" He gasped when Hueil lifted him off the floor.

"What is going on?" Ellan arrived wearing a dressing gown.

Hueil dropped Mannix, who barely caught himself to keep from completely falling to the floor. "Explain!" he commanded Mannix.

"The half-breed and the entire royal family left Garwood and are heading toward the Region of Sanctuary."

Her face lit up with a mixture of surprise and pleasure. "This is incredible. How many men do you have?"

"Myself, Locan and a dozen *madah-dune*."

"Give him Shadow Warriors to attack and destroy them before they reach the Fortress!"

"Kell and Vidar are with them," warned Mannix.

At her visible annoyance, Hueil said, "We will attack using enough force to give the half-breed something to consider and to feel out Kell. We are not ready to face them yet or tip our hand."

"Very well." She waved at Mannix. "Cause what trouble you can."

"Ay, my lady." Mannix vanished.

"Why do you trust them? They are two of most incompetent Guardians I've ever seen."

"I never said I trusted them." He sarcastically sneered. "Although, for warriors they are weak minded. Kell should thank me for weeding them out."

"Speaking of the captain, how do you plan to deal with him? Surely not just using those two fools."

"Hardly, my dear. By the means I freed the Shadow Warriors I will unlock Dagar's nether dimension."

Surprised apprehension showed on her face. "Dagar?"

"Afraid?" He moved beside of her and stroked her cheek. "No need to fear. What he created I can command and they won't hurt you."

"As long as I do what you want, I suppose?"

"Did our union prove nothing to you?"

"That a Guardian is surprisingly passionate."

"Not that I have feelings for you?" He leaned down to kiss her neck. She whispered in his ear, "No."

He took her face in his hand and deeply looked into her eyes. "I do care for you with a deep sense I have never felt for a mortal before."

For a moment she stared at him. The usual iciness to his blue eyes somehow gone making her mildly confused. "Do you really mean that? And do I dare believe you?"

"The choice is yours. Just like it was to leave when I offered you freedom."

Chapter 8

WREN AND RIDGE LED THE ROYAL GROUP THROUGH THE FOREST. With too much traffic on the main roads, less traveled roads were more suitable for a large company to pass unnoticed.

The lead riders consisted of Chad and the half of his company, including Fraser. Tyrone, Angus and Nigel followed on horseback. Avatar and Kell walked behind them. Valery rode between Mirit and Tristine. Armus and Virgil escorted the women with Cody alongside Valery's horse. Tristine wore breeches like Valery and Mirit. Eli and Jillian rode with Daria and Mikaela in a nondescript carriage. Jade sat by the carriage driver while Skylar sat on the back bumper. Titus and Ellis rode behind the carriage, Egan and Kendrick with them. Necie and the other children rode in the second carriage. Mahon sat beside the driver. Finally came a combined troop of royal soldiers, Jor'ellian Guards and Angus' men.

A fourth time Wren glanced back to those following.

"Problem?" asked Ridge.

She faced forward to answer. "With this many to shield, I tried to enlarge the barrier and felt something pushing back against it." She scanned the terrain with narrow eyes of concentration.

"I offered to lend my strength, but you insisted on acting solo."

She cocked a wry smile. "I thought only warriors were so arrogant, not one of my own caste."

"Better than constantly trying to prove myself."

"I proved myself long ago."

He leaned closer, a twinkle of challenge in his eyes. "Then why refuse my help if not your own arrogance?"

She took stock of him. "You may not a bad as they say."

Ridge's brows furrowed with uncertainty. "I guess I'll take that as a compliment. We've worked together in the past, in case you forgot."

"I haven't. I was just recalling what Avatar said about you in Natan." She made a mischievous smile and he rolled his eyes.

"He told you about my tracking. Well, I wasn't wrong, and the group reunited."

Her smile faded as she turned her attention to the road ahead. "I think I will need your help," she said out of the corner of her mouth.

"Ay. It's closer this time." He touched her arm as they continued to walk. "*Na sgiath bho suil at cunnart.*" He repeated the phrase twice.

After a moment she relaxed. "It worked, the sense is fading."

"Taking our combined powers means it's powerful."

"We'll stop before dark and establish a defensive perimeter. If it returns, it may be stronger and more determined. I'd rather have everyone together than strung out. Keep the point." She spoke a brief word to Chad before continuing to where Tyrone rode.

"Sire. With so many, night travel is hazardous. We will have to stop to make camp within the hour."

"We haven't gone that far." He turned to Kell. "What do you say?"

"This is Wren's province, Sire. If she says we should stop, we stop."

"I hoped to be further along."

"Considering the late start and large numbers, we've done well," she said. "Tomorrow, we'll make better time."

"Very well. Return to the point, I'll tell Tristine." Tyrone rode the short distance to the women. "Wren suggests stopping within the hour."

"I'm not surprised. However, we can't take too long to reach the Fortress. This cool weather and cold nights will be hard on Mikaela."

"Have Jade take her to the Fortress and she won't have to endure it."

Tristine grinned. "I mentioned that earlier. She likes Jillian and says she doesn't get enough adventure like her brothers. I told her, if she shows any sign of distress, Jade will take her there without argument."

He laughed and kissed her cheek. "Always one step ahead of me with the children." He noticed Valery. "How are you holding up?"

"I'm fine, Sire," was her modest reply.

"She's had enough adventure," said Mirit, a kind smile at Valery.

"Although the three of us are becoming well acquainted. I've been telling her about our family," said Tristine.

"The queen and princess have been most gracious, Sire."

"Sometime soon, you and I shall have to talk." He smiled at Valery then tossed a wink at Tristine before rejoining Nigel and Angus.

"I don't know what more I could tell him," said Valery, bashful.

Mirit laughed at the shyness. "Don't be intimidated by Tyrone's size. With family, he is generous, tenderhearted, and," she leaned closer, "has a mischievous side that comes out at the most unexpected times."

Tristine laughed in agreement as Mirit continued.

"It took several months after marrying Nigel for me not to be caught off guard and to counter him."

"Oh, if you had seen him and Father when they were in a jovial mood. They were a pair. Next to Darius and Allard, they could spar or make hapless victims of anyone in their vicinity."

"He and Nigel do well together. Angus gets in a jab now and then."

"Not to the level Father and Tyrone could reach."

Valery wore a small considering smile in watching Tyrone speak to Nigel and Angus. "Hard to picture so strong a king possessing such humor. Prince Nigel on the other hand, has a gentler demeanor."

Tristine and Mirit laughed so loud that the men looked back. Tristine shook her head and waved at Tyrone. He and the men turned forward.

"My brother is sarcasm incarnate."

"No, in that, I trump Nigel. At least when we first met," said Mirit.

Tristine spoke to Valery while gesturing between Mirit and Nigel. "According to Avatar, they had to marry or would kill each other."

"Really?" Valery made an impulsive glance back, trying to look past the second carriage.

Mirit smiled. "Are you looking for someone in particular?"

Valery turned forward in her saddle, the flush of embarrassment on her face. "Eh … no, Highness."

"Not Lord Ellis?"

"Lord Ellis? What makes you ask that?" she stammered. Her flush grew brighter.

"The way he's been attentive to you since you arrived."

She avoided eye contact, though her words irritated. "I think it is guilt."

"What would he have to be guilty of?"

"I didn't mean Lord Ellis." She tossed a sheepish glance to Tristine.

"Titus," she said without offense or accusation.

"Ay, Majesty. He uses Lord Ellis to act as a buffer."

"Well, you two do repel each other."

"I don't mean to be rude to the prince, Majesty. He's just—" She clamped her mouth shut.

At the reticence, Tristine said, "You don't need to be afraid to speak to me. I have no delusion regarding my son's shortcomings."

"Well, he can't stand the thought of a woman doing better than he," she declared, which made Tristine and Mirit laugh.

"He takes after his uncle," said Mirit. "When I first met Nigel, I used my skill with the sword to entertain. I acted brash and quick to refute or fight anyone. At the time I didn't know he was a Jor'ellian, only that he secretly came to Tunlund to rescue his nephew."

"You're Baron Mathias' daughter. What were you doing in Tunlund and being an entertainer?"

"At age sixteen, Tunlundian pirates kidnapped me in a raid on the West Coast. My father's fleet engaged the pirates and I suffered a head injury during battle. I woke with no memory of who I was or anything about my life. The captain took pity on me and sought refuge with his cousin's tribe of gypsies to raise me as his own. Meeting Nigel began a series of events that eventually led to my memory returning."

Valery spoke in recollection. "Grandfather told me about his adventures in Tunlund. I never put a face to what he said. You sacrificed your life to save Prince Titus."

"Ay. Jor'el showed mercy in restoring my life." She looked ahead to Nigel, and a tender smile appeared. "Eight months later, we married."

"Are your children among those in the carriages?"

Mirit's smile turned plaintive. "We have no children, nor can I conceive. A side effect of my restoration."

"I'm sorry."

She patted Valery's hand. "Don't be. I couldn't ask for a better husband, kinder in-laws, or such precious nieces and nephews. Well," she snickered, "maybe a little more restraint on the eldest nephew's part."

Tristine chuckled. "What of you? What will you do now?"

The change of subject caught Valery off guard. "I don't know, Majesty. I haven't thought past what is happening."

"Understandable. What would you like to do?"

She thought before answering. "Hard to say. I've always been contrary, according to my father."

"Mirit and I know what that is like. If my father told me to wear a gown, I wore breeches. If he told me to ride, I walked." Tristine smiled. "There are times I still miss him terribly."

"At least you and your father got along. Mine threatened to kill me. He did my mother." Her voice cracked with a sob but her features harsh.

"I'm sorry. I didn't mean to upset you."

"I wish I could have stopped him instead of running!"

"You informed the king, and that is of great importance for all."

Valery nodded and wiped the tears from her face and eyes.

Mirit considering glance moved from Valery to the weapon the girl wore. "Do you know how to use your sword?"

"Some. I never had formal lessons. I mimicked what my father's men did in practice. It gave me something to do and stay out of his way."

"Would you like to learn? So you can help to stop him?"

Valery straightened in the saddle with resolution. "Ay, Highness."

For a moment, Mirit locked eyes with Valery to study the determination of the younger woman. "Very well. You shall be my personal squire and I will teach you all I know."

"I would honored, Highness."

By the time the conversation ended, those ahead turned off the road. Wren and Ridge instructed the Jor'ellians and soldiers to form a perimeter with the royal family and nobles in the center.

Once the carriage stopped, Avery, Galen and Spencer emerged as bundles of energy and began playing a game of tag. Avery slapped Eli and teased him about being slow. Eli responded by chasing the boys.

"Eli! Keep them within the perimeter!" shouted Angus. He helped Necie with the twins.

"Ay, Uncle!" Eli reached for Galen, and pretended to miss. The boy scurried off, giggling about being fast.

Suddenly Spencer and Galen circled Valery. She tried to move aside. When Eli rushed by, she tripped. Hands caught her. Ellis. She had not seen him since they left Garwood.

"They are a rambunctious lot. Are you hurt? An ankle perhaps?"

"No. I'm fine."

"Well, what's this?" said Titus with a teasing smile.

"Nothing." She moved from Ellis and straightened her doublet.

"The boys weren't watching where they were going. She tripped and I caught her," said Ellis.

Titus kept smiling. "Very well, if that's the excuse you choose."

Valery huffed and walked off.

"I thought you were going to be nicer to her?" chided Ellis.

"I was only teasing. See my smile." He motioned to his face. "No malice or sarcasm to my words or tone."

"A subtle distinction. Even I had difficulty telling the difference."

Titus frowned. "Very well. I will restrain myself to only kind words."

"That will be a first."

Hearing Mirit's call, Valery changed course. "Ay, Highness?"

"Help Jillian with Mikaela since Eli is occupied elsewhere."

She masked her surprise at the request then made her way to the second carriage. Not that she disliked Jillian. Her association with Titus made socializing difficult.

Jillian sat on a log next to Mikaela trying to make certain the girl's cloak stayed closed. Daria waited beside them.

"My lady, Princess Mirit sent me to help you."

Jillian's wary gaze passed to Cody. "You may help, but the wolf will have to go. I don't want him scaring the girls."

The girls warily eyed the wolf.

Valery kindly smiled and knelt to pet Cody. "He's friendly. He won't hurt you." The girls remained unconvinced so she said to Cody, "Find a place nearby to lay down." He moved off to a spot close-by.

"He did what you said," said Daria in awe.

"I told you he's friendly."

Jillian's skepticism reflected in her words. "A fire needs to be built. Can you do that? Or should I have a soldier do it?"

Valery stiffened at the obvious dig. "I can build a fire. I also hunt, clean and cook what I kill. Can you?"

Jillian frowned when Mikaela and Daria giggled. She gave Valery a dismissive wave. "Then do so. The little princess must be kept warm."

Valery smiled and bowed to Mikaela before going about her duty.

While Tyrone, Tristine, Avatar and Nigel conversed about the journey, Mirit observed the scene between Valery and Jillian. "Avatar, when we reach the Fortress, take Valery to be properly outfitted and equipped as my personal squire."

"Of course. May I ask what brought this about?"

"Our conversation on the journey."

"Does she have skill?"

"Some, but more importantly, she has the heart and determination to learn." She turned her full attention to the others. Her tone changed to relaying a confidence. "She displays the signs of abuse I saw too often in Tunlund."

"Abuse? You mean physical?" asked Nigel.

"Along with mental and emotional."

"Allard would not have tolerated it," he refuted then lowered his voice when she motioned to Valery, who prepared a fire.

Mirit turned her back further from Valery, and her voice discrete. "I don't believe he knew or suspected."

"How? She's his granddaughter."

"From my experience, some instances of abuse are obvious and well-known. Others not, and most surprising when discovered, even to other family members. I believe this is a case since I agree Allard would have protected her. Unfortunately, intervention is rare. The orphans in Stamos' tribe weren't all orphans. He made the claim to cover his actions and save the tribe from any repercussions for intervening."

"You said she displays all the signs. I don't recall anything unusual during our conversation," said Tristine.

"When speaking, she battles between shyness, withdrawing and wanting to strike back at what causes the pain, her father. For too long she felt trapped and forced to suppress her feelings so when they surface, she retreats because of pain. Ay, she grieves for her mother, her face lights up speaking about Allard. He was the kindest person in her life."

"Since Braden assumed responsibility for the Meadowlands, Nixie sensed something amiss with his family," said Avatar.

"She told you?" asked Mirit.

"Ay, before she returned to the province."

Tristine swallowed back emotions of regret. "I wish Nixie told us. I would have been more careful when discussing our fathers."

"There is a fine line we Guardians walk in respect to intervening in the lives of mortals. Sometimes we take the initiative to act and successfully prevent disaster. Other times, our actions cause more trouble while there are times when inaction is the best."

"Not in this case," she groused.

"Nixie acted as soon as she knew and deeply regrets being unable to prevent Lady Florie's death."

"I still wish I knew."

"If Allard didn't, then there was no way for anyone else," said Mirit.

"You did."

"Only because of my experience. And why I made the offer, to give her focus and direction. Perhaps by doing so, she has a chance to heal."

Tyrone listened with thoughtful interest. "What you say makes sense. She went between those emotions during our interview and even grew hostile toward Titus. It may help to tell him."

"No!" snapped Mirit then lowered her voice, though no one else nearby seemed to notice. "I want to see how she responds to me and her training before informing anyone else."

"Mirit's right. Titus knows enough, and Wren told us how Ellis helped her when learning about her mother. There is plenty of general knowledge without revealing specifics," said Nigel.

"Nor should we compound her feeling of shame by speaking of it to others," said Mirit.

"Valery has nothing to be ashamed of," said Tyrone.

Mirit looked directly at him. "Don't you feel some *shame* when one of your children acts wrongly or willfully against you?"

He nodded with understanding. "Braden's actions reflect upon her. Very well. We'll leave the situation in your hands."

<hr />

By nightfall, the fires were built and food cooking. They didn't erect tents since they traveled light. The children would sleep in the carriages and the rest on bedrolls.

Not much conversation transpired between Valery and Jillian. Valery built the fire and cooked the dressed fowl given her by a soldier. Even eating, Jillian focused on the girls. Mikaela ate slowly, appeared tired and coughed a few times. When Jillian asked about summoning the company surgeon, Mikaela declined.

"Then sleep. Rest is the best for your condition." Jillian helped Mikaela get into the carriage.

Daria went with them and removed a blanket from the compartment under the seat. "Here." She handed it to Jillian.

"Sit beside her and I'll put the blanket on both of you." She made certain the girls were sufficiently comfy and cozy. "Now, try to sleep." She returned to the fire and sat opposite Valery. "I don't know if she'll sleep well."

"What exactly is her illness?"

Jillian didn't look at Valery while answering. "Any number of things. Being born too early, she suffers from a variety of illnesses, but is a sweet child." She smiled and glanced at the carriage.

Valery became startled when a hand holding a cup appeared in front of her face. She relaxed at seeing Ellis.

"I thought you might like some mulled cider to ward off the chill."

She took the cup. "Thank you."

He sat next to her. Titus sat beside Jillian and handed her a cup of warm cider. Cody arrived and lied down next to the log where Ellis and Valery sat.

Wary, Jillian eyed Cody. "I thought you told it to go someplace else?"

"To not frighten the girls." Valery scratched Cody behind the ear. He turned his head, his eyes closing with a contented noise.

"Isn't this cozy," said Titus and promptly received a warning glare from Ellis. "I mean it sincerely and not otherwise." He sipped his cider.

Valery stopped petting Cody to sip her cider. Her skeptical reaction was enough to convey disbelief.

"Princess Mirit asked Valery to help me with Mikaela and she has done so," said Jillian.

Titus swallowed his drink. "How is Mikaela?"

"I'm fine! But I can't sleep if you're going to talk all night," she said from the carriage.

Ellis laughed and Valery smiled.

Jade stopped Titus from rising by placing a hand on his shoulder. "I'll see she sleeps." The Guardian approached the carriage and waved her hand while speaking in the Ancient.

"I wish I understood what they were saying," whispered Ellis.

"A command to sleep undisturbed," said Titus.

"You speak Ancient now?"

"Part of my training." Titus smugly smiled and drank.

"Then I too shall be learning to speak it," said Valery.

"You? How?" asked Titus after a hard, surprised swallow of cider.

"Princess Mirit graciously appointed me her personal squire."

"Squire? But you're a woman."

Valery sat up straight and scowled. "I'm a woman who can best you in strategy. And maybe someday match you with a sword."

"Easy." Ellis took hold of her arm. She shook him off, slammed down the cup and left. He placed his cup down to go after her.

Valery didn't go very far; just enough to not see Titus. His comments infuriated her. Cody circled her legs.

"Titus didn't mean it," said Ellis.

She made a contrary grunt, looked away and crossed her arms.

He stepped in front of her so she couldn't avoid him. "It's true. Since learning you are related, he is trying to change."

"You expect me to believe that?"

"Have I ever lied to you?"

She grew flustered at the challenge. "I don't know you well enough to say for certain. All I know is you intervene and speak for *him*. Maybe if you spoke on your own behalf for a change I would know."

At her rebuttal, his jowls tightened and he gripped the hilt of his sword. He looked to the ground in an effort to compose himself. "You think so little of me?"

She tried to soften her tone in reply. "I said I don't know you."

He lifted his head. For the first time sternness filled his teal blue eyes. "Know this, I do not lie, not even for him." He walked off.

Cody whimpered and took a few steps to follow Ellis. He stopped and looked up at Valery.

She winced in regret. "Wait!" She ran after Ellis only he kept walking. She seized him to stop. "I'm sorry. I don't know why I said that. I'm still trying to comprehend everything that's happened, I suppose."

"At least he is trying to put the past behind."

Unable to endure the sincerity in his eyes, she swallowed back her emotion and awkwardly said, "I'll try too. I need to get back."

Drawing near the fire, Valery saw Titus with his arm around Jillian and they were laughing. Although they were betrothed, she had not seen any displays of affection. Her observation was short-lived when Cody walked past her to the fire. His approach caught their attention.

"Where is Ellis?" asked Titus.

She balked, as Ellis' statement about not lying made her consider her own words.

"I'm here." Ellis wore a small smile as he appeared beside Valery.

With a mix of surprise and curiosity, she regarded him. He steered her back to log where she sat. He remained standing.

"I think it is time we bid the ladies goodnight. We have a long journey in the morning," said Ellis.

"Ay." Titus kissed Jillian's cheek. "Goodnight."

"Goodnight." She smiled, her blush noticeable even in the firelight.

"Lady Valery."

"Highness." She looked at Ellis. "My lord." He didn't smile like earlier, rather bowed and left with Titus. She stared after him, chewing on her lower lip in regret.

"What did my brother say to you?"

The question made Valery turned back to the fire. "Nothing … I mean, we did speak." She snatched up the log she used to poke the fire.

"I'll prepare the fire for sleep while you get settled in your bedroll." She dared not look at Jillian.

Jillian made herself comfortable. "What about you? Your bedroll looks thin. Will you be warm enough?"

"Cody will help me."

Jillian rolled on her side and propped herself on her elbow. "I must admit he's not as wild and fearsome as I first thought."

"Oh, he can be. For some reason, he has attached himself to me and I've been most grateful for his help and company."

"Well, goodnight." Jillian settled down.

"Goodnight." After stoking the fire, Valery settled down. Cody lay next to her. She stared up at the stars. Her mind lingered on her exchange with Ellis. Why did she act so combative? He behaved chivalrous, helpful and kind. Indeed, he spoke no falsehood. Whatever the reason, she would try to keep her temper. *With Ellis it'll be easier than with Titus, but I'll try.* She closed her eyes and fell asleep.

A short time later, Tristine returned to the fire around which she, Tyrone, Nigel and Mirit slept. All lay awake on their bedrolls. Kell, Armus, Avatar and Vidar surrounded the royal couples. Kell and Vidar stood watch. Avatar and Armus sat in the Guardian meditative position, legs crossed, swords resting on their laps, hands folded and eyes closed.

"Another fit?" asked Tyrone.

"No, a nightmare. She sleeps now. For a moment I wondered about summoning the surgeon." She looked to the Guardian captain. "Kell, how much longer before Eldric is fully recovered?"

"Two or three days. Even as a physician, a healing is taxing on his life force. I rather Wren would have healed naturally, yet under the circumstances, I had to honor her request despite Eldric's objections."

"He didn't want to heal her?" asked Mirit with some confusion.

"No, only the more serious the wound the more energy is required. Eldric told me afterward if left untreated even for a day longer, Wren would have succumbed to her injury."

123

"I didn't realize it was so serious," said Tyrone.

"Nor did I when I ordered him to heal her. Because of the personal danger, any exercise of a Guardian's ultimate power must be used with discretion. I have seen Eldric use his power without hesitation. However, overuse can consume and destroy a Guardian who goes beyond capacity."

"You think Eldric did so?" asked Nigel.

"No. He'll join us at the Fortress when he is able. It was not knowing the extent of the personal danger to him that I regret." Kell glanced at the sky. "Try to go back to sleep. It's four hours until dawn."

Tristine yawned. "I don't sleep outdoors like I once did."

"You didn't sleep well then either," snickered Nigel. He settled down next to Mirit, whose eyes were already closed.

"I got a boar on my first night out. It took you three times for a kill."

"Really?" asked Tyrone, turning to face Nigel. "Boar or deer?"

Nigel frowned and muttered, "Rabbit."

"Outdone by a female even in youth," said Mirit, eyes still closed.

Tyrone laughed and Nigel turned away, grumbling, "Go to sleep."

At the carriage, Jillian slipped back into her bedroll. "Throw another log on, it's cold." She told Valery and snuggled further down.

Valery blew on the fire to get a flame going then placed a small branch on the pile.

"Is that all? It won't burn hot enough," complained Jillian.

"Use anything larger and the fire will smother, and no warmth at all. You'd know that if you had any experience outdoors, like I do."

Jillian turned away from the fire, but soon rolled back to get closer to the heat. "Don't gloat," she chided.

"Me?" Valery snickered under her breath.

"Go head, say it. You don't like me."

Valery placed aside the prodding stick now that the fire burned on its own. "I don't know you well enough to say." She went to her bedroll.

"Not true. Everybody has an opinion even after a first meeting. We've met on a number of occasions."

"I hardly call those meetings." Valery pulled up her blanket and lay down on her back.

"What else could you call them?"

"Competition, sport, purposefully trying to intimidate and insult."

The answer surprised Jillian. "You think those were planned?"

"What else? All for the prince's benefit."

"So you don't like me because of Titus."

She glanced at Jillian. "You are his betrothed."

"True. What about my brother? He is being nice to you. Do you repay his kindness by scorning me?"

Pricked by the question, she faced skyward. "No, and I'm sorry."

Jillian propped herself on her elbow. "You're a hard person to understand. One moment you scorn me, the next you apologize."

"Then maybe you shouldn't try to understand me," she spoke with a slight quiver in her voice then turned away.

For a moment, Jillian watched Valery before speaking again. "Titus and Ellis told me what happened to you and I'm sorry." Valery didn't reply so she continued. "I suppose we've acted harsh toward each other without cause. You with me because of my association to Titus and I with you because of jealousy."

Valery glanced over her shoulder. "Jealous of what?"

She grew sheepish. "You're very intelligent and articulate, and engage Titus in a way I can't. Oh, we talk and I enjoy his company, and love him dearly, but I have no interest or inclination toward strategy and politics."

Curiosity made Valery roll over to face Jillian. "You were jealous of me because of that?"

Jillian avoided eye contact as she admitted, "Ay."

The confession stunned Valery. "I don't know what to say. I didn't mean to make you jealous and," she began to laugh but tried to suppress it, "I never tried to win Titus' affection." She couldn't stop from laughing. "Me and Titus!"

Now Jillian became curious. "Then you have no feelings for him?"

Valery tried to contain her amusement to answer. "No! We'd kill each other before sharing mutual affection." She smiled at Jillian. "He's all yours." Again she burst into laughing, and this time, Jillian joined her.

Suddenly it started: a low, eerie howling that surrounded them.

Fearful, Jillian sank under her covers. "What's that?"

Valery tossed aside her blanket. She reached for her sword, which lay by the bedroll. "They found us."

"Who?"

Cody snarled, his hackles bristling. The howling grew louder, more intense and frightening.

"Get inside the carriage and stay with the girls! Cody, go with her."

Jillian scrambled out of the bedroll and hurried to the carriage.

The whole camp woke at the painful volume and pitch of the howling. Mortals and Guardians cringed.

"*Madah-dune!*" shouted Wren. She had a finger on the trigger of her crossbow ready to fire at the slightest movement. She no sooner finished the warning then multiple male, mortal cries of surprise and pain came from around the perimeter. Darkness obscured the cause.

"What's happening?" asked Tristine. She grimaced in her attempt to withstand the noise.

"They are picking off the sentries before attacking," said Kell.

Armus moved beside Tristine with his sword poised and ready. He scowled against the pain and his eyes scanned the trees for movement.

Tyrone gripped the hilt of his drawn sword and gritted his teeth to withstand the pain. Nigel showed signs of distress at the howling. He held his sword in both hands so tight, his knuckles turned white from effort. Mirit held her sword ready, yet also tried to shield one ear. Tristine gasped in pain, she dropped to her knees to cover her ears. Mirit knelt beside Tristine for support.

Tyrone groaned in annoyance, unable to move to aid Tristine due to the immobilizing noise. "Kell! Get the women and children out of here!"

Before Kell could comply, the howling stopped, much to everyone's relief. Barely a moment of eerie silence passed and the attack launched. Primitive Spears and large rocks flew from the darkness striking soldiers and Guardians alike. Spears killed three soldiers while several others were struck in the head by the rocks and injured. Skylar sustained a gash to his left shoulder when a spear grazed him while shielding Eli. A large rock stuck Jade at the base of the skull and knocked her to the ground in front of the carriage. She fought to remain conscious.

"*Astair de am bhais!*" a cry from out of the trees followed by a blur.

The squad of Angus' soldiers at the carriage to protect Necie and the younger children fell, as if struck by something in the passing blur.

Kell snarled with intense anger. "*Mannix! Anns Jor'el's ainmean, sgur!*"

The captain's command made the blur fade into the shape of Mannix, who stumbled into a tree. His naked sword was stained by blood. Kell charged. Mannix ran further into the forest. With Kell nearly on top of him, Mannix disappeared. Kell swung and his sword passed through the light. He didn't know if he succeeded or Mannix escaped. The sounds of battle drew him back to the main group.

A wolf-man raced toward the carriage. The door stood open from when Jillian climbed inside to be with the girls. Valery slammed the door closed and turned to confront the wolf-man. It was closer than anticipated. She dodged a swinging club, which smashed into the side of the wagon. Jillian and the girls screamed. Cody snapped at the beast's leg. A backhand swipe of the massive paw sent Cody tumbling into the trees.

Jade became lightheaded and dizzy upon standing. She ignored the sensation to draw her sword and race to Valery' aid. Her sword blocked the beast's second attack. Jade became the focus of the beast's attack.

Valery's reprieve was short-lived when the girls screamed again. Another wolf-man arrived on the opposite side of the carriage. It flung open the door and to reach into the carriage. "Jade! One's inside the carriage!"

Jade was too involved with battling the first wolf-man to reply, so Valery ran to the other side of the carriage. The beast dragged a screaming and struggling Jillian from the carriage. Valery's blade cut deep into its hide. It howled in pain, dropped Jillian and turned upon Valery.

Valery jumped back to avoid a swipe of both massive hand/claws. Her sword proved useless against such a wild abandoned attack. One blow caught her in the upper left arm and sent her flying sideways about ten feet. She landed hard on the ground. When it reached down for her, she snatched her sword and thrust up. The blade caught it in the middle of its chest. The momentum made the beast fall forward. She wasn't fast enough to roll out of its way. The dying form pinned her to the ground where she struggled to breathe under its smothering weight.

"Valery! Jillian!" shouted Ellis and Titus in near unison.

"*Imich dhiom!*" Egan thrust out his left hand toward the beast.

The wolf-man flew off Valery and landed a few yards away from her. Cody pounced upon it and sank teeth into its throat. The jaws closed to choke the remaining life out of the offending beast.

"Valery?" Ellis skidded on his knees beside her. She sat up, groaned in pain and bent over to cradle her left arm. He held her in support, careful of her wound. "Egan!" he called.

The Guardian joined them to examine her arm. The beast's claws ripped open the sleeve and left a very large, angry welt. "A nasty bruise, down into the muscle. Nothing broken. The surgeon can give you something for the pain."

She took a deep breath before replying. "Maybe later. Help me up," she said to Ellis. Once standing they saw Titus with Jillian and the girls. Titus held Mikaela and Jillian carried Daria.

Jade arrived. "Is everyone all right?"

"Ay. Thanks to you and Valery," said Jillian. She turned to Titus. "It drug me out of carriage and would have killed me, but Valery saved me."

"It could have killed us all!" Mikaela sobbed and hugged Titus' neck.

Titus held his sister close. A sympathetic eye on Jillian and Daria passed to Valery. "Thank you. We wouldn't have arrived in time."

Valery awkwardly smiled. She drew her left arm close to her body.

"You should see the surgeon," insisted Ellis.

She shook her head. "I'm just sore."

"Where's Mother?" Mikaela asked Titus.

"We'll find her."

Mirit stayed down to shield a recovering Tristine. Tyrone and Nigel parried club blows from the wolf-men. Virgil and Avatar intercepted several more creatures and killed them. Vidar killed another. The attack ended after a few brief moments.

Mirit helped Tristine sit. "Is it over? Or could there be another wave?"

"Hard to tell." Nigel watched the trees for signed of movement.

Angus came running with Fraser and Eli at his heels. All three carried bloody swords. "Is anyone hurt?"

"No," said Tyrone. "Necie and the children?"

"All are well, just very frightened."

"Do you think there are more out there?" asked Fraser.

"No," said Kell.

"How can you be certain?"

"The earlier shout in the Ancient was Mannix using his power of blinding speed by which to kill. I tried to catch him but he vanished."

Angus sneered with jowls tightened. "So that's how they died. Some of my best men, cut down without a chance to fight."

"They died protecting your family."

The others arrived; Titus carried Mikaela, Jillian with Daria, Ellis, Valery, Egan and Jade.

"Mama," said Mikaela.

Tristine took her from Titus. "Thank Jor'el. Everyone is alive and unharmed."

"You can also thank Valery and Jade. Ellis, Egan and I would not have reached them in time," said Titus.

"Already proving your mettle. Well done," said Mirit with a grin. She noticed Valery's torn sleeve. "You're wounded?"

"A bad bruise, nothing serious."

Chad arrived. "Sire. Six royal soldiers are dead and six injured, three very seriously. No fatalities among the Jor'ellians or Guardians, only minor injury. We counted twelve dead creatures."

"Only twelve did all this?" asked Fraser with disturbed surprise.

"It could have been worse," said Wren. "Sire, Ridge is using his power to shield the area. I don't know for how long. It took our normal combined energy to form a protective barrier the creatures breached."

"Tell Ridge he can stop. All the women and children are to be taken to the Fortress immediately. I don't care if takes every Guardian present! The rest of us will ride," said Tyrone firmly to Kell.

The captain saluted and left to comply.

"I'm staying," said Mirit. "Tristine will be safe at the Fortress."

Although his expression showed disagreement, Tyrone didn't argue rather said to Chad. "Take what baggage can be packed on any extra horse, leave the rest with the carriages. Order a detail to bury the dead."

"Ay, Sire." Chad saluted and left.

Ellis gently took Valery by the right arm to escort her after Kell.

She balked and stopped. "What are doing?"

"I'm taking you to the Guardians."

"The princess stays, I stay. I'm her squire." She removed her arm from him.

"Weren't those the same creatures that attacked you and Wren?"

"Ay. Horrid creatures," she said, a look of disconcertion passing over her face. At his disapproval, she became determined. "I'm staying."

His expression shifted between concern and vexation as he searched for words. "You're injured."

"It's just a bruise. I've had far worse and recovered."

His brows levelled in momentary discomposure. "Very well, if that's the way you want it." He left to aid Titus in helping the Guardians with the younger children.

Mirit came along side Valery. "He's only trying to help."

"I know. He's been kind and I'm grateful. I'm simply tired of running. I must take a stand." She swallowed back her rising emotion.

"You may want to tell him that rather than rebuff him."

A flash of light caught their attention. One-by-one the Guardians left with Tristine, Niece and the younger royal children.

"We should join the others for departure."

"In a moment." Mirit didn't detain her, so Valery went to find Ellis. He checked his horse's harness. "My lord," she said with shy awkwardness. "If your service is still available, I would appreciate your company for the journey."

"I thought you'd be with the princess. After all you are her squire."

He replied in a more cutting voice than she expected, which made her search for words to respond as Mirit suggested.

Titus arrived, and leading his horse. He wore one of those smug expressions Valery found irritating and she immediately grew defensive.

"Better a squire than a lackey." She turned on her heels and left.

"What was that about?" asked Titus.

Ellis shook his head in befuddlement. "I'm not sure. She asked me to ride with her, then you show up and she walks off in a huff."

"I heard you two arguing and came to stop it."

Ellis scowled. "Your interference doesn't help. She only sees me speaking for you and not myself. As if speaking to a woman isn't hard enough, now I'm nothing more than *your* parrot."

"I was wrong to put you in such a position."

He heaved a hapless shrug. "Part of my retainer duty. But did you have use Jillian to make it more compelling?"

Titus winced at the question. "I regret that more than I can say, especially since Valery saved Jillian and the girls." He stopped Ellis from returning to fix the harness. "Have you tried to convince her that you can speak for yourself?"

"Of course. But every time we talk she either says something I can't reply to or I fumble over the words I want to say and it comes out all wrong. Like I did just now. Again!" He gathered the reins and mounted.

Titus also mounted his horse. "It's the effort you stumble over not the words, and have for years."

"What do you mean?"

"You have always spoken straight to me, no pretense or façade. In that, I have found a true and honest friend. You might try the same with Valery. No flowery words, just straight, simple, honest speech."

Ellis spoke in recollection. "I told her the same when she wondered if straightforward, forthright speech is appreciated from a woman."

Titus grinned. "Then take your own advice and don't try so hard in speaking your mind. Or maybe, your heart?" Ellis shifted awkwardly in the saddle so Titus continued. "I see what is happening between you two. If you truly have feelings for her, don't let the past between she and I interfere. Or her present misconception."

Whereas Ellis's normal reticence on the subject registered on his face, he spoke clearly. "Where I *may* admit to feelings, I don't want to presume upon her at this difficult time. If she is ever to reciprocate, I'd rather it be genuine and not from gratitude for kindness."

Titus smiled. "Well said."

"Only if I can repeat a similar sentiment to her."

"You will, when the time is right."

"Move out!" shouted Tyrone.

Wren took the lead, followed by Tyrone and Nigel with Kell behind them. Mirit rode beside Angus; Virgil followed then came Valery, with Cody trotting alongside. She glanced to Titus and Ellis, as they moved to into formation.

"Go, ride with her. I'll join Fraser," said Titus.

"I just said I didn't want to presume."

"You said she asked you. By her glance, the invitation is still open." He didn't wait for an answer, and turned his horse to join Fraser, in Chad's company of Jor'ellians.

Ellis moved his horse beside Valery. She noticed his arrival but didn't say anything, yet he saw a small smile when she faced forward.

* * *

The captain of the Fortress Guards rushed to receive the unexpected arrival of the queen and the others. Tristine, Jillian, Necie and the children were taken to the apartment of the Knight of the Temple. Nigel and Mirit stayed in the apartment when at the Fortress. The entire third floor of the armory consisted of a main living area, a dining area, a private office, and two bedrooms, each with a privy.

A young woman in her mid-twenties with raven hair and hazel eyes arrived. "Majesty. Whatever you need, I will gladly see to it."

Tristine flashed a weary smile. "Thank you, Magan."

"Is Chad with you?"

"No. He remained with the king and will be here in a few days."

"The captain is rousing Grandfather. In the meantime, I'll send for food and drink. And extra blankets," she chuckled at seeing the children.

A short time later, Tristine, Jillian and Necie sat in the main living area drinking the tea Magan served them. Uriah arrived. He looked ten years younger than his sixty-seven years, healthy and spry. Eli, Armus and Mahon remained with the women. The younger children retired.

"Majesty. Highness. My Lady. Forgive my lateness."

"I understand. We arrived unexpectedly."

"Are recent events responsible for this visit?"

"That's putting it mildly, Vicar. Please, sit." She proceeded to tell him what occurred since Avatar and Chad left.

He wasn't unsettled by the tale rather regretful. "I'm afraid there may be worse to come. All is unfolding according to Prophecy. A time of upheaval will test the royal house in preparation for the building of *Jor'el-l'ahair* and the return of the Almighty to dwell among His people."

"Kell says she may have a legitimate claim to the throne. Does she?"

"I will consult the law books and find the answer before the king arrives. For now, you must rest to strengthen your heart and resolve for what is to come. Be assured, Jor'el will supply the answer." He rose, kissed Tristine's hand and tenderly smiled at Necie. He gave a formal nod to Eli and Jillian. "Magan." He motioned for her to leave with him.

When the door closed, Tristine spoke her frustration. "That wasn't what I wanted I hear!"

"He will find the answer, and so will Kell," said Armus.

"Just the thought of Ellan for one moment reigning is intolerable!"

"Father will do all he can to prevent it," said Eli

She touched his face, a tender smile on her lips. "I'm grateful you don't know what she's like and I pray you don't find out." Her voice turned urgent and imploring. "Promise me, no matter what happens, stay true to what we've taught you and don't be swayed by lying tongues."

"I promise."

She kissed his cheek. "Now, stay with Mikaela and the children. We depend upon your gentle manner to help them not to be frightened."

"I'd rather help you and Father. I can fight."

She smiled. "I know your skill and heart, but it is just as important to keep our family reassured and whole as it is to wield a sword. Fraser doesn't have your patience with the children and Titus—"

"Is heir and must face his future," he finished, a smile appearing. "I'll do as you ask." He kissed her cheek and went to the bedchamber.

"I'll help Eli," said Jillian and left.

"He's such a dear heart," said Necie.

"Ay. I think of my sons, Eli … well, I try not to play favorites."

"They are all special in their own ways. And you and Tyrone have not failed to let each know they are loved."

Tristine had difficulty keeping her temper and emotions. "I didn't want to do what Father—"

Necie seized Tristine. "You haven't! So why scorn his memory? He too was blinded by Ellan, Musetta and Sullivan." Tristine went to object, but Necie continued. "Ay, you weren't fooled, but Father regretted his actions and mourned the consequences. He more than made up for it during his remaining years—"

"I know that!" she interrupted. "Still, you can't deny he favored Ellan and it caused tension between he and I. That is what I try to avoid with my children: favoritism and the resulting tension. What's happening isn't about Father. It's about Ellan, so let's not argue."

"Then please don't speak so harshly against him."

Necie grew emotional and Tristine hugged her. "I don't scorn his memory. I miss him, and at times more than I can say."

"I think the Vicar is right about resting," said Mahon. He escorted Necie to the other bedchamber.

"It'll be hard to rest until Tyrone and the others arrive."

"Try."

"I will, when you return to tell him we are safe."

"Since when is this up for negotiation?" he said with a wry snicker.

"Since I became queen." The humor was momentary. "Oh, Armus," she whimpered. "Why can't she leave me alone?"

He tilted her head. "You must rest. Tyrone needs you to be strong, and so do the children." He led her to the room. Necie was already in bed. "I'll leave once you are asleep. Mahon will remain."

Tristine sat on the bed, and let Armus help her take off her boots and doublet before slipping under the covers. She closed her eyes and he blew out the candle. The sooner he believed her asleep, the sooner he would leave. However, sleep was something she really couldn't do.

She heard the door softly close and managed to see a shaft of light under the threshold flare then fade. At least something went right. They endured so much turmoil over the last week she found it difficult to think. Old feelings resurfaced, stronger and more intense.

During the five years they believed Nigel dead, she endured Ellan's vicious spleen, constantly goaded and inciting arguments between her and their father. The tension grew when Musetta arrived in disguise. With her son Sullivan, they spurred the jealous sibling rivalry to the breaking point before launching her coup. It was an act of revenge for Ellis defeating Dagar and killing Latham, who was Musetta's lover and Sullivan's father. Tristine suspected Ellan's involvement and tried to warn

Ellis. Kell and Darius also made attempts to warn him. Not until Ellan put the poison in his wine, did Ellis finally realize the truth. He survived and put down the coup at great cost to the family.

True Tristine met Tyrone, Nigel reunited with his family and his health restored. None of that changed the years of animosity and pain she endured from Ellan. Now, everything came crashing back. She wouldn't let it touch her children! Alas, Ellan and Sullivan were crowned.

Surely Father's decree annulled their coronation. Jor'el, don't let her win. Grant us wisdom to find a way to stop her! She wiped away the silent tears.

Mahon knelt beside the bed. "You're supposed to be asleep."

"It's hard."

He smiled and stroked her head. "Jor'el is still sovereign. Be at peace. *Fois et caidil.*"

She closed her eyes, and soon she slept.

In a hidden hollow, Locan wrapped a bandage around Mannix's left thigh wound. "You're fortunate Kell's sword only grazed you."

"I didn't think he was so close." He rubbed his wound

"What now? We can't tell Hueil that we lost two dozen *madah-dune* while she lives and he's not in our custody."

Mannix titled his head in consideration. "I need a day for my leg to heal, and they'll be expecting another attack. We'll wait to lure him away after they've reached The Fortress."

Chapter 9

FIVE NIGHTS ON HORSEBACK WASN'T WHAT ERIC WANTED TO DO. However, Alrick said he couldn't dimension travel three to Waldron. He tried to privately convince Alrick to take Karly and Bryson while he continued to Waldron. He dreaded what effect explaining the situation to Wess could have on his wife and wanted to spare her. Alrick stressed keeping the family together for safety, along with preserving the rings.

At age eight, Bryson rode by himself between Karly and Eric, who kept the rear guard. Alrick led them. To avoid being seen, they traveled at night. During the day, Alrick found places for them to hide and rest.

They arrived at Waldron as the grey light of dawn broke on the sixth day of travel. The castle was shut with royal soldiers on the battlements. About a quarter mile from the gate they were accosted by a mounted patrol of six soldiers, two of them carried torches. Although lamps lit the road for a mile, torches helped when patrolling off the road. They met the soldiers between two lampposts, with shadows separating them.

"Halt! Who are you and what do you want?"

"I am Alrick, Trio Leader of the Delta. This family seeks shelter."

The soldier glanced past Alrick to the others. His eyes narrowed to see clearly in the dim light. "Only General Wess can authorize admittance and I'm not sure I want to wake him."

Karly moved her horse forward, which placed the soldiers on guard. She stopped inside the light. "He'll wake for me, Lieutenant Cameron."

"Indeed, my lady! Corporal, tell them to open the gate."

"Sir?"

"Do as you're told, or the general won't be pleased."

"Ay, sir." The corporal rode to Waldron.

"Please, follow me." Cameron led them through the gate, into the Grand Courtyard and to the armory where Wess had private quarters.

Inside the general's office on the first floor, Cameron ordered a soldier to light some candles. "I'll fetch the general," he said to Karly and then told soldiers, "Have rooms prepared." He left.

Bryson rubbed his arms. "I think it's colder in here than outside."

Karly wrapped her arms around him to help him get warm. "You'll be warm soon enough."

"I hope Grandpa Wess doesn't take too long to wake up." He yawned. "I want to go to sleep."

"I usually rise an hour before dawn. See? I'm fully dressed." Wess smiled and motioned to himself in teasing Bryson.

"Father." Karly embraced him, unable to stop some sniffling.

Her emotion concerned him. "Why the tears?" He wiped her cheeks.

"My father sent us, sir," said Eric.

"I thought as much when Cameron told me of your arrival." Wess turned to Bryson when the youngster yawned. "You said you wanted to sleep, will my bed do for now?"

"Ay, sir."

He ruffled the boy's hair. "Cameron, take my grandson upstairs and have someone remain with him."

"Ay, General. Master Bryson." He took the boy's hand in leaving.

Wess encouraged Karly to take a seat in front of his desk. He motioned to Eric. "Start at the beginning and tell me everything."

"It's rather difficult, sir. The situation is greatly disturbing. In fact, I didn't want to leave, but my father insisted," said Eric.

"So did Uncle," she stressed for Wess' benefit.

He gave a sober nod. "The king sent word concerning some of the Council and Ellan."

Karly took hold of Wess' hand. "Uncle deeply regrets the situation and wanted me to make certain you understand."

He patted her hand. "I'm sure he does. Unfortunately, his choice places us on opposites sides."

"What about Dylan and Garrick?" asked Eric.

"Oh, I almost forgot." She reached into the pocket of her cape. "Uncle gave me this and said for you to give it to whoever survives."

Wess fought back emotions in accepting the ring. "Dylan and I spoke at length when he chose to remain in the army. Garrick, I'm sorry to say, has sailed with Hollis and the East Coast Fleet against the king."

Unable to fight tears any longer, Karly rose and hugged Wess. For a moment he, held her. When he finally did speak, his voice was hoarse.

"This is something I hoped would never happen again. Now that is has, we must deal with it." He kissed her cheek and stroked her hair.

"Neither of them bears you ill feelings. They sent us to you for safety and as reassurance," said Eric.

Wess sighed before being able to ask, "What of you?"

The question caught Eric off guard. "I bear you no ill will, sir. I respect you as highly as my father."

Wess kindly smiled. "No, I meant how are bearing up with this?"

"It's hard." He reached into his pocket and pulled out the signet ring. "Father gave the Delta to me, so I can offer allegiance to the king. I will honor his wishes and do what he feels he cannot because his prior oath."

"Put it away." He waited for Eric to pocket the ring before speaking again. "You'll be safe here until I can arrange for escort to the king."

"He's not here?"

"No."

"Father, I don't want to leave you!"

"Waldron isn't safe! This is the first place Ellan will attack. I've ordered defenses made while the royal family is en route to the Region of Sanctuary. That is where I will send you, after some rest of course." He forced a grin. "Bryson didn't appear to like night travel, which I assumed you did to arrive here just before dawn."

"Ay, General," said Alrick. "I made certain they were hidden during the day. However, an eight year old mortal boy doesn't like being inactive during daylight hours."

Wess chuckled. "Bryson is a bundle of energy. If you can delay returning to the Delta, I can use your services again."

"Alas, the combined strength of my Trio was unable to help the baron prevent Hueil from securing the Delta."

He pursed his lips in frustration. "Kell won't like hearing that."

"Nor is it something I want to tell him."

Wess regarded his daughter and Eric. "Under the circumstances, resting for the day is all that can be spared. Hueil's grip is causing a strangle hold among the Guardians while Ellan is snatching up Council Members right and left."

Seeing Karly weary and upset, Eric placed a supporting arm about her waist. "We'll be ready to leave we you say, sir."

Wess kindly smiled at his daughter. "Courage. Remember, you are a general's daughter, and of noble birth."

"Ay, Father."

"General, a room is ready," said Cameron from the threshold.

"Go with Cameron."

After the door closed, Wess sat on the corner of the desk. He closed his eyes with an audible sigh of dejection.

"General. The baron and Lord Bosley do this with heavy hearts," said Alrick.

Wess nodded since speech proved difficult. "Thought of arm conflict and facing Bosley as the enemy pains me more than I can say."

"Uncle … General," Dylan corrected himself since Wess wasn't alone.

For a moment Wess stared at Dylan. At age twenty-six he bore a strong resemblance to Bosley in his younger days.

Dylan made no comment to the regard, rather said, "I saw Karly and Eric going upstairs when I entered from the training room. Trouble?"

Wess nodded. "Bosley and Erasmus sent them for safety along with words of deep regret. I intend to send them to the Fortress to carry those regrets to the king. I want you to lead the escort."

"I'd rather stay here and help you defend Waldron."

"Karly would be grateful for your company. And with this news, we both have some reconsidering to do."

"Reconsidering?"

He took a long deep breath before replying. "I'm not certain I can withstand having my family divided again. We barely survived three coups. The one against my uncle, King Marcellus, which restored the House of Tristan to the throne; Owain's rebellion's, when Bosley and I helped save Queen Shannan and then infant Prince Nigel," he said with a small smile, which faded as he continued, "and the first time Ellan attempted to seize power. We were divided over her then, and suffered great and painful losses. I don't know if I have the heart for a fourth."

"I understand you wanting to reconsider. What about Aunt Callie and Uncle Grant?"

"They arrived safely in Tunlund." He grew somber. "I'm glad Tyrone gave Grant the ambassadorship, as Callie mourned so when Cassie died. Now this … No, let her remain blissfully ignorant unless it become absolutely necessary." He placed his left hand on Dylan's shoulder. "I want to do for you what Bosley would and keep you safe to spare our family more grief. The same Erasmus is doing with Eric."

"What about Garrick, he's the eldest?"

He looked his nephew in the eye. "You know he sailed against the king."

Dylan's voice barely rose above a whisper. "I still can't believe it."

"Go with Karly and Eric, and give your father and I some solace on behalf of our children." Wess opened his right hand to reveal Bosley's signet ring. "And take this. He sent it to me to give to whoever survives. *You* are going to survive, Dylan! You must."

Dylan fought against tears in taking the ring. "I won't fail. I promise."

"Prepare a squad to leave after dark. Night travel is the best." He cocked a grin. "Although Bryson won't be keen on it after coming here."

Dylan chuckled. "Don't worry, I'll find a way to distract him. Or better yet, tie him to the saddle to keep him from falling off." The humor faded. He placed the ring in his doublet pocket and left.

At nine o'clock that night, six mounted and armed royal soldiers waited at the postern gate. They were all Wess could spare for escort. He walked with Eric, Dylan, Karly, Bryson and Alrick. Bryson lagged behind then balked at mounting another horse. Alrick lifted him into the saddle.

Eric stood by Bryson's horse. "I know this is difficult and you don't understand, but we must continue. It is important we reach the king."

"Why does Grandpa Erasmus what to hurt the king?"

"He doesn't!" insisted Eric and gripped Bryson's hand. "That is what I must tell the king."

"Bryson," began Wess. "Do you recall during your lessons what I said about your sparring opponent? How even though he isn't your enemy, you must fight him like an enemy in order to improve your skill?"

"I remember."

"Well, your grandfather Erasmus is in a similar situation. The king is not his enemy, but he must fight like he is."

Bryson's face grew forlorn. "It doesn't seem right."

"No, and it is the duty of you and your parents to inform the king of Erasmus' true feelings. By doing so, a fight may be avoided. That would please everyone, including Erasmus."

"Ay, sir."

Wess patted Bryson's leg. "Good lad."

Eric flashed a smile of thanks to Wess before mounting.

Wess drew Dylan aside to speak in private. He pulled out a thick sealed letter from his doublet pocket. "Give this to the king. It is a letter detailing their story along with my resignation."

"What? No, Uncle, you can't resign."

"Keep your voice down." He tossed a glance to the others. "I thought long and hard about this. Although I have great affection for Tyrone and Tristine, I don't have the heart for another coup. I'll defend Waldron, to the death if need be, but in open battle, I can't take the field against my brother, just like I won't have you fight him."

"I don't think the king will accept it."

"Doesn't matter, my decision is made. Now put it away." Once Dylan pocketed the letter, Wess steered him to his horse. "Jor'el watch over your journey."

"And may He protect you, Father."

Wess signaled for the postern gate to be opened. He watched until they disappeared into the forest then ordered the gate closed.

Alrick led the group in a north-by-northwest direction. Dylan and two soldiers followed then came Karly, Bryson, Eric and the remaining four soldiers. For several hours they travelled through the woods, avoiding the main roads. The trek proved difficult for the mortals to steer their horses, weaving in and out of hollows and densely wooded areas.

Frustrated, Dylan shoved a thin branch of overgrown bush from his face. "Are you sure you know where you're going, Alrick? I think Wren or a forest Guardian would be better for navigation."

"He would rather used his sword to hack the enemy than cut his way through the woods," said a new voice.

Alrick stood ready to strike. Dylan and the soldiers drew their weapons. A tall shadow moved out from between the trees.

"No need for violence, Alrick." He held his hands up to indicate he was unarmed and snapped the fingers on his right hand. A small flame appeared on his fingertips to reveal his identity; a male Guardian with white hair and violet eyes wearing a russet and tan vassal uniform with modest ornamentations, including a jeweled hilted dagger.

Alrick scowled and came off his defensive stance. "Gresham! You could have found a less dramatic way to let us know you were here."

"And miss seeing you overreact? Too much fun." He blew out the flame on his fingertips.

"Gresham?" asked Eric.

"Trio Leader of Midessex. I've been watching since you left Waldron."

"Why didn't you show yourself earlier?"

"Because you weren't the only ones I was watching." He spoke to Alrick. "You must change course. Keep going in this direction and you'll venture too close to the ruins."

"Ruins?" asked Bryson with boyish enthusiasm.

"Ravendale."

"Why does that sound familiar? Oh, ay, Grandpa Wess lived there as a boy. Can we see it, Mama?"

"No!" snapped Gresham before she replied. "That's what I've come to tell you. Evil stirs the ruins."

"What kind of evil?" asked Dylan.

Gresham's gaze grew intense. "A sense of coming alive. Of rebirth."

Karly gasped with a visible shudder.

Eric took her hand. "We'll change course."

"But, if it's where Grandpa Wess once lived wouldn't he want to know?" asked Bryson.

"We'll leave Gresham to tell him."

"Not entirely," said Dylan. "You, Karly, Bryson and half the squad continue. I'll take the Guardians and the rest to investigate. We'll rejoin you when we're done."

"Oh, Dylan, no, it's too dangerous," protested Karly.

"I'm a soldier, cousin. I'll do reconnaissance, no confrontation. Bryson is right. Wess needs intelligence. So will Kell and the king. Sergeant, continue on the forest path. We'll catch up as soon as we can."

"Ay, Lieutenant. Royce, keep the rear. My lord, my lady, follow me."

After separating, Gresham took Alrick, Dylan and the rest in a more west-by-north direction. The autumn nights grew chillier. Dylan shivered in the saddle and drew his cloak closer about.

"Is it getting colder?"

"I think you're right, Lieutenant," said a soldier. "I was raised in the woods, but this doesn't feel like a natural cold to me."

"It's not," said Gresham in a harsh whisper. "Keep quiet and dismount. We'll continue on foot."

The mortals tethered the horses to low hanging branches. Gresham drew his dagger, signaling for Alrick to do the same with his sword. The mortals mimicked the Guardians in arming themselves.

Gresham whispered. "There is a small plateau overlooking the ruins."

"How far?" asked Dylan.

"A quarter mile, with the ruins a mile and half further."

"And the sense is this strong?"

"Ay. Any closer than a mile and whatever force is there will be able to sense Alrick and me. Follow closely and stay low and quiet."

Gresham led them on the path to the plateau with Alrick in the rear. After several hundred yards, he crouched down for a few steps then finally went on all fours. He signaled the others to do the same and they inched forward, laying flat on their bellies for the last fifty feet to the brush line. The smell of smoke lingered in the night air from several large fires lit at the ruins. The light allowed them to see well enough even at that distance.

"Shadow Warriors," sneered Alrick.

"And *madah-dune,*" said Gresham.

"Those hairy creatures?" asked Dylan. He lay between Alrick and Gresham.

"Ay. Nasty and vicious," said Alrick.

Gresham's eyes narrowed in staring at the ruins. "No, something else. More than the *madah-dune* or Shadow Warriors."

Surprise made Alrick rise up on his elbows. "By the west fire. Hueil."

"Wretched turncoat," sneered Gresham.

"Where? I can't see anyone this far without a spyglass," said Dylan.

"Guardians have keener eyesight. He's the blonde male standing between the Warriors," said Alrick.

"What is he doing?" chided Gresham. Hueil gestured and spoke to what appeared to be a large fallen stone.

"I can't make out the words," said Alrick.

"I thought there was a Jor'ellian trick to eavesdropping," said Dylan.

"No trick, a skill. Yet hazardous to attempt under the circumstances."

An ear-pierce screech-like scream made them cringe in pain. From the ruins, a creature shot up about a hundred feet into the air, did a flip and came back to land. It stood on two legs, and taller than the Shadow Warriors by a foot with a body shaped like a man but scaly, armor-like skin of a lizard. The head resembled a dragon, wings folded against its back and a spiked tail. A sword hung at the side

Gresham's eyes went wide in fearful recognition then his head snapped to Alrick. "A wyvern! That's what I sensed."

The warrior stared in dread at the creature. More screams and several wyverns shot up from the ruins.

"Back to the horses!" ordered Alrick.

They retreated from the edge. Continuous screaming came from the ruins. They didn't stop until reaching the horses.

"Gresham, take the point. Ride on and don't look back," said Alrick.

The mortals pushed their horses to follow a speedy Gresham. Alrick lingered, watching for signs of pursuit. None came. He raced after them.

❦

Royce turned in the saddle at upon hearing hooves. A horse neighed. "Sergeant! Someone's coming," he called and drew his sword.

"It maybe the others," said Eric.

"Or maybe not." Royce turned his horse to face whatever bore down on them. The other soldiers joined him. "Keep going, my lord, we'll engage them."

Before Eric, Karly and Bryson could leave, "It's us! Gresham and the others," came a shout from the direction of the approaching horses.

"Thank Jor'el," said Eric.

The returning group pulled to a stop. Alrick arrived and waved them on. "Keep them going, Gresham!" the warrior ordered.

"Why?" asked Eric.

"No time to explain, just ride! And don't look back."

Gresham took off in a run with Dylan taking the lead to follow him.

Hearing a distant scream of a wyvern, Alrick paused to looked back. Although there were still no signs of pursuit it wasn't worth taking the risk of stopping. He glanced up to see a few thin clouds through the bare branches. No wyvern. He ran after the others.

<hr />

By dawn the mortals and horses faltered, all in need of rest. Bryson fought to stay awake and not fall off his mount. Karly tried to help him, despite her head occasionally drooping due to great weariness.

"Eric, we must stop before Bryson and I swoon with fatigue."

Alrick moved between their horses to take the reins and lead the animals. "Gresham has found shelter. Just a few moments then you can rest."

By the time they arrived, Gresham had a fire going and a small boar hanging on a spit. He also arranged pallets for sleeping. Eric stiffly dismounted then helped his wife. Alrick lifted Bryson off his horse and carried the boy to a pallet. Once lying down, the boy fell asleep.

"I suppose I'll save him some meat for he wakes," said Gresham.

Eric helped Karly sit on a pallet. He nearly fell when his tired legs gave way. "Smells good, but I wonder if I can stay awake to eat."

"Be ready in about ten minutes."

"Impossible. It's a boar. Granted a small one, but a boar."

Dylan wryly smiled as he sat opposite Eric and Karly. He and his men didn't appear as fatigued. "Not so impossible. Guardians can catch and cook game very quickly. How? I don't know, but they do."

"And the best tasting boar to be found anywhere," said Gresham.

Alrick laughed. "Don't let Gresham fool you, my lord. He's a vassal. Any skill he learned from Wren, Ridge or any forest Guardian. I'm surprise he's kept us on course."

Gresham smirked in annoyance. "This is my province, warrior. I know every square mile better than any forest Guardian."

"As long as we're away from those wyvern creatures and the boar is edible, then we're doing just fine for me," said a soldier. He took a whiff of roasting boar and smiled with satisfaction.

"A wyvern?" asked Eric.

"A creature from the ruins. That's why we were running," said Dylan.

"It is one of the most evil and formidable creatures Dagar ever created. Not only strong and powerful, but also intelligent." Alrick's brow leveled in recollection. "The last time I saw one was at the Great Battle. It took Barnum and I together to vanquish one. Kell won't like learning they have returned."

Dylan looked to the horizon and the morning sun. "I reckon it's near seven o'clock. Five hours should be enough rest."

"Some how I don't think Bryson will agree," said Eric.

"Once at the Fortress, he can sleep an entire day if he likes. I'll even make sure no one disturbs him. Or you, dear cousin," said Dylan.

She barely managed a smile due to fatigue.

"Eat your fill first then get some sleep." Gresham took the boar off the fire and hung it to carve off generous portions with his dagger.

Chapter 10

WITH SPEED REQUIRED, TIME TO REST AND EAT PROVED MINIMAL. This made any private discussions nearly impossible, thus little conversation passed between Ellis and Valery on the ride to the Fortress. Most comments concerned the journey. During the stops, Valery spent time with Mirit for some task and Ellis tended his duty to Titus. When back in the saddle, they rode together.

Once through the river plain of the Southern Forest they crossed the border into the Region of Sanctuary. They slowed their mounts to a walking pace for some rest. The spires of the Temple and battlements of the Fortress rose over the distant trees.

"At last," said a weary Valery. "I can't ride much longer at this pace."

"We won't reach the Temple until tomorrow," said Ellis.

"Really? It's doesn't look that far."

"The Temple and Fortress are enormous. Haven't you been there?"

She shook her head, still staring at the horizon. "No."

"Not even for the annual High Holy Festival?"

"No, but I always wanted to go. It sounds grand from what my mother and grandfather told me. She went every year until she married.

Grandfather remained faithful in attendance, but my father made excuses to stay home."

"It is grand. A heartwarming and fun celebration in honor of Jor'el and Allon's history. I attend every year, and find the older I get, the more I understand its significance and enjoy it more."

"Grandfather promised to take me when I turned thirteen and could officially attend Court as his guest. Something my father couldn't prevent since Grandfather said he would use his rank if necessary."

"His memorial service was held a month before the festival, correct?" He spoke in more of a statement than a question. She simply nodded so he tried to sound encouraging. "Well, you'll see it now."

"Hardly the same atmosphere."

The call came to resume a gallop.

"That was quick. My horse is still breathing hard," said Ellis.

They looked up at hearing an eagle's cry.

"Maybe it warned Wren of something." She kicked her protesting horse into a gallop when those in front of them picked up speed.

Again conversation lapsed due to urgency. This time the horses labored to keep up the pace. Not until everyone entered the forest and under cover did they halt and dismount to walk the horses.

When Valery's feet touched the ground, she held onto the saddle to keep from collapsing. Already on foot, Ellis caught her about the waist.

"Are you all right?"

"I just need to get the blood back into the my legs."

He chuckled. "I know the feeling." He shook his legs out one at a time and began to walk. "You need a drink."

She shook her head. "I wasn't able to refill my flask at the last stop."

He took his flask off his saddlebow, but frowned in disappointment upon shaking it. "Mine's empty also."

"Here. She can have some of mine." Fraser brought his horse between them. He held his flask out to Valery. Cody growled and Fraser paused in the offering.

"He wants to inspect you first," said Ellis, a pleased smile at Cody.

"Why? He's seen me before." Fraser again tried to hand her the flask and Cody nudged it.

"Easy, Cody. It's only water." Valery took the flask and felt the lightness. "There isn't much left. Are certain you want me to have it?"

"Ay. I just had some."

Valery took a swallow and returned the flask. Fraser offered it to Ellis. When he finished, Fraser put the flask back on his saddlebow.

"Never let it be said I didn't help my brother's retainer," he said in a begrudging manner. "Or a lady in need," he said with a friendly smile.

Ellis forced a grin. "Of course not, Highness."

Valery smiled sheepishly at Fraser.

"I admire the way you're bearing up under all this. I think my aunt chose wisely to take you as her squire."

"Thank you." She caught Ellis' watchful eye of the younger prince. Fraser didn't seem to notice and continued speaking.

"In fact, when we reach the Fortress, we may be training together since I'm a Jor'ellian Cadet and my uncle's squire."

"That would be interesting, Highness." Again she saw Ellis' guarded expression. Fraser still appeared oblivious.

"Oh, I almost I forgot. Titus requests your presence," he said to Ellis.

"Did he say why?"

"Does he have to?" said the young prince in firm tone.

"Of course not. I just thought he might have given a reason. Highness," he said with a nod. "My lady." He warmly smiled at her.

She returned his genuine smile and watched him dropped back to join Titus among the Jor'ellians.

Titus appeared curious when Ellis arrived. "Did Valery talk your ear off, or did you run out of things to say and retreated for solitude?"

Ellis became suspicious. "Fraser said you requested my presence."

"Oh, did he?" Titus watched Fraser speak to Valery. "My brother is taking liberties. Only I'm not sure whether it's with me or Valery."

Ellis' jowls flex in annoyance. "Either way, I'm the dupe."

"I don't think you need to fear, if you followed my advice and spoke honestly with her."

"We've barely had time to talk, much less discuss affection."

"Fraser's doing a lot of talking."

"I'm going back." He stopped when the call to mount-up came.

"Later, I'm afraid." Titus pulled himself up into the saddle.

Ellis narrowly eyed Fraser, who helped Valery mount. Hearing Titus call, Ellis sprung into the saddle and snapped the reins to urge his horse into a gallop.

⁂

Late the following afternoon, Tyrone and the others reached the Fortress. By their scuffed, dusty and weary appearance, the group rode hard the past four days. The horses didn't look any better, lathered in sweat and unsteady with fatigue. Under normal conditions it took a week to travel from Garwood in the Southern Forest to the Fortress located in the middle of the Region of Sanctuary. The courtyard buzzed with activity to receive the arriving group.

Ellis pulled his exhausted horse to an unsteady stop as close to Valery as possible. He tried to dismount in time to help her. Fraser beat him. To his modest reprieve, Fraser wasn't alert to Valery's weariness when she stumbled in taking her first step. Ellis caught her.

"Don't have your land legs yet," he teased.

"No," she chuckled and held on to him. "Thank you."

"Hey! Get that wolf out of here," yelled one of the Fortress guards.

"He's with Lady Valery," said Wren.

The guard looked skeptical, shrugged and went back to duty.

Tristine, Necie and Jillian rushed over. Tristine threw her arms around Tyrone. Necie greeted Angus and Jillian met Titus.

"We were so worried something more would happen," said Tristine.

Tyrone wearily grinned. "Thank Jor'el nothing did, but we'll talk after I bathe and change into some clean clothes."

"All the guest rooms are prepared, Sire," said the captain.

"I'm sure Tristine has already claimed our apartment," said Nigel, smiling. Tristine made an affirming smirk in reply.

"Supper will ready and waiting, Sire," said Magan.

"Thank you."

"I'll take you to our rooms." Necie held Angus' arm.

"Valery." Mirit motioned for her.

Titus gabbed Ellis' arm on the way and dragged him from greeting Jillian to proceed upstairs.

Magan found Chad. After an ardent welcome, he inquired about the boys. "Rambunctious as ever," she replied. "But Galen and Spencer are rivals in energy."

He laughed. "Better running off the energy here then on the road."

"The queen told me what happened. It sounds frightening."

"We'll find a way to stop them." He kissed her again then sighed. "Alas, I must first tend to my men. Duty before pleasure."

"I'll have your bath ready and waiting," she said with teasing smile.

"Do." He smiled and went his way.

After two hours, everyone assembled in the large formal dining hall for a good hearty meal. Uriah joined them along with Avatar, Kell and Armus. The rest of the Guardians stood post around the hall. The table easily accommodated fifty people, so the younger children were included in the gathering. They were excited to see their fathers, brothers, uncles and cousins. Even in dire circumstances, there was genuine pleasure and enjoyment in the presence of the unspoiled, innocent love and silliness of children. Mikaela climbed onto Tyrone's lap after the meal. He sat at the head of the table relaxing and participating in light conversation.

Valery sat between Ellis and Fraser, opposite Titus and Jillian. Her clothes were replaced with the uniform of Jor'ellian cadet. Cody stretched out behind her chair sleeping after eating from a mutton leg. Conversation between Valery and Ellis was minimal, since Fraser talked non-stop about his eagerness to begin training. He also addressed Valery with comments and questions regarding her new position. She was gracious and polite, often drawing Ellis into the discussion. However, Fraser ran over Ellis' speech.

Even Titus attempted to corral his younger brother by either diverting Fraser's attention or engaging Ellis. Jillian offered her support, but no more successful than the others. Soon Fraser's voice dominated the group.

Galen scurried about the room pretending to be riding at break-neck speed with three year-old Spencer attempting to keep up with him. Avery made inquiry of Angus regarding the situation, at least from the perspective of an eight-year old. Daria ran to Mikaela and whispered something in her ear.

"Oh, ay." Mikaela squirmed to get down. "Father, can you put me down? Daria and I have important business."

"Far be it from me to keep you from your business." Tyrone chuckled and set her on her feet.

She and Daria promptly huddled together speaking in hushed voices with a few giggles. Tyrone tossed a curious glance to Tristine, who sat to his left. She shrugged with a grin of ignorance.

Daria reached into a pocket hidden in the folds of her skirt and pulled out a shiny kind of material. She hid it between her hands when she noticed Tyrone. "Uncle," she lowly scolded. "No one is supposed to see it until it's presented. It's a surprise."

"I don't even know what it is," he said, trying not to laugh.

"You'll know soon enough."

Mikaela took Daria's arm. "Now, she's not looking this way." They approached Valery. "Lady Valery."

"Princess. Lady Daria."

Mikaela assumed a regal air. "In gratitude for your bravery, my cousin, Lady Daria, and I wish to present you with this medal in token of our appreciation."

Her speech drew the attention of everyone at the table. Tyrone leaned forward to see better and smiled when Daria handed Mikaela the object. Mikaela in turn gave it to Valery. A piece of fabric was badly sown onto a coin at the end with a hole through which the fabric was attached and a pin at the other end.

"It's not a real medal, we made it using what we had."

"Eli helped us by making the hole in the coin," said Daria.

Eli sat a few chairs from Valery. He nodded and smiled.

"I think it's the best medal I've ever seen. Thank you," said Valery.

"Will you wear it?" asked Daria.

"Of course." Valery pinned it on her uniform and both girls beamed.

Tyrone started clapping. The others joined in the applause. Titus winked at Mikaela, who giggled.

Valery bowed her head to Mikaela and Daria. "I'm pleased to have been of service, Your Highness, Lady Daria."

Mikaela assumed her regal expression and curtsied. Daria mimicked her, then the girls returned to the head of the table.

Ellis widely smiled. "Well, your first honor as a squire."

"And perhaps the nicest gift I've ever received."

"I think it looks good on your uniform," said Jillian.

Chad entered and approached Tyrone. "Sire. Lord Eric, Lady Karly and their son have arrived, escorted by Alrick, Gresham and Lieutenant Dylan. General Wess sent them."

"Show them in. I'm sure they're hungry."

"I wonder why Wess sent them here?" asked Tristine.

"For safety, I would assume."

Everyone turned attention to the arriving group.

"Sire. Majesty," said Eric. He, Karly and Bryson paid their respects. Their great fatigue obvious in expression and movement.

"Please, join us. We just finished eating, but there is plenty of food left. You also, Lieutenant."

Exhausted from travel and stress, Karly began to weep. Eric held her. "With all due respect, Sire, my wife is exhausted and must rest."

"Captain Chad, see they are cared for with room and food."

Karly barely took a few steps before nearly fainting. Dylan aided Eric in assisting her from the hall. Bryson followed, concerned for his mother.

"Must be something terrible. I've never seen Karly so shaken," said Ellis in grave concern.

"I'm sure she'll be fine after resting," said Valery.

"Wess is well since he sent them," said Nigel with encouragement.

Ellis fought irritation to reply. "We both know Bosley is the cause of her distress!"

Tyrone put up a stiff hand to silence Ellis. He spoke to Jade and Mahon. "Take the children to their rooms."

The Guardians gathered the younger children. Mahon picked up Spencer and held Galen by the hand. Jade escorted Mikaela and Daria.

Tyrone spoke to Alrick after the children left. "What happened?"

"The Delta is under Hueil's control—" A throaty growl from Kell interrupted Alrick, who continued in defense. "I sent Cort and Kent to start a delaying action. Alas, I've not heard from them and fear the worst. I reported the problem to Baron Erasmus, that's when he and Lord Bosley instructed me to bring Eric and his family to General Wess for safety and shelter. The General felt they were safer here."

"The news we discovered along the way here is far worse than losing the Delta," said Gresham, his face mirroring the dread in his voice. "Hueil somehow breeched the seal of Dagar's nether dimension and called forth *wyverns*."

Shock and anger brought Kell to his feet. Armus also stood. Avatar, Virgil, Wren, Vidar and the other Guardians showed degrees of surprise and concern.

"What are wyverns?" asked Tyrone at their reactions.

"Dagar's most evil and formidable creation," said Kell. "Sire, whatever we are to do, we must do it quickly."

Tyrone rose to speak but Uriah bolted up and declared, "You can't!"

"I can't what?"

The reluctance and anguish on Uriah's face matched his speech. "I didn't want to inform you this way. I have searched the laws and diligently inquired of Jor'el to find an exception. There is none." Tyrone stared at him in wary anticipation, prompting Uriah to continue. "You don't have the authority to issue any orders. Ellan *is* the rightful Queen of Allon."

Tristine gasped in horror and seized Tyrone's hand. His whole body went rigid, grey eyes glaring mercilessly at Uriah.

Irate, Nigel warned Uriah, "Mind your words, Vicar!"

"I'm sorry, but it is true!" he said in desperate apology.

Tyrone's voice was tight. "Sorry? What about Ellis' decree disavowing her claim?"

"It must have been a misinterpretation of law. Only under two circumstances can such a decree be made without the person's consent, in the event of death, or the murder of another royal family member."

Tristine was incredulous. "She tried to kill father with poison!"

"He survived," said Uriah.

"Mother died," insisted Necie.

"My father also," added Angus.

Uriah tempered his reply with compassion. "Darius wasn't of royal blood and by his own lips, said Musetta killed him. Queen Shannan died by Morrell's hand."

"With Ellan as their ally!" snapped Tristine. Passion brought her to her feet. "If not for her they wouldn't have succeeded as far as they did."

"True, but she had no direct hand in anyone's death. She bears responsibility for conspiracy, but is only directly guilty of treason and *attempted* murder. Neither of those are permissible exceptions to warrant the decree. Although at the time, I can understand why King Ellis believed he had the right. Technically he was wrong."

The coldness in Tyrone's grey eyes made the Vicar retreat a step. "You expect me to stand by and let this happen on a technicality?"

"Far from a technicality."

"Enough!" shouted Nigel, his patience ended. "This isn't helping. Division is threatening the stability of Allon. We must find a way to confront it regardless of legalities, or *everything* that's been accomplished will be destroyed!"

"You know I don't want that," said Uriah.

Tyrone closed his eyes, and took several deep breaths to regain his composure. He then spoke to Uriah. "None of us do. If it is still permissible, I would like a chapel prepared for a night of solitary prayer."

A smile of relief appeared on Uriah's face. "I can willingly grant your request, for you are still a prince."

Tyrone felt Tristine squeeze his hand yet spoke to everyone. "All of you are free to seek guidance and strength as your conscience dictates."

Uriah and Tyrone left together.

Nigel confronted Kell. "Captain! You haven't said a word, why?"

"I will make diligent inquiry for an answer, Highness."

The evasive answer did not satisfy Nigel, so Mirit tugged on his hand. "Tristine and Eli are leaving. We should help her." He didn't immediately yield, rather kept staring at Kell. "Nigel, please," she urged. He gave a curt nod and marched from the table with Mirit matching his stride.

"I need to help my mother," said Titus to Jillian.

Fraser rose, bowed to Valery and hurried after them.

"I should attend the princess. You and Jillian do what you feel necessary, " said Valery in tone of quiet compassion to Ellis.

"See to Karly. I'll help with the children," said Jillian to Ellis.

With the mortals departed, only the Guardians remained.

"That didn't go well," chided Armus.

"Did you avoid answering Nigel because you knew about the decree being illegal?" Avatar asked Kell in not-to-friendly tone.

"No!" Kell stoutly refuted. "I advised Ellis on the legalities."

"Then why suggest the family come here?"

"Especially with Ellan making threats in her letter to Tristine," said Armus, bolstering Avatar's argument.

"I admit, I wondered about Ellan from time to time. Only because of Jor'el's mercy in granting his request to spare her life, not a problem with the decree."

"Jor'el wanted immediate justice? That goes against the law to take the life of a royal," Avatar continued in dispute.

"*If* the crime only went against mortals, but by involving the Dark Way, it was an affront to Jor'el." Kell continued after a sober sigh. "Despite all she did, Ellis couldn't bring himself to execute her."

"I wish you'd told me when placing her in my keeping," groused Vidar.

"I didn't see the need since it wouldn't affect her imprisonment."

"It might have saved the lives of my Trio mates!" argued Wren. "And what about Hueil? Why wasn't he destroyed after Tunlund?"

"Ay," said Avatar, his temper not cooled by Kell's responses. "He enslaved a nation and killed Guardians by way of unholy sacrifices!"

Kell was slow to answer. "I don't know. But I'm sure there is a reason. As we all must be that Jor'el has a purpose for all this."

"Easier said than done," complained Avatar.

"I need to tell this to Tyrone before he begins his prayer so he can be *fully* informed," said Armus.

"No, I will. I bear responsibility for advising Ellis. You help Tristine." He looked to Avatar. "Tell Nigel I didn't know and meant what I said—I will find out."

Uriah escorted Tyrone to the private chapel connected to his house. A rich, yet modestly decorated room of rosewood paneling with four pews before a small altar. Four stained glass windows faced in each direction. Each window depicted symbols of Jor'el, Allon, the Temple, and the throne. With reverence, Uriah spoke a prayer in the Ancient while lighting all the candles and lanterns in the room.

Kell arrived. "Sire. I need to speak to you."

Uriah stopped lighting a lantern at hearing the address.

Tyrone noticed the reaction. "We'll dispense with formality," he said for the Vicar's benefit.

Uriah placed the candle he used back in its place on the altar. He spoke to Tyrone. "Understand; I harbor no ill will or intention towards you. I know that is an issue since you assumed the throne, only not from me. I truly want the best for everyone, but my first duty is to Jor'el and the sanctity of His law and the preservation of Allon."

"You think that is not my priority? I wish you had come to me in private."

"Perhaps this is best. Whereas you can handle the situation public or private, Tristine needs more support. She endured so much back then. Now, I will leave you. My door is open should you have need." He withdrew.

"Uriah is a good and faithful servant," said Kell.

Tyrone made no comment to the statement, rather said, "You wanted to speak to me?"

"To explain what happened when Ellis stayed in seclusion."

"He said he was mourning Darius and Shannan, along with seeking Jor'el's council on what to do with Ellan."

"Put simply, ay. What he didn't want known was Jor'el deemed Ellan worthy of execution for her crimes."

"He said the law forbade the taking of royal blood."

"For mortal crimes. Using the Dark Way went against Jor'el's sovereignty and called for the ultimate penalty. However, Ellis couldn't bring himself to do it. He spent those three days pleading for her life. Jor'el granted the request by ordering her imprisoned in the nether dimension."

"If Jor'el spared her then why isn't the decree legal?"

"I don't know. I advised Ellis and believed in the legality."

"Why would Uriah refute you, Jor'el's Captain?"

"Uriah would not have said what he did if not convinced of the validity of his findings. Also, Hueil helped to write the law, not me."

"Wonderful," chided Tyrone. "He couldn't defeat me in Tunlund, so now he uses a legal loophole to jerk the throne out from under me. And Uriah says I must stand by and let him!" His passion again rose to irate.

Kell's restraining hand gripped Tyrone's shoulder. "You are the Great King of prophecy. So while you seek guidance in prayer, I intend to find out directly from Jor'el. There must be a way to confront Hueil."

"Let's hope we find the answer quickly."

"I leave immediately." Kell stepped back and vanished.

Tyrone knelt on one knee before the altar. "Jor'el, hear your servant on behalf of people you appointed me to govern and protect. Show me why this is happening and what must be done to defend your name and stop the evil from overtaking your people." He sat on the front pew to begin a night of remembrance and contemplation.

He intended to begin his consideration on the day he met Tristine, only his memory went back to the days of his youth when his grandfather Fraser and mother Mikaela were alive. He suffered cruel teasing and taunting from people upon discovering his father was a Shadow Warrior. King Marcellus and Grand Master Latham employed them in a ruthless effort to subdue the people and stop the Son of Tristan from assuming the throne. In fact, his birth occurred the day of Ellis and Shannan's coronation. His grandfather, a former priest, named him Tyrone and said it meant 'sovereign' in the Ancient. At the time, none of them knew of the destiny linked to his name.

His mother died when he was eighteen, not seeing her son's future. Two years later, he and his grandfather saw what they believed to be a glimpse of the future when King Ellis' horse threw a shoe. He and Prince Nigel sought a smith to repair it while on a hunting trip, the fateful trip where Nigel was believed killed. His grandfather mourned the fate of his country without a strong king. So great did he mourn that he died a few months later at the age of eighty.

For the first time, Tyrone faced life alone. He survived on his blacksmith skills and lived isolated outside the town. People came to him for business due to his superior workmanship. He heavily leaned upon the faith instilled in him by the grandfather and mother.

A year to the day that his grandfather died, a wandering cripple by the name of Waymon sought shelter from a harsh winter storm. Over the next four years they formed a close friendship born from adversity and the commonality of being outcast and devoid of family. Or so he initially believed. He suspected something different about Waymon. Despite his deformities, nobility showed in his manner, speech and knowledge. He learned Waymon became crippled by a horrendous accident. Waymon didn't elaborate and he didn't press for answers. He understood the pain associated with the hardships of life. Waymon directed Tristine to him when her horse threw a shoe. Later he discovered Waymon's true identity, Prince Nigel. Their friendship eventually became a brotherhood.

Tyrone softly smiled at the thought of Tristine. Although they met under dire circumstances the attraction was immediate and deep for both of them. His love and concern for her gave him the courage to leave his life of isolation and walk straight to his destiny. He could see how his whole life prepared him for that time. As the Great King he ruled for ten years, but why was this second attempted coup being allowed?

His half-breed parentage irritated some on the Council. He knew the rumors of Zebulon's distain at being named Ellis' heir. It didn't surprise him when the old curmudgeon caused trouble during Council meetings, nor Gareth's support. However, some names among those who supported Ellan did surprise him. After all they been through and how well Bosley and Erasmus knew the royal family, they of all the others were the most painful to hear about. Where the situation with Ellan proved troublesome, Hueil's involvement was dangerous.

Events in Tunlund flashed across his mind. He began to break out in a cold sweat when recalling the vision Hueil gave him of Titus' sacrifice in an effort to defeat him. Joined with the cries of anguish from the Guardians Hueil killed in previous sacrifices, made him shudder. So real, painful and frightening, he couldn't let it happen in Allon!

Suddenly a new vision appeared, and one of fire and chaos. Screams and images of his family grew among the flames.

"No!" He gritted his teeth and held his arms across his chest in a desperate fight against the sensation. "Jor'el! Help me to find a way to defeat him," he cried out before falling to his knees, then passing out.

Against the black of night, flames from a fire a Ravendale rose higher and intense in red-hot light and heat. Hueil stared into the flames and wickedly grinned.

"Despite your Guardian heritage, you suffer the same mortal weakness, half-breed. We shall see how long you can endure what I have planned this time."

A grim-looking Shadow Warrior arrived. "My lord. We are ready to leave."

Hueil winced then blinked. The flames reduced to a normal size fire. "Proceed to the rendezvous. Oh, Phelan, have you heard from those two fools yet?"

"No, my lord. Shall I pay them a visit to encourage their progress?"

"After we have fully assembled our forces. If they haven't succeeded by then, make your visit a final calling."

"With pleasure, my lord."

Chapter 11

TITUS SPENT MOST OF THE NIGHT WITH HIS MOTHER AND BROTHERS. He finally convinced Tristine to go to sleep around three o'clock in the morning. He left the apartment to wander the compound. So much happened in such a short time that listening to the argument between his parents and Uriah about Ellan's legitimate claim unsettled him. His entire life became null and void in a matter of moments. The question now is what to do about it? His father wouldn't just hand the throne over to Ellan no matter what Uriah said. However, no one has seen or spoken to Tyrone since last evening. Then again, no one wanted to disturb him, but Titus grew increasing uncomfortable about the situation.

At dawn, he went to the armory. Nigel and Mirit practiced the Jor'ellian forms to release tension and focus their minds for the day. They remained until Tristine fell asleep then left, to rest they said. Titus knew better, which is why he went to the armory.

Nigel broke form when Titus arrived. "Has she woken already?"

"No, she still sleeps. I just wonder what are we going to do if an answer isn't found?"

"I'm confident between Tyrone, Kell and Uriah an answer *will* be found. My concern is the impact this is having upon you, your brothers and Mikaela."

"Jade is making certain Mikaela knows enough to satisfy but not be scared. Fraser is spouting his usual complaints and Eli counters him for Mother's sake."

"Hopefully the Jor'ellian training will curb Fraser's tongue."

Titus scowled to the contrary. "What about Father? Will you go to the chapel and speak to him?"

Nigel shook his head. "Tyrone will speak when he is ready. We must be patient and trust Jor'el."

It was obvious the response didn't satisfy Titus so Mirit spoke.

"For the sake of your mother and siblings, you must exhibit the strong faith in Jor'el you did in Tunlund."

"The same faith you must someday possess as king," added Nigel.

Both statements hit him hard and deep. He left the armory. Absorbed in thought of their parting words, his wandering brought him near the Vicar's residence. He didn't enter the house, rather made his way to the private chapel, also accessible from the outside.

Tyrone knelt at the altar, his head bent in prayer. Titus sat on the last pew to watch his father. So physically strong and mentally sure, yet always bending a knee in times of crisis. The paradox wasn't lost upon him. Since the journey to Natan five years earlier, he saw his father differently than as a youth. In fact, he viewed many things differently than he did back then.

After his rescue from Tunlund, he idolized Nigel. That idolization drove him to scorn his father. Everything changed in Natan when his actions forced Tyrone to take on the part of a soldier, submitting for the safety of others. On that fateful journey, Allard died helping Titus flee the rival warlord attacking their host.

Although others told him Allard's death wasn't his fault, he still felt responsible. The guilt intensified at seeing Braden, Florie, Valery and the rest of Allard's children and grandchildren in mourning. Since then he accepted the fact Allard died in service to his king and country. Guilt faded, but some regret remained concerning the death of a loyal family friend. Regret disappeared when he and Valery began clashing a few months after the memorial. What exactly placed them at odds was a mystery. Or rather something he didn't want to admit, pride. She proved very intelligent, inheriting Allard's wit and quick tongue, which tended to infuriate him.

Since Valery informed them of the betrayal, Titus came to understand why using Ellis to counter her was wrong. He smiled at the thought of their budding relationship. Learning about her being family and caught up in events, gave him pause to rethink their relationship. It gave him pause to rethink everything in his life. He concluded that the only constant is Jor'el, all else changes.

Tyrone rising from his knees and sitting on the pew broke Titus thoughts. His father appeared unaware of anyone's presence. For a brief moment, Titus wondered about letting him know then thought better of it. Nigel was correct; his father would speak when ready. Thus Titus sat, his gaze and thoughts shifting between Tyrone and the altar. Startled, he flinched when someone sat beside him. Fraser.

"What are you doing here?" he whispered.

"Looking for you," replied Fraser, also whispering. "Mother wanted to know where you went."

"I thought she still slept."

"She woke at dawn."

"Does she need me?"

"She wants to know if you've spoken to Father. It's not like him to be so quiet."

"Unlike hissing and whispering boys." Tyrone turned in the pew.

"We didn't mean to disturb you, sir," said Titus.

He grinned. "Considering how long you've been here, you did well."

"You knew I was here?"

"From the moment you entered."

"Why didn't you say anything?"

"Just as you did not wish to disturb me, I did not wish to disturb you. Now, I have a task for both of you."

Tyrone entered Avatar's office and found Kell waiting. "They should be here momentarily," he said. He no sooner finished speaking than Tristine rushed in. Nigel, Mirit, Armus, Virgil and Armus with her. She greeted him with a hug and questions of concern. "I'm well. When the rest have joined us, I'll explain why I summoned everyone."

They didn't wait long as Fraser and Titus were prompt in their task. With only a few chairs available, Uriah, Jillian, Necie and Karly sat.

Tyrone began his explanation. "Why I called you all here is in regard to what must be done to counter our current crisis. First, I want to discuss what brings Lord Eric, his family and Lieutenant Dylan to the Fortress for it is related to the issue." He turned to the named parties. "You told Captain Chad that General Wess sent you. Is it because the Delta is now in Hueil's control?"

"Ay. My father wanted to save some of his family while he and Lord Bosley told me to express deeply their regret," said Eric.

"After agreeing with Ellan?" asked Tristine, not hiding her hurt and anger.

"Madam, he is compelled to stand by his earlier oath to your sister, though it pains him to do so."

"Compelled?" asked Tyrone.

"He means Ellan used threats," said Tristine with a hard edge.

"Indeed, Madam." Eric stepped towards her while reaching into his pocket. His action brought Armus to stand between him and Tristine. "My father's signet ring." He held it up for Armus.

Tristine nudged Armus to move aside.

Eric got down on one knee before her. "As a sign of remorse and affection, he gave the Delta to me with instructions to pledge my allegiance to you and the king, which I freely do." He kissed her hand.

She became misty eyed. "In my heart I did not want to believe Erasmus would betray us."

"In his heart he has not, Madam! He wishes for another way, but this is all he could think of to save part of his family and reassure you and the king of his loyalty and affection."

"Ay," began Dylan. "Father also sent his ring to uncle for safe keeping. Wess in turn gave it to me, charging me with my cousins' safety and to pledge the same loyalty. I am grieved by Garrick's choice."

Tristine's smile wavered slightly. "Rise, Eric. Your message is greatly appreciated, and affection mutual for Erasmus and Bosley."

Eric stayed on his knee. "I'll rise when my duty is complete." He addressed Tyrone. "Sire, I carry out my father's wishes along with following my own conscience in pledging fidelity." He began to bow his head when Tyrone pulled him to his feet.

"As much as I desire to accept your fidelity, under the circumstances, it is to another you must make that pledge."

"Sire, I cannot! No, I will not bow to Ellan!"

"Not Ellan. The one person whose claim exceeds her." Tyrone turned to Nigel, who said nothing rather stared at him.

"Tyrone, what are you saying?" asked Tristine with trepidation.

His eyes never left Nigel to reply. "As first born, he is the only person upon which she has no claim. If the crown is to be passed, it will be to Nigel and no other."

"Abdicate?" she could barely speak the word.

This time he looked at her. "Ay."

"No!" declared Nigel. "You are Jor'el's appointed to be king."

Tyrone seized Nigel's arm to press his point. "Don't you understand? If Allon is to be saved from Ellan and Hueil, it is by *you*. Not me, not Kell, not Tristine, *you!* First born of the Son of Tristan, Jor'el's chosen before me. It is the answer I received from Jor'el last night."

"As did I," said Kell in confirming Tyrone's assertion.

Nigel pulled from Tyrone and moved behind Avatar's desk, his back to them. Mirit joined him in an attempt to offer support and comfort.

Uriah crossed to where Nigel could see him. "Your Royal Highness," he began by using Nigel's former title as heir. "I too sense this, but until Tyrone spoke, did not feel at liberty to broach the subject."

"I have not been crowned," said Nigel in feeble objection.

"We could hold the abdication and coronation together at the Temple with Uriah presiding," said Tyrone.

"Then what? Take to the battlefield and destroy my sister?"

"To protect a sister." Tyrone placed an arm around Tristine's shoulder. "Two sisters, your wife, brothers, nephews and nieces. To do as Jor'el commands to save the kingdom!"

Overwhelmed, Nigel leaned on Avatar's desk with head lowered and screwed his eyes shut.

Mirit spoke in a firm voice unwilling to accept objection. "I think it is best everyone leave."

Kell and Armus ushered the others out.

"Nigel," said Tristine, her voice low and pleading. When he looked at her, the conflict in his eyes made her mute. Tyrone steered her to the door where Armus took her out into the hall.

Tyrone lingered. "Time is short. Don't focus so much on Ellan that you forget Hueil, who once killed your wife. His grip is darker and far more reaching."

Avatar closed the door behind Tyrone and remained. Nigel sat in the desk chair. Mirit knelt beside him and took his hand.

"You know Tyrone would not ask this of you if he weren't completely convinced." For a brief moment, she gazed into his eyes. "Are you afraid of the responsibility?"

"No."

"Of facing Ellan?"

"Pause for thought and concern since she is my sister, but not fear."

"Then what?"

Nigel pushed himself out of the chair. "Aside from being caught off guard, I'm the Knight of the Temple and the King's Champion. The last thirteen years I have defended Allon and the throne. The thought of

Tyrone and Tristine abdicating is unsettling, not just to me, but to anyone. He is Jor'el's chosen, not I."

"You will still be defending Allon, only with a different title."

Nigel didn't answer. His eyes focused on the floor.

Avatar approached. "I never told you this, but in my spirit, I knew there was a specific reason for what happened to you. Certainly returning proved beneficial for all, but that wasn't it. Hearing Tyrone, I suddenly realized the reason."

Nigel quizzically regarded Avatar, and some anger crept into his voice. "To be king? You know I never felt I would be king."

"Not in the permanent sense." Avatar placed his hands on Nigel's shoulders to get his full attention. "Everything that has happened to you, all the hardships, the experiences, even Mirit's one time death, has been to mold and prepare you to fulfill your destiny. Tyrone is right: *you are* the only one who can save Allon. To do so, you must wear the crown. Once the threat is over, you can abdicate. And I will be by your side."

"We both will," said Mirit. "Or should I should say three, for Chad would hardly be left out. Then there is Fraser. Perhaps Titus—"

"No! I draw the line at Titus," said Nigel.

Mirit regarded him, careful yet hopeful. "You will do it?"

"Ay, since it will protect my family and defend Allon. Jor'el give me strength, as it goes against my better judgment and oath."

⁘

Bells rang out from the Temple in a notifying cadence. Golden lamp stands forged by metal workers in the Highlands illuminated the gold, white and crimson interior. Tapestries from the Lowlands hung on the walls. A crimson carpet from the Meadowlands led to the High Altar. Sun cascading through the windows made a bright mosaic of color on the white marble floor. Each window represented a province with six on each side of the Temple. The incense was supplied by the West Coast, exclusive importers of such finery. Not to be outdone, the exquisite Altar furnishings were donated by leading merchant families of the East Coast.

Wood for the High Altar came from the oldest tree in Allon, which was found in the Delta.

Priests, Jor'ellians, servants, cadets, squires, nobles and officials filled the Temple. On the front row stood Nigel and Mirit, both dressed in state royal attire, and bareheaded. Avatar flanked Nigel.

For this occasion, Tyrone sent Avatar to fetch Mathias to witness his daughter's coronation. Mathias stood beside Mirit. His hair and thin trimmed beard were now totally white. His face and body started to show his age of seventy-eight, but with the clear, steady eyes and the bearing of seasoned soldier and statesman. Tyrone also sent for Fagan and Ned, to ensure all loyal Council Members were present.

Tyrone and Tristine waited on the opposite side of the front row from Nigel and Mirit and also regally dressed. They wore their crowns. Finely bedecked in priestly robes, Uriah climbed the steps of the raised platform and paused before the altar. Two attendants flanked him. Kell and Armus waited at the bottom of the altar steps dressed in their white uniforms. Royal soldiers, Temple guards and the Guardians were posted around the Temple for security.

After the sounding of trumpets from outside, Uriah spoke. "We gather on this solemn occasion to bear witness to Jor'el's will in the abdication of one in favor of another." He put up his hands to stop some murmuring. "This is done for the purpose of confronting an enemy, who threatens to end the reign of House of Tristan and replace Jor'el with the Dark Way. This cannot be allowed! United, Guardians and mortals, we bear witness and lend our unwavering support to what must be done." He nodded to Tyrone and Tristine.

Hand-in-hand, they mounted the altar steps and faced the crowd for Tyrone to speak. "This is both a sad and hopeful day. Yet know that what we do, we do for the good of Allon and the honor of Jor'el."

They approached the altar, removed their crowns, placed them on the altar then knelt. Tyrone again spoke. "This day we relinquish our crowns and claim in favor of another, and trust that Jor'el will use his courage and strength for the salvation of Allon. Jor'el's will be done."

Taking Tristine's hand, they descended from the altar. He tried to catch Nigel's glance, but Nigel stared straight ahead. Still, the tension and pain showed on Nigel's face. Tyrone did catch Mirit's distressful gaze.

"Prince Nigel, come forth with your wife Princess Mirit," said Uriah.

They too mounted the platform hand-in-hand. When they turned faced the crowd, Nigel looked over their heads, his jowls clenched.

Cody trotted down the aisle with two guards trying to catch him. He stopped at the row where Valery sat.

"Leave the beast!" said Uriah. "It is a good sign, since a wolf helped the Daughter of Allon and Son of Tristan." The guards backed off.

Uriah continued, more to the crowd than to Nigel. "As first born of King Ellis, the Son of Tristan, and Queen Shannan, the Daughter of Allon, you, Nigel, are rightful King of Allon. This day receive the crown of your father and the charge from Jor'el to hold, defend and protect the heritage and throne to which you were born. Do you accept this charge?"

"On behalf of my father and Jor'el, I accept this charge," Nigel spoke with clarity.

"Kneel and take from the hand of Jor'el's captain your father's crown."

Nigel knelt. Kell took the king's crown from off the altar and stood in front of Nigel. He looked up to the Guardian captain.

"Nigel, Son of Ellis, the Son of Tristan, by will of Jor'el and right of birth, I crown you king of Allon."

Nigel bent his head and Kell placed the crown upon his head. When he looked up again, Kell stepped back.

Uriah spoke, "Mirit, daughter of Mathias of the Council of Twelve, princess by marriage. Do you accept the charge of Jor'el to serve as faithful queen to your husband and lord king?"

"By Jor'el's will, I accept the charge," she replied.

"Then kneel and accept from the Guardian of Allon your crown."

Mirit knelt beside Nigel. Armus went to the altar and took the queen's crown. He stepped in front of her, and she looked up.

"Mirit, daughter of Mathias, by marriage and pledge, I crown you queen of Allon." She bowed her head. He crowned her and moved aside.

"Rise to the fidelity of your subjects," said Uriah.

They stood and everyone in the Temple knelt.

"Hail Nigel, King of Allon!" declared Kell.

"Hail Nigel, King of Allon," said Tyrone and all the rest repeated.

Uriah held up his hands for silence. "According to law those members of the Council of Twelve or their representative will now affix their seal alongside their province in a pledge of fidelity to King Nigel." He motioned to a table at the left side of the altar. Two royal guards flanked the table with Vidar behind it. "Those present come forward and join me in recognizing Jor'el's chosen king."

Angus, Mathias, Fagan, Ned, Dylan and Eric came and stamped their ring into wax beside the name of the province they represented. Uriah spoke a word of blessing and they returned to their places. When complete, he picked up the document and returned to the platform.

"A majority of the Council of Twelve recognizes and pledges their fidelity to you, King Nigel."

Nigel formally nodded and addressed the crowd. "Your fidelity is appreciated. For myself," he said with a slight quiver as he looked for the first time at Tyrone and Tristine, "I thank those who served before me and swear to uphold all they accomplished with honor and dignity. I further pledge to all present, the queen and I will not rest until the threat is put down and Allon safe again." He took Mirit's hand, descended the platform and walked the center aisle to exit the Temple to the shout, "Long live the king.'" Virgil and Avatar accompanied them.

Being twilight, lamp and torchlight illuminated the Courtyard where Royal soldiers, Jor'ellians Guards and Knights assembled. Chad sat mounted and called for attention when Nigel and Mirit emerged from the Temple. He saluted.

"Ready for your inspection, Sire."

Nigel grinned. "Later, Captain. Begin preparation for a morning departure to Waldron."

"Ay, Sire." Chad saluted and returned to his troops.

Nigel and Mirit proceeded to the Fortress. Along the way, respect was paid the royal couple. They didn't stop until reaching their apartment. He moved to stand in front of a fire in the hearth.

"I realize this isn't easy for you," she said.

He didn't answer.

"It isn't easy for me. I love them as much as you do and pains me, but it must be this way."

At a knock on the door, Nigel signaled to Virgil.

"Lieutenant Dylan, Sire. He says he needs to speak to you."

"What is it, Lieutenant?" asked Nigel.

The young man's expression and demeanor showed regret. "I hoped to speak to either you or Prince Tyrone before the ceremony, and loath to bring it to your attention now. I have a letter from the general." He pulled it out from his inside doublet pocket. "It is addressed to *King* Tyrone. Alas, I think the effect will be more so with you." He held it out to Nigel.

Curious, Nigel took the letter, broke the seal and read. The first part dealt with Eric, Karly, Dylan and confirming the loss of the Delta. The second half of the letter stunned him and he sat, staring at the letter.

"Nigel?" asked Mirit in concern.

He ignored her to confront Dylan. "He can't mean this."

"As I said, he wrote to King Tyrone."

"What is it?" She reached for the letter, which he yielded.

"Wess' resignation."

Surprised, she read the portion regarding the resignation. "This is incredible. What will we do for a general?"

"I won't accept it, that's what!"

"Sire, my uncle is determined not to face his brother in battle. Although he will defend Waldron to the death if needed."

Nigel stood, his rebuke sharp. "I know your uncle's mettle better than you!"

Mirit gripped Nigel's arm and said, "Remember Bosley is his father."

"I know," he said in frustration. "Neither do I want face Bosley in battle, but I will not accept Wess' resignation. I cannot. I need his help, if not his friendship."

"My uncle spoke with fondness when recalling what happened when you were an infant. He also expressed that he doesn't have the heart for a fourth coup. Knowing him as you do, you are acquainted with his adversities, yet he faithfully serves those who desposed his family."

At first, Nigel glared at Dylan for the brash response then softened his expression. "I understand more than you realize. My father owed his life to your grandfather Hugh. The same debt I owe Wess and Bosley. Outside of my family, I hold them in highest affection. This," he took back the letter from Mirit, "comes from a man weary and fearful. Like you said, he wrote it to Tyrone, not me. Since the situation is changed, I want to allay those fears and offer him a chance to help me secure Allon. If he still feels the same after I've spoken to him, I will grant his request." He clapped Dylan on the shoulder. "I not only understand, I sympathize with Wess. It is *my sister* we must defeat to save Allon."

Dylan became thunderstruck with regret. "I'm sorry, Sire. I don't know what made me forget your pain in favor of my own."

Nigel flashed a poignant smile. "You're young."

"I'd like to come with you to Waldron and help convince him."

"Wess wants to spare you. Will you go against his wishes?"

"I'm a royal soldier as my uncle and his uncle before him."

Nigel grinned in genuine pleasure. "Very well. Find Captain Chad and tell him you're joining my retinue."

Dylan saluted then asked, "Sire, could I beg a favor, for my uncle's sake? That Eric, Karly and Bryson be taken to the Highlands for safety."

Nigel chuckled. "I'll make arrangements."

"Thank you, Sire."

Tyrone, Tristine, Angus, Necie, Mathias, Fagan and Ned arrived as Dylan left. He flashed a smile at Fagan in passing.

"Did Dylan bring more news, Sire?" asked Fagan.

Nigel held up the paper. "Wess' resignation."

"What?" said Tristine with astonishment. She took the letter from Nigel to read. Tyrone looked over her shoulder at the letter.

"He wrote to Tyrone. Dylan gave it to me since he didn't have time before the ceremony. I hope to convince Wess otherwise."

"That might take some convincing." Tyrone gave the letter to Fagan.

After a brief moment to read, Fagan spoke. "He thought about retiring after the Soren invasion. When Glenda died, he needed to occupy himself. Or rather Cassie convinced him not to be idle. Her death shortly after hit him doubly hard."

"If I can't convince him, I will accept the resignation and wish him all the best." Nigel took back the letter from Fagan. "Dylan asked for Eric, Karly and Bryson be taken to the Highlands for safety."

"Naturally, I would never turn them away."

Nigel smiled. "Virgil, see to their safe conduct."

The Guardian saluted and left.

"Chad said you plan to leave in the morning," said Angus.

"Ay. The sooner I become visible the better. Maybe news of my coronation will convince Ellan to back down."

"If not, then the fleet can make her think twice," said Mathias.

"How many ships?"

"Forty compared to Hollis' thirty. Five have forty-guns, twenty armed with thirty guns, ten with fifteen and five frigates for supplies and medical treatment." Mathias shook his head in sober regret. "I don't like the idea of firing on my second-in-command."

"He didn't give us much of a choice."

"Ay. The *Protectorate* is waiting for my return to join the others. Sire." He bowed to Nigel then hugged and kissed Mirit before leaving.

"Sire," began Ned. "My men, along with Fagan's, are en route to Waldron. Fifty thousand strong."

"Add my twenty thousand, and thirty thousand royal forces, for a total of one hundred thousand," said Angus.

"The others can combine for half as much more, making one hundred and fifty thousand. Along with Shadow Warriors and wyverns is a considerable force to face," said Tyrone.

"Doesn't change the fact Jor'el will defend what is right," said Ned.

Nigel flashed a grateful smile. "Your loyalty and courage is appreciated."

"We're not so faint of heart as to forget the debt we owe your father, nor the love we bore him—like some on the Council."

Fagan stirred with anger at his brother. "Don't judge Bosley and Erasmus! She threatened them, yet they sent their rings by way of their sons to show where they true heart lies. How else could the majority of the Council support Nigel's coronation? It could have easily been us."

The forcefulness made Ned recanted with a sober nod.

"Avatar, see they are returned as they came," said Nigel.

Avatar escorted Ned and Fagan to threshold and spoke a quick word to several Guardian warriors in the hallway. He barely shut the door after giving instructions, when Kell arrived in a rush.

"We need to act quickly and seal the breach."

"I'll change clothes so we can leave immediately," said Tyrone.

"What makes you think you can go?" asked Tristine.

Nigel intervened. "There is something we haven't told you. Since I'm king, Tyrone is now the King's Champion."

Tristine confronted Tyrone. "You agreed? Without asking me?"

"I don't need your permission to defend Allon. The switch is natural since we must stand united. Fraser will be in the Jor'ellian Guards accompanying Nigel while Titus and Angus will be with me. Eli shall remain here with you, Necie and the children."

"No. I'm going also, and as the Queen's Champion. If you can change places, so can I."

"This isn't up for debate."

"No debate, I'm stating the new reality."

Mirit had to swallow back a laugh, which made Tyrone suspicious.

"You put her up to this!" he chided.

Tristine intervened. "No, she tried to talk me out of it. Necie and I agreed." She upped her argument at his annoyance. "You said the switch is natural to stand united. We ruled together, so why can't we defend Allon together?

Her challenge made him wince and look for help. "Nigel?"

He shrugged, his expression hesitant. "She has a valid point. We defend Allon together." He motioned between he and Mirit.

When Tristine took hold of his arm, Tyrone sighed in resignation. "Very well." He then spoke to Kell and Angus. "I'll join you in the Courtyard." He kissed Tristine's cheek and entered the bedroom.

Angus hugged and kissed Necie before leaving.

"Look after for them, Kell," said Necie.

"Always. Just as Mahon will be looking after you."

In the Courtyard, Avatar, Chad, Wren, Ridge, Vidar and Mahon tended to preparation for the early morning departure. A rider arrived. He suffered minor wounds and reined a tired and sweaty horse.

"Commander Avatar, I'm Sergeant Conner." He saluted. "Lieutenant Mayers requests your immediate presence at the Redford Crossing Outpost. It is in danger of being overrun. I barely escaped alive."

"Chad, have Lieutenant Brewster's platoon mounted and ready to leave immediately."

"No, just you, Commander," said Conner in dispute. "That's what the lieutenant said. There's something strange about it." He rocked forward in the saddle. Ridge grabbed him and helped him to dismount.

"Take him to the infirmary," said Avatar.

"Bad timing," said Wren as they watched Ridge leave with Conner.

"What? The outpost being overrun?" chided Avatar.

"No, the request. You're to accompany the king to Waldron."

"I'll go to the outpost," said Mahon.

"What about the duke's children?" asked Vidar.

"He's tired of being a nanny," snickered Wren.

"The children are safe here. Besides, if he's asking for Avatar, whatever it is requires a Guardian and not more mortals," said Mahon.

Avatar pursed his lips. "Chad, tell Brewster to meet Mahon at the outpost."

"Where exactly is this outpost?" asked Mahon.

"Near the northern crossing of the River Tulach on the border of Midessex and the North Plains." Avatar looked steadily at Mahon and added, "Ten miles from the ruins of Ravendale."

"That could be why Mayers sensed something strange."

"Ay, so be careful. Do reconnaissance but wait until the platoon arrives for any action. Hueil is clever and I don't want you to take any unnecessary risks. Report to me at Waldron."

Mahon cocked a grin of bravado. "I'm always careful. Consider it done." He took a step back and vanished.

Kell, Titus, Angus, Ellis, Egan and five royal soldiers arrived and leading eight horses. Tyrone wore the uniform of the King's Champion.

Avatar cast curious eye up and down at Tyrone. "Is there's a explanation I should know about?"

"Simple. Nigel and I switched roles."

"As did Mirit and Tristine, I suppose?"

"Of course."

Avatar snorted with sarcasm. "I was joking."

"I'm not."

Kell chuckled and said, "We're going to seal the ruins."

"I just sent Mahon to Redford Crossing Outpost about ten miles away due to a report of *trouble*. Lieutenant Brewster's platoon is getting ready to leave shortly."

"Why Mahon?"

"They requested me. Since I'm leaving with king, he volunteered."

"Then we must be quick." Tyrone mounted his horse.

Kell smiled when seeing Ridge returned to the group. "Ridge, if Wren can bear to be without you, we need your help."

"Oh, I can bear it. Take him, please," she dryly said.

"Well, I guess it's nice to be wanted."

"Titus!" Jillian rushed from the armory stairs. Valery followed, only she didn't appear as fretful as Jillian. "So it is true. You are leaving."

"To help stop Hueil."

"When will you be back?"

"I don't know."

She fought becoming emotional so he hugged her.

"I'll make sure he stays out of trouble," said Ellis.

Jillian hugged her brother. "You be careful too."

"I will." Ellis kissed her cheek. When they separated, he caught Valery's eye. "You'll be leaving tomorrow with the queen."

"Ay. Perhaps I'll see you at Waldron."

"Time to go," said Kell.

Ellis went to mount when Valery caught his arm. For a moment they looked at each, but neither spoke.

"I'll make sure *he* stays out of trouble," teased Titus.

Ellis flashed a cavalier smile at Valery and mounted his horse.

Standing side-by-side, Jillian and Valery watched them leave the Fortress.

"Kell, Egan and Ridge will protect them," said Avatar.

"Ay. Come," said Valery to Jillian. "We have out duties as well."

Chapter 12

MAHON REAPPEARED IN THE WOODS FIVE MILES FROM THE Redford Crossing Outpost. Although he teased Avatar about expressing concern, he knew to proceed on foot rather than be detected immediately upon appearance from a dimension travel. Besides, if Hueil was at the ruins, Avatar needed to stay clear. He suffered too much when Hueil nearly killed him in Tunlund. No telling how Avatar would respond to a direct confrontation, which is why he volunteered and not for being tired of the duke's children. In fact, he always had a soft spot for mortal children. Something his imprisonment in the nether dimension had not changed.

He and Avatar rarely spoke of the incident leading to his capture since he made the choice to provide cover for Avatar's escape. Still, his three-hundred-year apprenticeship to Avatar helped hone Mahon's warrior skills to the point of being able to endure hundreds of years of torture and torment. Their relationship started as mentor and apprentice, but became a friendship of fourteen hundred years. Thus, for a multitude of reasons, if there were any signs of the Dark Way at the outpost, he would be the one to discover it and not Avatar.

Twilight faded, yet the sense of evil grew with each passing mile. The smell of smoldering ashes floated on the cold night air. Although his breath turned to white vapor, weather didn't affect Guardians.

A mile from the outpost, Mahon held the hilt of his sword. He looked for signs of wyverns or some winged creature Hueil might employ. Indeed, whatever Mayers sensed came from the Dark Way.

At hearing what sounded like a twig snap, Mahon stopped and crouched behind some brush. For a moment he listened. Hearing nothing else, he slowly moved to the tree line. The outpost lay two hundred yards from the trees in a small meadow. Several thin trails of smoke rose from behind the walls. He saw no sentries or sign of life. He took a deep breath, closed his eyes and carefully stretched out his senses. He felt cold, darkness and death, but no imminent danger.

Mahon ran to the outpost. The shattered front gate hung partially off its hinges with large gouges in the wood. He touched it for examination and quickly withdrew his hand at the sharp sense of evil.

"Wyverns."

He drew his sword and entered the compound. Dead mortals lay everywhere. He knelt to examine one and noticed the epaulets. "You must have been Lieutenant Mayers. Rest in Jor'el's peace."

Light flickered and a murmur came from a building with a broken door. Perhaps a mortal survived the carnage. He went to investigate. Upon stepping inside, the candle became extinguished by a gust of wind. Not that he needed light to see in the dark. Something hard and fast struck him in the back of the head sending him into the rear wall. He turned to make defense when a blast slammed him into the wall on the far side of the room. He struck his head and fell unconscious.

A booted foot kicked Mahon's sword away. It slid across the floor and under a fallen table. Locan knelt and turned Mahon over. "Wonderful! It's not him. I know I made Mayers request the commander."

Mannix squatted for a better view just.

Locan drew his dagger. "Well, he won't do us any good."

Mannix stopped Locan. "Wait! His name is Mahon. He was Avatar's apprentice. Kill him and Avatar will be merciless in hunting us down."

"Avatar's apprentice?" Locan gazed at Mahon in consideration and sheathed his dagger. "I have an idea. We'll take him to Hueil—"

"He'll say we failed and destroy us on the spot."

"Not when I explain who he is. We couldn't get Avatar, so we the got the best thing to thwart him."

"Risky."

"It's either that or total failure."

Mahon groaned and began to stir with recovery.

"Quick! Before he wakes." Locan pulled Mahon to his feet. Mannix grabbed Mahon by the other arm and they vanished.

<hr />

They reappeared in a small dimly lit room. Mahon suddenly woke, only to be clouted unconscious by Locan.

"Bind him. I'll fetch Hueil," said Locan.

"I hope this works." Mannix dropped Mahon onto a wooden table with shackles. After carefully placing Mahon's wrists and ankles inside the shackles, he used the hilt of his sword to hit them closed.

At the sound clanking metal, Mahon again woke, groggy, yet aware of restraints on his wrists. He tugged against them and felt searing pain. More pain came from his ankles and pain shot up his legs.

"I wouldn't move if I were you. Stygian shackles hurt."

Mahon swallowed back the pain. "Who are you? What do you want?"

"I'm of no significance. What is wanted is different, but I'll wait for the master to tell you."

Mahon sneered. "You and your master will get nothing out of me."

"Don't be so sure about that," said a new voice near Mahon's feet.

Mahon lifted his head. In doing so, his shoulders and arms moved. Searing pain shot thorough him. His head fell back and he bit his lip to stop an outcry. The newcomer appeared beside him. "Hueil."

"Nice to see I'm remembered, even by one as young as you, Mahon the Mighty. That is your title, since your power is the strength of ten Guardians."

"What do you want?"

"Personally, the thought of killing you is quite appealing. However, Locan has a better suggestion," he indicated Locan, "being as you were Avatar's apprentice after all."

Mahon didn't reply.

"You know what I did to him in Tunlund, don't you?"

Again Mahon didn't reply. His eyes narrowed and jowls taut in anger.

"I see you do. That will make your substitution for him all the more delightful."

"Substitution?"

"Using you instead will cause him more pain. And *that* is the delightful part."

"I won't do your bidding so kill me now and be done with it!"

"Oh, no. I heard you survived Dagar's reconditioning chamber." Hueil wickedly smiled and pulled the device from his pocket. "You should know what this is."

Mahon's expression showed the dread of recognition. He strained against the shackles, ignoring the pain. Hueil seized his head by the hair, stopping the futile effort. He jerked Mahon's head back and grabbed his chin to force open his mouth.

"Give him the potion!"

Cup in hand, Locan poured the liquid into Mahon's mouth. He tried to turn away but couldn't because of Hueil's hold. He gagged on the liquid. It took effort to force him to drink the potion.

Satisfied, Hueil released him. "There, not too difficult."

Mahon eyes screwed shut. "I won't do what you want. I survived, I can resist."

Hueil leaned down, and maliciously whispered, "I don't think so!" He rammed the device into Mahon's skull behind the ear.

Mahon cried out with intense pain before fainting. Mannix impulsively stepped away at the outcry and balled his fists to maintain his composure. Locan saw the reaction, but not Hueil.

"We'll give the potion and device time to work before reconditioning him to carry out my instructions." Hueil laughed. "Oh, to see it happen."

"Is that possible?" asked Locan.

Hueil's humor faded. "No, but we will know when it is done. Watch him and let me know when he wakes." He left.

Locan moved beside Mannix, who remained fretful in his staring at the unconscious Mahon. "How long should it take?"

"I don't know," murmured Mannix.

"I thought you witnessed reconditioning during your imprisonment?"

Mannix nodded. "Depends upon the Guardian." He abruptly crossed to a far corner, turning his back to the table.

Concerned at Mannix's mounting discomfort, Locan joined him. "Are you having second thoughts?"

"This is bringing back horrible memories."

"It was your idea to help Hueil. I agreed because we are Trio Mates."

"To help him escape! Not everything else," he argued. "True, I wanted to be useful again and not stuck in guard duty because of suspicion from the past, but not attempting to kill a girl or the king. And certainly, not—the torture of another Guardian!" He grew discomposed. "I experienced too much of that."

"This is no time for remorse or uncertainty. If you back out or show weakness, it could mean our lives."

Mannix shook his head, a look of befuddlement on his face. "With each passing day and encounter, I become more confused, unable to think clearly." He suddenly became frightened. "Maybe Dagar succeeded, and did recondition me!"

Locan seized Mannix. "Get a hold of yourself."

"You'll have to take the lead, I can't anymore."

"All right, but calm down."

Mahon began to stir with sounds of waking. Locan hurried back to the table. Mahon's eyes opened with a vacant gaze and blank expression. "Why does he look so strange?"

"The potion," said Mannix, his voice thick with remembrance. "It's reached his subconscious. He's not awake in the sense of conscious knowledge."

"I'll fetch Hueil. Watch him." Mannix focused on Mahon, so Locan jerked his arm to get his attention. "Can you do it while I fetch Hueil?"

"Ay."

Locan left and Mannix returned his attention to Mahon. Even at fourteen hundred years, Mahon was a youthful looking warrior. His light, bright blue eyes stared at the ceiling. "Can you hear me?"

Mahon turned to face him but didn't reply.

"Do you recognize me?"

Again Mahon didn't speak, just continued to stare. The life and strength normally present in a Guardian's eyes were gone.

"You can't react. You are prepared."

Mannix sent an anxious glance to door. At no sign of return, he reached behind Mahon's right ear and loosened the device. Mahon flinched, his brows knitted in pain, but his eyes remained on Mannix.

"I don't know if that'll help. Act as if I didn't do anything."

The place Mannix and Locan brought Mahon was a small obscure manor house across the Midessex border inside the Lowlands. It had been abandoned since Gareth's son was executed for his part in the kidnapping of Titus and starting the war with Tunlund. With the family ruling the adjoining South Plains and Lowlands, their holdings overlapped into both provinces and proved the perfect place to hide a fugitive, or at least keep from being seen.

Ellan sat at a vanity in the bedchamber in a dressing gown when Hueil returned. "I hope whatever it is won't upset our plans."

"It will require a bit of altering, but accomplish the same result."

"What do you mean, alter? I thought they reported his capture."

"No. They sprung the trap, only snared a different prey—Mahon."

"Mahon?" she said in surprise. "He served as Necie's Overseer. How could his capture produce the same results?"

Hueil smiled and plopped into a chair next to a small table upon which sat a decanter of wine and two glasses. He poured himself a glass. "He was Avatar's apprentice." He drank. "Imagine the look on Avatar's face when Mahon completes the task and he has to destroy him."

"So you kill three birds with one stroke."

He swallowed more wine and laughed. "Delightful, isn't it?"

"What makes you think Mahon can get close enough to the half-breed?"

"Once a Guardian is reconditioned nothing will or can stop them. Take Morrell for example. For years he lay conveniently hidden among your family until he fulfilled the mission on which Dagar sent him."

"To kill my mother," said Ellan with a twinge of regret.

"You sound remorseful. The Daughter of Allon would have destroyed Musetta and Sullivan if discovered."

"They were discovered by Tristine! And my husband Sullivan, killed by the half-breed," she painfully sneered. "All the same, with the plot thwarted, Morrell didn't have to kill my mother."

He shrugged and poured more wine. "As I said, nothing can stop a reconditioned Guardian, including reason or change in circumstances. When he is ready, Mahon will be unleashed."

"Before or after our formal declaration of war?"

"The timing doesn't matter, it's when he's broken and ready. Although," he said, thoughtful, "he survived Dagar's reconditioning, so he may be quite strong. I instructed them to fetch me when he wakes, by then the potion and device will have begun the process."

"Hopefully you'll be done with him in time to leave for Roxbury. The forces should be gathered there by the end of the week."

"If not, you go on ahead and I'll join you."

"My lord. Majesty." Locan bowed to them. "His eyes are open."

"So soon? Interesting," mused Hueil. "He may not be so strong after all." He smiled at Ellan. "I'll be back shortly."

Mannix remained beside the table. Mahon's vacant eyes stared at the ceiling, almost unblinking. The arrival of Locan and Hueil drew Mannix's marked attention from Mahon.

"Has he said anything?" asked Hueil.

"No, my lord. He just stares."

Hueil smiled. He turned Mahon's head to look straight into his eyes. "So much for your prior experience. It didn't help your resistance, mighty Mahon. Now, you shall bend to the will of your new master, Hueil, soon to be god of Allon. Can you understand me?"

Mahon's head moved in a slight nod.

"Then say it."

Mahon's lips moved to speak with some difficulty at first. His voice sounded hollow. "Ay, master."

Hueil grinned. "Excellent. Now whom do you serve?"

Mahon licked his lips before speaking. "The king."

Hueil seized Mahon's shoulder with a jerk. Mahon cried out due to intense pain. "Whom do you serve?" he demanded.

"The king!" he said between gritted teeth. More pain at another jerk.

"Tyrone is dead! You will kill him."

Mahon screwed his eyes shut and shook his head. "Ni ... Ni-gel!"

"Nigel?" Hueil turned to Mannix and Locan for confirmation.

"It sounded like he said Nigel," said Locan.

Hueil returned to Mahon. "Are you saying Nigel is king?"

"I serve King Nigel," said Mahon before fainting.

Hueil slapped Mahon's face to rouse him.

At the abuse, Mannix turned aside. Locan stopped further retreat.

Hueil focused on Mahon and didn't notice. "Wake up!" Mahon's eyes opened. Hueil held Mahon's face. "Who is your master, worm?"

Mahon tried to resist answering when movement caught his attention. He darted a side-glance to see Mannix make a slight shake of his head. Hueil seemed ignorant of the brief distraction when he squeezed Mahon's face and repeated his question.

"Who is your master?"

"You, my lord Hueil."

"Now we are making progress." He released Mahon. "The king is the enemy of your master. Say it!"

"The king is the enemy of my master."

"Good. *Avatar* is the enemy of your master."

"Avatar?" repeated Mahon, his face showing confusion.

"Avatar!" He stuck Mahon's shoulder. The movement caused more pain. "The king and Avatar are the enemies of your master."

Mahon's eyes screwed closed and his breathing labored as he said, "The king and Avatar are the enemies of my master." He fainted again.

"Will you wake him again, lord?" asked Locan.

"No. Let his subconscious digest what it has been told. When next he wakes, we'll continue the process."

"How many sessions does it usually take?"

"Depends upon him. We made good progress for the first session. Fetch me when he wakes." Hueil left the room.

After the door shut, Mannix felt for Mahon's pulse. "His fight to resist has weakened him."

"I saw you shake your head at him, what was that about?"

The question caught Mannix off guard and he forced a reply. "For him not to resist. The more resistance the greater the physical danger."

In the bedchamber, Ellan slipped under the covers. "Any progress?"

"Ay. There's been an interesting development. Tyrone isn't king any longer, your brother Nigel is."

She gaped in momentary astonishment. "Nigel? How?"

"Abdication, of course. After all, he is first born."

It took a moment for her to digest the news. "What do we do now?"

"Continue. Does this change your desire for revenge?"

"No, but, as second born, I have claim over Tristine, not Nigel."

"That is why the half-breed did it, to confound you. Are you going to allow him to succeed?" When she didn't immediately answer, he continued. "You sent your letter and successfully divided the Council, who are at this very moment providing you troops and ships."

"Ay," she said, but still thoughtful.

He sat on the edge of the bed to make her face him. "Did you not tell me that when you believed your brother dead and you became heir, you're father attempted to mold you into Nigel's image?" Her face grew stern but a hint of thoughtfulness remained, so he continued his reasoning. "About how you came to hate his memory because of that? Even as children, Nigel favored Tristine over you. Now, he defends her against you."

Her look became sharp. "He shall curse the day he returned!" Then a sly tilt appeared on her face. "There maybe a way to undermine him."

"What?"

She smiled and touched his cheek. "Just as you seek to use subtlety with Tyrone, I can do so with Nigel. True, he became hated, but in some ways by default. Yet, he possesses a weakness I could always exploit: his soft spot and love of family."

"I don't see how you can do that under the current circumstances."

She lightly laughed. "Guardians are very intelligent and powerful, yet with one flaw, the tendency to underestimate a mortal's heart."

"Despite being unpredictable creatures, I'm not ignorant of a mortal's fickleness of emotion. I have used it against them in the past."

"Didn't you tell me that it was the bonds between Avatar and Nigel, Nigel and Titus, and eventually Mirit that led to your defeat?"

Hueil scowled with a low throaty growl.

"Dear one," she said with an affectionate smile. "I'm not insulting you, merely pointing out another means to help us succeed."

"How do you plan to do it?"

"First we must get confirmation of what Mahon said is true. If so, I'll find a way to speak to Nigel privately."

"Too risky. You could be captured."

"Hardly in the presence of a Shadow Warrior." She stroked his cheek. "Trust me, just like you want me to trust you."

He began to laugh. "You are a unique mortal, my dear. Intelligent, shrewd and ambitious." He began to kiss her when Locan arrived.

"My lord, he's awake again."

"You must pretend to give in," urged Mannix. "It's the only way to save yourself." Mahon stared at him, which made Mannix fretful. "Do you understand?" Mahon's gaze turned to stare up at the ceiling. "If I remove it, he will know and kill you." Mahon kept staring at the ceiling. "I'm sorry, if I acted too late." He stepped back from the table just before Locan and Hueil arrived.

Locan joined Mannix while Hueil dealt with Mahon.

"Welcome back, my loyal warrior. Who is your master?"

Mahon's gaze turned from the ceiling to Hueil. "You are, my lord."

He smiled in brief satisfaction, before sneering and asking, "What of the king and Avatar?"

"The king and Avatar are your enemies, my master."

"Excellent. What do you do to the enemies of your master?"

He turned to look at ceiling again and said, "Destroy them."

"Look at me and say that."

"Destroy them," he repeated, but again his eyes looked away.

"I said, look at me and say it!" He seized Mahon's shoulder.

Intense pain shot through Mahon's body and he jerked a moment before settling down. His eyes were screwed shut and teeth set against the pain. Hueil seized his face and Mahon's eyes snapped open. Hueil's face was only inches from his face.

"Look at me and say it, worm!" he said in harsh command.

Mahon swallowed back the pain to speak, "Destroy them."

"Very good, my loyal warrior. You may rest now."

Mahon closed his eyes.

"How much longer until he is ready, my lord?" asked Locan.

"The next session will determine his fate."

"His fate?" asked Mannix.

"If he can't be turned, he will be destroyed." Hueil left.

Mahon didn't wake for three hours. When he heard footsteps, he gave his attention to the one who entered, Hueil. He kept his eye on Hueil even when the cunning Guardian stopped beside him.

"Who is your master?"

"You are, my lord," said Mahon clearly and without hesitation.

"Who are the enemies of your master?"

"The king and Avatar are your enemies, my lord."

"How will you prove your loyal to me, your master?"

"I will destroy your enemies."

Hueil held Mahon's eye. "Whatever the cost?"

"Whatever the cost."

"Excellent. When the time is right, you shall act. Rest until then."

"Ay, master." Mahon closed his eyes.

With a satisfied smile, Hueil spoke to Locan. "I must admit I wasn't convinced at your initial suggestion, but he may prove a better choice. He was certainly easier. With Nigel as king, Avatar will experience double the pain of loss when Mahon kills him!"

"Could the ease of reconditioning be due his prior experience?"

"Some survivors suffer lingering affects that can be enhanced."

Mannix winced at the statement. Locan covered for his friend's discomposure by asking, "When will you unleash him?"

Hueil sarcastically chuckled. "Oh, you'll know. All of Allon will know when the king is dead. Now, return to watching the half-breed."

Locan and Mannix saluted and vanished.

Chapter 13

MEANWHILE AT THE FORTRESS, FOUR HUNDRED JOR'ELLIAN Guards, Knights, the remaining royal soldiers and duke's men gathered in formation just after dawn. Wren, Virgil, Vidar, Avatar, Armus and Kendrick waited by the main gate. Tristine wore Mirit's old uniform. Nigel and Mirit arrived.

"Sire, we're ready to leave," said Avatar.

Nigel simply nodded; distracted by Tristine.

She noticed his wariness. "Is something wrong?"

He took her aside to talk privately. "I want you and Armus to remain."

"We're been through this. I can fight and I won't stay behind."

"No, no." He took her by the shoulders to get her full attention. "This is something different, something unsettling I sensed in my meditation last night. I need you to stay here in charge of defense, not forcing you into inaction."

His urgent tone made Armus join them. "What did you sense?"

"If Hueil is picking off outposts this close to the Region's border, he could breach security and threaten the Temple and Fortress. Remember, our father faced Dagar on the Temple plain."

"You think because we fled here from Garwood he might try to take the Fortress to destroy the family," she said.

"Ay. Tyrone has left and we're heading for Waldron. Hopefully, we can draw his attention. This leaves Necie, Jillian and the children vulnerable, and neither knows how to fight. Ay, Skylar, Jade, Uriah, Temple Guards and Jor'ellians will make a stand. However, I want someone here I can depend upon and trust implicitly."

Her eyes never left him as he spoke. "Armus and I will remain."

"Thank you." He kissed her forehead. "Now we must go."

Fraser held the reins of his horse and Nigel's horse. Valery held the reins of her and Mirit's horses.

Once all were mounted, Uriah raised his hand to speak a prayer. All bowed their heads. "Merciful Jor'el, we ask you to watch over the king and queen from this day forth as they undertake the task of ridding Allon of your enemy. Grant them traveling safety and wisdom. *Tangiel.*"

"*Tangiel,*" all repeated.

For this journey, Avatar, Virgil, Vidar and Kendrick also rode horses. Wren lead the group on foot. Nigel and Mirit followed her with Avatar and Virgil behind them; then came Fraser and Valery with Cody alongside. Vidar and Kendrick were behind Fraser and Valery with Chad and his troops in the rear.

After traveling a mile, Mirit glanced over her shoulder to Avatar and Virgil. At her look, Avatar moved his horse beside Nigel's horse.

"I still think I should take you and the queen to Waldron rather than travel in the open."

"We can't show fear, and the more visible I am the better."

"Not fear, I'm talking sense. Hueil breached the nether seal, making Ravendale active again. It's only thirty-five miles from Waldron. And," he added with emphasis, "we come within twenty miles of it by travelling on the main road."

"Which is why I told Wren to take an alternate route at the North Plains split."

"You're being stubborn."

Nigel grinned. "Is that anyway to talk to the king?"

"I feel like I'm talking to the obstinate prince of your youth and not the wiser man I thought you had become."

Nigel's smile vanished. "That's going too far, Avatar!"

"Why, because I'm not your Overseer anymore? I'm Commander of the Jor'ellian Guard and speak as openly as I ever did. Kell did so with your father, as does Armus with Tyrone. You find fault that I do the same with you, *Sire?*"

"Of course not. You're asking me to take the easy way out when there isn't anything easy about this."

"Avatar's right, you are being stubborn," said Mirit. "Being installed at Waldron will send the same message and be safer for everyone."

"And more time for training and planning," added Virgil.

"Ay, more time for training and planning," she repeated.

Nigel became suspicious. "Why do I think the you three discussed this beforehand?"

"Because we did," she said. "You're not the only one who can sense things. I may not be a Jor'ellian Knight, but remember my experience in Natan? Riding like this is a needless risk. The Guardians should take us, Fraser and Valery to Waldron. Let Chad and the troop continue on bearing the royal standard. It'll serve the same purpose of visibility but be safer for you."

Nigel saw their united determination. He looked ahead to the trees across the clearing. "Once we're undercover, we'll stop and explain the change in plan to Chad and Wren. Unless of course, they already know."

She grinned. "Would I exclude dear Chad? Or Wren?"

He snorted a laugh. "Why did I think becoming king would change things?"

"Because you're a hopeless optimist and love your life the way it is."

"Bound and gagged on all sides."

"No, loved and supported."

Wess sat in his office partaking of luncheon. Cameron rushed in.

"General, the king and queen have arrived!"

Wess swallowed hard the drink he took. "When? How?"

"Dimension travel. Avatar said the king is in his study and sends for you."

Wess grabbed his hat on the way out. Cameron did his best to keep pace with Wess, whose long strides were well known. Once inside the main building, they made the trek past the Great Hall to the grand stairway up to the galley way and the King's study overlooking the Grand Courtyard. Virgil stood outside the study door.

"The king sent for me," said Wess.

He opened the door. "General Wess, Sire." Cameron began to follow when Virgil stopped him. "Just the general."

Inside, Wess met Avatar, Vidar and Mirit. "The king sent for me."

"Indeed he did, General." She nodded to the far side of the room where Nigel stepped forward so Wess could see him.

"Highness, I thought the king was here."

"He is. You're looking at him."

Wess flinched, stunned and confused. "You? What happened to Tyrone? Tristine?"

"Nothing. They are safe, as is the rest of the family. Only there's been a dramatic change, and one we hope will counter Ellan." He motioned to a chair in front of the desk. "Please, Wess, have a seat."

Wess did so, and cautiously watched Nigel sit behind the desk. Nigel reached for some papers Wess recognized as his letter by the seal. "You want me to reconsider my resignation."

"It is one of the matters we need to discuss. I hope after hearing what has happened, you will reconsider. Jor'el knows I need your help."

Wess pursed his lips and reclined to get comfortable. "I'm listening."

Together with Mirit, Vidar and Avatar, Nigel related every detail of the events since leaving Waldron. Wess asked a couple of questions, but more intent on listening. He studied Nigel even when the others spoke. Nigel never wavered from the inspection and a long moment of silence followed the conclusion.

Nigel indicated for Avatar, Vidar and Mirit to leave, no doubt to speak in private. Now came the moment of truth. A moment Wess wanted to avoid, only this was not the same situation of a few days ago.

After the door closed, Nigel spoke. "Wess, I know all you have endured during your life. I cannot begin to express my personal admiration and deep gratitude for your loyalty and friendship."

"But that's not enough."

"I didn't mean that."

"Under the circumstances, it is what you think."

"No, Wess. You completely misunderstand. I owe you and Bosley my life. I'm not making platitudes to convince you to stay. By the heavenlies, I don't want to fight Bosley or Erasmus!" Agitated, Nigel paced. "Nor Ellan. I had to take the crown to protect one sister against another, so I understand your reluctance. Do you understand the harsh reality I must face?"

Wess chewed on his lower lip while listening. "Not at first. And I wrote the letter to Tyrone," he said with a feeble wave of protest to the papers on the desk.

Nigel sat on the edge of the desk in front of Wess. "If after hearing everything, you still feel unable to help me, I will accept your resignation this instant and you are free to go. No hard feelings."

Wess stared at the letter in a moment of consideration. "You said Dylan is on his way here with Chad."

"Ay. To carry on the family tradition of being a soldier—"

"Family and tradition!" Wess bolted out of the chair. "Two words difficult to hear right now."

"For me too. My family's heritage and future depend upon me. This situation forces many to make difficult choices. Ellis is with Tyrone and Titus."

"Ellis has been attached to Titus for years."

"Eric, Karly and Bryson are safe in the Highlands," continued Nigel, not phased by Wess' outbursts.

A look of relief passed over Wess' face. "How long will you reign?"

"Until the threat is ended. Tyrone is the Great King of Prophecy. I never desired to be king, only to serve Jor'el and protect my family and Allon. Wess, I need your help to do that."

Wess stared at Nigel. The man now king was once the infant he and Bosley saved; crippled by a failed assassination and restored the risen to King's Champion. Not once did he show jealousy or a selfish desire for the throne. At length, he spoke. "For as long as you are king, I will remain your general. When you relinquish the crown, I retire."

Nigel smiled with relief and gratitude. "Agreed. Thank you, Wess."

Wess cocked a grin. "What now, Sire?"

"Recall Avatar and Mirit. Send Virgil to fetch Fraser, Valery and all high-ranking officers. We have planning to do."

Wess slapped his sword in salute and left.

The meeting lasted into the evening and fell into a pattern of repetition and arguing. At Mirit's insistence, it adjourned, leaving her and Nigel alone in the study.

"That didn't go as I hoped." He plopped into the desk chair.

"Give them time to get used to the idea of you being king and how you handle things. Tyrone listens but is more forceful in corralling them and making decisions."

"I'm hardly a light touch."

She sat on the desk to speak to him. "How did your father conduct such meetings?"

"Why ask? You just said they are used to Tyrone's manner."

"Tyrone isn't the son of Ellis, *you* are."

He lightly chuckled. "I see your point."

"Good. Because you are a natural born leader. In order to be an effective king, even for a short time, you must shed your reluctance to deal with this matter and embrace your heritage."

He pulled her onto his lap. "Right now I'd like to embrace my wife."

"That can be arranged." They kissed.

"What's that?" he asked at hearing a low grumble.

"My stomach. It's well past suppertime."

He laughed. "I suppose food is in order."

"If the supper I ordered hasn't grown cold."

Kendrick escorted Fraser and Valery to the family dining room at the back of the main building. Inside, four servants arranged plates and platters of newly prepared hot food.

"Will the king and queen be joining us?" asked Valery.

"Ay. You heard the queen was quite insistent," said Kendrick.

"Well, let's not stand on ceremony and wait. I'm famished." Fraser sat and helped himself to the food.

Valery sat opposite Fraser. "Do you at least say a word of thanks?"

"You sound like my mother," he grumbled with a mouth full of food.

She bowed her hand and spoke a few words of thanks before partaking of the food.

Fraser reluctantly paused in eating and briefly bowed his head.

"It wasn't necessary for my benefit," she said.

"You are so contrary. I see why you and Titus clash. What I don't understand is Ellis' attraction."

Her temper flared at his insult. "You're bold and presumptuous to question Lord Ellis in his absence."

"I'm a prince. I have a right to question anyone."

"And insult them too, I suppose?"

Fraser shrugged, since his mouth was too full to reply.

"For being a prince, you have much to learn about manners and treating people with respect."

"I get enough lecture from my parents and Kendrick. I don't need it from you."

"You don't listen to them."

"Why? I get little respect. I'm second born and made aware of that."

"You are your uncle's squire and he is now king. What more do you want, to wear the crown yourself? Isn't that what your *Aunt Ellan* wants and why she is pushing Allon to civil war?"

Irate, Fraser bolted to his feet, which made her stand in defiance.

"Peace!" said Kendrick. "She's right. You can't command respect. You must earn it. Something your father has tried to tell you, and your uncle is hoping to help you achieve."

Nigel, Mirit and Virgil arrived.

"Don't stand on our account. We don't need to have too much ceremony," said Nigel, unaware of the exchange. "Sit." He took a seat one end of the table with Mirit at other end.

Valery and Fraser complied. He immediately changed his attitude.

"I think your plans are well thought out, Uncle—*Sire*," he corrected at Nigel displeasure.

"I said too much ceremony, not negate it all together. Remember, you are still a cadet in the Jor'ellian Guard. I haven't forgotten I said you could call me *Uncle* in private, *if* allowed."

"I'm sorry, Sire."

"Excuse us a moment." He and Mirit bowed their heads and offered a word of thanks.

Valery and Fraser didn't resume eating until Nigel and Mirit finished.

"Tomorrow will begin your training, Valery," said Mirit.

"I look forward to it, Majesty."

"You'll find it grueling and exhausting."

"I doubt anymore so than battle."

Mirit chuckled. "Well said. Fraser? Are you ready for such training?"

"I'm ready for anything, Majesty." He tossed a challenging eye to Valery that was noticed by Nigel and Mirit.

"Indeed," said Nigel. "We'll see if either one of you can keep to our training schedule."

"I make no pretense about my skill or endurance, Sire. Both are limited since I am self-taught," said Valery.

"I'm sure you will make a good effort. You've already shown your mettle."

"Thank you, Sire."

"Now, finished eating. Afterwards you may retire. We rise at dawn."

Virgil escorted Valery to a room in the family quarters. Although of nobility, she was unaccustomed to such luxury and splendor of the large, regal room. On the occasions she visited Waldron, she saw only the Grand Courtyard, the Great Hall, Chapel and small guest rooms.

"Impressive, isn't it?" asked Virgil.

"Ay. A person could get lost in such a enormous room."

Virgil wryly grinned. "The privy is at that end of the room with a dressing area. There's a small balcony out that window overlooking the garden. The sitting area is opposite the privy." He stopped when Valery waved, unable to catch her breath for laughing.

"How do memorize everything? I scarcely remember what fork to use at a formal dinner," she said between breaths.

"This is Prince Eli's room. The queen insisted you make temporary use of it to be closer if she needs you rather than the guest quarters."

There came a knock at the door. Virgil admitted a maid, who carried some garments. "Mistress Madison will attend you, my lady. If you have any problems, I'll be in hall. Goodnight." Virgil bowed.

"Goodnight and thank you for the map."

"I brought more suitable night clothes, my lady," said Madison. "If your ladyship will change behind the dressing screen, I'll take your uniform to be cleaned and pressed for the morning."

Valery exchanged garments with Madison by handing them over the screen. When finished, she moved from behind the screen and began undoing her hair.

"My lady, I can will brush out your hair before taking the uniform to be cleaned."

"No, thank you, I like doing it myself. Just turn down the bed and that will be all."

"Very good, my lady."

Valery sat at the vanity to take down her hair. It had grown knotted and tangled from lack of proper attention. She tried to deal with it at the Fortress, but under the circumstances, personal attention was minimal.

"Goodnight, my lady," said Madison when finished with the bed.

Valery made an acknowledgement then began brushing out the tangles. Seeing her reflection in the mirror brought Fraser's cutting comment to mind. *What I don't understand is Ellis' attraction.* She stopped brushing to gaze at herself. In truth, she wondered the same, being plain in feature with strawberry blonde hair, common green eyes, a bit on plump side, not fat, rather healthy and strong according to her mother. Yet compared to the wiry, glamorous women at Court, she didn't consider herself pretty. Despite Ellis' reticence and occasional fumbling in speech, he was handsome with teal blue eyes, brown hair and a pleasant smile. What made him keep company with her? She grew frustrated at her self-evaluation brought on my Fraser's mean-spirited comments.

"Fraser is a big-mouth, pompous ninny of a prince!" Her frustration translated into the harsh brushing of her hair and catching a large knot. "Ouch! … Oooo."

"A rather interesting way of describing him."

She gaped at seeing Mirit's reflection in the mirror. "Majesty! I didn't hear you come in."

Mirit wore a dressing gown with her full wavy brown hair loose. "I came to see if you were settled for the night."

"Ay. At least I will be in a moment." She gently massaged her head where she jerked out the brush.

Mirit took the brush from Valery, turned the girl's head to face the mirror and began to gently brush Valery's hair.

"Majesty, you shouldn't."

Mirit stopped her from moving. "I want to. Now, relax. Hasn't anyone brushed your hair before?"

"Only my mother. And when I was a little girl."

"You have servants, don't you?"

"Some. Father is rather frugal."

Mirit grinned at the discreet comment. "Well, frugality can be good." She gathered some of Valery's hair in her hand to ease the brushing out of tangles near the end. "What did Fraser say to upset you?"

"Nothing."

Mirit's soft yet firm expression showed the contrary when looking at Valery in the mirror. "Then why risk tearing out such pretty hair?"

"Pretty? My hair is scrawny. The only part of me that is."

"Ah! So he said something about your appearance."

"Not exactly."

"Fraser has a loose, indiscriminate tongue. We hope his Jor'ellian training will help him to tame it. Now, please tell me what he said."

"We started to quarrel about what is happening. He said I was contrary and understood why Prince Titus and I clash, but," she became downcast, "he could not understand Lord Ellis' attraction to me."

Mirit paused in brushing for outraged surprise. "He said that to you?"

Valery shyly looked away from the mirror.

"What nonsense!" She knelt for Valery to see her, and not in the mirror. "You're right in describing Fraser for he is most certainly wrong to question Ellis or any man who finds you attractive. You are a fine looking young lady."

"Not compared to many at Court my age."

"Who? Lady Tricia? She spends hours teasing her thin hair to make it stand up and she doesn't have as beautiful texture or color as you. Lady Patrice wears so much make-up I don't even know if she remembers what she looks underneath. While Lady Beryl stuffs herself into her dresses hoping to appear smaller." She stood and turned Valery's face to the mirror. "Your color is striking between your strawberry hair, green eyes and pink complexion. You can tell when you blush."

Valery shyly smiled.

"And you have a pretty smile. There is much to admire, only you need the confidence to let people see it." She piled the hair on Valery's head. "Your hair adorned and wearing an emerald green gown, you would turn any man's head."

"We don't have the time for a ball."

"No. Our uniforms will serve for now. One day we'll make certain Ellis and others see you for the beautiful young woman you really are."

Valery grew misty eyes. "Thank you, Majesty."

Mirit softly smiled. "Now it's late. Do you sleep with your hair loose or under a cap?"

"I usually wear it in a braid."

"Let me finish brushing and I'll braid it; then off to bed for both of us."

Chapter 14

LATE AT NIGHT, ELLIS AND TITUS SAT BESIDE A CAMPFIRE DRINKING the hot tea Eldric prescribed to help against cold nights in the wilderness. The soldiers were stationed around the perimeter of the campsite. Tyrone, Angus, Kell and Egan stood off to one side discussing how to approach the ruins. From over the rim of his cup, Ellis observed the group. He turned to Titus, who was more interested in drinking his tea than the conversation.

"Your father is a brave man."

Titus grinned. "He's faced Hueil before."

"I mean his abdication." Ellis leaned closer. "I admire your uncle and I don't wish to speak against him, but what assurance does your father have that he'll give back the crown when this over?"

"None," said Tyrone. He sat on a log across from Ellis, catching the young man off guard.

"Sire … Sir, I meant no disrespect."

"I know. Still, it is a legitimate question." Tyrone took a cup and helped himself to tea from the pot hanging to one side of the fire. He took a drink before continuing. "I met Nigel a year after his accident when he was a wandering cripple. You've heard about his past, correct?"

"Ay, sir."

"He was seventeen and I, twenty-one. Back then I didn't know his identity. We were both outcasts with no hope for the future. We struck up a friendship. Since then, our friendship had become a brotherhood. We've known each other for twenty-two years." His story became interrupted when Angus joined them.

"Boring the boys with family talk?" he teased, and fetched some tea.

Tyrone chuckled. "I could tell them about your wedding day jitters."

He laughed. "Not like Nigel. He couldn't choose what suit to wear."

"I remember," snickered Titus.

"Back to your question," said Tyrone to Ellis. "Knowing Nigel as I do, I can't see a situation where he wouldn't yield back the crown."

"Heavens, no," said Angus. "Is that what this is about?"

"Ellis asked a legitimate question regarding my abdication."

"With all due respect, sir, no one expected the present situation with Ellan's return," said Ellis.

"True. However, Ellan is ambitious, Nigel is not. You've joined Titus in training with him at Waldron. Has something made you doubt him?"

"No, sir," said Ellis in sudden awkward. "I just—"

"Just looking at all sides of the issue," said Titus.

"Ay. I admire the prince … the king."

Tyrone grinned at the reticence. "This is an awkward situation for everyone. Jor'el willing, it won't last for long and everything can get back to normal." He tossed a teasing glance from Ellis and Titus to Angus.

"You mean wooing or arguing?" said Angus on cue.

"With some there isn't a difference."

Even in the firelight they saw Ellis blush. Titus poked him and laughed, which made Ellis' flush brighten with embarrassment.

"We jest," said Tyrone. "Lady Valery is a fine young woman." He grew reflective. "I see Allard in her. Not just her physical coloring, but in spirit. Along with intelligence, he could be stubborn and determined. A shame he didn't realize Braden's abusive nature."

Angus gave Tyrone a quick warning jab and used his cup to gesture at the young men. Both regarded Tyrone in curious surprise. Tyrone frowned in regret at his miscue. Angus shrugged and drank his tea.

"What do you mean, abusive?" asked Titus.

"Surely not physical abuse toward Valery?" added Ellis.

Tyrone nodded. "I'm afraid so. Only it's not widely known."

Ellis' initial disturbance turned to outrage. "Her own father!"

"How long have you known?" asked Titus.

"A few days. Mirit recognized the signs of how Valery battles between boldness and withdrawing. Like she did during the interview, going being feeling trapped and suppressing her feeling to wanting to strike out at what causes her pain."

"I thought her outburst rather odd," said Titus in recollection. "Did she confirm Aunt Mirit's assessment?"

"No, she hasn't spoken. Perhaps due to feeling ashamed."

"She has nothing to be ashamed of! It is his behavior," chided Ellis.

"He is her father. And his actions reflect upon her. Just like the actions of children reflect upon their parents."

Titus took a drink to cover his disturbance. He understood the reference to his dishonorable behavior in Natan.

Ellis reacted differently, horrified by recent conversations with Valery. "She said her father always acted critical of her and her mother, and his behavior intensified after her grandfather died. I tried to get her to leave with the Guardians due to her wound, but she said she suffered worse and survived. I didn't think she meant abuse. Nor did I even consider it. The thought of harming a woman is abhorrent!"

"No one knew, including Allard," said Angus.

"How's that possible?"

Tyrone replied, "Mirit encountered similar situations while living in Tunlund. According to her, some were obvious and well known, others not, and when discovered, surprised even other family members. If

Allard knew or suspected, he would have protected Valery. Of that Mirit and the rest of us are certain."

Ellis sat poised on the log as if ready to bolt up. "What can we do to help her now that we know?"

"Don't tell her you know," said Angus. "At least that is Mirit's suggestion."

"Why?"

"She asked Valery to be her squire to help her heal by learning to be more focused and gain confidence."

"Valery hardly lacks confidence," said Titus.

"Oh, but she does," said Tyrone. "Perhaps not obvious to the casual observer, but neither is Ellis' lack of confidence readily seen."

The comment briefly stymied Ellis. "How are we comparable? I have not suffered abuse."

"Among your peers you display great confidence and skill in weapons, conversation, etc., but alone with a woman or any situation you feel ill-equipped to handle, you become tongue-tied and awkward." Tyrone put up a hand to stop Ellis' protest. "Don't deny it. I've known since you were a babe. Earlier you balked when I asked you a question and there was no need. You have nothing to fear from me, whether king or prince. I value your friendship to my son. Similarly, Valery shows great confidence in areas she is well versed but retreats and becomes awkward when feeling threatened or uncertain."

Titus clapped Ellis' shoulder. "I told you to act more confidently."

"My personality flaw doesn't change her situation or provide instruction on how to help her."

"Just act normal," said Angus.

"It'll be hard to act as if I don't know," he refuted.

"I said, normal, not ignorant. We can tell you have feelings for her. Act on those feelings, only with kindness, tenderness and patience." Angus glanced to Tyrone before asking Ellis, "Unless our telling you changed your feelings for her."

"No!" Ellis blurted out before realizing it.

Angus smiled. "I didn't think so."

"Use your feelings with confidence and compassion. Perhaps by doing so, you can help her heal without revealing what you know," said Tyrone.

"I think I can … No," he added at Tyrone's askew glance, "I can and I will."

Tyrone grinned. "Good. Now—"

"Highness!" Ridge rushed into camp. "Hueil is no longer at the ruins. If we hurry, we can be there by dawn."

"Let's go." Tyrone tossed his remaining tea onto the fire, making the flames hiss. Angus did the same with what tea remained in the pot.

"I can do it quicker." Ridge waved his hands out toward the fire and said, "*Lasair bi a mach.*" The fire was immediately extinguished.

"Show off." Angus shoved the pot into Ridge's hand.

Within moments they abandoned the campsite, Ridge leading the way. The mortals pressed their horses at a gallop to keep pace with the forest Guardian.

The gray light of dawn broke over the eastern horizon. They reached the rim of trees on top of a small plateau overlooking the ruins. Ridge raised his arm to signal a halt.

"Do you sense something?" asked Tyrone.

"No, cautious. Anything could have happened in the past few hours. Kell and I will look around." He signaled Kell right and he went left.

"Do you sense anything, Father?" asked Titus.

Tyrone stared at the ruins and didn't answer. The area covered about a square mile radius. Most parts were heavily overgrown while others exposed, and some showed evidence of recent activity. His eyes narrowed on a spot near the crumbled western wall, the spot where Alrick and Gresham saw Hueil and wyverns. As if stuck, Tyrone flinched and tugged so hard on his horse's reins that the animal reared. He swayed in the saddle.

Egan steadied Tyrone and the horse. "Highness?"

"I'm all right. Hueil's presence is strong, so are wyverns."

Ridge and Kell returned. "All clear, Highness. We can proceed." He headed down a step and rocky path to the ruins. He paused at a section near the middle. "I think this is where the breach happened."

Tyrone continued west. The ranger tossed a curious glance to Kell, but the captain hurried after Tyrone. The rest followed.

At the spot where Hueil called forth the wyverns, Tyrone dismounted. Portions of fallen stone pillars lay near the charred wood from a large fire. He moved around a stone to approach the fire site. In slow, deliberate steps, he circled the remains, never taking his eyes off the wood. His brows leveled and grey eyes narrowed in concentration. His breathing grew labored from effort. Finally, he stopped, squatted, reached out to touch the wood.

"Be careful, Highness," warned Kell.

Tyrone paused at hearing the warning then continued reaching until his hand touched the wood. "What are you up to this time, creature of darkness?" He no sooner finished speaking when a vision sprang up before his eyes. The charred wood was on fire, the flames high and intense. He heard screams, but not of creatures, rather mortals, females and children. Individual faces of his family appeared in the flames ending with Hueil's face laughing with mockery. Fearful, Tyrone jumped backwards, tripped and fell on his back.

"Father?" Titus ran to Tyrone, who labored to breathe and his face covered in sweat. "Are you hurt?"

Tyrone didn't answer and reached for Titus to aid him. Ellis came alongside to help. Once on his feet, Tyrone ordered, "Seal it, Captain! Seal it so it can never be opened again."

"With pleasure." Kell moved to the charred wood.

Tyrone drew Titus and Ellis away from the fallen pillars.

"How will he seal it?" asked Ellis.

"Watch," said Egan.

Kell drew his sword and placed the hilt in front of his face. He spoke in the Ancient. "By Jor'el's power, I, Kell, Captain of the Guardians, call upon the forces of heaven and earth to come together and seal forever the darkness that has marked this place."

Egan and Ridge stepped up to the pillars. Egan drew his sword and Ridge readied his staff. They spoke in unison. "We so come together."

Kell thrust his sword over his head. "By your power, Jor'el!"

Thunder erupted in the cloudless sky. Kell touched the charred wood with his sword. Lightning from heaven struck the wood. For several moments, Kell held his sword on the wood for the lightning to funnel down and scorch the wood and surrounding pillars. The tremendous effort and strength for Kell to remain in place showed on his face. Soon smoke from the searing began to obscure him from the others.

A sudden blinding brightness and deafening crash startled the horses and mortals. When the light faded and the sound stopped, the smoke vanished to reveal Kell. He knelt and leaned heavily upon his sword. The charred pile of wood gone, but the earth between the pillars now blackened with the symbol of Jor'el etched in the middle. Egan and Ridge helped Kell to stand. The captain looked weary and unusually pale.

"Are you all right, Kell?" asked Tyrone.

"I will be shortly. It is done, and never to be opened again."

"But you sealed it before and Hueil opened it," said Titus.

Kell motioned to the etching. "This time it bears Jor'el's seal of permanence. Nothing will grow here again, and once we leave, a supernatural barrier will forbid anything from moving past the pillars."

"Why wasn't that done before?" asked Angus.

Kell took a deep breath of recovery before replying. "My guess is Prophecy regarding the testing Uriah mentioned. I thought I sealed it well enough for the testing to come from somewhere else. I was wrong."

"That's a first, you being wrong," said Ridge.

Kell ignored the comment and waved for everyone to move. Once they stepped outside the rim a rumbling began, coming from beneath the earth. Out of the ground between the fallen pillars, new stones formed to connect the sections and create a complete enclosure.

"The barrier." Kell sheathed his sword. "What did you see, Highness?"

"The same disturbing vision I had the night of prayer."

"What?" asked Titus.

Tyrone shook his head. "I'd rather not say at the moment since I'm unsure of the meaning. When I understand, I'll let you know."

"What now? Return to the Fortress?" asked Angus.

"Waldron. Nigel should be there by the time we arrive. First, let's find a place to get some real sleep. Kell looks like he could use it."

Angus laughed. Ellis and Titus chuckled as they went to the horses.

"Well, you do look like a mortal with a hangover," said Egan.

"Next time you try being a conduit for such power."

<hr />

After finding a suitable spot several miles away from the ruins and getting five hours of sleep and meditative rest, the group moved again. This time Ridge led them to a main road for easier travel.

Late in the afternoon, all felt a cold sense of evil. The mortals grew uneasy and the Guardians alert. A peculiar smell hung in the air.

"Hueil again?" asked Ellis.

"No, but some evil is close by," replied Titus. His eyes shifted from one side of the road to another.

"I need to start learning how you and the Jor'ellians can sense things." Ellis carefully placed a hand on his sword, ready for trouble.

"Remind me to speak to my uncle about giving you lessons."

Ellis wrinkled his nose. "What is that horrid smell?"

Titus mimicked Ellis' sour expression. "Doesn't smell like wood, coal or oil."

Ahead, Ridge stopped at an intersection. "This road leads to the Redford Crossing Outpost."

"Avatar sent Mahon to do reconnaissance with Lieutenant Brewster's platoon," said Kell.

"Let's see what happened." Tyrone turned onto the north road.

The sense of evil and the smell grew more intense. In fact, smoke rose over the treetops.

Ellis grimaced at the pungent smell. "Definitely not wood."

Tyrone and Angus exchanged cautious, knowing glances before Tyrone turned in his saddle and said, "A funeral pyre."

Titus and Ellis look stunned and disconcerted. "You mean for burning mortal remains?" said Titus.

"Ay. In some cultures, warriors are cremated rather than buried." He turned forward and spoke Angus. "This may be too much for them."

"I'll hang back and detain them if needed." Angus discreetly slowed his horse for Titus and Ellis to draw alongside of him.

"It could be very bad, couldn't it, Uncle?"

"Ay, yet a sight one must endure, especially during battle."

"You're riding with us to make sure we can."

"Or help if you can't."

Soon the pyres grew visible through the trees, along with activity of Jor'ellian Guards in and around the outpost.

"Highness." Brewster moved from the front gate to meet Tyrone.

"Lieutenant. Any survivors?"

"Alas, no."

Tyrone dismounted to inspect the shattered gate, particularly the deep gouges in the wood.

"Wyverns," said Kell.

From behind came coughing and what sounded like retching. Ellis and Titus were dismounted. Ellis hunched over with Angus beside him for support. Titus appeared on the verge of joining Ellis. He turned away just when Tyrone arrived and desperately tried not to retch.

Tyrone held Titus's shoulder. "Steady."

Titus took several deep breaths and managed to stop himself.

Angus helped Ellis to straighten up. He looked sickly pale. "Sorry, Highness," said Ellis to Tyrone.

"Nothing to apologize for. I'd be concerned if you didn't react. We discovered the presence of wyverns, which is the reason for the pyres."

"How so?" asked Titus.

"Death by supernatural creatures is gruesome, and can be infectious. Burning is the only way to stop the evil poison from spreading. Remain with Angus while Kell and I speak to Lieutenant Brewster."

"Are they all right?" asked Brewster.

"Ay. Do you know what happened here?"

"No. We arrived too late."

"What about Mahon? What did he say happened?" asked Kell.

"He wasn't here when we arrived, Captain."

"Maybe he reported to Avatar," said Tyrone at seeing Kell's frown.

"Avatar told him to wait for Lieutenant Brewster."

"Perhaps what he discovered was worth reporting immediately. We'll find out when we reach Waldron. For now I want to investigate."

Brewster fell in step as they entered the compound. "We didn't find anything other than dead bodies and those gouge marks. Although by the looks of the men, it happened fast and without warning."

Soldiers carried fallen comrades to the pyres. Some of the dead still wore sheathed swords.

"They didn't even have time to draw their weapons," said Tyrone.

"Ay. Others looked surprised at the time of death."

Tyrone turned from the grim task to focus on a building with an open door. He examined the door before entering. "Mahon was here."

"Ay," agreed Kell. "There was a confrontation."

"With Mahon or the wyverns?" asked Brewster.

Kell didn't answer and moved to search the room.

Tyrone backed into a table. His weight made it move with a metallic sound. He reached down to pick up a sword. "Kell. Mahon's sword."

Kell took the weapon, closed his eyes for a moment, and winced in pain. His eyes snapped open. "He's alive, but injured."

"Where is he?" asked Brewster.

"Not sure. He probably sought refuge to heal if he couldn't dimension travel to safety."

"Should we look for him?"

"You won't find him. When a warrior is injured and seeks refuge, it's a place well hidden. When he's ready, he'll find us." Kell stuck Mahon's sword in his belt. "We shouldn't stay too long, Highness."

"Ay. When finished here, head to Waldron," Tyrone instructed Brewster. He and Kell rejoined the others. Ridge, Egan and the soldiers helped with the pyres. "Time to leave," he called and mounted his horse.

"What is that?" Titus asked Kell.

"Mahon's sword."

"Is he dead?"

"No. Injured and in hiding to heal. I'll keep it for him. We need to find a place for the night. Ridge, take the lead." While the ranger followed instructions, Kell stared at the outpost as if sensing something.

Egan drew along side him. "Are you sure about Mahon?"

"Being alive, ay. But there's another presence close by."

"Should I make a search?"

He shook his head. "Too risky."

"Kell?" called Tyrone

The captain nudged Egan for them to follow the others. Before losing sight of the outpost, Kell again looked back. He then ran after Tyrone, reducing his speed to walk beside the horse. "Highness, I suggest making a detour to Arundine and speak to the Trio Leaders before going to Waldron. They need to be informed of the change in leadership and what we're up against."

"Ay. Let Ridge know and we'll follow your lead."

***

Mannix drug Locan deeper into the forest. "What are you doing? Any closer and Kell would have seen us."

"I wanted to learn if he discovered anything at the outpost. It's bad enough he sealed the ruins. Hueil won't like hearing that."

"Ay, but we were only supposed to watch the Fortress."

"You told me to take the lead. Following Tyrone is important. We have confirmation that Nigel is king and on his way to Waldron.

The answer annoyed Mannix. "I don't like any of this. It's getting far too complex and dangerous."

Locan tried to be reassuring. "I won't take unnecessary risks, but we must see this through. If not, Hueil will find us and destroy us."

"Not if we leave Allon."

"Leave? You think he can't find us?"

"He's not omniscient like Jor'el."

"No, but he has long reach and ruled as a god for centuries. I don't know if any place is far enough."

Mannix's agitation mounted. "Surviving for however long we can is better than continually facing destruction every time we see him."

"If the situation becomes too hazardous, we'll leave." He made Mannix face him. "Trust me, as I trusted you enough to forfeit my station."

For a moment Mannix didn't reply. "All right. What now?"

"We report this finding to Hueil." Seeing Mannix grow weary, he added, "I'll make the report, you wait someplace he can't see you."

Chapter 15

A T A SECLUDED MANOR HOUSE IN THE LOWLANDS, ELLAN AND Hueil met with Gareth and Zebulon over dinner. Servants ringed the table ready for when called upon. Zebulon's steward entered and bowed to Ellan.

"Madam, Lord Bosley and Baron Erasmus have arrived."

"Send them in."

Booted, spurred and road dusty, they presented themselves.

"You seemed to have made haste," said Ellan.

"You wanted our troops within twelve days, Madam," said Erasmus.

"At Roxbury but not here!"

"They are at Roxbury. We proceeded here to inform you that all the troops are assembled. Including Malcolm."

"What is the total troop count?" asked Zebulon.

"Just under one hundred and sixty thousand," said Bosley.

Ellan smiled. "That is good news, gentlemen." She motioned to the table. "Please, join us. You must be hungry and thirsty."

"Thank you." Erasmus and Bosley assumed seats at the table and servants brought them plates of food and drink.

They proceeded to let Erasmus and Bosley eat without too many comments until Ellan said, "Gentlemen, do use usually eat with your gloves on?"

"Oh," said Erasmus, a quick glance at Bosley. "It's been such a hectic day we forgot." He began by taking off his left glove. Bosley did the same, and deliberately tugged at each finger. When Erasmus began removing his right glove, he noticed Locan in the threshold. "Someone to speak to you, Madam."

Ellan went from watching them to Locan. Bosley stopped removing his right glove and reached to take a drink.

"What news?" she asked the Guardian.

"The information is correct. Prince Nigel has been crowned king."

Bosley almost choked on his drink. "What? Nigel is king?"

"We heard a rumor that Tyrone abdicated and Nigel crowned, but wanted the information confirmed before making it known," began Ellan. "Why look so forlorn, gentlemen? This changes nothing."

"Madam, this changes everything! Nigel is firstborn and takes his rightful place," said Erasmus.

Annoyed, she leaned forward. "His coronation comes years after mine, which was legitimate, performed by the Vicar and confirmed by the entire Council! Were any of you present to confirm his coronation and pledge fidelity?"

They hesitated, so Gareth declared, "No, none of us were."

"Then it changes nothing," she said. "I expect all to uphold their oath regardless of my brother's choice to stand with the half-breed against my legal claim."

"In fact, he could be viewed as the usurper," said Gareth.

"How do you figure that? He *is* firstborn," said Bosley.

"Based upon the circumstances the queen described of her prior coronation. This move cannot be viewed any other way."

"Any alteration to the plan will also be considered treason," said Hueil. His icy gaze focused on Bosley and Erasmus.

Bosley shrank back in his seat and Erasmus turned away.

Ellan fought a smirk of satisfaction to ask, "Lost your appetite, gentlemen?"

"Maybe their nerve as well," scoffed Zebulon.

Erasmus barely looked at Zebulon, but with enough ire and wounded pride that Zebulon sneered in response.

"Return to your troops and await my orders," commanded Ellan.

Erasmus stood, stiff and square-shouldered. Bosley rose, also appearing putout. They offered her marginal bows.

"Oh, gentlemen," her voice stopped their departure, the tone full of ominous warning. "If I find you absent upon my arrival at Roxbury, remember, Shadow Warriors have a long reach and are relentless."

"We will be there, Madam," said Erasmus, and they left.

"I'll keep an eye on them," said Gareth.

"Finish eating first. Let them think they are not being watched."

Gareth smiled and resumed eating.

Neither Erasmus nor Bosley spoke as they sent their horses into a full gallop. After a mile, Erasmus slowed his horse and Bosley pulled alongside him.

"That was too close," said Erasmus.

"Never mind our gloves. Nigel is king!"

"Don't be fooled. She suspects us. Discovering we no longer have our rings will confirm her suspicions. We must be more careful."

"What about Nigel?"

"Doesn't change what we must do. Hopefully Eric and the others have reached Wess and he will carry the news to Nigel."

"That's some consolation, I suppose."

"It's all we have." Erasmus glanced back over his shoulder. They rode far enough to not see the manor house. "No one is following us."

"With Shadow Warriors, we wouldn't know," groused Bosley.

"Ay. But we must keep her from discovering our supply shortage."

"We're playing a dangerous game of deception. Missing rings, short supplies, what next, illness among the ranks?"

"That's a possibility," said Erasmus with humorless grin. "We agreed passive resistance is only way to help the king, whether Tyrone or Nigel."

"I know. But, the closer we come to battle, the more I dread the thought of facing Wess."

"I share your feelings. Jor'el willing, our efforts will avoid battle. The sooner we return the better." He kicked his horse to pick up the pace.

Roxbury was only a four-hour ride from the manor house. When they returned to Erasmus' tent, they found Malcolm waiting. He appeared very pale and more fragile than the last time they saw him. He sat at the table with his cloak and a blanket wrapped around him.

"What are you doing here? You should be in bed," said Erasmus.

"He shouldn't even be here, he should be home," said Bosley.

"I had to speak to you both." Malcolm waved them closer due to his weak voice. "I heard a rumor about Nigel being crowned king."

Erasmus sat on his cot. "No rumor. Ellan confirmed it. Tyrone abdicated and Nigel crowned."

"Oh, merciful heaven," moaned Malcolm. "What do we do now?"

"First you must calm down and take your medicine." Bosley poured wine and offered it to Malcolm.

He pushed the cup away. "No time."

"Make time." Bosley put the cup in Malcolm's hand.

"I mean I don't have any more time. I'm dying."

Thunderstruck, Bosley sat beside Erasmus. The latter also disturbed by the news and said; "Has this been confirmed?"

"Phoebe told me I wouldn't live long past harvest. When this started, I stopped taking my medicine. I don't want to live to see civil war."

A poignant silence followed before Erasmus spoke again. "We don't know what to say. You've been a good friend, Council Member ..."

Malcolm's feeble shake of this head stopped Erasmus' speech. "There is nothing to say. I just wish I had the courage to do what you and Bosley are doing."

"We're not doing anything," said Bosley.

Malcolm smiled. "My body maybe fragile, but I still have eyes and a mind." With a shaky hand, he held out his ring to Erasmus. "I have no heir. Whomever the king appoints, I pray he is stronger than me."

"I'll make certain he gets it." Erasmus pocketed the ring.

Malcolm swooned and Bosley moved to support him. "Let me take you to your tent." He tried to help Malcolm stand, but Malcolm fell back into the chair.

"I can't move," his voice barely above a raspy whisper. He fainted.

Erasmus called for one of his men to fetch his surgeon the said to Bosley. "We'll lift him to a cot." Being ill for so long, Malcolm was easy to lift and move, his body the shell of what it was.

Instead of the surgeon, Malcolm's personal physician, Bevan, arrived. "You send for me, my lord?"

"Lord Malcolm fainted."

"I feared something like this." Bevin made a quick examination and somberly shook his head. "I advised him not to travel since it would tax what strength he had left."

"Is there anything you can do?" asked Bosley.

"No. Doubtful he will survive the night. All we can do is to make him comfortable."

Bosley took an extra blanket from the footlocker at the end of Erasmus' bed and placed it over Malcolm.

"I'll arrange for him to be taken home," said Erasmus.

"No need. He did so while waiting for you and Lord Bosley. His only concern was you would not return in time so he could speak to you."

"He collapsed after we spoke."

Bosley sat in the chair Malcolm occupied and drank the wine he poured for him. "How many more of us will die before this is over?"

"We'll stay with him." Erasmus motioned for Bevan to leave.

"I would be derelict in my duty if I left. Also," he began, a prompting gaze shifting between Bosley and Erasmus, "I am under strict instruction to say he left his ring at home. He feared that in his weakened condition, if anything should happen, it could fall into the wrong hands."

"Very wise of him. Now, make yourself comfortable." Erasmus sat in the other chair at the table with Bosley and helped himself to the wine.

Bevan sat on the trunk at the foot of the bed. They no sooner became settled then Gareth arrived, booted and spurred from travel.

"What are you doing here?" asked Erasmus.

"I came to inspect the troops."

"At this hour?"

Gareth noticed Malcolm. "What's wrong with him?"

"He's dying. He won't last the night. Tell that to Ellan!" chided Bosley.

Gareth straightened with insult, which brought Erasmus to his feet.

"It's been a long, tiring and now sorrowful day," he said.

"What about his troops?"

"He placed them under my command."

Gareth scoffed. "I don't think so. The queen will decide."

Incited by Gareth's insensitive manner, Bosley stood toe-to-toe with him, his eyes direct and voice harsh. "Even if you never respected him in life, at least let him pass in peace!"

Without a word, Gareth turned on his heels and left.

"Their suspicion is growing." Erasmus' strong grip stopped Bosley.

"I'm sure there is something to fetch from your medical supplies to make Lord Malcolm more comfortable," Erasmus said to Bevan.

He nodded in understanding. "In fact there is." He left.

"His ring can't stay here with Gareth as her watchdog," said Bosley.

"I sent Bevan on a errand so he can't say what he doesn't know regarding its whereabouts." Erasmus leaned closer to speak low so they couldn't be overheard. "When Hayden first took over the Lowlands, he wanted advice on how to deal with Derwin and the Guardians. I told him about how I let Alrick know when I need to speak to him. Hayden implemented the same system. I just have to get to the signal point."

"I take it you know where it is."

"Ay. If Bevan returns before I do, tell him, I've gone to make my nightly rounds." Erasmus left.

Outside, no one looked in his direction, so he ducked into the shadows to make his way to the camp's perimeter. Hayden constructed a second signal point in a grove about a quarter mile from the house. Erasmus didn't have far to travel, and only needed to avoid patrols and Shadow Warriors.

Jor'el, please let this work, he prayed.

Once he reached the perimeter of trees, he scanned the area before darting into the woods. He occasionally glanced back to see the encampment and house through the trees.

Erasmus reached the grove and found the signal point, a hollow stump with a false top made to avoid the casual eye. He wrapped Malcolm's ring in his handkerchief, lifted the false top, placed the ring inside the hollow stump and replaced the top. Beside the stump, he found a makeshift branch matching the stump and fitted into a burnt out hole on the side of the stump.

Finished, he made his way back to camp, again pausing at the perimeter to see if any eyes were watching. This time he assumed a casual pace in returning to his tent. He was gone about twenty minutes.

Bevan sat on the trunk. "Was all in order on your rounds, my lord?"

"Indeed," replied Erasmus. He smiled and resumed his seat.

⚜

Ellan and Hueil conversed in the drawing room when a flash of light appeared. Hueil didn't react while Ellan stiffened in anticipation. From the fading light the Shadow Warrior, Phelan, appeared.

"Majesty. Lord Gareth reports Lord Malcolm collapsed, and is at this moment, dying. He is not expected to survive the night," said Phelan.

"And his troops?"

"Lord Gareth placed them under your command, Majesty."

"One less troublemaker," said Hueil.

Ellan laughed with scorn. "Malcolm couldn't lift a finger much less cause trouble. His passing places the North Plains under my control. I should move my command there and not depend upon hospitality."

223

"It is too far with so many troops, and tip our hand," said Hueil.

"Ay." She made a frustrated wave. "Back to our discussion. I think the visit to my brother would be beneficial before armed conflict. With Phelan there is no fear of capture."

"Phelan can use a shielding medal to gain access to Waldron, kill him and be done with it," he argued.

She narrowed her eyes in annoyance. "Don't insult my intelligence. You are too clever to make such a haphazard statement and I too smart to fall for it. If Nigel suddenly dies it will upset everything and cast suspicion on me for assassination, undermining an already fragile alliance. Not to mention handing the crown back to the half-breed and giving him further motivation. At least with Nigel alive, the half-breed is contained."

Hueil laughed, which annoyed her.

"You can be so infuriating with your condescension!"

"I'm simply doing what I was created to do, probe mortals and get them to think, not act on fickle emotions and passion. However," he changed to warning. "The half-breed has not been inactive. He visited the ruins and ordered Kell to permanently seal it."

"I thought you finished with the ruins?"

"That's beside the point. By abdicating, he is free to act independent and unpredictable."

"Are you admitting to a miscalculation?" she said with caustic teasing.

"Hardly," he shot back. "While at the ruins, I reminded him I'm still a threat. We must keep him occupied and not allow them to reunite."

"Sounds like you're beginning to agree to my plan. You delay the half-breed while I play upon Nigel's sympathy."

Hueil cocked a grin, reached into his pocket and pulled out a shielding medal. "Shall we discuss all the details before acting?"

Chapter 16

SHORTLY BEFORE DAWN, NIGEL AND MIRIT WERE IN THE ROYAL bedchamber with servants helping them dress for the day. Both wore breeches and doublets suitable for training. Mirit sat at the vanity where a maid finished pinning up her long braid. Nigel sat on the end of the bed pulling on his boots a male servant handed him.

"I'll fetch Valery and meet you and Fraser in the armory," she said.

He nodded since he yawned.

She chuckled and approached the bed. "Don't let them see fatigue. What impression would that give?"

"I'm not tired. I just didn't sleep for being pleasantly occupied." With a teasing smile, he pulled her to sit on his lap.

"Now, now. We must set an example of promptness and dedication." She rose when there came a knock at the door followed by Fraser's voice. "Your pupil is already." She dismissed the maid and headed for the door when Virgil admitted Fraser. "Good morning," she greeted him.

"Majesty." Fraser bowed.

"You're old, tired uncle is still dressing," she said with a light chuckle. "We'll meet you at the armory." She and Virgil left, shutting the door.

"Aunt Mirit's in a good mood this morning."

Nigel laughed. "Some women are morning people. She's one of them." He stood for the servant to close his doublet.

"Avatar said something about preparing an initiation. What is that?"

"The testing of a new cadet. That's all," he said to the servant. The man bowed and left. Nigel looked in the mirror and straightened the doublet to his liking. He fetched his sword and belt off a nearby chair.

Within two feet of the door, they heard a clicking sound. Nigel tried the handle to discover the door was locked. "That's strange." He tried to use the key but it wouldn't turn.

"I hope you're not going somewhere and miss our reunion," a female voice spoke from behind.

Nigel and Fraser whirled about and both reached for their swords.

"No need for violence, brother." She stepped out from the corner.

Surprised, Nigel let the sword fall back in the scabbard. "Ellan?"

"Hello, Nigel."

"She is my aunt?" asked Fraser.

"Aunt? Is he your son?"

"Tristine is my mother."

"Hold your tongue," warned Nigel.

"There is no need. I mean no harm to you or the boy."

"Really?" Nigel's gaze shifted to Phelan, who held a shielding medal. "A Shadow Warrior and shielding medal. So that's how you got in here undetected." He pushed Fraser toward the door.

"Phelan is helping me."

"You expect me to believe a Shadow Warrior is helping a mortal? I'm a Jor'ellian, I know better."

"I also heard you are now king."

"What do you want?"

She grew fretful. "I came to explain what is happening."

"You said enough in your letter."

"No!" she said in pleading voice. "Hueil forced me to write it. He's forcing me to do everything."

"Why?"

"Revenge for Tunlund."

"So why involve you?"

Her voice became desperate. "I don't understand it all! Only that he hopes to use me to destroy our family."

"You nearly did a good job of that yourself once," he chided.

"No, no! It was Musetta, Morrell and Sullivan. I didn't know what I was doing. I swear!" Overcome with emotion, she sat in a chair, weeping. "I've spent the last eighteen tormented by those horrid memories."

Fraser withdrew a handkerchief from his pocket and started to approach her. Nigel intercepted him. "She's crying."

"At least the boy is considerate to my pain," she sobbed.

He released Fraser, who gave her the handkerchief.

"Thank you." She wiped her eyes and gently blew her nose. She gazed at him. "I see Tristine in you. Although we had our differences, I do love my sister."

Nigel scoffed with a humorless chuckle. "I don't think you'll ever convince Tristine of that." He pulled Fraser away from Ellan.

"No, you're right." She stood with pleading eyes on Nigel. "As children, you mediated between us and we always made amends. Now, with you're help, she may listen and understand my position."

He grew incredulous. "Childhood squabbles are one thing, but asking me to act as peacemaker now, isn't possible. Your actions divided the Council, forced Tristine and Tyrone to abdicate and me to take up arms!"

Ellan wept, nearly uncontrollable. "No, no, not me! Hueil. Oh, how can I make you believe me?" In desperation she turned to Fraser. "You can speak to your mother on my behalf—"

Nigel stepped between them. "Leave the boy out of this!"

"I can't. Hueil wants everyone destroyed."

Nigel jowls tightened. He glanced to Phelan then back to Ellan. "You have overstayed your welcome."

"You dismiss me when I came to you for help and safety?"

"Safety? You mean sanctuary?" asked Fraser.

"Ay! He can't turn me away."

"Uncle—"

"Quiet!" he snapped, but his eyes never left Ellan. "If you want me to believe you are sincere, then leave."

"How will that prove sincerity if she's Hueil prisoner?" argued Fraser.

"I said, quiet, cadet!" This time Nigel glared at Fraser.

At the rebuff, he gripped his sword and took a step back.

"You turn an innocent boy against me? You've grown cruel," she said with distress. "I misjudged you, remembering the brother I loved."

Nigel squared his shoulders, and a brief pricked expression passed over his face. "And you a sister I once loved, who tried to kill our father and now threatens the same to Tristine and Tyrone. Not to mention civil war! This is your final warning, take the Shadow Warrior and go before I call Avatar and fulfill my Jor'ellian duty!"

She sniffled, and tried to regain some dignity. She held out the handkerchief to Fraser.

"Keep it, Aunt."

"Thank you." She lifted her chin with wounded pride and moved to Phelan. They vanished, no light, just gone.

Click! Nigel found the door unlocked. He didn't leave the room, rather stared at the spot Ellan and Phelan occupied a moment earlier

"How could you be so cruel to your sister?" demanded Fraser.

"You don't know what you're talking about."

"Nigel!" Mirit rushed in, flushed and worried. Avatar, Virgil and Valery were with her, all armed and ready for confrontation. "Are you all right? Avatar and Virgil sensed trouble."

He took a deep calming breath before saying, "Ellan was here."

"What?" she exclaimed in dreadful surprise.

Avatar's silver eyes blazed in anger. "How?"

"A Shadow Warrior and shielding medal."

"She tearfully pleaded for sanctuary and you turned her away!" argued Fraser.

"Sanctuary," said Avatar with a huff of disbelief.

Fraser continued his passionate argument. "She said Hueil is forcing her to help his act of revenge for Tunlund. Uncle didn't believe her."

"Enough!" snapped Nigel. His temper exhausted, he shoved Fraser to Virgil. "Take him and start the initiation!"

Fraser resisted. "You cast me aside like her?"

"Wait!" Nigel's command made Virgil pause in removing Fraser. Nigel stood toe-to-toe with his nephew. The young man's face showed a stubbornness that had to be broken. "The purpose of training is to help you restrain your tongue and teach you to think like a warrior, not to cast you aside. More than once you spoke thoughtlessly, giving her information to bring back for Hueil to use against us."

"I didn't mean to. She's my aunt, your sister. I thought family was important. At least that's what I've been told."

"Family is important, but so is duty! Twice you ignored my order of silence. I'm not only your uncle, but also your commander and king!"

"I'm sorry, Sire," he said with restraint and gripped his sword.

Nigel stared at Fraser in an attempt to see beyond the stubbornness. "Go with Virgil. We'll be down shortly."

Fraser made a stiff bow and complied.

Mirit motioned for Valery to leave then spoke to Nigel. "I'm certain meeting Ellan again was very difficult for you."

"A bit. It was harder to hear Fraser's comment about being cast aside. I suppose I let my temper get the best of me."

"No," refuted Avatar. "He needs to learn self-discipline. You and Tyrone are doing all you can and should. At some point, Fraser must take responsibility for his words and actions."

"I'm afraid of what can happen if he doesn't learn soon. He was completely taken in by her." He snorted in irony. "She tried to play upon my sympathies by invoking childhood memories with passionate tears."

Mirit noticed twinges of remorse on his face. "Did she succeed?"

"Not entirely. Still, there may have been some truth to her words."

"Ellan has always been a manipulator. Even as a child, she twisted things to her favor," said Avatar

"Ay, ay," said Nigel in frustration. "I won't deny that her plea for sanctuary was tempting, even if only to corral her and keep her from Hueil. I probably could have taken the Warrior without help."

Avatar grabbed Nigel's arm to get his full attention. "No! Any aggressive move and she would have ordered you both killed, and no one would have known until it was too late because of the medal."

"I wonder why she didn't," said Nigel in quiet voice full of dread.

Mirit hugged him, tight. "I'm glad she didn't." A soft sob escaped.

For a moment he held her. "Well, it's over, and now we know for certain where we stand." He smiled and wiped her tears away. "Care for some training?"

She couldn't help a chuckle. "Ay. If only to release some tension."

"Only don't envision poor Valery as Ellan."

"No. I'll warm up with Virgil."

<hr />

Back at the manor house, Hueil listened to Ellan's report of the encounter. "So your brother isn't as soft as you remember."

"No," she said with disappointment. "He reminded me of our father and how he dealt with us as children, stern and unyielding."

"It sounds like you accomplished nothing but to irritate him."

"Nigel, perhaps." She removed a handkerchief from her skirt pocket.

"Where did you get that?"

"Fraser gave it to me as kindness to a distressed aunt."

Hueil laughed. "Your act hit a target other than the one intended."

"Tristine's son, no less." She toyed with the handkerchief. "He most willingly defended me to Nigel. If I can speak to him privately, I can gain his support against Tristine." She laughed in malicious delight. "It would be delightful to turn him against her."

Hueil flashed a keen smile. "You may not have to turn him completely, just use him as a thorn in her side."

"What do you mean?"

"You said he *willingly* spoke."

"Ay. Twice he disobeyed Nigel's order to be quiet." She scowled with sarcasm. "So like his mother, contrary."

"Use that to your benefit. Only not at Waldron, some place comfortable and isolated to cultivate his willingness."

She smiled with understanding. "You mean make him a spy?"

"While not making him aware he is spying by convincing him he is helping a distressed aunt to thwart her evil captor," said Hueil, who then laughed. "Oh, I couldn't get one son, but we can use another."

Ellan smile also increased due to pleasure. "Give him a day or two. If he truly is his mother's son, he'll brood about it and when given a chance to act, he'll seize it! Tristine always did after she and father clashed."

"I thought you helped those clashes?"

She giggled. "Ay. They were so predictable in their responses."

"I have just the means to aid us." He lowered his head, closed his eyes and after a moment a flash of light appeared in the room. From the fading light appeared a male vassal Guardian by his modest clothes and lack of sword. "This is Fitch. He is one of the remaining shape-shifters. Guardians who can change between a heavenly and any given mortal." he said to her look of confusion. "Mona, the Trio leader of the North Plain is a Guardian with such capabilities. Only a few remain, most were destroyed during the Great Battle. Fitch became trapped in Dagar's nether dimension when Kell first sealed it."

"Why didn't you flee like the others after Dagar's defeat?" she asked.

Fitch looked to Hueil, who replied. "He can't speak; a result of reconditioning. He bears no love for Kell or the others since they left him to be captured and face hundreds of years of torture then trapped with the creatures of *infrin*."

"He told you this? But you said he can't speak."

"Guardians communicate in ways other than speech."

"How will this help with Fraser?"

"Simple. Fitch will return to Waldron with Phelan under the protection of the shielding medal and switch places with your sleeping nephew. After your discussion, Fraser will be returned."

She remained uncertain. "Won't the others notice he's gone? He can look like Fraser but will he act like him? And I thought Guardians were sensitive to each other's presence."

Hueil simply grinned. "The Guardian essence is masked by the mortal persona. Although, Fitch will still possess power, being discovered can only be done by the most astute, and *only* if there is any suspicion will they even try. To the casual observance, he will be Fraser. Our questioning shouldn't take too long so the risk of discovery is minimal."

"Will you use the same potion with him you did with Mahon?"

"No need if he is as willing as you say. In the end, he will be returned unharmed and unaware of anything more than a dream."

"Turn him without him realizing it," she said with a sly smile. "Then in two days I will meet with my nephew. What about our other plans?"

"As I said, the half-breed knows I'm still a threat. I think while he's away and the new king not yet established, I'll unleash my new faithful warrior. If he can eliminate Avatar first, Nigel will be more vulnerable."

Chapter 17

THE FIRST DAY OF TRAINING WAS BROKEN UP INTO THREE TWO hour-long sessions: endurance and strength training, memorizing the Jor'ellian attack and defensive forms, and limited bouts with Mirit and Nigel. In between the morning and afternoon sessions, Kendrick took Valery and Fraser to the chapel to receive instruction from Master Hampton on Verse and Prophecy. After lunch, another training session in the armory, followed by instruction on Court etiquette from Sir Reynold and his wife Lady Chesley, the advisors of royal protocol. Following the evening training session, they prepared for a formal meal with the king and queen.

By ten o'clock that night, Valery was exhausted and overwhelmed by all the instruction. Although her mother taught her manners and some protocol, what she learned the first day far exceeded anything previous. Of course being familiar with much more than her, Frasier became distracted and chided by Kendrick about staying on task and not disrupting the session. The prince didn't like the Guardian's interference as told by his reluctant submission. However, the more time Valery spent in the company of Guardians the more fascinating she found them.

Naturally she knew about Guardians from her time at Court, but never interacted with them on a personal level. For all their large size and strength, they could be humorous, kindhearted, compassionate, and gentle, especially dealing with children.

Of the Guardians, Valery felt closest to Wren after what they experienced. Being Mirit's squire and constantly around the royal couple, she found Virgil possessed a wonderful sense of humor, and Avatar dry-witted and very intelligent. Now, being paired with Fraser for training, she came to regard Kendrick as one of the most patient beings she ever met. To endure Fraser's endless jabbering and fits of willfulness took great self-control. Kendrick rarely displayed anger or annoyance, but there was no escaping the reproving and deep probing in the Guardian's bright copper eyes on those occasions he dealt sternly with Fraser.

She yawned upon reached the bedchamber. Someone opened the door. Virgil grinned and asked, "Can you make it to the bed?"

She chuckled. "I honestly don't know. They do this everyday?"

"Just about." He ushered her inside. "Shall I send for Madison?"

She plopped on the bed. "No, I think I'll sleep in my clothes."

He laughed and crossed to the wardrobe. "Not a good idea if you want to be comfortable." He pulled out the nightclothes and brought them to her. "Do you need help undoing the corset?"

"Ay," she grumbled and went behind the screen to remove the gown. "How long have you been with the queen?"

"Since Natan. Although I've served at Court since being freed from captivity in Soren and the invasion."

"Captivity?" She stepped out from behind the screen in the second layer of corset and petticoat. She turned her back to him when he made a swirling motion using his finger.

"I spent a little over five hundred years as a prisoner."

"Five hundred years?" she echoed in surprise and nearly turned around. He stopped her to finish undoing the laces of the corset. "How old are you?"

"Sixteen hundred years give or take a decade."

"I didn't know Guardians lived so long."

"Our spirits are immortal. We only die in the physical when killed by another Guardian or a Shadow Warrior. Loose enough?"

"Ay." She turned to face him, the corset loose but still on her. "I heard Wren would have died if she wasn't healed."

"Those creatures were created by the Dark Way, thus possibly lethal. We can be injured by mortals, but heal quickly on our own, though there are exceptions. My twin, Jedrek, died when a mortal used a stygian arrow when he tried to protect Prince Titus from his kidnappers."

"What is a stygian arrow?"

"One of the two elements capable of either rendering us helpless or killing us. Spurean is other element. They were forged in the fires of heaven by Rune, chief metal smith of the Guardians. Unfortunately, he joined Dagar and overtime revealed his secrets. That's how they held me captive for so long, bound by spurean manacles and chains."

"I'm sorry to hear about Jedrek and your captivity." She yawned.

"Enough talk. Finish changing and go to bed."

"Ay. Dawn comes early."

"No, they rise the same time regardless of the sun," he quipped.

She waved him off. "Goodnight."

At the following morning session, Valery and Fraser employed the previous day's lessons in a bout. Here she felt Fraser had the advantage after years of training while she was self-taught. Still, under the watchful eye of Nigel and Mirit, she made a good show of what she learned.

Once they assumed the first position, Nigel said, "Take it slow at first. We want to see forms one through three. Begin."

Valery and Fraser exchanged the first three counts.

"Good. Now four through eight."

They did so then stopped and went back to the first position.

"Good. Now with speed on my cadence. Begin." Nigel began counting one through eight and they responded. "Again, only faster." He counted. "Again." He counted for a third time and they kept pace. "Very good. Let's try fighting speed."

They assumed position. Before Nigel gave the signal, Fraser launched at Valery. She dodged out of the way only his blade caught her left sleeve and ripped it open.

"Fraser!"

"I'm sorry. I anticipated your count."

Mirit examine the tear. "He only cut the sleeve. No injury."

Nigel examined Valery for himself. "What about this bruise?"

"That happened when the wolf-men attack the camp," she said.

"You're fortunate you have the quickness to get out of the way." He sent a side-glance at Fraser as he continued. "Let this be a lesson to both of you, don't be anxious and jump into battle prematurely, but expect your adversary to be unpredictable. Take a few moments for refreshment and we'll start again." He waved them to move on.

"Unpredictable is an understatement," she chided under her breath.

"I'll give you a warning next time," he grumbled in reply.

With expressions of equal determination, they went their separate ways to each get a drink.

"I don't like the way they're reacting to each other," said Nigel.

"If she can beat him, maybe it will help him to curb his tongue."

"It didn't help me when I discovered you were my equal with a sword. In fact, I married you," he teased.

She began to laugh, only stopped at seeing Valery and Fraser's attention. She turned from their view to speak privately to Nigel. "Won't happen with them. Where he needs a lesson in humility, she needs to gain confidence."

"You think beating a man will give her confidence?"

"A man beat her," she said in low but firm voice. "She can't grow past her wounds if she shrinks from confrontation. Once she learns she can win and is able to control her responses, I hope she can begin the road to complete healing."

"I won't let it get out of hand."

"Agreed. I don't want to turn her into a fighter, only to gain a sense of victory over her past. I needed to experience that before I could return your love. If she and Ellis are to have a future and not live with the dark shadow of her father looming over them, she needs this."

"Very well." He noticed they finished with refreshment. "Time for a bout." He waited as they took the first position. "At fight speed. Begin!"

As anticipated, Fraser attacked and Valery made a good defense. He was the aggressor and she on the defensive, yet keen to what he tried to do. She made a miscue at his fourth attack. When she moved past him, he struck her aside with the flat of his sword on her rump.

Fraser laughed. "Maybe Ellis likes a woman who can fight and not talk since he really can't do either."

"One day your conceit will get you into trouble!"

They exchanged a good series of blows until he made a move she parried by ducking to one side. This time when he passed her, he sent an elbow into her bruised arm. She retreated in pain and grabbed her arm.

Nigel moved to intervene but Mirit stopped him. "No. Let's see what she does."

Angry, Valery went after Fraser. Her forcefulness drove him into a corner. He snatched a cloak off a hook on the wall to distract her. She tried batting aside the cloak. Finally she yanked it from him. When he swung his sword at her, she ducked and came up flipping the cloak to catch his sword arm and pull it down. Rather than lunging, she brought up her right elbow to clip him under the chin then used her foot to sweep his legs out from under him. He fell on his back with a hard thud. He lay winded and stunned, a groan escaping.

Nigel knelt to examine Fraser. "Nothing broken. She knows how to fight and you got the bad end of that bout."

Upset at the result of her violence, Valery balked. "I'm sorry! I don't know what came over me." She dropped her sword and ran outside.

Mirit caught Valery in the yard. "You have nothing to apologize for or to be ashamed of. Fraser provoked and you responded, but with control."

"I knocked him down!"

"You pulled what should have been a fatal blow in battle. You didn't want to hurt him, you just wanted the pain to stop."

Tears swelled when Valery asked, "You know, don't you?"

"Ay."

She grew emotional so Mirit took her to Wess' office in the armory. The room was unoccupied. "You don't need to fear him any more."

"He killed my mother!" She bitterly wept and Mirit held her.

"She helped you to escape and get beyond his reach." She tilted Valery's head. "The bout showed you have the strength to let go, to overcome and be free from the past."

Valery wiped her eyes. "Right now the situation is a hindrance."

"No excuses. Jor'el has given you strength, use it to heal—despite the situation." She softly smiled. "Not just for yourself, but also for Ellis. Don't deny your feelings for him, or let them be ruled by the past."

She winced at the mention of Ellis. "He can't know about it!"

"Why? Do you fear it will change his feelings for you?"

"I—I don't know, but ..." She balked and shied away.

Mirit gently turned Valery to face her. "I don't believe it will change anything. Since you arrived at Garwood, he's demonstrated tender concern for your wellbeing. Rebuffing him has been guided by fear."

"I don't want my father to hurt him!" she said in a protective voice.

Mirit fought laughing at the change from uncertainty to defense. "No need to worry. Ellis maybe shy and awkward with women, but he equals Titus in mock combat. Nigel helped to instruct him, so I know Braden would suffer the worst, more so with you involved. The same protectiveness you feel for him, will drive Ellis—for your sake."

"You're that certain?"

Mirit held Valery's gaze. "So are you. Only you shift between letting him get close and keeping up him at a distance. I acted the same with Nigel in the beginning: fearing to love someone and of him loving me."

"What changed?"

Mirit flashed a smile that quickly faded. "He nearly drowned and the thought of losing him made me realize I didn't want a life without him."

Valery lowered her eyes and chewed on her lower lip, considering the answer. There came a happy bark. Cody entered. She knelt to greet him.

"The troop has arrived," said Mirit.

In the Grand Courtyard, Chad and his men joined Brewster and his platoon. Avatar and Vidar greeted them when Nigel and a very sore Fraser arrived. Brewster saluted Nigel.

"Sire."

"Lieutenant. What news of the outpost?"

"All dead, Sire. A wyvern attack."

"What did Mahon say?" asked Avatar.

"He wasn't there when we arrived, but Prince Tyrone found his sword."

"Tyrone? Did he go to the ruins?" said Nigel.

Brewster shrugged. "I don't know about that, Sire. We were tending to the dead according to Jor'ellian rite concerning the Dark Way when he arrived with Captain Kell and others. The prince wanted to search the outpost and found Mahon's sword behind a fallen table. Captain Kell says Mahon is alive, but probably injured and in hiding."

Avatar spoke with thoughtful concern. "If he faced wyverns then he would be injured and retreat for healing."

"I volunteered to search for him only Kell said I wouldn't find him."

Avatar flashed a partial grin. "Ay, Mahon has his own way of dealing with injury so interrupting him isn't a good idea."

"With your permission, Sire, my men and I would like to clean up and get something to eat."

"Of course." He returned Brewster's salute.

"Do you believe Mahon will be fine?" Chad asked Avatar.

"If I believed otherwise, I'd be searching for him. Since Kell sensed he is alive, that's good enough. See to the men."

At the unusual dismissal done in the king's presence, Chad tossed a questioning glance to Nigel. He nodded so Chad complied.

"Why do I think you said that for Chad's benefit?" said Nigel.

"Mayers requested my help. I should have gone, not Mahon."

"Then it would be you out there we'd be concerned about rather than with the king as you should be. No, Mahon was right to go," said Wren.

"If Hueil is picking off the outposts we'll need to reinforce the Region's border. Dispatch Bryce and Broisus to warn the outpost commanders and perhaps they can find Mahon," said Nigel.

"No, I will. As his mentor, I can hone in on his spirit quicker than anyone." Avatar took a deep breath and closed his eyes. His brows leveled in the effort to stretch out his senses. He gritted his teeth and clenched his fists. His eyes snapped opened. "I sensed a sudden fluctuation in his spirit, like he died but isn't dead. I must find him before it's too late."

"Go!" said Nigel.

"Vidar, stay with Nigel. Wren, we'll start near the outpost on the main road." They stepped back from the others and disappeared.

<hr />

Avatar and Wren reappeared at the intersection where the main road from the North Plains traversed Midessex.

"He's nearby," said Avatar. "I'll head to the outpost and get a bearing of where he's gone. You make a wide arc to search for any visible signs and come in from the north. Be careful, something is not right."

She readied her crossbow. "You too."

Avatar drew his sword and waited until she was out of sight before starting up the road. He smelled the lingering odor of the pyres. Although on the lookout for wyverns or other creature of Hueil's making, he couldn't shake the sense that whatever was wrong dealt with Mahon. However, he discovered no indication Mahon used the road.

He arrived at the outpost and viewed the evidence of the wyvern attack and the smoldering funeral pyres. The sense of evil and Mahon increased. Suddenly alert, he whirled around and barely blocked the blow that sent him staggered back a few steps. He gaped at who attacked him.

"Mahon?"

Mahon came at him again and Avatar turned aside the attack.

"What are doing?"

"Destroying the enemies of my master!"

Avatar noticed the evil glare in Mahon's eyes and realized what happened. "Hueil!" he swore.

Avatar dodged another attack and sent Mahon stumbling forward with a vicious kick to the back. Mahon regained his balance and charged. The Dark Way enhanced Mahon's special power, and Avatar felt the increased strength. Being an elite warrior of the High Trio and Jor'ellian Commander, he had the ability to counter Mahon. However, such fierce blows tested the limits of their strength and the strain was evident on their faces. When they parted to catch their breath, Avatar spoke with dismay and vexation.

"You don't recognize me, do you? It's me, Avatar!"

Mahon snarled but his eyes narrowed in focused concentration.

"That's right. Look at me and remember! I trained you. We are friends!"

"Avatar!" Wren ran from the woods but pulled up when Mahon turned to her. At first, he appeared to be thinking then fiercely snarled. "Mahon? What's wrong?"

Avatar waved a warning hand at her. "Stay back, Wren! Hueil's gotten to him. He doesn't recognize us."

"What—?" She barely spoke when Mahon attacked Avatar with such force that he was driven back and stumbled over one of the pyres. "Mahon, what are you doing?"

"Destroying the enemies of my master, Lord Hueil!" He leapt up in the air over the pyres and landed in front of Avatar, who just got to his feet. Avatar raised his sword in defense. A blast from Mahon's hand sent Avatar hurtling through the air. He slammed into the outpost wall where he head snapped back and hit hard. Stunned, he slumped against the wall.

"Mahon, stop!" She raised her bow. He continued to advance on Avatar. Her finger encircled the trigger. "Don't make me shoot!"

Avatar looked up at hearing her warning. Mahon veered off and headed toward Wren. Still groggy, he use his hand to brace against the wall, he pushed himself up.

"Wren, back off!" Avatar's voice brought Mahon's attention back to him and a new charge. He placed the pommel of his sword in front of his face. "Don't make me use my power," he pleaded with clenched teeth.

Mahon raised his sword above his head. Avatar began to speak in the Ancient when … *Twang!* Mahon cried out in painful anger as an arrow pieced his right hand. He dropped his sword and turned. When he advanced toward Wren—*Twang!* Another bolt struck in him in the left side and brought him to his knees. In hurtful surprise, he turned from the wound in his side to her.

"Wren? Why?" he asked in confusion.

She halted in loading the third bolt. Painful regret welled up at seeing his befuddled expression. He appeared on the verge of collapse. "I didn't want to shoot! You gave me no choice."

Cautious, Avatar approached Mahon from behind. Mahon began to rise. "No, stay down! Don't force us to take any further action."

At Avatar's voice, Mahon's puzzled expression changed to a sneer.

"Please, Mahon! Do as he says," she pleaded.

Again his expression altered to confusion when looking at her. He cried in sudden agonizing pain, bent over and grabbed his head.

"Yield your sword and we'll take to Eldric," she said.

Mahon moaned in pain again, and this time with a bewildered whimper. He spoke in confusion to Wren. "What's happening to me?"

"Let us take you Eldric, so he can tell us."

"I don't think Eldric can't help me! But I need help."

"Yield your sword, Mahon!" said Avatar, urgent.

Mahon used the heel of his pierced right hand to push his sword aside, yet kept his hunched back to Avatar. When Avatar kicked the sword aside, Mahon sprung up and tackled him. He landed on top with a dagger pressed against Avatar's throat.

"No!" Wren raised her bow.

"Don't shoot!" said Avatar. He stared at Mahon, who appeared unusually pale and sweaty. The mental conflict and physical pain visible in dulling light blue eyes. A trickle of blood flowed from Mahon's right nostril. Although Mahon dagger pressed dangerously close to cutting his throat, in the eyes the battle took place. Avatar focused his attention and spoke. *"Cuimhne, Mahon. Cuimhne!"*

For a long moment, Mahon stared in concentration at Avatar. The strain of trying to remember turned the trickle of blood to a darker stream. "Avatar?" he murmured with a hint of recognition.

"Ay. And if you're going to kill me, do it quickly."

An expression of sheer horror overcame Mahon at seeing his dagger at Avatar's throat. He let go of the hilt then cried out with intense pain. He fell to one side convulsing, with his hands ripping at his ears.

Avatar scrambled to his feet to stop Wren from approaching Mahon.

"He's in great pain!" she protested.

"I don't think we can help."

A loud agonizing gasp, and then Mahon lay motionless. Streams of blood ran from both nostrils and his ears.

Wren knelt and felt his face. "He's cool. He won't last much longer if we don't take to Eldric."

Avatar lifted Mahon in his arms and vanished.

Wren picked up a broken piece of metal on the ground where Mahon lay. She put it in her pouch and vanished.

At Waldron's infirmary Avatar and Wren waited in the corridor. She sniffled a few times. He touched her shoulder and she began to weep.

"I didn't want to shoot him, but I thought he was going to kill you."

He held her. "You had no choice."

"It doesn't change the fact that if he dies, I killed him!"

"As I would have if he continued advancing on you."

He spoke with a voice void of emotion and she searched his face. "I pulled my shots. Would you have pulled your blow?"

He winced and released her, his voice strained in reply. "It's not that simple. Somehow Hueil altered him, and that's not the Mahon I trained and have known for so long!" When she looked away, pricked and uncertain, he seized shoulders to make her face him. "He held a dagger to my throat and I stared into the face of a friend ready to kill me! Ready to kill both of us without hesitation. If he hadn't stopped I—"

"He did stop."

Avatar took a deep breath to regain his composure. "The question is why and how? Morrell didn't stop when the coup failed. So why did Mahon heed my command to remember?"

"Because he too stared into the face of his friend and mentor. Whatever Hueil did, it wasn't enough to change him completely. Oh, I pray he doesn't die."

"Either way, it wouldn't change the end for Hueil the next time I see him. I swear in Jor'el's name!"

His fierceness troubled her. "Don't destroy yourself for vengeance. Mahon wouldn't want that, and neither do I."

He shook his head, a small wry smile appearing. "No, I'm the Jor'ellian Commander. Hueil won't escape justice."

Nigel, Mirit, Fraser, Valery, Vidar, Kendrick and Virgil arrived, all showing signs of concern.

"What's this about Mahon? We heard he turned on you and Wren wounded him," said Nigel.

Avatar nodded, grim and lips pressed together.

Eldric emerged from the infirmary. "I confined him to his own room only he insisted upon seeing you," he said to Avatar.

"Will he survive?" asked Wren, tentative.

"Ay, but in what state and capacity, I don't know."

"What do you mean?" asked Nigel, his temper rising. "This is Mahon we're talking about."

"I understand, Sire. I believe Avatar should speak to him first."

"I want to hear from him what happened. If not, how can I explain this to Necie, Angus and the children?"

Avatar placed a steady hand on Nigel's shoulder yet spoke to Eldric. "Is he of any threat?"

"I don't believe so."

"Then we will all speak to him."

Eldric frowned with disapproval, but yielded at Avatar's determination. "Very well, Commander. This way, Sire."

Mahon sat up in bed with his torso and his right hand bandaged. His face and ears were clean of blood. He appeared very pale and weary.

"You sent for me?" asked Avatar in a hollow voice.

"I wasn't expecting anyone else." Discomposure filled his eyes in regard of Nigel. "I'm sorry, Sire. I don't know what came over me." He closed his eyes and swallowed back the dryness in his throat.

"Do you remember anything?"

He shook his head. "I arrived at the outpost, but the next thing I remember is Wren, a bolt, and seeing my dagger poised …"

Wren grabbed Mahon's left hand. "I didn't want to shoot!" Her voice cracked with emotion.

"I know."

"What could cause his memory loss and odd behavior?" asked Mirit

Eldric shook his head. "I couldn't find anything physically wrong with him other than the wounds."

"Wait. I found this on the ground after Avatar picked him up." Wren took the metal piece from her pouch and handed it to Eldric.

Eldric scowled, angry and disgusted. "A mind-reconditioning device."

"No!" exclaimed Mahon in horror. He snatched it from Eldric. He stared in angry disbelief at the device.

Vidar tried to take it from Mahon. "You didn't know! Please, give it to me."

Mahon let go and fell back against the pillows with a lamenting sob. He closed his eyes in an attempt to regain his composure.

"What it is?" asked Mirit.

Vidar's jowls grew tight and copper eyes narrowed in wrath. "Dagar used these to break more stubborn Guardians. It works by being placed behind the ear to connect with a pain nerve. If the Guardian didn't follow instruction, they became subjected to intense pain. This would continue until they submitted or died resisting its influence."

"Some who escaped Dagar's imprisonment and suffered from the device I have helped, others," Eldric paused, "Jor'el had to set free. Their minds ... gone."

"That's what you meant when you said you didn't know what state he would be in," said Fraser.

Eldric replied with sobriety. "Ay, and the fact those who gave in, did so of their own free will."

Mahon looked to Avatar. He hadn't spoken since arriving and his expression remained stoic. "I did not consciously seek to kill you."

Avatar didn't reply.

"You don't believe me."

"I didn't say that."

"I'm not sure if I can believe myself."

"Mahon, Eldric has helped others, he can help you," said Wren.

"No. There is only one way to know for certain if I harbored evil against you or Avatar." He pushed aside the covers, stood at attention to speak clear and direct. "As is my right, I request of you, my mentor, *feucha le teine*."

Avatar's reaction came in the form of increased scrutiny in his silver eyes directed at Mahon.

"*Trial by fire?* What is that?" asked Mirit, only to be ignored.

"Now!" insisted Mahon.

Avatar seized Mahon and they vanished.

"Where did they go?" demanded Nigel.

"To The Fringe. The Trial by Fire is conducted there," said Vidar.

"What is it?" Mirit repeated her question more forcefully.

"The ultimate test of a Guardian's heart and mind. When questions are raised about a Guardian's motive or devotion and the Guardian insists the questions are wrong, they have the right to request Trial by Fire either from their mentor or Kell. The trial will prove the accusations one way or another."

"It is a permanent solution," droned Wren.

"How so?" asked Nigel.

She faulted in answering so Vidar explained. "The Guardian passes through divine fire. If innocent, they survive, if not, they are consumed."

"How many Guardians have survived?"

Vidar somberly shook his head. "None."

***

Suspended between time and space, between the physical world and the heavenlies, they arrived at the Fringe. Avatar held onto Mahon to keep him from swooning, his wound making him weak, almost unconscious.

"Mahon?"

He groaned and lifted his head, eyes blinking to focus. "We're here."

"Are you sure about this?"

Mahon cocked a humorless grin. "No, but it's the only way to be certain." He stood on his own. "Begin."

Avatar stepped forward and looked up into the heavenlies. "Jor'el, I, Avatar, seek an audience on behalf of one who needs your judgment."

A brief pause followed his call during which they waited. A bright light of swirling haze appeared in front of them but no distinguishing facial features only opalescent eyes gazing out from the haze. Avatar knelt. Mahon tried to kneel but barely kept his balance to stay on his feet.

"Your audience is granted. I know why you and Mahon are here."

"Will you test Mahon with your divine fire?"

"Mahon's heart is set on it. What about you?"

"I—I am uncertain. I want to believe, yet I fear the answer."

"Would you hesitate to make the request of Mahon if the situation was reversed?"

"No."

"Then let it be so for him."

"As you command." Avatar rose and stepped back to join Mahon.

The eyes disappeared and the swirling white hazy became a pillar of fire stretching from the Fringe floor up into the heaven. With a deep commanding voice, Jor'el spoke. "Step into the fire, Mahon!"

Before complying, Mahon spoke to Avatar. "No matter the outcome, it has been a honor serving with you and calling you friend."

"And I you."

Mahon took a deep breath and stepped into the fire.

Avatar gripped the hilt of his sword until his knuckles turned white. The flames intensified to the point of obscuring any sign of Mahon. At Mahon's ear piercing cry, Avatar screwed his eyes shut against its meaning. The Fringe exploded in brilliant orange light. The force threw him back twenty feet. He blinked to bring his eyes back into focus. He could only rise to his knees, as his head hurt and his vision spotty. After a moment, he noticed the Fringe returned to its grayish hue with no sign of Jor'el or Mahon. He was alone. Avatar hung his head, as all the pent-up emotions came forth in sobs of sorrow.

"Need some help?"

Avatar's head snapped up at hearing a voice. Momentarily speechless, he gaped at Mahon, who wore a new uniform. "You?"

"I don't look that different." Mahon helped Avatar stand and became engulfed in a bear hug.

"Never scare me like that again!"

Mahon eyes sparkled with his usual impishness swagger when he smiled. "This shows it won't happen."

"If anyone dares to question you, they will answer to me! Now, let's return. Wren will be very relieved."

Chapter 18

K ELL WENT TO ARUNDINE AHEAD OF THE GROUP TO ARRANGE
the meeting. He summoned all Guardian leadership to assemble,
not just Trio Leaders. Waiting on the portico, he watched
Tyrone and the others arrive.

The large domed building of gleaming white marble was located in
the most central part of Allon. Even when dismounting, Ellis stared in
awe at the splendor of Arundine.

"Impressive."

Titus chuckled. "Wait till you go inside."

They followed Tyrone into Arundine. Twelve pillars held up the
dome. Between the pillars stood marble chairs. Under the dome lay a
marble floor interlaid with a map of Allon and the name of each province
in front of its respective chair. Standing beside each chair was the
Guardian Trio leader of the province. Armus, Avatar and Vidar waited
near the elevated platform near the high chair. Tyrone, Angus and Kell
moved to the platform while Titus and Ellis hung back.

Titus whispered to Ellis as he indentified the Trio Leaders. "Priscilla
is Guardian of The Fair Winds from the East Coast."

"She's beautiful," said Ellis. She wore a flowing sea foam and dark green gown perfectly complimenting her fair hair, skin and emerald eyes.

Titus grinned and continued. "Mona, Guardian of Legends of the North Plains. She's a vassal who can change personas to suit any given situation. Callie is a female warrior from the Northern Forest. Elwood is a ranger, who took Auriel's place in the South Plains. You know Nixie from the Meadowlands, Wren of the Southern Forest, Gresham of Midessex and Alrick from the Delta. The grizzled one with the beard is Barnum of the Highlands. He's actually friendly despite his appearance. Chase of the West Coast is the opposite of Gulliver, a quiet mild-tempered sea Guardian. Derwin of the Lowlands and Zadok of the Region of Sanctuary." He stopped at hearing Tyrone speak.

"Thank you all for coming so quickly. Please, be seated."

"We are at your command, Sire," said Barnum.

Tyrone flashed a tolerate smile. "That is one issue for which you were summoned. I am no longer king—" The stunned reactions and comments forced him to call for silence. Once he had their attention again, he proceeded. "Doubtless you heard of Hueil and Ellan's escape. In order to ensure the safety of the royal family and preserve Allon, I chose to abdicate in favor of the only one whose claim can outstrip Ellan of her right to the throne—Nigel."

"Has he accepted?" asked Mona.

"Ay. The abdication and coronation took place at the Temple with Vicar Uriah presiding and seven of the Council Members bearing witness. For the time being, I'm once more Prince Tyrone, only with the extra title of King's Champion." He flashed a wry smile and motioned to his uniform.

"We wondered why you were wearing it," said Mona of herself and Priscilla.

"Complete role reversals on all fronts. Tristine is now the Queen's Champion and still at the Fortress. *King* Nigel and *Queen* Mirit have returned to Waldron to rendezvous with royal troops, Jor'ellians, the forces from Angus, Fagan, Mathias and Ned. Gareth, Zebulon, Braden,

Malcolm, Hollis, Erasmus and Bosley have sided with Ellan. In fact, Mathias launched the West Coast fleet in direct opposition to Hollis and the East Coast fleet. In short, Allon is poised on the brink of civil war."

"What about Sir Hayden?" asked Zadok.

"Driven out of the province by Gareth's troops and Shadow Warriors. They acted before I knew what happened," groused Derwin.

"The same in the Delta," said Alrick.

"Wait," began Callie in thought. "If the Council of Twelve is divided how did seven witness the coronation since the majority went to Ellan?"

"Ellan and Hueil are employing forceful tactics to enlist the aid. Despite that, Erasmus and Bosley sent their signet rings by way of their sons, Eric and Dylan, urging them to pledge their loyalty. As legal representatives, they stood in for their province," said Tyrone.

"Dangerous for them to do. I hate to think what has, or could happen, if they are discovered," said Angus.

"They followed their heart and conscience. For that, Jor'el will look kindly on them," said Armus.

"Time for the Guardian leadership to take our place beside the new king," said Kell

Zadok frowned in dispute. "His highness is our king, not Nigel."

"Nigel is rightful born heir! The Son of Ellis, the Son of Tristan! Jor'el's chosen before me," rebuked Tyrone.

"I don't dispute his heritage. I was there when the Son of Tristan defeated Dagar, but that doesn't change who you are, king of mortals and Guardians."

Tyrone moved from the high chair to accost Zadok. "Do you think I easily yielded the throne? That I didn't want to take to the field and face Hueil? Or have you forgotten Tunlund? You were there also."

"Peace, Zadok!" commanded Kell when the warrior went to reply. "This was done according to Jor'el's law and with the Almighty's blessing. The decision is not open for dispute or debate."

The warrior slapped his sword and bowed his head. "It will be done, Captain. And I'm sorry, I didn't mean to argue."

Kell motioned to Tyrone.

Zadok knelt on one knee. "I apologize, Highness. Sometimes my mouth speaks inadequately what I really mean."

"Rise, Zadok," said Tyrone. "Anymore questions or comments?"

No Trio leader replied, none dared.

"Good, because there is more. Hueil gained brief access to Dagar's nether dimension and called forth wyverns. We permanently sealed it." He motioned between himself and Kell.

Zadok stiffened for action and his eyes betrayed surprise. In fact, all showed signs of surprise and wary concern.

"Wyverns," muttered Mona. She shivered and paled. "They destroyed many of us at the Great Battle."

"And why we must be prepared and united to face them," said Kell.

"How?"

"It will require most of us using our powers to combat whatever Hueil unleashes." Kell turned to Priscilla. "Can you face them again?"

She appeared uneasy in remembrance. "Maybe. But just before your summons arrived, Gulliver sent word that Mathias needs my help."

"We shouldn't prevent her," said Tyrone.

"There is an alternative." Kell closed his eyes.

After a brief moment, a light appeared and revealed a female vassal. She was slender with long black hair of ringlets and bright silver eyes. Priscilla sighed in relief upon sight of her.

"You sent for me, Captain?"

"Highness, this is Wyndy, a weather Guardian like Priscilla. She will be one of our main defenses against the wyverns."

"Wyverns?" Wyndy snorted in annoyance. "You couldn't call upon me for something simple or fun. Just out of blue, I'm supposed to face wyverns. You've got a lot to learn about timing, Kell."

Tyrone suppressed a chuckle. "She is as contrary to you as Priscilla."

"Worse, she's a whirlwind of emotion."

Wyndy forced a toothy grin. "Please, ignore the captain's cynicism, Highness. I'm happy to be of service to you."

"We have a lot to do before that happens," said Kell. "All Leaders are to gather their forces and meet at Waldron as quickly as possible to begin planning. You also report to Waldron," he said to Wyndy. "Along with the Shadow Warriors and wyverns, Ellan can muster at least one hundred and fifty thousand mortal troops."

"Combined we can only support Nigel with one hundred thousand," said Tyrone. He soberly sighed, his face growing disconcerted. "This will be a bloody and deadly conflict among our people."

"Fighting and killing Allonians goes against why we were created," said Barnum.

"Even when we fought Marcellus and Dagar," added Zadok.

For a brief moment, Tyrone studied Zadok. This time the Guardian appeared sympathetic. "Now, go," he barely spoke above a whisper. He turned to approach the high chair, unable to watch their departure.

"Indeed, he is a brave man," said Ellis in admiration.

Titus joined Tyrone. No words spoken as father and son regarded each other. Nothing could be said since both knew what had to be done. After a moment, Tyrone spoke. "Time we left for Waldron. I'm certain Nigel must be wondering about us."

"Highness," began Avatar. He, Vidar and Wren approached Tyrone. "There is something we need to tell you and Kell about Mahon."

"Mahon?" echoed Angus. "Has something happened to him?"

Ellis, Armus, Egan and Ridge waited to one side, listening.

"I don't know all the details since he can't remember, but somehow he was captured at the outpost. As a result, Hueil altered him—"

"What?" exclaimed Kell. Armus drew alongside Kell, mirroring his concern. Egan and Ridge came to Armus' shoulders, equally curious.

"Lieutenant Brewster reported that Mahon wasn't at the outpost, and how you and the prince believed him injured. I used my sense to confirm it. Only I felt something terribly wrong, as if he died but wasn't dead. Wren and I went to the outpost and … he attacked us."

"He attacked you not me," said Wren. She explained to Kell and Armus, "We were forced to take action and bring him down."

"He's dead?" asked Angus, shocked.

"No! Thank Jor'el, but I had to shoot!" She turned back to Kell, pleading. "To disarm and disable not kill. He had Avatar on the ground, a dagger to his throat. He looked so surprised at me," Her voice cracked.

"You had no choice. I would have done the same," said Vidar.

Kell's compassionate focus shifted to Avatar. "He tried to kill you?"

Avatar gave a curt nod. "By the look in his eyes when he first attacked and proclaimed destruction of his master's enemies. Yet throughout the ordeal, he waivered between attacking and confusion."

"How?" asked Tyrone.

"Wren found this." Vidar pulled the device from his pouch.

Kell went rigid with intense anger and snatched it from Vidar. Armus' rage showed in gripping the hilt of his sword and a fierce sneer.

"What is it?"

"A mind-reconditioning device," said Vidar. "Without the Guardian's knowledge, it is placed behind an ear and pressed into a pain nerve. Then the reconditioning starts. Obey and all is well, disobey or resist and suffer intense pain until the Guardian either yields or is destroyed."

Avatar added, "For some reason it didn't completely hinder his reactions or inhibit his conscience. When Wren's action prompted a bewildered response, I commanded him to remember me. He became horrified at seeing his dagger at my throat. He collapsed and we took him to Eldric."

"So, he's just badly injured," said Angus.

Avatar frowned and said, "Not exactly. When he came to himself at the infirmary he demanded his right of Trial by Fire." He added an explanation for the benefit of the mortals. "It's a divine instrument of judgment to determine a Guardian's true heart and state of mind. Since Mahon couldn't remember anything, he questioned himself whether he yielded willingly or was forced to act against his will. He claimed his right to determine the guilt or innocence of his actions."

Armus, Ridge and Egan all looked in dreaded anticipation to Kell.

The captain remained focused on Avatar. "Has it been done yet?" he asked in a thick voice.

A small smile appeared on Avatar's face. "Ay, and he survived! Which proved him innocent and Jor'el restored him to his position."

The relief on Kell's face was immediate. Armus released his sword with a loud exhale. Egan smiled and Ridge said, "Thank Jor'el."

"Indeed," agreed Angus. "For a moment I feared I would have terrible news to tell Necie and the children."

"It is bad enough what Mahon suffered," said Wren.

"And having him turn on you," said Kell.

Avatar's silver eyes narrowed in wrath. "One more reason to stop Hueil once and for all."

Kell gripped Avatar's shoulder. "With Jor'el's help, we shall."

"We should return to Waldron. Nigel wants to know everything as soon as possible," said Vidar.

"Nigel? Tristine," said Armus with a chuckle. He spoke to Tyrone, "She told me to tell you not to do anything foolish in front of your son."

"Too late!" said Titus. He laughed and Ellis tried to hide a smile.

Tyrone took hold of the back of Titus' neck. "Tell her, we're fine."

"Ay, sir," said Titus. His teeth gritted against the corrective squeeze.

Armus grinned, bowed and stepped back from the group to vanish.

"Do you want us to take you, the duke, prince and Lord Ellis to Waldron?" asked Avatar, indicating himself, Wren and Vidar.

Tyrone thought before answering, "No. We're not done yet. There is a sense I need to investigate and perhaps learn the source of my vision."

"Vision?"

Tyrone waved aside Avatar's question. "Return to Waldron and report to Nigel. Tell him, we'll join him as soon as possible. Give this to Eldric to be destroyed." He gave Avatar the device.

"Willingly." Avatar stepped back with Wren and Vidar. Their vanishing created a brighter flash of light than a single departure.

"What do we need to investigate?" asked Angus.

"The sense is vague, but I want to head north."

"To the ruins or outpost?"

Tyrone shook his head. "I'm not sure yet. Images of them are in the vision along with fire. The sooner we get started the better." He led them outside. The sun sank in the afternoon sky.

"Three hours until sundown, Highness," said Ridge.

"Then we'll travel north for three hours." Tyrone mounted.

When all were ready, Ridge led the way from Arundine. Again, Kell lingered to scan the perimeter. He ran to catch up to Tyrone.

"We're being followed. My guess is Mannix and Locan."

"I wondered when you would say so."

"How long have you sensed them?"

"Since arriving at the ruins. You?"

Kell scowled. "At the outpost I got a strong sense of their presence. Although I suspected the possibility when leaving the Fortress."

"Ay. Perhaps they were involved in capturing Mahon. Before then it was vague and more suspicion."

"Nice to know I'm completely inept."

<hr>

Mannix and Locan retreated from their vantage point near Arundine and vanished when Kell nearly spotted them. They reappeared outside Roxbury. Tents and banners of various mortal forces stretched across the fields. Nearest the manor house were the Shadow Warriors and wyverns. They warily sidestepped the beasts to enter the manor.

Gareth, Zebulon, Erasmus, Bosley and an unfamiliar mortal left the study before they entered. By various maps, tankards and instruments of planning scattered over the table it was a long and involved meeting. Ellan stood by the window, an impatient expression on her profile. Hueil hovered over the table, his arms folded and staring at a map of Allon.

"Majesty. My lord," said Locan.

"At last. Some intelligence. Report," snapped Ellan.

"Kell and the half-breed met with the Trio Leaders at Arundine. No doubt to inform them of state of things. At least that is our guess."

"Guess? You don't know?" demanded Hueil.

"We couldn't use our power to eavesdrop or alert them to our presence. Our orders are to follow and keep watch on the half-breed."

"Where is he now?"

"Heading north and not toward Waldron."

Hueil grinned with pleasure. "My visions are having the desired effect. He wants to know what I'm going to do."

"Maybe, my lord, however," said Locan with caution, "we were surprised to see Avatar at Arundine."

"What? Mahon failed? How is that possible?" Her frustration propelled her to confront Hueil.

"He may not have acted yet. Any word of Mahon?" asked Hueil

"No, my lord."

Ellan became irate. "If Mahon doesn't succeed—"

"My dear, there are other ways to deal with Avatar before battle."

"I hope so." She stormed back to the window.

Locan and Mannix warily watched the interaction. Hueil sneered at them. "Return to following the half-breed!"

"What good are spies if they bring back useless information?" she complained after Locan and Mannix vanished.

"Not useless to know about the Trio Leaders or that the half-breed isn't on his way to Waldron. In fact, this may be the time to implement the next phase in our plan by interviewing your nephew this evening."

"Ay, dispatch Phelan and Fitch."

Chapter 19

FRASER FELT SORE AND TIRED AFTER TWO DAYS OF GRUELING training. Valery tripping him hurt more then he wanted to admit, including his head snapping back and hitting the floor. Still, he attended dinner and made polite, if short, conversation. He sighed in relief when slipping under the covers and into his nice soft bed.

"Are you sure you don't want me to fetch a pain remedy from Eldric?" asked Kendrick.

"No," moaned Fraser with a yawn. "I just want to sleep."

"Very well. Goodnight."

Fraser grumbled something, rolled over and fell asleep.

Kendrick extinguished the lamp. He moved to his customary place when something struck him from behind and rendered him unconscious.

"Be quick," said Phelan to Fitch. He held the shielding medal.

Fitch touched Fraser's head. The boy stirred but didn't wake. In an instant, Fitch shape-shifted into Fraser. "You can take him now," he said to Phelan.

"You can speak?"

"In mortal form, ay. Hurry, before the Guardian wakes."

Phelan muttered a few words in the Ancient and lifted Fraser out of bed. The young man remained asleep. Phelan stepped back from the bed and vanished. Fitch got in bed and assumed Fraser's sleeping position.

A flash of light woke Kendrick. He bolted up and reached for his sword. He blinked to focus his eyes and saw no one other than Fraser, who slept peacefully. Something briefly knocked him unconscious. Why? Although Fraser appeared unharmed, he sensed uneasiness about the boy.

Kendrick took a deep breath, closed his eyes and stretched out his senses. Indeed the boy's essence went from the room to someplace else. That didn't make sense with Fraser in bed. Still, something didn't feel right. He opened the door and looked out into the hall. Royal guards stood their post undisturbed.

"Corporal. Have you seen anyone unusual in the hall?"

"No, sir. All is quiet. Is there a problem with the prince?"

"No. Under the circumstances I wanted to make certain all is well."

"Ay, sir. Is there anything else?"

"No." Kendrick closed the door and went back to the bed. "You're here, yet not here. With what happened to Mahon, I don't I like that," he thought aloud.

He could alert Avatar. With the boy in bed, how could he explain his concern? All appeared well and guards saw nothing. The only option was to quickly follow the strange sense to discover the reason, and hopefully return before anyone noticed his absence.

He placed a hand on Fraser's head and spoke the Ancient. "Sleep so deep as to remember nothing until I return." At first, he felt a tensing to his voice, then a fading into the relaxation of a very deep slumber. Satisfied, he vanished.

Kendrick reappeared in a dimly lit unfamiliar hallway near a window. Boisterous voices came from outside. He carefully looked out the window. Down in a small courtyard, Shadow Warriors taunted a wyvern!

He pulled back from the window. Where did the sense lead him? Even without stretching his senses, he felt Fraser's essence down the hall.

Quietly drawing his sword, he stayed close to the wall and avoided any light. Near a room with the door partly opened, he heard a female speaking. He positioned himself to peek inside. To his surprise, Fraser lay on a couch asleep. How could the boy be in two places at once? His befuddlement was short-lived at hearing a familiar male voice speak.

"Quiet! Someone is nearby."

"Hueil!" hissed Kendrick, he thought low enough not to be heard,. That wasn't the case. Hueil's head snapped around to the door. Kendrick acted. He kicked in the door intent on rescuing his charge.

The sudden noise woke Fraser. "Kendrick?" he asked in confusion.

By a wave of his hand, Hueil sent Kendrick flying across the room into the far wall. Phelan rushed in, sword drawn and attacked Kendrick.

Fearful Fraser watched. Ellan moved to block his view. "It's all right."

"Aunt Ellan?"

"Ay, my dear boy. Lie back down." She tried to coax him as he fought to see what was happening.

"It's Kendrick. Where am I?"

Hueil touched Fraser's head and said, "*Cadail.*" The boy fell asleep.

Kendrick avoided Phelan's attack by diving under the Shadow Warrior's blade. He managed to get to one knee when Phelan charged. He shoved the Warrior back and stood to go the offensive. Again Hueil sent him flying, only this time out the door, across the hall and crashing through a window. He landed in the small courtyard below where he saw the Shadow Warriors and wyvern. He lay winded and dazed. He took a large gulp of air.

"Well, what have we here?" said a Shadow Warrior.

Phelan appeared at the broken window. "Kill him!"

The Shadow Warriors drew their swords. When one thrust down at him, Kendrick rolled away and would have kept rolling but hit a pillar of an archway. He scrambled to his feet and gripped his sword in both hands. He parried blows from two Warriors and thrust to make them retreat so he could advance.

While his companions engaged Kendrick, one Warrior smiled and moved toward the chained wyvern. The creature growled and gurgled at him. "You want to have fun with a Guardian?" The wyvern grew still so he unfastened the chains and quickly stepped back. "The wyvern's loose!" he shouted in warning.

An ear-piercing war cry filled the courtyard. The wyvern drew its sword. The other Warriors vanished in dimension travel, giving it a clear path to Kendrick. Vanishing wasn't a bad idea. Suddenly, a dagger struck Kendrick high in the middle of his chest. The Warrior who freed the wyvern threw it.

"Goodbye, Guardian." The Warrior vanished.

The wyvern swung at him, forcing Kendrick to make clumsy defense. It sent him sprawling to the cobblestone. The impact drove the dagger deeper into his chest, up to the guard. He gasped in great pain. He grabbed the hilt and yanked it out, crying in angry agony. He was lifted into the air and came face-to-face with the salivating wyvern. He thrust the dagger into the wyvern's body. The creature screamed in furious pain, dropped him and backed away to deal with the dagger. He didn't have the strength to battle the wyvern. Although risky to life-force, he used what strength he had left to vanish in dimension travel. He reappeared in a small grove near a hollow stump and immediately fainted.

"Is he dead?" Hueil asked Phelan when the Warrior's return.

"They set the wyvern on him."

Hueil chuckled then looked to Ellan. She sat on the couch beside the sleeping Fraser. "You can speak to him now."

"Are you certain he will believe this is a dream? Especially if his Guardian is dead."

"Don't worry. The boy is weak minded. He obeyed me and went to sleep immediately. Not to mention being swayed by your performance."

She grinned. "You should leave. Remember, he thinks you are my evil captor."

"We'll be right outside the door."

Once alone, she tapped his face. "Fraser. It's time to wake up."

He stirred and opened his eyes. He became confused at seeing her. "Aunt Ellan?" He glanced around. "Where am I?"

"Don't you know? You came to see me."

"I did?"

"Ay. You said you had news of your mother." She helped him sit-up.

"My mother is at the Fortress. At least she was when we left."

"You promised to speak to her on my behalf. Have you not kept your word?"

"I haven't seen her since we left. How did I get here?"

"Kendrick. You fainted from dimension travel."

"Kendrick? Oh, ay, but I thought he was in trouble."

She seized him and drew close to speak. "Hueil," she spoke his name with dread, "discovered Kendrick's presence and he left for safety."

"Then how will I get back? And without Uncle knowing."

"Have no fear. I told you Phelan is helping me. Now what did you want to tell that you took such a risk?"

He thought for a moment, still befuddled. "I can't recall."

"Oh, Fraser, there is no time for hesitation! Hueil may arrive at any moment," she said in despair.

"Truly, I don't recall."

"There must be something or why come here? You said your mother is at the Fortress, is she alone?" she spoke with hurried, urgent prodding.

"No. Eli and Mikaela are with her, along with Aunt Necie and her children. Oh, and Jillian."

"Jillian?"

"Lord Fagan's daughter. She is betrothed to Titus."

She cast a nervous glance toward the door and asked, "Anyone else? Guardians?"

"Armus. But he's always with mother. Jade and Skylar are with Eli and Mikaela. That's all the Guardians. The rest are priests and a few Jor'ellians. The majority of Knights came with us to Waldron."

She kept her up fretful act of speech. "What of Tyrone? Surely he wouldn't just leave Tristine."

"Father is doing reconnaissance. Something about ruins."

"Oh, Fraser, can't you tell me anymore? My life depends upon it!"

"Honest, Aunt, that's all I know. I would tell you if did. In fact, I'd help you to escape if I could."

"You don't understand! Hueil wants to take the Fortress. Our family is in danger."

"We must warn them. I'll tell Uncle and he'll send word to the Fortress." He scrambled to get off the couch when she stopped him.

"He won't listen, especially if he learns I gave you the information."

"I'll make him listen," he said with determination and stood.

"Wait. I may have a better idea. How well do you write?"

"Well, enough."

"I mean like Nigel." She grabbed his right hand upon which he wore his royal signet ring. "To use this to send a warning."

"You mean forge Uncle's hand and seal?"

"He won't listen, so what choice do we have? You don't want them to die, do you?"

"No!"

She ushered him to a desk. "If we save them, Nigel will think better and believe me. Believe *us*. You do believe me, don't you, dear Fraser?"

"Ay. Why would you willingly subject yourself to such evil?"

"Indeed, why?" she repeated with a wry smile. "Now, sit." She grabbed paper, pen and ink. "Write what I tell you."

He arranged himself to take dictation. "I'm ready."

"How does he normally address your mother in a letter?"

He smiled and wrote while speaking, "My dearest sister."

Ellan forced a smile and repeated, "My dearest sister, I hasten to write and warn you of a plot to take the Fortress. Unfortunately, Tyrone has been unable to seal the ruins and Hueil's strength grows. I fear there is no place safe in Allon for you, Necie, Jillian and the children. I urge you all to head for Melwynn by way of the Highland road. Alas, I can't spare any forces to help you, so take only the bare necessities and do not hesitate." She watched him write. "How does he sign it?"

"As always, your loving brother, Nigel." Fraser signed it. "How do you know about Father and the ruins? I haven't heard."

"It doesn't matter!" she hastily said and reached for the sealing wax. "Warning them is of paramount importance. Now, hurry, use your ring. We've taken too much time already."

He just finished making the seal with his ring on the seam of the folded letter when they heard Hueil's voice.

Ellan gasped in fear and snatched the letter. "He's coming!"

Fraser bolted to his feet. "Let me get you out of here."

"No time." The door opened and both froze in fearful anticipation. Phelan appeared. Ellan shoved Fraser toward the Warrior. "Return with Phelan and try, try to convince Nigel and Tristine I mean no harm! I will do what I can to stall Hueil with misinformation."

"I will, Aunt, I promise. What about the letter?"

"I'll take care of it. Now, you must leave."

The door burst open and Hueil stood in the threshold.

"Go!" she snapped. In a flash, Phelan and Fraser vanished.

Once the light faded, she laughed, long and loud.

"What a marvelous performance, my dear. If I didn't know you better, you could have fooled me."

"He was too easy." She produced the letter.

"When Fitch returns, he'll execute part two."

⁕

Back at Fraser's room in Waldron, the door opened and Virgil arrived in making his nightly rounds. After taking a few soft steps into the room he didn't see Kendrick. Fraser lay in bed, so he approached.

"Highness. Prince Fraser." No response so he shook the young man by the shoulder. "Fraser?"

There came a groan and a groggy answer. "What?"

"Is everything all right? I don't see Kendrick."

Fraser lifted his head and his brows furrowed at not seeing Kendrick. His fell back on the pillow. "Oh, headache. Need remedy."

Virgil grinned. "I see, too much fun at training so he went to Eldric. Well, I'm sorry I woke you. I just wanted make sure all was well." He left.

The door just closed upon Virgil's departure when Phelan arrived in the room near the terrace doors carrying an unconscious Fraser. This time with no light, they just appeared after removing the shielding medal. Phelan carefully looked about the room.

"Fitch. We're back," he harshly whispered.

"Eh?"

"You look awful, are you all right?"

"Kendrick put me to sleep. Rather, him to sleep."

"Well, you won't have to worry about Kendrick for phase two."

Fitch/Fraser got out of bed. He held back the covers while Phelan put the real Fraser back in bed.

When the boy began to stir, Phelan spoke in the Ancient and Fraser went back to sleep. He and Fitch stepped back. Holding Fitch by the shoulder, Phelan put the shielding medal on and they disappeared.

<hr />

Tyrone stirred uneasily in his bedroll. Several hours ago they stopped for the night. Although he didn't anticipate sleep, he fell into a deep disturbing dream. This time the fire became more distinct with frightened and screaming children. Some were being chased by Shadow Warriors, while others trapped by flames. The faces became clearer: Mikaela, Eli, Daria and the other children! Tristine cried out for him. He couldn't wake up and he couldn't help. He thrashed about in an effort to reach them. The flames grew larger and intense until they finally obscured the children and Tristine. Hueil's face appeared in the fire laughing and mocking then transformed into Nigel's face. Someone grabbed him and he sat up. He breathed heavy in fear and drenched in sweat. For a moment he stared at who woke him.

"Titus? You're here? And unhurt."

"Ay. Father, what is it? You look horrible."

Kell, Angus, Egan, Ridge and Ellis gathered about, also concerned.

"The vision again?" asked Kell.

Tyrone nodded, trying to regain his breath and composure. "The Fortress, fire, they are all in danger! We must leave immediately." He held onto Titus and tried to rise, but fell to his knees in pain. Titus supported him. "I can't move."

"Why? What's wrong?"

It took moment to reply, as Tyrone appeared he would faint. "I don't know. You and Ellis must go to the Fortress immediately. Have Egan and Ridge take you by dimension travel. I'll follow with Angus and Kell as soon as I can."

"I can't leave you like this."

"Kell is with me. Your mother, Jillian and the rest need help. Now, go! Egan." He motioned to the Guardian, who responded by drawing Titus to his feet.

Chapter 20

T RISTINE DIDN'T WANT TO WAKE WHEN SOMEONE NUDGED HER shoulder. She hadn't slept well since Tyrone, Nigel and the others left so Armus had the Jor'ellian physician fix her a sleeping draft.

"Go away," she muttered into the pillow and turned from the light.

"You can't get rid of me that easy." Armus held her shoulder. "Besides, Fraser is here."

"Fraser," she sleepily repeated then her eyes snapped open. "Fraser!"

"He says Nigel sent him."

She sat up and became blinded by the light. "Let him in."

For a moment the light was out of her eye then she heard a voice.

"Mother, Uncle sent me with this letter for you." He gave it to her.

"What time is it?" She rubbed her eyes before reading the letter.

"Four o'clock, I think."

Armus held the lantern for her to read. She blinked a couple of times to focus on the letter's contents. "Oh no," she murmured.

"What?" asked Armus and she gave him the letter.

"He says Tyrone failed at the ruins and Hueil is heading this way. He wants me to take the others to Melwynn immediately."

"The Highland road is the fastest and safest route. I'll see what Jor'ellians Uriah can spare." Armus placed the letter by the lantern on the bedside table and departed.

"You must hurry, Mother!"

"Ay." She tossed aside the covers "Go wake Necie and Jillian while I get dressed."

Fraser moved quicker than normal in following instructions. Eli woke Mikaela while Jillian went with Fraser to the other apartment to help Necie and her children. Fraser quickly returned to find Eli and Mikaela in the main room.

"Where are Jade and Skylar?" asked Fraser, somewhat annoyed.

"They went to help Armus. Fraser, what is this about?" asked Eli.

"No time to explain, we must hurry."

"Where are Father and Titus?" asked Mikaela, trying not to yawn.

"Stop asking so many questions, just do as you're told!"

Hurt, she pouted. Eli scolded Fraser. "No need to be mean. It's bad enough to wake her and travel in the cold night."

Fraser snarled with great annoyance.

Tristine emerged from the bedchamber and fastened the quiver over her shoulder. "Is everyone awake?"

"Ay. Jillian is helping Aunt Necie." Fraser spied the dark metal arrows in the quiver. "Stygian arrows?"

"Of course. I'm not going hunting." She noticed Mikaela upset and knelt. "I know this is difficult, but it is for our safety."

"Fraser yelled at her," said Eli.

Irate, she scolded her sons. "This isn't the time for childish arguing!"

"Fire!" they heard shouting from the hallway.

"I smell smoke," said Eli.

Mikaela screamed and pointed to the room where she and Eli had been sleeping.

"Quickly! Get out." Tristine lifted Mikaela and handed her to Eli.

Fraser reached the door and flicked his fingers. Click. "It's locked!"

Tristine pushed him aside. "Find the key!"

"Now your room is on fire!" said Eli.

Tristine tried the open the door, but felt the heat and had to let go. Smoke filled the room. Mikaela coughed and buried her head in Eli's shoulder.

"I can't find it!" said Fraser, making as if looking around.

The flames from both bedrooms were now in the main room.

Tristine banged on the door and shouted, "Armus! Armus!"

"What about the windows?" asked Eli between coughs. He used his hands to shield Mikaela's face.

"Too high."

A flash of light and Armus appeared.

"Get the children out!" she said, her words choking.

Armus took Eli and Mikaela and vanished.

"Fraser?" she called. The smoke grew thick and heavy. She fought to breathe and see. A diffused flash of light pierced the smoke. She started gasping, sank to her knees then collapsed.

The courtyard buzzed with chaotic activity. Priests, soldiers and servants ran to put out the fire engulfing the top two floors of the armory. Armus laid Tristine on the ground nearest the stable where the family gathered. Her eyes closed, face and clothes smudged with smoke and ash.

"Mama?" sobbed a worried Mikaela. Jillian held her while Eli helped Necie, Jade and Skylar with the younger children.

"She just fainted," said Armus with a soft reassuring smile.

Uriah rushed over. "Is she all right?"

"Ay." Armus urged her to wake. "Tristine."

She moved then opened her eyes. "Armus. Where are the children?"

"They're here and safe."

She held onto him and sat up to look at the children. "Fraser? You did get him out of the room, didn't you?"

"No. When I went back for you he was gone."

"But I saw a light!"

"Probably Kendrick."

"Ay," she said a bit calmer.

"Are you well enough to travel, Highness?" asked Uriah.

She motioned for Armus to help her stand. Once on her feet, she took a moment to catch her breath and check her balance. "Ay. What about the fire?"

"We'll take care of it. All is ready for your journey. Unfortunately, I can only spare a dozen knights and one wagon for the children. I don't travel in a carriage, and other resources went with your brother."

"With the Guardians and having to travel fast, that should be enough. Jade, Skylar, take Necie and children to the wagon. The rest of us will ride."

It took fifteen minutes for everyone to be situated. From the saddle, Tristine watched priests, guards and servants battling to contain the fire.

"I suppose Kendrick took Fraser back to Waldron," she said.

"Most likely," said Armus. "Hopefully we can put some distance between us and the Fortress before dawn."

"Lead on."

Armus ran through the open postern gate. Tristine, Jillian and Eli kicked their horses into a canter to keep pace with the Guardian. Skylar drove the wagon. He snapped the reins for speed. Mounted Jor'ellians guarded the rear.

After their departure, Uriah noticed the fire gaining strength. He raced to where his assistant supervised the attempt to deal with fire.

"I though it was under control?"

"We did too, but it somehow reignited."

"If the flames reach the gunnery storehouse the gunpowder will explode!" Uriah raced to the storehouse adjacent to the armory. Someone ran to the back of the storehouse. "You there!" He pursued the individual when a small explosion knocked him back a few steps. Flames rose from the west end of the gunnery storehouse. "Get that fire out before it ignites the whole building!"

They scrambled to carry out his orders. Uriah continued after the person. He reached the corner and caught a glimpse of a person resembling Fraser, and who vanished in a flash of light.

"Vicar!"

Uriah heard the call, yet hesitated in replying for being baffled.

"Vicar!" the voice grew closer.

"Highness?" he said, surprised at seeing Titus, Ellis, Egan and Ridge.

"Where are my mother, Jillian, Aunt Necie and the children?"

"They left. Out the postern gate a few minutes ago."

Titus and Ellis began to leave when Uriah called, "Wait! Is Fraser with you?"

"No. He should be at Waldron."

"He was just here."

"Why would he be here?"

"He said the king sent him. But why start a fire?"

Titus grew defensive. "Are accusing Fraser of starting the fire?"

Uriah became insistent in speech. "It's all confusing. As Jor'el is my witness, he ran from the gunnery storehouse a mere few seconds before it exploded. I followed him here, and he vanished."

"Was Kendrick with him?" asked Egan.

"No, *and* mortals just don't vanish."

Ear-piercing cries came from above. Wyverns dove from various directions. Priests, Jor'ellians and Guardians scrambled to repel the attack. For the priests, it was a futile gesture against the sword-wielding beasts. The Jor'ellians faired better, lasting longer against the Dark Way creatures. It took the combined strength of Egan and Ridge to keep the creatures from reaching Uriah, Titus and Ellis.

The Guardians killed four wyverns when the hissing and whizzing of arrows came from over the walls. Ellis fell to his knees and grabbed his left arm when an arrow shot passed him. Titus moved to help his friend when Egan jerked him out of the way. Two arrows landed where Titus had been standing.

"Ellis?" called Titus.

Ridge examined Ellis. "Nasty flesh wound. No serious damage."

"Shadow Warriors!" shouted a Jor'ellian.

Through the front gate Shadow Warriors rushed in.

"Egan! Get them out of here! Find Tristine," shouted Uriah before rushing to join the defense.

Tristine and the others traveled a half-mile from the Fortress when ear-piercing cries halted their progress. In the light of dawn, Wyverns dove at the Fortress and flames rose over the walls. Then came the sound of whizzing arrows.

"The Fortress is under attack!" said Eli.

"Nigel warned us," said Tristine.

Armus drew his sword. "Jor'ellians, form on me! We'll make a defensive line. Go! And don't look back." He slapped the rump of Tristine's horse.

She obeyed. Mikaela and Daria screamed when the wagon lurched forward. Avery tried to comfort his sister and cousin. Galen and Spencer whimpered in fear at being jolted about. Necie held the twins. Tristine's horse was the first to cross the bridge over a small river swollen by the recent rains. Jillian and Eli came after her with the wagon behind him.

A familiar voice shouted, "Now!"

From the shadowy side of the road, rushed three Shadow Warriors. Tristine violently jerked the reins. The horse skidded and reared, tossing her hard to the road. Eli veered his horse aside to avoid trampling her. Jillian screamed when a Shadow Warrior seized her horse, stopping the animal. She fell off and knocked unconscious from impact with the ground.

Two arrows killed the wagon horses in mid-stride. Skylar tried to keep the wagon under control, as the momentum made it slide sideways. The rear end behind the right wheel slammed into the first bridge rail. The hatch broke off and flew down the steep incline to the river. The wagon didn't stop moving until both rear wheels were off the edge. Jade grabbed Galen and Spencer to keep them from falling out.

"Avery! Slowly move toward me with the girls. Easy!" said Necie.

Skylar started to get down from the seat when the wagon slipped.

"No! Stay!" shouted Jade. "Your weight is all that is holding it still." He sat back down. "I'll get them off, you stay put."

Already holding Galen and Spencer, Jade carefully lifted the boys out of the wagon and onto the road beside the bridge.

Up ahead, Shadow Warriors attacked the others. Skylar saw it the same time Jade did.

"Hurry! They won't last too long," he urged.

The Shadow Warrior released Jillian's horse and it bolted. He drew his sword and advanced upon Jillian.

"Leave off!"

The Warrior felt Titus' sword slice open his side. With a great growl of anger, he went after Titus. Egan intercepted the Warrior.

Titus fell to his knees beside Jillian and gently turned her over. She was very pale with a bloody gash on her forehead. "Jillian?" He gathered her in his arms and heard a loud groan. Her eyes blinked and opened.

"Titus?"

"Ay. Thank Jor'el, you're alive."

"Look out!" she cried.

He ducked and shielded her as another Shadow Warrior attacked.

Ellis jumped the Warrior in an effort to protect Titus and Jillian. The Warrior tossed him aside like a rag doll. Ellis landed hard on his back, completely knocking the wind out of him. The Warrior advanced. Ellis couldn't move and desperately tried to recover his breath.

"Stay down," Titus told Jillian and raced to Ellis' aid. His sword swipe clipped the Warrior's arm enough to deflect the blow at Ellis. The Warrior turned his attention to Titus. Although being part Guardian made him stronger than most mortals, it was still difficult handling a Shadow Warrior, but Titus wouldn't yield.

Ellis slowly regained his breath and turned over onto his side. Someone stood near a tree. "Fraser?" Upon meeting his gaze, Fraser fled into the trees. Ellis pushed himself up, intent on following, but halted at hearing a girl scream.

At the bridge, four Shadow Warriors attacked Jade and Skylar. Necie and most of the children were huddled at the end of the bridge. Mikaela remained in the wagon.

Tristine scrambled to her feet when Ridge blocked the Shadow Warrior from reaching her. She didn't have time to react to the ranger's arrival for seeing what was happening at the wagon. She armed her bow and fired at one of the Shadow Warriors attacking Jade and Skylar.

The arrow flew between the Guardians and struck the Warrior squarely in the chest. The force sent him into the wagon. His weight shoved it over the edge before he vanished in the grey light of demise.

"Mikaela!" shouted Necie.

Ellis raced to the bridge. Part of the wagon sank beneath the water, while other parts floated on the current. A head broke through the water. "Mikaela!" He rushed down the incline, lost his footing and slipped the whole way to the shore.

Mikaela grabbed onto a piece of the wagon lodged between two rocks in the middle of the river about three hundred yards from the bridge. "Ellis! Help!"

Despite the swift current, he knew how to swim. He took off his sword, cloak and boots. He waded out as far as he could before starting to swim. It proved difficult, as his arm ached from the earlier wound. Fortunately, the current helped to carry him toward her.

"Hurry! I'm slipping!" she called.

Just when she came within arm's reach, she fell off the board, pulled underwater by the current. Ellis dove after her. A few seconds later, he broke the surf with an unconscious Mikaela in tow. He started for shore. A large part of the board wedged in the rocks broke loose and struck him in the back of the head. They slipped underwater.

"No!" cried Tristine. "Jade!"

Before Jade could act, a flash of light appeared in the water near where Ellis and Mikaela submerged. Armus. He dove underwater and brought them up. Jade appeared on the opposite shore to help Armus. Ridge joined her. She took Mikaela, the girl unconscious. Ridge helped a gasping and staggering Ellis. Not wanting to climb the incline, Armus, Jade and Ridge vanished. They reappeared with the others, now gathered at the end of the bridge near the wagon. Weak kneed, exhausted and pale, Ellis collapsed onto his rump, breathing hard.

Jillian sat beside him. "Are you badly hurt?"

He couldn't answer. Instead, he leaned on her and she held him.

Ridge knelt to examine Ellis. He flinched when the ranger touched his head. "Along with the arm wound, you have a bump on the back of your head."

"Mikaela?" Ellis managed to ask.

Jade and Tristine tended to Mikaela. She regained unconsciousness, very pale, felt cool with lips and eyes lids blue. She shivered and jerked.

"I'll take her to Eldric." Jade picked up Mikaela, stood and vanished.

"We need to get the rest of you to safety also," said Armus.

Upon closer inspection, Tristine noticed Armus' battered and bruised appearance. Concerned, she looked passed him. "Where are the others?"

"Dead," he said in sober reply.

"Oh, merciful heaven," murmured Necie. "By why attack children?"

"I saw Fraser," said Ellis.

"Where?" asked Titus.

He sat up to reply. "Like Uriah, I saw him in the trees during the attack." He pointed across the bridge.

"Of course Uriah saw Fraser. He came with a letter from Nigel warning of the attack and urging us to leave for Melwynn. Kendrick took him back to Waldron so you couldn't have seen him," said Tristine.

Ellis stood, yet unsteady. "No, Highness. The Vicar said Fraser ran from the gunnery storehouse before it exploded. When he followed, Fraser vanished. The Vicar didn't see Kendrick."

"Kendrick rescued him from the fire in our apartment," she insisted. "Did you see him?"

She paused in though then said, "No. I assumed so by a flash of light through the smoke."

"But Uriah and I saw Fraser." He blinked at pain caused by passion.

She became frustrated yet compassionate due to his injury. "It's too dangerous for us to stand out here arguing."

"It is rather odd he is seen where disaster happens."

Armus stepped in before Tristine's anger exploded. "We can figure it out at Melwynn." He took hold of her arm, only she pushed him off.

"Take Necie, Jillian and the children. I'm going to Waldron to speak to Nigel and Fraser and get to the bottom of this."

"Ellis and I will go with you. After all, Father sent us to help."

"Where is he?"

"On his way. He sent us ahead when he sensed danger, and was incapacitated."

"How so?"

"No wounds, just something to do with a vision he had of a fire. Kell is with him."

The news made her more determined. "Do as I say," she told Armus.

"It will take all of us and I won't leave you vulnerable."

Titus intervened by placing a staying hand on Tristine's shoulder. "We'll wait in the cover of the trees until Armus returns."

She scowled at him and spoke in reluctant agreement. "Ay."

Back at the Fortress, Kell, Tyrone and Angus arrived. The lightning-quick attack ended and most of the fires lay smoldering. Tyrone stood near the main gate, surveying the dead priests, Jor'ellians and servants. Angus and Kell moved among the bodies.

"Shadow Warriors, stygian arrows and wyverns did this," said Kell.

Angus squatted at seeing something among the debris. Daria's doll. He fought a sob of sorrow and stood. "Tyrone," he said in a thick voice.

Tyrone recognized the doll: the birthday present he and Tristine gave Daria. She took it everywhere with her. Anxious, he turned to view the terrible aftermath of fire at apartment. The stairs were charred and in places fallen. He raced across the compound and climbed up to the third floor to find the apartment totally gutted inside.

Among the smoldering beams and seared furniture hung a sense of death. The faces of Tristine, Eli and Mikaela sprang before his eyes like in his vision. Fear like he never felt before, welled up inside him. He took an impulsive step backward and stumbled on a beam. He fell on his rump, his hand slipping on something in an effort to catching his balance. Pieces of paper lay among the ashes, the edges burned off, but the contents intact. He blew off the ash and began to read a letter from Nigel. What was this about his failure to seal the ruins? Nigel knew he succeeded, Avatar would have informed him. And how could Nigel know of the attack on the Fortress? He barely understood what his visions meant. Then again, Hueil played with his mind in Tunlund. Could this be the same?

Re-reading the letter, Hueil's mocking and laughing face appeared for a split second and changed into Nigel laughing with ridicule. Shocked, the letter dropped into his lap. For a moment he wondered what could it mean? *Was Nigel also in league with Hueil? No, impossible! Not after Tunlund.* Using his hand to brace himself to rise, he felt a soft garment under his fingers. Instead of standing he pulled it out from the rubble. Tristine's nightgown. Tyrone wept and hugged the gown.

"You believe they're dead too," said Angus, in a husky voice. He entered the apartment. His painful, watery eyes scanned the room. "Everyone in the compound is dead. No one could have survived."

Tyrone grabbed the letter and stood. He held the nightgown in one hand. "I found this." He gave the letter to Angus. "It's from Nigel. He says I *failed* to seal the ruins and warned Tristine of the attack."

"How could he know about the attack?"

Tyrone's face grew harsh and determined. "I don't know. But he has some explaining to do."

277

"Highness!" Kell rushed in. "I found Uriah and he's still alive."

Tyrone dropped the nightgown, snatched the letter from Angus and stuffed it in his pocket before leaving. Kell led them to the chapel behind the Vicar's private residence. Uriah lay on the ground unconscious with burns on his hands, his neck and the left side of his face; his garments charred and bloody.

"He needs immediate attention," said Tyrone.

They heard whimpering and soft crying. For a moment they listened to determine the direction.

"Sounds like it's coming from under him," said Angus.

Tyrone put an ear to the ground. "Someone is alive down there. Kell."

Kell carefully moved Uriah to one side to reveal he lay upon on a hatch. Tyrone stood to pull the hatch open. A muffled female cry came from below.

"Hello? Is anyone there?"

"Who's there?" the female voice quivered.

"Prince Tyrone." She appeared and he recognized her. "Magan."

"Highness," she said in great relief. "Grandfather hid us. Is he dead?"

"Alive, and badly injured. Are any of you hurt?"

"No, thank Jor'el."

He extended his hand to help her. Instead, she fetched her sons. First she handed up Chandler and then Ephraim. Tyrone gave the boys to Angus, who took them to one side. Kell stood in front of Uriah so they couldn't see the Vicar. Finally, Tyrone helped her climb out.

"Where is Grandfather?"

Tyrone stopped her from finding Uriah. "He will be cared for by the Guardians. Do you know what happened to our families?"

She shook her head. "No, but I heard shouting from the apartment and some knights tried to go upstairs. They couldn't reach the apartment due to the flames. Then the attack." She began to cry and went to her boys to hold them close. "I'm glad Chad wasn't here. He too would have been killed."

"He'll be glad to learn you and the boys are alive."

"We need to find someplace safe for them," said Angus.

"The Temple," said Kell. "Even now, some of the priests are arriving and will take care of the dead."

"I'm surprised they didn't attack the Temple too."

"Even during the darkest days of Allon, the Temple was spared."

Tyrone held Magan's shoulder. "Angus will take you and the boys to safety." He waited for Angus to continue with Magan and her sons before speaking to Kell. "Take Uriah to Melwynn then join us at the Temple. We're going to Waldron from there. Nigel has some explaining to do!" He gave the letter to Kell before leaving to join Angus.

Chapter 21

I N THE MORNING, FRASER WOKE FROM A FITFUL NIGHT'S SLEEP. The light of dawn filtered through the open window of his bedroom. He turned away from the light to go back to sleep. Images of his dream flashed across his mind. Frustrated, he sat up and yawned.

"What a night," he complained. "I think hitting my head gave me nightmares. Kendrick, get me a glass of water." He didn't receive a reply. After rubbing his eyes, he noticed he was alone. "Kendrick?"

He tossed aside the covers and rose to make a search of the room. Although large, there were only two separated areas, the privy, the sitting area and dressing area. Both were through open archways. *Why would a Guardian use the privy? Maybe he's in the hallway?* He opened the door. Royal guards stood their posts and Virgil waited outside his aunt and uncle's room. He summoned the Guardian.

"Where is Kendrick?"

"You told me he went to fetch you a headache remedy from Eldric."

"I did?"

"Ay, Highness." Virgil looked quizzically at Fraser. "Are you all right? Or is your headache worse?"

"Worse. And I had a horrible nightmare."

Virgil curbed a grin. "Losing will sometimes do that. Eldric doesn't like being disturbed at his nightly meditation unless it's urgent. He's probably taunting Kendrick by making him wait."

"And me," groused Fraser, rubbing his temples.

"I'll learn what's keeping him. Meanwhile, I'll send Holden to you."

"Ugh, more training. Maybe I can convince Uncle I need a day off."

Virgil laughed. "Somehow I don't think so."

Fraser closed the door and went to the privy. He splashed water on his face in an effort to wake up. He looked into the mirror and became surprised when the faces of his family and Kendrick stared back at him. They faded into Hueil and Ellan, and both laughing. Frightened, he ran from the privy. Feeling dizzy, he sat to keep from fainting.

"Highness."

He jumped to his feet in fright. "Holden!"

"I didn't mean to scare you. Shall I help you dress?"

He nodded, though confused by the images, nightmare and Kendrick's absence.

"Virgil," said Valery. She emerged from her room, inadvertently stopping his trek from Fraser's door.

"My lady. Sleep well?"

"I did, thank you."

He smiled. "Apparently the prince didn't and had nightmares. I think due to the knock on the head you gave him."

She tried not to laugh and said, "It's nothing to laugh about."

"Right. I'll stop when you do."

"Virgil." Nigel and Mirit emerged from their chamber. "Have breakfast sent to the armory. We'll eat while training."

"Ay, Sire." He left.

"You look fresh and chipper this morning," said Mirit. They began making their way down the hall from the royal quarters.

"Thank you, Majesty. I slept very well, but according to Virgil, Prince Fraser didn't sleep so well," she said with a teasing grin.

"I assume he said why."

"Something to do being defeated by a woman."

Mirit laughed and looked past Valery to Nigel. The girl walked between them. "Seems I remember someone acting just like that."

He smiled. "My ego bruising days ended when we married. And I won," he said the last sentence in triumph to Valery.

"Then I should go easy on the prince and not give him wrong ideas."

He laughed. "No, do your duty and leave Fraser to me."

Nothing more was said as they made their way to the armory.

Wess practiced his morning exercises with Avatar. "Good morning, Sire. Majesty, Lady Valery," began Wess. "Where is the prince?" They laughed, which made Wess curious. "I take it there is an inside joke?"

Nigel waved Valery toward the floor. "Start your warm-up exercises while I explain to the general."

Valery completed her stretching when a blurry-eyed Fraser arrived. He was met by smiling glances and muttered snickers, including Wess and Avatar.

"Morning, Sire. Majesty. General," he said in a quiet unsure voice.

"Good morning." Nigel wiped the grin from his face. "Do your warm-ups. Valery is already done and breakfast should be here shortly."

Fraser grumbled an affirmative reply and moved to begin his exercises. He passed by Virgil, who approached Nigel.

"Breakfast is on the way, Sire, only I couldn't find Kendrick."

"What do you mean?"

The blustery arrival of Tyrone, Angus and Kell interrupted a reply.

"How could you? Your own family!" Angus shouted at Nigel.

"What are you talking about—?" Nigel stepped toward them when Tyrone drew his sword and leveled it at him. Nigel stopped in surprise.

"Tyrone, what are you doing?" exclaimed Mirit.

"Stay back, Mirit!" ordered Angus, who also drew his sword.

Avatar rushed to Nigel, ready to draw and defend. Virgil stepped up to protect Mirit; hand on the hilt of his sword. Wess joined them, cautious in viewing all sides. Valery and Fraser watched in speechless bewilderment.

"Kell, what is this about?" demanded Avatar.

Kell didn't reply. He remained fixed in place with a steely expression.

"You'll have the answer when we do, and we want it now!" declared Tyrone, grey eyes mercilessly on Nigel.

"Very well. Put down the sword and tell me what this is about."

"They're dead!"

"Who?" Nigel asked with wary anticipation.

"Tristine, Necie, Jillian and the children!"

Dumbstruck, Nigel stared at Tyrone, unable to speak or move.

Mirit paled in horror. "No," she muttered on the verge of tears.

In fearful disbelief, Fraser moved toward Tyrone.

Wess intercepted him. "Be careful."

Fraser ignored Wess. "Father, they can't be! Not all."

Tyrone barely looked at Fraser, his primary focus on Nigel. "We just came from the Fortress where we witnessed the horrible aftermath. How did you know about the attack?"

"What attack?" Nigel managed to ask, still befuddled and grief-stricken.

Tyrone thrust the letter at Nigel with his left hand, the sword in his right staying level. "The attack *you* warned Tristine about! Along with lying by saying I failed at the ruins. I know Avatar told you I succeeded!"

Tentative of the sword, Nigel took the letter. He read then shook his head in denial. "I didn't write this! Surely, you recognize my handwriting? This a is bad forgery!"

Fraser's eyes grew wide in alarm. "Father, where did you get that?"

"It lay among the charred ruins of what *was* the apartment."

Nigel spoke in great distress. "As Jor'el is my witness, I didn't write this! And how could you even think I would want Tristine, Necie—any of them dead?"

Tyrone fought his own emotions. "Why should I believe you?" He pressed the blade closer toward Nigel.

In a quick move, Avatar drew his sword, knocked Tyrone's blade aside and stepped between Nigel and Tyrone with sword ready.

"Stand down, Avatar!" commanded Tyrone.

"Only if Kell tells me to!" His eyes flashed to Kell, who remained grimly silent. "Captain?" he urged, hoping for an answer.

"Tyrone! What are you doing?" called a familiar female voice.

Bewildered, he turned. "Tristine?" She entered the armory with Ellis, Titus, Egan, Ridge and Armus. He dropped his sword to embrace her. He wept, touching her face and hair. "You're alive!"

"Necie and the children?" asked Angus.

"Safe and at Melwynn, as is Lady Jillian," said Armus.

Angus' whole body sagged in relief and eyes swelled with tears of joy.

"Mother." Fraser moved from Wess, which brought him into view of the others.

"Traitor!" Ellis rushed Fraser when a stiff arm from Kell caught him in the chest. He stumbled backwards and fell to his knees in distress.

Valery knelt to aid Ellis yet scolded Kell. "Why did you do that?"

"No one advances upon a royal in anger."

Ellis gritted his teeth in painful rage. "Doesn't change the fact he is a traitor!"

"Beware of what you're saying, boy!" warned Wess.

"I swear it's true, Uncle! He was there when we were attacked."

"What are you talking about? Nigel wrote the letter causing all this," chided Tyrone.

"Fraser gave me the letter and said it came from Nigel," said Tristine.

"Me?" said Fraser, stupefied then became confused. "I didn't know it was going to be delivered. She didn't tell me," he said in hasty defense.

"She who?" demanded Tyrone.

Fraser balked, momentarily speechless. He then shook his head and murmured, "It can't be real. It was all a dream. She was in the dream."

Tyrone seized Fraser. "Stop babbling and answer me! Who?"

"She ... her ... Aunt Ellan."

The answer stymied Tyrone.

Nigel loudly swore. "Foolish boy! What have you done? Bad enough you couldn't keep your mouth shut when she was here."

"What? Ellan was here? At Waldron?" asked Tyrone.

"She came to explain how Hueil is forcing her to act against her will. Fraser happened to be with me when she arrived in the company of a Shadow Warrior using a shielding medal to avoid detection. His mouth kept going even when I ordered him twice to shut up! He showered her with compassion, saying he believed her lies!" Irate, Nigel waved the letter in the boy's face. "Tell me about this!"

Such fierceness made Fraser recoil in fear. "I swear! I thought it was a dream when she asked me to write."

"Asked? Not forced?" Nigel seized Fraser's right hand to draw attention to the signet ring. "You willingly forged my handwriting and used this for the seal?"

Completely undone, tears freely fell. "I thought it was a dream!"

Furious, Nigel shoved Fraser's away. "You betrayed our family in reality not a dream!"

With Valery's help, Ellis stood. "I wasn't dreaming when I saw you at the attack where Mikaela and I nearly drowned!"

"Drowned?" repeated Valery in a shocked whisper.

Ellis didn't hear, as he focused on the others.

"Mikaela?" asked Tyrone with renewed vigor.

Tristine diverted Tyrone's marked attention from Ellis. "They both went underwater when Ellis tried to rescue her. Armus saved them and Jade brought her to Eldric. She will recover."

Tyrone showed initial relief at the report then sneered at Fraser. "First the letter then you place your sister's life ... No, your mother and everyone else's life in jeopardy?"

"No! I couldn't have been there. I was in bed! Kendrick can tell you."

"I can't find Kendrick," said Virgil in firm voice. "When I spoke to Eldric, he said Kendrick never came to fetch you a headache remedy."

"But he was there—in the dream, fighting, trying to rescue me." His voice trailed off as he paled in horrible realization.

Tyrone accosted Fraser so hard the boy fell backwards to the floor. "In your gullible stupidity, you helped the enemy to almost destroy our family and possibly cost the life of a loyal Guardian!"

"No! I'd never want to hurt anyone. Certainly not Mikaela."

Tyrone stormed from the armory.

"Mother?" he sobbed.

Tristine turned from him and ran after Tyrone.

"Uncle Angus!" he said in desperation.

Angus sneered. "The only consolation for your treasonous behavior is the fact my family is alive. Alas, the same can't be said for those at Fortress, most were killed."

"Uriah?" asked Avatar.

"Badly injured and burned while saving Magan and the boys. He hid them is small root cellar behind his house. Tyrone and Kell found him lying unconscious over the hatch. Kell took him to Melwynn."

Avatar made a throaty growl of pain. "I need to speak to Chad and the Jor'ellian commanders."

"I'll take Lord Ellis to the infirmary, Majesty," said Valery.

Mirit nodded. She remained silent during the unsettling exchange.

Nigel glared at Fraser while the others made their departures. "You better find a place to stay out of your parents' way and my sight!" He turned on his heels to leave, the crumbled letter dropping from his hand.

"Uncle, please!"

"He won't listen this time," said Mirit, stern and unfriendly. "You caused him shame and dishonor by including him in your stupidity."

Disconcerted, Fraser looked at Titus, who never spoke. By his expression, the feelings of hurt, anger and disappointment went deep. Fraser raced from the armory.

"Should I follow him, Majesty?" asked Virgil.

"Why? Doubtful he'll leave Waldron. Let him stew. Maybe, he'll finally learn something." She took Titus' arm. "I want to visit Mikaela."

Fraser ran to the furthest corner in Waldron he could find; near the sewer outlet where few people, even the lowest servants rarely went. He bitterly wept. He had been used in the foulest way only not by coercion or torture, rather by his own weakness! The times his parents, aunts, uncles and Kendrick warned him echoed in his mind along with his excuses and indifference. Suddenly, he remembered everything clearly about his encounter with Ellan, every word, every sound, and even every smell.

Indeed, his mouth gave her the information she needed, and his hand willingly wrote what she said. But being at the Fortress? He had no memory of that incident. *What does it matter? I am responsible. Oh, poor Mikaela!* "Please, Jor'el, don't let her die because of my stupidity! Kendrick, I'm sorry. Help me to make it right somehow. Oh! How can I do that? How can I not?"

Foolish boy, Nigel's curse screamed in his brain. He gritted his teeth in painful repugnance. "I was a fool. No longer! I won't ever be weak and foolish enough to be deceived again." He peeked from the corner.

Although people rarely came to this corner, there was unusually high activity at Waldron in preparing for battle. When the opportunity came, he would leave and find a way to set things right even if he died trying.

Nigel paced the study in anger and agitation. He fought to control his reactions and emotions during the encounter. He could only suppress his feelings for so long. Hurt, grief, anger, pain, disappointment, worry and fear spewed forth in an outburst of rage. He swept everything off the desk and kicked over a chair in front of the desk. Passion vented, he collapsed into the chair behind the desk. How could Tyrone even think he wanted their family dead? To pull a sword on him? Then Fraser. They tried to curb his impulsive and reckless tongue. Now it led to deadly consequences. Not that Fraser was totally responsible for the attack, rather giving aid to the enemy.

"Enemy," he muttered and painfully added, "Ellan." He hadn't experienced first-hand the depth of her spleen rather withstood her for the sake of those he loved. This incident showed she hated enough to kill, and the lengths she would go to do so.

Tyrone's words came to mind. *Time is short. Don't focus so much on Ellan that you forget Hueil, who once killed your wife. His grip is darker and far more reaching.*

"Oh, Jor'el, why are you allowing this? Why must we go through this again?" He waited for an answer; longed for an answer. None came. He placed his head on the desk and wept. He flinched when someone touched his head with a gentle, stroking hand. He hadn't heard anyone come in and looked up. "Mirit?"

"No, Son of Ellis," said a voice from behind the chair.

Wary, Nigel stood. A warm yellow hazy of light with kind, smiling opalescent eyes gazing at him. "Jor'el."

"You seek answers you were already told. You just won't believe."

"You mean what Uriah said about the testing of my family?"

"Ay. Your father asked me the same question years ago when he didn't want to believe the truth about Ellan either."

"He also asked you to spare her life and you did."

"Ay. However, mercy doesn't negate the need for divine justice."

Nigel shivered and sighed. "So I must do what Father could not?"

"Would you rather leave it to Titus or Fraser?"

Pricked by question, he shook his head. "No. Because of this I understand the pain, conflict and grief my father experienced. I don't want to pass on such a burdensome legacy."

"Do not be cross concerning your father."

"I'm not. I'm just weary."

"Courage, Son of Ellis. I am with you and have given you help in your fight. Now, be strong for those depending upon you." Jor'el vanished.

Nigel sat on the corner of the desk. "Be strong," he repeated, and closed his eyes in an attempt to regain his composure.

"Strength is something I can lend you."

Nigel's eyes snapped at hearing Tyrone's voice. For an awkward moment they regarded each other. "How is Mikaela?"

A small, relieved grin appeared. "Awake, but tired. She asked Mirit if you were coming to visit her."

"I will," said Nigel with a smile a shrug. "I had to calm down first."

"Nigel," began Tyrone in heartfelt contrition. At a loss for words, He pulled Nigel to him in a tight embrace. "I'm so sorry!" he said in a choked voice. He held Nigel by the shoulders, to look directly at him. Tears in his eyes as he spoke. "I did something I never thought I would in drawing my sword on you. Although it is no excuse, Hueil used his power of inducing visions to influence me. Repeatedly your face kept appearing in flames, laughing, mocking."

"I would never do that to you."

"I do know that," said Tyrone, his voice filled with emotion. "But when I thought Tristine, Necie and the children were dead, I lost all reason. Grief made you the focal point. I think that's what Hueil wanted, to drive an irreconcilable wedge between us." He wiped his eyes.

"He nearly succeeded. Fraser may have reached that point by his actions."

"I'll deal with Fraser when I can think more clearly. First we must reconcile. Can we do that? Can you forgive me?"

"You know I can."

Tyrone hugged Nigel again. "Thank you, brother." He sniffed and wiped his eyes again. "Tristine will be relieved too. After visiting Mikaela, she scolded me for what I did, and Angus also."

"I can't recall seeing Angus so outraged, much less moved to violence due to anger."

"Just like me, he let grief guide his actions, not knowledge. That's what Tristine reminded us about—our knowledge of you, the Dark Way and Hueil. With an added admonishment to Angus about Ellan's past."

Nigel grew sheepish. "I confess, I didn't realize how hatred consumed her and guided her actions. Mind you, I believed what was said and I acted to help, even to the point of accepting the crown. Now, I fully understand."

"Nor did I realize it."

"She's not your sister so you have no history. That aside," he said with frustrated wave, "there is no longer the smallest hesitation to do what must be done, and to whatever extent! She and Hueil will face mortal and divine justice."

"As you command, Sire."

Nigel flashed a wry grin. "I can't wait till this over and you're once again king. I can't get used to the title." He glanced up and down at Tyrone. "I want my uniform back. Even if you did stretch it out."

Tyrone chuckled more with relief than humor. "What now?"

"As soon as I get some food and ease this headache, planning will begin. With your arrival, all parties are here. I received word shortly before dawn that their forces left Roxbury heading north."

"Angus was so mortified by his behavior, Mahon suggested taking him to Melwynn for a quick visit. To ease his mind about his family, and while I spoke to you first to gauge your reaction."

"He has nothing to fear from me."

"Under the circumstances, we're all more sensitive than usual. Mahon said they would be back my suppertime."

"Good, let him enjoy some time with his family."

Tyrone nodded with a grin. "I'll fetch your breakfast."

"No. Let's join our wives and eat together. I have some explaining and apologizing to do then I'll visit Mikaela."

At the infirmary, Valery paced the hallway while awaiting word of Ellis. Upon departure for breakfast, Mirit and Tristine informed her of the good prognosis for Mikaela. She didn't see Titus. Then again, he could have left unseen while she paced. Naturally she felt relief about Mikaela. However, the thought of Ellis nearly drowning hit her harder than anticipated. True, she looked forward to seeing him again. Due to the dangerous circumstances, she kept telling herself that wouldn't be for some time, if at all. Anything could happen in battle and that's what she was training for while Ellis remained with Titus.

Memories of recent events flashed through her mind as she waited. Ellis came to speak with her at Garwood, which turned in aiding her through a difficult interview. After the forest attack, he sought to protect her from further injury and their rode together to the Fortress. Through it all, he behaved chivalrous and kind. What did she do in return? Rebuff him, mostly. She tried to counter her impulsive reaction by implementing Mirit's advice, and found she enjoyed being around him. Although a defensive move by Kell, seeing Ellis struck down frightened her. When he spoke of nearly drowning, she recalled Mirit's story concerning Nigel. Could she face a life without Ellis?

"Eldric says you can see Ellis now," said Titus.

He startled her from her pondering. She flashed a retiring smile. "I'm glad to hear about Princess Mikaela. What about Lady Jillian?" She saw a brief look of distress.

"Eldric says the report from Melwynn is good, and she will recover."

"I'm glad for you and her."

For a moment Titus regarded her. "You mean that, don't you?"

"Ay."

He smiled. "As am I for you and Ellis. Now, don't keep him waiting." He gave her a gentle nudge toward the door.

She blushed and moved in the direction he indicated. Ellis stood shirtless with a bandage around chest, on his left upper arm, and around his head. The sight of the numerous injuries made her balk.

He put on his shirt and saw her. He smiled. "I don't look that bad."

"I didn't realize you had so many injuries. Here, let me help." She took the doublet and held it. He gingerly slipped his left arm thought the sleeve first then the right. She gently laid it on his shoulders. "I didn't hurt you, did I?"

"In helping me dress, no." He faced her, took her hands and held them tightly between his hands. "In other ways, ay."

Her eyes grew wide with concern. "How?"

"In here." He placed her hand over his heart. "After the ruins, Fortress and nearly drowning, I realized how much you are on mind. How I miss you when we were apart. And," he said, stroking her cheek, "pain at the thought of anyone harming you."

She stared at him in fearful realization. "You know?"

He held her hands to stop her withdrawal. "No, I won't let you retreat this time. There is too much at stake to let the past win, both with your father and Ellan. I won't let anyone hurt you again."

Tears welled up. He knew her deepest secret and wasn't repulsed. In fact, he kept holding her hands against his chest. Mirit was right. His knowing didn't change his feelings. Still, she voiced her thoughts. "No one has ever defended me before."

He lifted her chin. "I *will* because I love you."

She found herself beginning to laugh, more a relief of tension, and stopped. "You always could find a way to make me laugh at the most difficult times."

"I'm sure I sound funny. For all the words I stumble over, I had no problem speaking now. I do not jest with my heart or yours."

"I know. I didn't mean to laugh. I believe I feel the same about you, only the words are difficult for me to say."

"I understand. This will show you I'm willing to wait." He kissed her.

She responded to his kiss. He flinched when they embraced and they separated. "I'm sorry, if I hurt you."

He grimaced. "Not your fault. Kell's hit bruised my breastbone. Eldric said I was fortunate it didn't break. He gave me some medicine to help with pain and poultice to heal the bruising. The bandage is to remind me to take it easy and heal." He chuckled. "Whereas my chest is sore, my lips are fine."

She laughed then accepted his tender and careful kiss. After which, he grunted in frustration. "Oh, to heal quickly and hold you properly."

"You need *complete* rest from *all* activity," said Eldric. He sat working at a nearby table, not even looking at them.

"Then I take my leave of the infirmary and retire to my quarters." Ellis gathered the rest of his things.

"Alone," said Eldric, and this time looked at them.

Cody arrived, making Ellis smile. "Indeed, since I would not compromise my lady. Not to mention she has protection."

She laughed and took his hand to leave the infirmary.

In the quarters of the King's Champion, Avatar confronted Kell.

"Why didn't you intervene? Why let Tyrone draw a sword on Nigel? And me draw on Tyrone?"

"Questions needed to be answered," replied Kell, in a calm voice.

"At sword point?"

"Easy, Avatar," said Armus.

He shook off Armus' restraining grip. "Easy? Of all the mortals in this family, you, and *Kell*, should know Nigel not capable of betrayal. And certainly not of Tyrone, nor to cause harm to Tristine!"

"That is what I *hoped*," began Kell firmly. "After Hueil succeeded with Mahon, Nigel would be an easy target. The truth had to be learned." He grew concerned. "Virgil reporting Kendrick's absence is disturbing."

"So you stood silent on a *hope* and allowed me to draw upon *our* king?" Avatar's passion didn't allow for any response before declaring, "As Jor'el is my witness, if given chance I will use my position to render justice on Hueil!"

Kell took Avatar by the shoulders. Rather than a rebuke, he spoke in a serene voice. "*Bi aig fois, Avatar, agus dleasdanas deo treoraich thu.* Be at peace, Avatar, and duty will guide you."

"I *hope* you're right."

Kell grinned. "I don't hope, I *know* you are too stubborn and loyal to go against orders. Return to Nigel. I have some meditating to do."

The door closed a bit louder than normal upon Avatar's departure.

"He has every right to be upset. Your silence was unusual. Even I wondered if you'd let them come to blows," said Armus.

"I would only let it go until the truth was uncovered. Fortunately, that happened before any blow struck."

"Really? Blows aren't always physical. Tristine experienced another blow to the heart learning her son followed in her sister's wake of betrayal!"

"Keep your wits. This whole situation is about to explode."

"Ay! In battle."

"Which is why we must remain level-headed. The question is how did they get to Fraser? Kendrick would not have allowed it and the boy seemed confused about the sequences of events and Kendrick's whereabouts." Kell pursed his lips in thought. "I'll join you when I'm done meditating and trying to sense Kendrick."

Chapter 22

FOR THE NEXT THREE DAYS, WALDRON BUZZED WITH ROUND THE clock activity, as the plans for facing Hueil and Ellan went into full motion. Valery spent much of her free time with Ellis, while he tried to carry out Eldric's instruction of resting. They avoided speaking about the current situation due to its uncertainty and stuck to general topics. Yet when frustrated by some fighting technique she couldn't quite master he would start to demonstrate. She scolded him about aggravating his injuries and he stopped.

On several occasions the conversation led him to recount childhood escapades or memories. She enjoyed hearing them. She didn't speak much about her family and he didn't press her. What surprised Ellis was Cody chose to stay with him when Valery tended to duty. However, with so much going on he felt antsy about being idle. Eldric's daily remedies helped tremendously in his healing, faster than any mortal medicine. His restlessness wouldn't last too long since departure was set for the following morning.

Nigel declared a time of prayer and reflection at a service to be held in the castle chapel that evening. As duty required, Ellis and Valery attended Titus and Mirit. They managed to sit together during the service. With Uriah recovering at Melwynn, Waldron's priest, Master Hampton presided over the service. Being impossible for all to hear, simultaneous services were held throughout the encampment. At Waldron, royals, soldiers, priests and servants tried to fit into the chapel and the Grand Courtyard. Though they wouldn't be able to hear except by heralds relaying Hampton's words.

After Hampton's concluding prayer, Nigel mounted the altar steps wearing ceremonial clothes, the crown and the Sword of Allon.

"I know this is the time everyone expects to hear a rousing speech. I'm not one for flowery words or speeches. Action is what matters, and action is required, not more words. Jor'el is with us. It is for His divine honor and the salvation of Allon we march to battle." He drew the Sword, thrust it in the air and declared, "Long live Jor'el! Long live Allon!"

Those seated, stood and everyone echoed his words.

He sheathed the Sword and stepped down. People filed out through the main entrance. The royal family left by way of a side door reserved exclusively for them. It led to a private room and a tunnel connecting the chamber to a room in the main building adjacent to the Great Hall. They used the passage during celebrations and ceremonies to get from one place to another without being detained by the crowd. Virgil and Armus waited in the room.

"Anything?" Tyrone asked the Guardians.

"No sign of him. If he's still in the castle, he found a place to hide no one knows about," said Armus.

"Are you sure no one saw him leave?" asked Tristine.

"I think it is safe to say he found a way to leave unnoticed. Not unlike his mother in her youth."

She grew annoyed. "Why must everyone remind me of that?"

"Because it happened."

"If only Kendrick were here, he'd find him like you did me."

Armus cocked a grin. "I can still track and find any mortal."

"Your place is here. We can't waste time to find him," said Tyrone.

"Then what do we do? Just let him run off?" she argued.

"For now. Perhaps he can make good use of the time to think about what he's done and how his stupidity affected so many."

"What will you do if and when he does come back?"

He took a deep contemplating breath before answering. "I suppose that depends on his attitude."

"We can't make excuses for him anymore. We've done that for too long," chided Titus.

Tyrone kept his voice level, with an unmistaken rebuff in his eyes. "I'm not. True, he's done grave injury to many by his foolishness, yet despite his faults and weakness, Ellan and Hueil used him."

"That sounds like a excuse."

"They exploited his gullibility and lack of discretion. You acted on your own without coercion from anyone, and in direct defiance of me by going to Natan. Do you expect me to treat him with less compassion than I did you if he realizes his responsibility and seeks amends?"

The reminder of Natan embarrassed him. "No, sir." He made a curt bow and left the room by the Chapel door.

"We all must come to terms with Fraser: you and Tristine, as his parents; Titus as the eldest brother; and I as king, not just his uncle. You call his actions foolish. They were also treasonous," said Nigel.

Tristine became concerned. "What will you do if he returns?"

"Do you ask me as uncle or king? If he comes back repentant, uncle will gladly receive him without reservation. As king, how can I accept it without some form of punishment since he included me by his forgery?"

"You sound like Father when he accused me of treason for resisting Ellan and Sullivan."

He shook his head with insistence. "People didn't die as a result of your resistance. Many died due to his culpability! People I feel responsible for. How can I simply forgive him and look any of their relatives in the face?"

Tyrone drew Tristine back from Nigel. "I think enough has been said for now." They left the chamber by way of the tunnel.

Nigel regarded Eli, Ellis and Valery with twinge of melancholy. "Rest. Beginning at dawn, sleep and rest will be hard to come by until this is over." He and Mirit left, also by the tunnel.

"I'm going to find Titus. You coming?" Ellis asked Eli.

"No, I promised Mikaela to visit her. Besides, he listens to you. Fraser maybe gullible, but he thinks I'm too soft."

"He loves you both."

Eli gently smiled. "I'm speaking of brotherly disappointment, not love." He followed his parents and uncle through the tunnel.

Valery detained Ellis. "Will I see you before we leave?"

"Ay." He took her in his arms intent on kissing her but she resisted. "Your injuries."

He smiled. "Are much better since I've been a good patient." This time she didn't resist him. After they kissed, he sighed. "I pray the war doesn't last too long. This is much more pleasurable."

She blushed. "Go find Titus." She nudged him to the Chapel door.

Titus made his way to the royal garden. Fall and winter preparations were complete and the trees totally bare of leaves. He didn't notice or care. He hadn't spoken much since returning to Waldron. What could he say? Nigel was right; Fraser's actions were treasonous while his father's rebuke brought back painful memories. Indeed, he acted on his own. He recalled Fraser's response when they returned from Natan. Aside from the usual brotherly criticism and sarcasm, their relationship had not suffered. Then again, Fraser was ten years old and Titus so mortified, he sought to please everyone in his family with model behavior.

"I thought I'd find you here."

Titus glanced sideways at Ellis. He went and sat on a bench.

"Ah, I see. The cold shoulder treatment."

Titus rolled his eyes. Ellis sat beside him. Several moments of silence passed until Titus groused, "Well, go ahead, say 'I told you so'."

"Why? You just said it. And quite well, I might add."

"Oh, Ellis! Have we been too tolerant of him?"

"We?"

"All right, me! I have been too tolerant. I admit it. That should make you happy." Titus stood.

"I'm not happy. You should know better."

Frustrated, Titus passed a hand over his face. "This whole situation feels out of control. And there's not much I can do about it!"

Ellis rose. "There will be much to do on the battlefield. It is for that we must be prepared. Fraser is a distraction."

"Easy for you to say, he's not your brother."

Ellis fought to contain his annoyance. "His actions nearly cost my sister's life! Not to mention Mikaela and mine! So don't play self-righteous. And let's not argue. Not on the eve of marching to battle. Fraser will be handled when the time comes. Besides, you're always telling me how a Jor'ellian must focus on the task at hand and leave the rest to the Almighty."

Titus looked askew to Ellis. "Must you always remember everything I say? You sound as bad as Egan."

"Just for that, I won't tell you Mikaela requests a visit from both of you," said Egan. He and Jade walked up behind Ellis and Titus. The prince appeared put out.

Ellis laughed. "If you won't, I shall visit my little sweetheart."

"Should I tell Valery you have a secret love?"

"You do and I'll tell Jillian you only rebuffed Valery to hide your true feelings for her."

Titus laughed. "They wouldn't believe either of us."

Once out of danger, they moved Mikaela from the infirmary to her room. Eli propped her up with pillows. Valery sat beside the bed, an open book in her hand. Titus and Ellis arrived with Egan and Jade.

"I thought you retired," said Ellis to Valery.

"I stopped to look in on Her Highness and was asked to read."

"So much is going on that no one has had time to visit me. You've only been here once," Mikaela complained to Titus. "That's why I asked Jade to fetch you and Ellis. To visit me before you leave for war."

Titus sat on the bed, opposite of where Valery sat in the chair. "I apologize for being neglectful."

"What of Fraser? I haven't seen him in days!"

Titus balked. "Well," he awkwardly began. "He's been—"

"Sent on an errand by the king and isn't at Waldron," finished Ellis.

"Like Uncle sent him to warn us at the Fortress?"

"In a manner of speaking. Like your brothers, it will pain me to be away from my little sweetheart," Ellis spoke in a gallant manner.

Valery started to chuckle and pressed her lips together to stop. Mikaela smiled at Valery then made a fake pout at Ellis.

"I know the truth. Your heart belongs to another."

Ellis sat on the bed near Valery's chair. "There will always be a special place for you."

Mikaela had difficulty maintaining her fake pout, and smiled. "As long as I can come to the wedding, I'll forgive you."

The statement surprised Valery. "We haven't discussed marriage."

"Titus and Father said it is almost certain when this is over."

Valery and Ellis looked across to Titus.

He sheepishly smiled. "I suppose it may have sounded that way."

Ellis took Valery's hand. "Jor'el willing, I would consider it an honor to marry such a courageous lady."

"And I would be honored to have such a humorous husband." Valery tried to suppress her mirth, but both she and Ellis laughed.

"Then there will be a wedding?" asked Mikaela.

Before either Ellis or Valery could answer, Virgil arrived. "I'm sorry to interrupt, Princess," he said to Mikaela. "The king requires Princes Titus and Eli, Lord Ellis and Lady Valery to attend him in the study."

Mikaela pouted for real to which Titus kissed her cheek.

"I'll visit you as soon as we get back, I promise."

"So do I," said Eli, kissing her forehead.

"Take care, my little sweetheart." Ellis kissed her hand. Valery also showed affection with a tender hand caressing the girl's cheek.

"Will they be all right, Jade?" asked Mikaela, trying not to get upset.

"Jor'el will look after them."

Nigel, Tyrone, Tristine, Mirit, Angus, Armus, Kell, Avatar, Wess, Lord Fagan, Baron Ned, Chad, Hayden, Dylan, and two Jor'ellian commanders were in the study when they arrived with Virgil.

"Sorry to interrupt your evening. They are moving faster than anticipated. We leave in an hour to reach the plain by dawn and hope to establish our position prior to their arrival," said Nigel.

"No apology necessary, Sire," said Ellis.

"There is another change of plan." Nigel approached Eli. "With a shortened time, we can't evacuate many before securing Waldron. I want you to remain to look after them and maintain calm and order."

Eli's face fell with disappointment. "Of course, sir, but I can fight."

"This had nothing to do with your skill, courage or ability. If they break through our main line, I need someone here I can trust to make certain they don't take Waldron. Sir Edgar and Sir Merrill," he indicated the Jor'ellian commanders, "will remain with two thousand Jor'ellians to reinforce the five hundred remaining royal troops. Ewert and Bailey will command the hundred Guardians they handpicked to make defense."

Eli's brief disappointment turned to grim determination. "You can depend upon me, Sire."

A quick knock on the door was followed by Derwin entering, and along with a pale and weary looking—

"Kendrick!" said Tristine.

"Highness." Kendrick bowed and held it as he spoke in a husky voice of contrition. "I beg to report, I failed in protecting Prince Fraser."

Tyrone took the Guardian's arm to prompt him to stand. "No, the failure lies elsewhere: Fraser naturally, and me for not dealing firmly with his weakness. You suffered in the line of duty and I thank you."

"Do you know where Fraser is?" asked Tristine.

Kendrick grew a bit befuddled. "Actually, I'm not sure. He was physically here in bed, but also physically and in essence at the manor."

"What manor? What do you mean?" asked Kell.

Kendrick shrugged. "Everything is confusing, Captain. I escorted the prince to bed as usual. When I went to take my customary place something struck me in the back of the head and I blacked out. After coming to, I saw no one, only the prince asleep in bed, unharmed. Physically he appeared normal, but something waylaid me. I stretched my senses and discovered his essence went someplace else than the bed."

"Why didn't you summon me if you sensed trouble?" asked Avatar.

"Not trouble, something didn't feel right. If I called you, you would have seen, him in bed and undisturbed."

"I did, later," began Virgil. "He told me you went to fetch a headache remedy, only Eldric said you never came and I couldn't find you."

"I left to investigate the sense." He tossed a sheepish glance to Kell. "I know it was risky to abandon my post, but I had to find the source of the strange sensation. I didn't expect to go where it led me."

"The manor," said Kell.

"Ay. I didn't get my bearings before everything happened. According to Derwin, it is located in the Lowlands."

"I found him in a grove near Sir Loran's old manor house, where Sir Hayden put his signal post. It had been used," said Derwin.

"Not by me," said Hayden.

"I found this inside, Sire." Derwin gave Nigel a handkerchief.

Nigel felt the weight and unwrapped it to discover a signet ring. "The North Plains." He held the ring up to be seen.

"By the initials, the handkerchief belongs to Baron Erasmus."

Tyrone took the ring and Nigel examined the handkerchief to confirm the identity. "Why would Erasmus have Malcolm's ring?"

"After tending to Kendrick and hiding him for recovery, I did a brief reconnaissance. Lord Malcolm is dead, a result of his long illness."

"Oh no," murmured Tristine.

"Unfortunately, I couldn't discover how the ring came to be in the baron's possession."

"I can answer *how*," said a new female voice. Mona arrived. "I spoke to Master Bevan, Malcolm's personal physician after he brought the body home for burial. Malcolm knew he didn't have long to live and gave the ring to Erasmus for safekeeping. Erasmus tried to keep Bevan ignorant of his little jaunt from camp. It didn't work, he knew the baron carried out Malcolm's last wish."

"Dear Malcolm, fragile in body but not loyalty," said Tristine.

"Ay," said Nigel with sobriety. "Only Ellan commands his troops."

"As nice as this show of loyalty is, it doesn't explain what Kendrick said about Fraser," said Mirit.

"True. What happened when you got to the manor?" asked Tyrone.

Kendrick continued his story. "Fraser's sense was unmistakable. Then I saw him on a couch in the room with Hueil and Ellan."

"How could he be on the couch there but in his bed here?" asked Eli.

Kendrick shrugged. "I don't know. Unlike the sense in his room, it was him, physically and in essence. I tried to rescue him, only Hueil thought otherwise. He sent me flying through a window and into courtyard where three Shadow Warriors taunted a wyvern."

"A wyvern did that to you?" asked Virgil

"No, a Shadow Warrior," he chided. "When they loosed the wyvern on me, one threw his dagger. No doubt to make my destruction more certain. I pulled out the dagger, stuck it in the wyvern and vanished. I would have bled away my life force if Derwin hadn't found me."

"Wait," began Mona. "Am I to understand Fraser was here and in the manor house at the same time?"

"Ay," replied Kendrick.

"He was at the Fortress also," said Tristine.

"Ay. The Vicar saw him a second before he vanished, and mortals don't vanish," said Titus.

Mona shivered and crossed her arms as if warding off a chill.

"Mona?" asked Kell when an expression of concern and fear crisscrossed her face. "You think it could be another shape-shifter?"

"Ay, Captain. It explains the haunting and familiar sense I've not felt since the Great Battle. Fitch was here."

"How does that explain anything?" asked Angus.

"He took the prince's form to do whatever he was supposed to do."

Tyrone began to comprehend. "Fitch rendered Kendrick helpless long enough to take Fraser's place while he was taken to the manor house where Ellan worked her wiles on him."

"Two had to be involved, since Fitch isn't capable of rendering Kendrick unconscious *and* transporting Fraser someplace else while assuming his identity," said Kell.

"Phelan," said Nigel, drawing curious look from Kell. "The Shadow Warrior with Ellan when she called upon me via the shielding medal. Fitch stayed and he kidnapped Fraser."

"Then I spoke to Fitch not Fraser," said Virgil.

"And the Fortress? Was that Fitch also?" asked Tristine.

"Would make sense since the Vicar believed Fraser started the fire and didn't mention Kendrick when he disappeared. Fitch, I mean," Ellis corrected himself when Tristine glared at him.

"And how he disappeared from the apartment fire, when we assumed by way of Kendrick," added Armus.

"Along with coordinating the attack on us where Ellis saw him," added Eli.

Tristine turned to Tyrone. "Then Fraser had nothing to do with the tragedy at the Fortress."

Nigel spoke a word of caution. "He forged the letter with my name and seal that Fitch delivered and led you into a trap. He still bears responsibility for giving them the means to do so."

She scowled at the rebuff and asked Kendrick, "Can you find him?"

Kell intervened. "In Kendrick's present weak condition, it would be dangerous for him and the prince if they encounter trouble."

Tyrone placed a hand on Tristine's shoulder to get her attention. "At least we know the whole story. We will deal with Fraser later. Right now time is pressing and we must leave in an hour."

"Ay," she said in reluctant agreement.

"Everyone is dismissed to their assignments," said Nigel.

In near unison, they clasped their swords or bowed and departed.

The royal forces arrived at the plain of Arundine just after dawn, and before Hueil and Ellan. Scouts found no sign of the enemy within twenty miles. This gave them had time to move into position. The strong defensive line stretched the width of the plain and commanded the high ground and trees to the east and west.

It wasn't until twilight that a scout arrived to report the first sighting. Nigel, Avatar, Kell, Armus, Tyrone, Wess, Chad and Angus were under a canopy studying maps when the scout arrived.

"Sire. The enemy's been sighted six miles due south."

"Six miles? How did they get so close without being seen sooner?"

The question briefly stymied the scout. "I don't know, Sire."

"If Hueil is employing shielding medals, we're fortunate they were found at all," said Kell.

"He can shield that massive of an army?"

"When Sir Owain captured Waldron in the coup sending you and your mother fleeing, I used a single shielding medal to hide the approach of one thousand Guardians. Depending on how many medals Hueil has, he can manage it."

"You think Hueil will attack as soon as they arrive?" asked Angus.

"Doubtful. He'll want a report of our positions first."

"If he doesn't already know," said Avatar, which drew interest. "If he can use the medals to hide approach, he can use them for reconnaissance."

"There haven't been any reports of unusual activity," said Wess.

"Then maybe he thinks we're still at Waldron."

"Hold that thought," said Nigel to Avatar. "Also inform all commanders the enemy has been sighted and be on alert for anything."

Avatar nodded at Chad, who saluted and went to carry out the order.

Nigel spoke to Tyrone, Wess and Angus. "All we can do now is wait until morning and the moment of truth." He left the canopy and headed to where the royal tent had been erected.

When he arrived, Mirit, Valery and Tristine were inside tending to their weapons. Cody slept at Valery's feet. For a moment Nigel's gaze lingered on Tristine before speaking.

"They've been spotted six miles away. By dawn there will be battle."

She crossed to him. "Jor'el is with you, brother, as are we all." She hugged him and kissed his cheek. Taking her bow and quiver, she left.

"Valery, fetch us supper." Mirit waited until Valery was gone before taking his hand and having him sit beside her. "Doubts?"

"No, just the usual anticipation and angst before battle. If anything, I look forward to this being over and getting back to normal."

"That'll be hard, especially if something happens to Fraser. Did any of the scouts report seeing him?"

He shook his head. "I told them to inform me privately if they did."

"Perhaps you can spare Kendrick to find him."

"I will before dawn, with instructions to keep Fraser away from the fighting. I don't need him acting foolish."

"Like you did when you were younger?" asked Avatar. He entered carrying a tray of food and drink.

"Mirit sent Valery for supper," chided Nigel.

Avatar grinned. "Lord Ellis spotted her and I thought to help."

"You acting as a matchmaker? That's a new one."

Avatar looked askew at Nigel. "Oh? I had no hand in keeping you and Mirit from killing each other until you to realize your true feelings?"

Under a tree near where the cooks prepared food, Ellis and Valery sat to eat. Cody lay down next to her and gnawed on the meaty bone the cook gave him. She picked at the food on her plate.

"You should eat. You'll need strength," said Ellis.

"I know. I'm just—" she stopped.

"Scared?" She tossed a shy glance at him. He softly smiled and leaned close to say, "So am I."

"You? I thought you fought before?"

"No. I had no real fighting experience until those wolf-men. Seeing everyone dead at the outpost and the attack on the Fortress was disconcerting. Titus is the one with more battle experience than I."

"Did I hear my name?" Titus carefully sat on the ground with his plate of food and drink.

"We were talking of battle experience."

Titus swallowed a drink before speaking. "War can be a frightening and ugly thing." He became reflective. "Tunlund was my first time witnessing battle. I can't even begin to tell you how frightened I was."

"Grandfather said you were just a boy," said Valery.

"Ay, but you don't forget such intense feelings or vivid images. I thought it prepared me for Natan. I was wrong," he droned and looked directly at her in regret. "I never told you how I've felt responsible for Allard's death and how deeply sorry I am."

"Others, including your father and uncle, told me of his prior wound and the escape. They said you are not to blame. Although you and I haven't always been friendly, I believed them and never blamed you for his death. He died doing his duty, like many will do tomorrow."

Ellis took her hand. "You won't die. Not one of us here will."

"You can't be certain."

"I am certain of how devastated I would be if you did."

Titus put aside his plate to take a hold of both their arms. "Jor'el is the only certainty. He will be with us on the battlefield."

"Indeed, Jor'el will be present. Take courage in that," said Egan.

"Ay. Now let's finish eating." Titus took up his plate.

For the next ten minutes they ate in relative silence, except for comments about the food or nighttime weather from Titus and Ellis. Valery didn't say anything, though she did eat. When finished, she rose.

"I need to get back to the queen."

"I'll take care of your plate and tankard," said Egan.

Ellis also gave his plate and cup to Egan before escorting Valery. Cody followed, carrying his bone. Twenty feet from the tent, he stopped her and held her hands.

"Mikaela asked a question we laughed at then. I would like a real answer. If by Jor'el's will we survive, will you marry me?"

"Ay. For by surviving, I will know there is a future."

He kissed her then let her go to the tent.

Chapter 23

FRASER WASN'T CERTAIN HOW TO CORRECT WHAT HE HAD DONE, or where to go to think and consider. All he knew was he had to leave Waldron. He thought about confronting Ellan, but what could he say? *You deceived me?* She'd laugh in his face. Confronting Hueil was out of the question. The whole situation started with them, so it had to end with them. Thus he headed toward the Lowlands, knowing of the report that Ellan was with Zebulon. He managed to get some money before leaving, only enough to keep him fed but not hire a horse. It would be a long walk.

Several times he wished for Kendrick's help, even knowing the Guardian would prevent him from acting foolish. He remembered all the times he rejected Kendrick's advice or counsel and sorely regretted the way he treated him. Although fully aware of why Guardians were created and their function, it became so easy to take them for granted on a daily basis. Ironic to think he was part Guardian. Now, without his lifelong, loyal companion and family support, he faced a cold harsh reality, alone.

At dawn of the fourth day since leaving, he emerged from the thicket where he slept. He spied a large army about two miles away. Hearing ear-piercing cries and seeing wyverns, he ducked under cover. He took stock of the army. The numbers seemed endless with mortal foot soldiers and cavalry from the various defecting Council Members, wyverns, Shadow Warriors and Shadow Archers. The artillery appeared to be of the smaller variety. At that distance he couldn't distinguish individuals but reckoned Hueil or Ellan rode at the head of the army. With such massive numbers on the move, it would be impossible to get near them. He altered his plan to follow at a safe distance and await an opportunity.

After nightfall, Hueil and Ellan's forces arrived at the plain of Arundine to discover the royal army already encamped. Furious, she confronted Hueil in front of Gareth, Zebulon, Bosley, Erasmus, Phelan and several Shadow Warriors.

"How could you not know they left Waldron? Now they have established position!"

"There is nothing to be concerned about, Majesty. We have advantages they don't. Come the morning, they will feel our might."

"Don't pride yourself on your strategy, Guardian. Kell is with them."

He squared his shoulder with pride. "Kell was in Tunlund and did not detect the stygian arrows. There is nothing he can do to counter wyverns."

She was beside herself with frustration. "To your commands! You, come with me," she ordered Hueil. She led him to a small sheltered area. "Take heed, if you brought me to my ruin to serve your selfish end."

His temper flared. "Beware, my dear one, you accuse me wrongly."

"I will not suffer defeat! Revenge and the throne will be mine."

"It will be *ours*," he corrected. "You would not be here without me."

"Nor you without me!"

He smiled, tight and sarcastic. He went to touch her face and she jerked away. He seized her to make her look into his icy blue, narrow, probing eyes. "Only when we both have what we want will this end; you the throne and an heir, and me godhood and a son. So which will it be, dear one, united to achieve our goal, or fight each other for all to see?"

Pain on her face and the cold gleam in his eyes made her swallow back some fear. "United."

"Wise choice." He released her. "Now, no more public tantrums." He smiled and offered her his arm. "Shall we return?"

She accepted and they walked to where her tent was being erected.

Bosley and Erasmus set about placing their troops into position on the west flank. Zebulon and Malcolm's forces were on the east flank with Gareth and Braden's troops occupying the center. Shadow Warriors and Shadow Archers were spread among the forces while the wyverns were kept under control in the center. It took three hours to get into position. Once finished, they met in a tent for food and drink. Neither wanted to eat.

Erasmus sighed after taking a long drink. "I'm glad Erin isn't alive to see this. The thought of civil war would be more than she could bear."

"Ay," drone Bosley. "Although grateful our wives are spared, I can't imagine what Callie must be thinking with Wess and I on opposite sides."

"Tyrone sent her and Grant to Tunlund. She doesn't know."

"I pray she never finds out."

"Take heart. Our covert actions will give her, our sons and Wess some consolation."

Bosley shook his head. "The truth will be learned in the morning." He leaned closer. "Are you certain the ones designated were disabled?"

"By my lieutenant, your commander and Malcolm's artillery officer, but not Braden's man. Still, Braden only has seven of the forty guns. Besides, if our intentions had been betrayed we wouldn't be alive."

"That's something, I suppose," groused Bosley.

"It's everything. Alive we can still work, even during battle."

In the early soft orange glow of dawn, Nigel and Mirit emerged from their tent fully dressed for battle. He carried the gold helmet made to resemble an eagle's head with plumes of gold and purple. Upon the breast plate was the body of the eagle outstretched; the shoulder guards as wings protecting his arms. The arm and leg armor were gold fashioned to look like feathers, with boots as talons. Upon his white and gold shield was the crest of the House of Tristan: a flying eagle clenching a crown. On his left hip hung the Sword of Allon; the pommel the body of an eagle with head holding the blade with imbedded garnet eyes; the guard, carved wings protecting the hands. The master goldsmith of the Guardians, Rune, forged the entire suit in fires of the heavenlies before defecting to Dagar. Mirit's suit was fashioned in gold and royal blue and not as ornate as the famed Golden Armor.

Valery, Virgil and Avatar were also dressed for war and accompanied them to the command area. Valery wore the plain battle suit and armor of a Jor'ellian cadet. Avatar wore his commander's uniform and a breastplate of gold and silver with purple accents. Virgil wore the Guardian warrior's battle uniform.

Waiting at the canopy were Tyrone, Tristine, Kell, Armus, Angus, Wess, Fagan, Ned, Chad, Titus and Ellis. Tyrone and Tristine wore the complete battle uniforms of the King and Queen's Champions with breastplates and helmets. Kell looked impressive in his full captain's regalia; a gold cuirass emblazoned with the ancient symbol of Jor'el. From the shoulder clasps of the cuirass hung a short purple cloak. Instead of a belt, a purple sash held his scabbard. His face glowed warm, golden eyes sparkled with full power and authority. Armus was similarly dressed to Kell, only less ornate. Wess appeared every inch the general in his silver breastplate with the black and red family crest. The black and red undercoat was complete with gloves and knee-high boots. His sword was unusual with an intricate black hilt.

Angus wore the gold and brown of his house, while Titus and Ellis were dressed in the royal blue and silver. Ned's uniform consisted of green and black for the Northern Forest while Fagan' battle attire made of silver with white and black for the Highlands. Chad wore his Jor'ellian captain's battle gear. Some had their helmets on; other carried them while some were placed on the table. Everyone saluted the royal couple.

"All is ready, Sire," said Kell.

"Any sign of enemy movement?"

"They have taken up positions directly counter to ours," said Tyrone. He proceeded to point out positions to Nigel on the map in relation to the landscape. "Myself, Tristine, Valery, Wess, Virgil, and Avatar will remain with you and the royal forces in the center. Ned, and part of Fagan's force, will be on the left flank. Angus' forces and the rest of Fagan's men will be on the right flank. The Guardian archers have been divided into three units. Wren will command the left flank, Vidar the right flank, and Tristine in the center. The thousand Guardians and six Jor'ellian companies have been divided into three units, under the command of Avatar, Kell and Armus."

Nigel paid close attention, though the plan had been drawn up and the forces deployed before last night. It was always good to review in case something unforeseen occurred or new information required adjustment. Nothing had, thus the plan remained the same.

"Come full light, they could launch an attack," added Wess.

"Then to your commands and begin preparations to preempt them and lessen the impact. Jor'el's blessings go with all," said Nigel.

At the dismissal, they parted to go their separate ways.

A short distance from the command tent there was a brief moment of sober silence between Wess, Fagan, Dylan and Ellis.

Fagan broke the silence. "None of us wanted this, including Bosley."

"It doesn't change what we must do." Wess' voice sounded harsh.

"Uncle, please," urged Dylan.

Wess jowls flexed and eyes weary on his nephew. "I wish you had listened to your father and stayed with Eric and Karly."

"I didn't want you to face this alone."

"None of us are facing this alone. That should mean something, Wess," said Fagan.

"I can get permission to stay with the three of you," said Ellis.

"No, son, your place is with Titus."

"You're father's right. You need to keep an eye on him for Jillian's sake." Wess flashed a smile and clapped Ellis on the shoulder. "I want to see the wedding Cassie planned for her. Now, go. We'll meet up after."

Once separated, Wess didn't get far when someone called his name. Tristine hurried towards him. "Is something wrong?"

"No. I wanted to speak with you before it all started, to say thank you for staying. I know how much it means to Nigel. To me, to all of us to have you here." She grew fretful. "I don't know what I'd do if Ellan …"

He stopped her by placing an arm around her shoulders. "Don't let such thoughts cloud your mind. Distractions are dangerous in battle."

"And you? Are you able to set aside distractions?"

For a moment he stared at her, as if struck by a sudden thought. "You don't know how much you look and sound like your father."

"Is that good or bad?"

He smiled warm and generous. "Good. During my early days as his squire, he'd challenge me with such questions to get me to think and refocus. You have done the same. Now, let us go and face what we must with clear resolve." He steered her toward their assigned positions.

Nearby, Nigel observed the exchange between Wess and Tristine with a private smile. When they moved off, he summoned Kendrick.

"I know Kell said it was dangerous because of your wound, but can you find Fraser and keep him away? Not solely for his sake, more for Tristine and Tyrone."

"Ay, Sire," he said with confident smile. Not waiting for dismissal, Kendrick ran behind a tent, and a flash of light soon followed.

Nigel moved to where Avatar held the reins of a warhorse. The animal stood beside three wooden steps for ease of mounting. Virgil held the reins of two white spirit horses, noticeably larger than any mortal horse for carrying Guardians. Valery sat mounted and held the reins of Mirit's horse, which also stood beside three wooden steps for mounting.

Mirit waited on foot for Nigel's return. Nigel kissed her cheek before putting on the helmet. He moved up the steps to mount. Mirit put on her helmet and went to mount. With the royal couple situated, Avatar and Virgil mounted the spirit horses.

Valery said to Cody, "You must stay here. Battle is no place for you."

Cody made a barking whimper.

"Please. I don't want anything to happen to you."

Wren spoke to Cody. "Stay and watch, Cody. Avatar, Virgil and myself will protect her." At her words, Cody sat.

"Thank you," said Valery.

Nigel led them to the head of the centerline. Tristine, Kell and Armus stood at their commands, a few hundreds to either side of where he stopped. Tyrone sat mounted at the head of his troops.

During the night, the artillery moved in front of the army and stretched the length of the plain. By the sun rising, they saw the enemy arrayed in position.

"Give the order to commence firing, Commander," said Nigel.

At Avatar's signal, all thirty cannons opened fire.

Mirit and Valery's horses became startled by the noise but were quickly brought under control. The ground shook with the force of the cannonade.

In nervous anticipation, Bosley and Erasmus waited upon their horses for the start of the battle. They flinched when the royal cannons fired. Not until the second volley, did orders come to return fire. The moment of truth arrived. They would learn if the covert sabotage would be successful or backfire.

"Let's pray this works," said Bosley.

Erasmus issued the order to fire. Several of the cannons did, but by the commotion and activity a problem arose. He tried not to smile.

Bosley sounded less enthusiastic. "I'll wait to see about Malcolm's guns before being relieved."

On the east flank, only five cannons puffed with the smoke of fire, the rest silent. The crews scrambled to determine the cause or problem for not firing.

"You were saying?" asked Erasmus, allowing a smile.

In the center of the enemy line, Hueil and Ellan watched from atop horses. Both were handsomely dressed in regal armor. The black spirit horse was bigger and impatient, stomping the ground.

"Why aren't the fools returning full fire?" she demanded.

A messenger on horseback galloped over and tossed a hasty salute. "Lord Zebulon reports many of the guns are malfunctioning."

"Why?" demanded Hueil.

"I don't know, my lord."

Another rider arrived from the west flank. "Baron Erasmus reports some of the artillery is broken or misfiring."

"The fools!" she swore. "Tell them to make repairs and hurry!" She dismissed the riders.

"You don't think this a coincidence, do you?" he asked her in a tone decidedly sarcastic.

"Sabotage? Erasmus and Bosley, ay, but not Malcolm and Braden. Gareth took command of Malcolm's troops upon his death."

Meanwhile they watched the royal bombardment rain down a forth volley and inflict heavy casualties to the mortal troops. Gareth and Braden drew their horses to a sudden stop.

"It's doubtful we can fix the guns in time, Majesty. I suggest we charge before sustaining too many more causalities," said Braden.

"Have you found evidence of sabotage?" demanded Ellan.

"No, but we are unable look while under fire."

"Malcolm's cannons are old and outdated," groused Gareth. "In his frail condition, he didn't keep his army properly supplied. Erasmus and Bosley no doubt."

"Ay, but we can't argue about it," said Braden.

"Order the charge," snapped Ellan.

"Mortals only!" added Hueil before Gareth and Braden rode off.

"Why? Are you afraid your precious Shadow Warriors aren't up the task of facing Kell?" she chided.

He wore a tight sneer. "No, my dear, a strategic maneuver. Get the enemy to deploy most, if not all their forces, then move in for the kill."

At a trumpet sound, the cavalry line began to move forward.

"They're charging!"

Nigel heard Tyrone's call and acknowledged him with a wave. He drew the Sword of Allon and lifted it over his head as a signal for attention. He looked up and down the line to see all the commanders draw their swords or lift their bows to indicate readiness.

"For Jor'el and Allon!" he shouted and lowered the Sword to point straight ahead. He kicked his horse. He, Avatar, Mirit, Virgil and Valery led the spearhead charge into the center of the enemy's line.

When they rode passed the artillery, the royal guns ceased firing. Royal and Guardian archers launched a hail of arrows at the enemy to cover the charge.

Valery noticed her father a hundred yards to the west and leading his men. She couldn't think about him or what would happen if they met. Instead, she engaged an enemy soldier. Their skill levels were evenly matched. She managed to wound him and he fell from his horse.

There wasn't a moment's pause before another soldier attacked. She made a clumsy defense and barely kept herself from falling off her horse. She used the brief moment he turned his horse around to regain her balance and braced for more fighting. It soon became obvious he possessed more skill. She wouldn't yield. When he moved to knock her from her horse, she landed a blow to his mid-section that staggered him and he backed off. However, being off balance from dodging the counter-attack, she awkwardly slipped off her horse.

Out of the corner of her eye came a glint of steel. She lifted her sword to deflect the blow. The momentum of the rider's attack sent her off her feet. Her sword fell away on impact with the ground. Grimacing, she lay on the ground for a moment to catch her breath.

Near by, Ellis engaged two soldiers. Maneuvering a horse in battle proved frustrating. He repulsed an attack that made one soldier fall off due to overreaching. This left Ellis with only one foe to dispatch.

In turning around to deal with the fallen soldier, Ellis saw Valery knocked backwards. Unfortunately, his distraction allowed the soldier who fell from his horse to wound his right hand and knock his sword away. Ellis' reaction jerked his horse's head and the soldier fell back to avoid the horse. Ellis kicked the other soldier square in the chest and sent him stumbling away.

Fortunately, he suffered only a nick on his hand but couldn't locate his sword. The man bore down on Valery, who remained on the ground. She didn't appear to see the enemy. Having no weapon limited his options to either ramming or jumping at the man. He urged his horse in a rush to intervene.

Valery's eyes went wide in recognizing the attacker—her father! At the same moment, Ellis leapt from his horse. Both tumbled to the ground. Ellis ended on top and struck Braden in the face, rendering him semi-conscious. He snatched Braden's sword, stood and held it at Braden's throat. Cody arrived, hackles up and snarling at Braden.

"No, Ellis! Cody!" She scrambled to her feet.

Braden regained his senses enough to see a wolf, Ellis and Valery. He sneered at her. "You don't have the courage to kill me."

Cody snapped and Braden flinched in fear. Ellis pressed the sword point against Braden's neck, nicking the skin and drawing blood.

"We do!"

"No. He's not worth coming between us any more. Have him taken prisoner to face the king's justice."

Ellis grinned in approval. He noticed Ridge finish dealing with an attacking soldier. "Ridge!" The ranger hastened to the summons. "Take Lord Braden and secure him until the king can deal with his treachery."

Ridge jerked Braden to his feet.

"I knew you didn't have the courage," chided Braden.

Ellis seized Braden by the throat. "She has the courage to do what is right. Which is more than you, her father, ever did! Cody, go and don't let him out of your sight." He roughly released Braden.

Ridge left, securely holding Braden with Cody nipping at Braden.

The sounds of battle drew closer with Titus against three soldiers.

"I must get back to the Titus," said Ellis.

She grabbed him, kissed him and said, "I love you. Be careful."

He smiled. "Nothing will stop me now." He snatched the reins of his horse, vaulted into the saddle and raced to help Titus.

She retrieved her sword and horse to rejoin the battle beside Mirit.

Fraser followed the enemy to the plain of Arundine and discovered the battle raging. He began covert forays on the fringe of the west flank. He used a rock to strike one soldier in the head, knocking him off his horse. He tried to retreat when a second soldier spotted him, and forced to defend himself on foot. Fortunately his quickness came in handy. He slashed the soldier's leg so deep that the man fell off in agony. The wound must have severed an artery, as blood streamed out the leg. The soldier appeared on the verge of collapse.

"Mercy! Help before I bleed to death."

Fraser ripped off part of the soldier's uniform to wrap the leg. Blood immediately soaked the bandage. The soldier fainted and Fraser didn't know what else to do. The man's breath grew very shallow. Finally the soldier became still. Fraser felt for a pulse. None. For the first time, he killed. He became startled at hearing someone call a warning, "Tyrone!"

Angus fought two enemy soldiers. Just past Angus, his father engaged four mounted soldiers. Gripping his sword in determination, Fraser vaulted onto the dead soldier's horse.

While riding to help his father, he slashed the back of a soldier fighting Angus. The soldier swayed in the saddle and Angus finished him. He caught a sight of Fraser galloping toward Tyrone.

Fraser rammed his horse into another horse to get the enemy's attention. It worked. For the first time, he fought in mounted combat. With grit and resolve, he matched the soldier blow or blow.

"Fraser?" he heard his name and briefly caught his father's eye. He couldn't reply due to fighting. Unfortunately, this caused enough distraction for soldier to clout him in the left side of the head with the hilt of his sword. He fell from his horse, unconscious and bleeding.

"No!" Tyrone quickly finished his opponents. However, he couldn't find his son. Angus joined him. "Have you seen Fraser?"

"He rode past me to help you."

"He fell, but I don't see him now. Fraser!" He stood in the stirrups.

"He can't disappear, so he may have wandered back into battle."

A trumpet sounded and the enemy's west flank veered off the initial attack and headed for the center.

"Come! Nigel will need help against their reinforcements." When Tyrone hesitated, Angus gripped his arm. "We'll find Fraser later."

Tyrone jerked his horse around and rode to the center of the battle.

Kendrick reappeared in the wood some distance away from the battle and very unsteady on his feet. Fraser remained unconscious. Kendrick tried to be gentle in laying Fraser down. He grimaced and doubled over in great pain. The activity aggravated his wound and this was as far as he could bring his charge without causing further injury to either of them.

Although, he didn't know where they were, he heard no sounds of fighting. The boy could have fainted from dimension travel or the head wound. Either way, he would treat Fraser in the shelter of the trees until he regained enough strength to fetch help or take him back to Waldron.

Bosley led his men into the center. He had to fight to survive, but it was difficult to block out reality. Up until now, he fought Fagan's men on the flank. Bad enough fighting his brother-in-law, but in the center, he faced royal soldiers. At any moment he expected to meet Nigel or Wess. What he didn't expect to see was Dylan in the king's uniform, valiantly fighting. Before his eyes, his divided family faced each other on battlefield. He turned to leave, unable to bear it. However, what happened next, made him send his horse into a gallop toward the battle.

In the thick of fighting, Nigel used the Sword of Allon to make quick work of all enemy soldiers who came into range. Being engaged with the most recent foe, he didn't see the enemy archer take aim. He just finished the soldier when an arrow struck his right hand. Although the gauntlet deflected it from causing damage, the sharp impact made him drop the sword. He glared in the direction the arrow came. Not only did the archer loading for another shot, but a fast approaching rider struck the offending archer from behind. He barely recognized Bosley, when an arrow struck Bosley high in the chest near the neck where the armor didn't protect and sent him off his horse.

Nigel dismounted, threw off his helmet and hurried to Bosley. The arrow pierced deep. Bosley gasped for air so Nigel took off the helmet to help him breathe. Bosley's eyes were opened.

"Nigel," spoke in a raspy voice. "I'm sorry."

"Don't talk." He went to examine the wound.

Wess arrived and leapt from his horse. "Bosley!"

"We'll take him to Eldric," said Nigel, trying to sound encouraging.

Bosley gripped Nigel's arm and forced himself to speak. "We tried to stop them, Erasmus and I."

"Be still and let us take you to Eldric." Wess gathered Bosley in his arms when there came a great gasp and then stillness. He felt for a pulse. None. He screwed his eyes shut, trying not to weep, but a sob escape.

Nigel's voice was thick with sorrow. "He saved me again, only this time it cost him. Take him back to camp. I'll see he gets a proper burial."

Wess lifted Bosley's body over his horse's saddle and left the field.

Nigel stood, blinked and wiped his eyes clear. At a nudge on his arm, he reached for his sword, forgetting he was unarmed. He relaxed at recognizing Avatar, who held his helmet and the Sword of Allon.

"Don't let his sacrifice be in vain."

Nigel put the helmet on and took the sword. Staunch resolution replaced grief. "One more reason to stop them!"

Ellan stirred in the saddle. With annoyed impatience, she watched the dismal sight of her troops being cut down on every flank. "This is ridiculous! Why did you let them face royal soldiers and Guardians on their own? Send out the Shadow Warriors and wyverns."

"Patience, my dear. All is going according to plan."

"Whose plan? Yours? Well, I don't care a wit for your plan."

"Majesty!" called a rider, who was soiled and wounded from battle. "I beg to report Lord Zebulon is dead and Lord Braden taken prisoner. Sir Gareth is trying to hold the flank."

"What of Bosley and Erasmus?"

The rider shrugged ignorance. "I don't know. Their flank is divided."

She snarled at Hueil. "Enough! We end it before we are defeated!"

Hueil snarled, but shouted, "Phelan! Prepare the Shadow Warriors for advance and unleashing of the wyverns."

With a sharp salute, Phelan followed orders.

Occasional volleys of cannonade and arrows were launched unto the field from the enemy in a feeble attack. Mahon helped Angus to stand after a burst of cannon fire killed Angus' horse.

"Are you hurt?"

"Only my pride. Not to mention my backside."

They heard a very loud and distinctive trumpet that made Mahon jump to defense and look skyward.

"What is it?" asked Angus.

"Dagar used that call at the Great Battle to summon—," ear-piercing screams finished Mahon's sentence the same time he did, "wyverns!"

The sky filled with hundreds of wyverns heading in their direction.

Angus stared in dreaded amazement. "How many are there?"

Mahon shook his head. "I didn't think so many were left."

"Merciful heaven," said Valery upon seeing the approaching swarm. "What are they?"

"Wyverns," said Virgil. He steadied his agitated spirit horse when he moved between Valery and Mirit. Their swords bloody from battle.

"Come!" Mirit turned her horse to yell, "Nigel! Wyverns!"

He acknowledged her, and called out orders. "Tristine! Wren! Vidar! Stygian arrows!"

"Ay, Sire," came their reply.

"Shadow Warriors," said Avatar, indicating a new charge.

"Kell!" Nigel took his shield off the saddlebow. Mirit and Valery did the same with their shields.

Kell ran in front of them and shouted. "Guardians! Jor'ellians! Form on Armus and me!"

Armus stood one hundred yards to the left, and echoed the order.

"Avatar! Wyndy! Ridge! To your positions!" Kell placed his sword in readiness before his face. "Spare no power! Show no mercy! Give no quarter!" He thrust his sword in the air. "For Jor'el, for the king, for Allon!" When his call was echoed, he lowered his sword. "Now!"

Immediately a thousand stygian arrows were launched, some aimed at the wyverns, others arching toward the Shadow Warriors. The vanishing grey light showed the demise of some Shadow Warriors. The arrows had little affect on the swarm of wyverns.

Kell repeated the signal. A second volley of arrows launched. It had the same effect of vanquishing some Shadow Warriors and not hurting the wyverns.

"Armus!" Kell motioned to the enemy.

"Charge!" shouted Armus to his troops. He launched himself at the enemy while calling upon his overwhelming power. He plowed through the first rank of ten Shadow Warriors like a hot knife through butter.

"Now!" said Kell, and his troops raced forward to join the battle.

Engaged in battle with four Shadow Warriors, Mahon grunted under his breath in Ancient, "*An luths de fichead!*" His strength surged, and with a few swift strokes, all four Warriors vanished. Hearing someone approach, he whirled about ready to strike.

"Mahon?" exclaimed Mannix in surprise.

Mahon pulled his blow. For a moment, they stared at each other. Mannix appeared skeptical and wary, and Mahon to remember. At the indecision, Mannix fled. Mahon lowered his sword and faulted in step.

Kell rushed over to aid Mahon. "Did Mannix land a blow?"

He sluggishly shook his head. "No, I let him go."

"What? I commanded no quarter!"

The hissing and whizzing of enemy arrows interrupted Mahon's answer. One struck Mannix and he vanished in grey light.

"Stygian arrows!" chided Kell in warning.

Being mortal, the Jor'ellian fell under when struck. A handful Guardians vanished and others seriously wounded. Not good.

"If you can't handle battle then withdraw!" he snapped at Mahon.

"No, Captain—" he started to protest when Kell ran back into the fray. Angry, Mahon continued to fight.

A stygian arrow penetrated Tristine's breastplate and struck deep in the right side of her body. The force knocked her back ten feet. By the time Armus reached her, she was unconscious.

Tyrone and Nigel arrived. Tyrone jumped from his horse. "Tristine!"

Nigel's horse did not like the sudden stop and he fought to get it under control. "How is she?"

"It's a stygian arrow and must be removed quickly yet carefully. I'm taking her to Eldric." Armus lifted her in his arms and disappeared.

"Go with him," said Nigel.

Tyrone vaulted into the saddle and rode back to camp.

Nigel's horse remained contrary when he turned the animal to issue a command. "Wren! Vidar! Target the archers." The horse lurched in the direction he wanted and partly bucked. "Avatar! Now!"

Avatar drew his sword and rushed forward on foot. Wyndy and Ridge went with him. Avatar and Wyndy began to speak in the Ancient.

"*Lubach gaoth! Lucach goath! Milleadth de namh!*" Wyndy raised her arms to the sky. Immediately dark clouds appeared accompanied by fierce winds, swirling and twisting around the wyverns. A few funnel tails reached the ground. Some wyverns were tossed off course while others hurled to the ground.

"*An dealanach siuthad de namh!*" Avatar thrust his sword into the air. With a sudden clap of thunder, a shaft of blinding light flashed from his sword and raced up into the swirling clouds. Branches of lightning emanated from the clouds in various directions, striking wyverns and exploding them in mid air.

Kell heard Nigel's order. He placed the pommel of his sword in front of his face. "Jor'el's strength attend us now!" he said in the Ancient.

Ewert, Bailey, Nixie, Zadok, Derwin, and other Guardian Warriors formed behind Kell, saying, "Let it be so!"

With a war cry, Kell engaged a wyvern that fell from the sky. The others followed his lead in attacking grounded wyverns or Shadow Warriors.

The Dark Way man-dragon swung its spiked tail to stop Kell's advance. He dodged the spike and came up swinging his sword. He cut off the tail portion with the spike. The enraged wyvern charged Kell.

Sparks flew when the blades met and Kell didn't budge. He turned the wyvern's blade aside.

Instinctively, the wyvern used its partial tail in defense. This time when Kell ducked, it lunged at him, taking the captain to the ground. The impact knocked Kell's sword away and the wyvern's knee landed on his chest. The crushing weight made it hard for Kell to breathe. He snatched its arm to keep the sword at bay and held the chin to prevent being bitten by four-inch fangs.

"*Imich dhiom!*" he managed to say and shoved the wyvern off him. He took a deep gulp of air in attempt to regain his breath. At the beast's roar, Kell rose to his knees. His sword was not within reach. He stretched out his left hand and commanded in the Ancient, "Stop!"

The wyvern screamed in anger as the command brought it to an abrupt halt. Slowly, it moved forward. The effort to stop its approach showed on Kell's face. Still holding up his left hand, he took the dagger from his belt with his right hand. Risky, but with his command not working, he had to act. He bolted to his feet to throw the dagger, which released the wyvern from his command. It charged at full speed when the dagger struck, burying hilt deep in the left breast, briefly halting it. Kell snatched up his sword and swung at the wyvern, severing its jugular vein. Unlike Shadow Warriors, wyverns didn't vanish when killed.

It took a couple of moments for Kell to recover using a great deal of strength to deal with a wyvern singlehanded. He noticed Ewert and Bailey battled one very large wyvern. Ewert dodged the spiked tail as Bailey fought steel to steel with the creature. Finally Ewert sliced off the dangerous spike. The wyvern's angry retaliation sent Ewert sideways with a swing of its arm. That left it vulnerable to Bailey's special power attack. His sword nearly cleaved the wyvern in half.

Satisfied at that victory, Kell's attention was drawn to Zadok and Derwin surrounded by three wyverns. The warriors stood back-to-back with their swords poised and ready. One wyvern feinted an attack to engage the warriors and another swung its tail. The spike sliced across Derwin's abdomen and he fell to his knees.

Kell moved to intervene when a lightning bolt struck the offending wyvern and it exploded. At the same time he heard Avatar shout, "Now, Ridge!"

Ridge took his staff in both hands and lifted it the air with one end pointed toward the ground. He shouted in the Ancient. "*Talamh uir sluig de namh!*" He struck the ground with the end of his staff. From the strike point, cracks ran out onto battlefield. The earth opened under the feet of Shadow Warriors and fallen wyverns, dragging them under and quickly closing on top of them.

Kell avoided the cracks. Guardians and Jor'ellians also avoided the spreading cracks. The earth consumed the enemy until all were gone. Kell ran to where Zadok examined Derwin's wound. He was in great pain from a deep gash across his mid-section.

"We'll take him to field hospital."

Derwin hissed and gritted his teeth against the pain when Zadok and Kell lifted him to his feet. He doubled over, so they caught him under the arm and about the waist and carried him from the field.

Arriving at the front line in time to witness the attack, Ellan became speechless. Wyvern were struck from the sky by lightning bolts, caught in twisters or disappeared beneath the ground along with Shadow Warriors.

"This can't be happening!" she muttered in utter disbelief.

All her dreams of revenge ruined before her eyes. She turned away to regain her composure. Hueil spoke to Phelan, the Guardian mounted and the Shadow Warrior on foot. How unfazed he acted in the midst of certain defeat. What treachery was he planning? He didn't want her or a son. *He wanted the throne.* She knew it all along, but if it would help her get revenge, it was worth the risk. Not now. With defeat inevitable, she wouldn't let him have the throne. She carefully withdrew her dagger then spoke in voice feinting entreaty and beckoning.

"Hueil. Please reassure me this is going according to your plan."

He pulled his horse alongside her. She shouted in anger and launched at him dagger first. She landed a blow that penetrated his right breast. He caught her and pulled her off her horse. Both fell to the ground. Even wounded, she was no match for a Guardian and he tossed her aside. The dagger jerked out in the process. He hissed in painful rage. She scrambled to her feet, the dagger still in her hand and showed no fear only hatred and anger. She advanced. He threw out his hand and began closing his fist. She stopped in mid-stride, gasping for air.

"Foolish, mortal! I would have shared power with you, for a little while. Since you desire death." He clenched his fist and jerked his hand as if snatching something. A snapping sound followed. Her neck broke and she collapsed to the ground. Blank eyes stared up at the sky.

"What now, my lord? They have defeated the wyverns and Shadow Warriors." Phelan pointed to a clear sky, no clouds, lightning or wyverns.

"A strategic withdrawal." Hueil no sooner spoke then a stygian arrow struck Phelan and the Warrior vanished in grey light. Hueil noticed Wren the moment she fired. A stygian arrow hit him deep his right shoulder.

He staggered from the impact of a second wound. He groaned in anger when searing pain spread through his body. The arrow being stygian metal barely registered in his brain when a powerful backhand to the face sent him sideway and split his lip into his chin. Hueil managed to stay on his feet and indentify who struck him. Mahon! The warrior had his sword drawn and looked very nasty.

"I'm unarmed." Hueil raised his left arm, unable to lift his right arm. His watched Mahon and Wren. He couldn't disappear with arrow lodged in his body and stifling his energy. "Either of you kill me and you'll suffer the consequences."

Neither replied or moved. Hueil took advantage of their non-action to turn for a hasty retreat. Surprised disbelief registered on his face when a sword plunged through his chest. He looked from the blade to— "You?"

"As Jor'ellian Commander, I have the authority to execute immediate justice. You are finished!" Avatar jerked out his sword. Hueil collapsed to the ground and vanished in grey light. Avatar stared at the vacant spot. Mahon's hand on his shoulder made him look up.

"It's over, my friend."

Nigel, Mirit and Valery, Virgil arrived on horseback and halted beside Ellan's body. Nigel stared at Ellan, his face expressionless.

"Hueil is responsible. He is no more. I made certain," said Avatar. When Nigel met his gaze, the mortal's face remained void of emotion. Without a word, Nigel turned his horse and rode back across the plain. Mirit, Valery and Virgil followed.

"Will he be all right?" asked Mahon.

"I don't know," said Avatar.

"What should we do with her?" asked Wren.

"I'll find out. Meanwhile, secure the body from view." Avatar left.

Nigel, Mirit, Valery and Virgil dismounted at the field hospital. They found Tyrone and Armus with Eldric. Tristine remained unconscious and pale under a blanket pulled over her shoulders. She wore an undershirt with a bandage visible through the open neck.

"How is she?" asked Nigel in a near whisper.

"A very serious wound, and fortunate the arrow wasn't higher," said Eldric.

"Will she live?"

"Ay. I gave her something for the pain and to sleep. She needs rest." He made motion for them to leave.

Armus folded his arms in defiance. "I'm staying,"

Eldric frowned, to which Tyrone asked, "Will you make him leave?"

"Don't ask me to order him," added Nigel.

"Very well, Sire," said the physician with unabashed sarcasm, "but the rest of you, please leave. She will be fine."

Outside, Titus and Ellis rushed to meet them. "Mother?" asked Titus.

"The wound is serious, but she will recover. She sleeps and Armus is with her," replied Tyrone.

"Thank Jor'el. I feared the worst."

"Indeed. Thank Jor'el, for many more survived than were killed."

Ellis and Valery exchanged glances; he smiled and she blushed.

329

"Is there something we should know about?" asked Mirit.

"A question I asked Lady Valery last evening to which she consented, providing we survived. And we have," replied Ellis, his smile growing.

Mirit eyed the couple. "Have you obtained permission to wed?"

Ellis' smile vanished. "I don't know if her father would consent. He is a prisoner awaiting the king's pleasure."

"Who captured him?" asked Nigel.

"I did, at her ladyship's request. He was about to run her down."

"Better to face your justice than personal vengeance," said Valery.

Nigel nodded in approval. "Wisely done."

"Indeed," said Mirit, who fought a smile. "Only I didn't mean her father. As my squire and cousin to the king, she is a royal ward."

"Oh," said Ellis stunned and uncertain.

Titus poked Ellis and motioned to Nigel. "Well, ask, you ninny."

Valery took Ellis' arm. "Sire, I ask permission to wed Lord Ellis."

Nigel smiled and said, "Granted."

"Thank you, Sire," said Ellis with relief.

As the group moved toward the royal tent, Tyrone caught sight of Avatar's beckoning gesture. He discreetly left the others to join the Guardian. "What is it?"

"Ellan is dead. So is Hueil."

After a moment of relief, Tyrone grew sober. "Does Nigel know?"

"Ay. However, by his strange non-reaction, I don't feel he can discuss her dispensation."

Tyron grew thoughtful. "Although a royal, she shouldn't be buried in the family crypt. Any suggestions?"

"A proper burial where no mortal can find her."

"Do so. If Nigel asks, I'll assume responsibility."

"No need. I don't think he'll question either of us."

After parting from Avatar, Tyrone entered the tent and found Nigel holding a piece of paper and looking grim. Mirit wept and Ellis discomposed with Valery trying to comfort him. Kell, Angus and Mahon had joined them.

"Has something happened?" asked Tyrone.

"I told them about Bosley because of this." Nigel indicated the letter. "Mathias defeated Hollis. Most didn't want to fight and offered minimal resistance before surrendering, except Hollis. His ship was sunk with all hands lost. Now, I must tell Wess and Dylan that Garrick is also dead."

"No." Tyrone took the paper. "I'm the one who gave the order for Mathias to sail, so I'll be the one to tell them."

"I'm coming with you. I need to be with my uncle and cousin," said Ellis. He withdrew from Valery. She wouldn't be put off from accompanying him. They stopped at entrance when Fagan arrived.

"Sire. We captured Gareth. What do you want done with him?"

"How many prisoners are there?"

"One hundred officers and some lesser noblemen along with Braden and Gareth."

"Have them secured until I can convene a court of judgment."

"You shouldn't wait too long, Sire," said Kell.

"This evening, after a few hours of rest and prayer. Myself, Tyrone, Angus, you, Avatar and Vidar will serve as judges. By the way, where is Avatar?"

"Tending to duty, as we should be," began Tyrone. "I'll send him to you. Fagan, join us." He steered Fagan out of the tent with Valery and Ellis following.

Chapter 24

FRASER DIDN'T KNOW LONG HE REMAINED UNCONSCIOUS WHEN he smelled something burning. His eyes opened at hearing the crackling of a fire and realized the odor was smoke. He tried to sit up, only got dizzy and leaned back on his elbows hoping for the sensation to pass. A person sat beside the fire, poking the logs. In surprise, he sat up, ignoring all pain.

"Kendrick? Are you really alive or is this a dream? Oh, my head."

The Guardian moved from the fire. "No dream. I'm alive, though wounded. You suffered a nasty blow to head." He examined the crude bandage he made from the hem of his garment when Fraser hugged him.

"I thought Hueil killed you! I thought everything was a dream, a horrible dream. I've acted like a fool believing her."

"True. But why charge into battle like you did?" He took Fraser by the shoulders to look him in the eyes.

"I had to do something to make things right. Perhaps if I either killed the enemy or died trying, they'd believe I didn't mean it! The last thing I wanted is for you, Mikaela, or anyone to be hurt. I'm sorry. Can you forgive me?" he begged and hugged Kendrick again.

"I can forgive you. But getting killed isn't the way to seek forgiveness. Admitting and facing those you wronged is the way to true forgiveness and reconciliation."

"I don't think I can after seeing my parents' hurt and disappointment. I've never seen Uncle Angus so angry before. Uncle Nigel," his voice cracked, "he told me to get out of his sight!"

"Nigel sent me to find you."

The statement baffled Fraser. "He did? Why?"

"Some love is so strong it can overcome mistakes. Nigel learned that lesson when he ran away because he thought he couldn't face his family after his crippling. Now, *you* must face those mistakes and not run away."

"He came back and they were reunited. Mother told me."

"After five years and through great adversity. Will you wait to speak to your parents and risk losing precious time?"

"I don't know." He moaned and held his head. It hurt from the blow and confusion.

"I wish I could give you something for the pain, but that's Eldric's specialty."

"What about my stomach? I'm hungry."

"I was about to cook a rabbit when you woke."

"Good. Then I think I want to sleep some more."

Kendrick returned to the fire and placed on a prepared rabbit on a skewer over the flame. "What about returning to Waldron?"

"Ask me in morning after I've slept on it."

***

Nigel wished he could sleep, but that wasn't practical or possible. He, Tyrone, Angus, Avatar, Kell and Vidar took their seats for the court of judgment. As they waited for the first prisoner, Tyrone told Nigel about Wess and Dylan's reaction. Wess did most of the talking while Dylan was somber for having lost his father and older brother.

"I wish I could have spared them," sighed Nigel.

"You're not to blame for the choices of others."

"Ay." He sighed with lament. "Bosley protected me *again,* only this time he died. For that, I feel regret and sorrow for Wess and Dylan."

"Sire, the prisoners are ready for judgment."

Nigel just nodded, and the proceedings began with the lowest ranking prisoners. Wess was excused from duty, so Chad acted as the lead officer in presenting the prisoners. He read their names and charges then asked for a plea. If they pleaded guilty, a sentence was passed befitting the crime. If they plead not guilty, they were required to make defense. Only a handful pleaded not guilty, most unable to make adequate defense to defer sentence. Two men made sound cases by offering evidence of coercion by Ellan or Gareth, and showing proof of aiding Bosley and Erasmus in their efforts to sabotage. They were artillery officers, one from the North Plains and the other from Midessex. In the end, the charges were dismissed and the men released.

Finally came time for the Council Members. Nigel ordered them brought one at a time instead of groups like the soldiers and lower noblemen. The first to appear before the court was Erasmus. This proved surprising since his name had not been mentioned. He was soiled and weary, yet humble and contrite in posture.

"Sire. Highness. Your Grace," he addressed and bowed to each.

"Baron Erasmus. We were not aware of your capture," said Nigel.

"I surrendered to Captain Chad an hour ago."

"Indeed, Sire. Only I did not have time to tell you before the proceedings," confirmed Chad.

"Sire, may I inquire if you received what Lord Bosley and I sent?"

"Everything arrived in good order, Baron."

Erasmus smiled in relief. "I'm glad."

"However," said Nigel, growing sorrowful. "Bosley died in battle."

Erasmus turned pale with grief. "It pains me more than I can say."

"I too am deeply grieved. Before he died, he told me what you and he did to try and help me."

Erasmus' voice was thick with regret. "Before heaven, we didn't want to fight you!" he said to Nigel then to Tyrone, "Or force you and Tristine to such action. We did everything we could to prevent it."

"Speaking to Malcolm and Braden's artillery officers, we found proof to support your claim. Unfortunately, the uprising can't be ignored."

"I know, Sire, and I am prepared to face my punishment. However, I ask you to spare my son and his family."

"You can be assured of their safety and well-being. By proxy, Eric witnessed my coronation." Nigel grinned, poignant and short lived. "As for your punishment … " he looked to his colleagues for consensus.

"The prison island of Glyndower needs a new steward," said Kell.

Nigel grew curious. "Glyndower?"

"Ay. It is isolated with only one way on or off the island by ship."

"Not much trouble he could get into there," said Tyrone, to which Angus added his agreement. Vidar and Avatar gave consenting nods.

"Very well. Baron, you are to exiled to the island of Glyndower for the remainder of your life to act as royal steward."

Erasmus smiled in relief. "Thank you for mercy, Sire."

Nigel signaled Chad to escort Erasmus from the proceedings. Barely a moment passed before Gareth faced the judges. For this encounter, Nigel's demeanor changed to grim and unyielding.

"Well, Sir Gareth, your true colors have finally been seen. If you think you can talk your way out of this one, you are wrong!"

He sneered in disdain. "Don't flatter yourself that I would even try. At least with the half-breed I had some hope of intelligent argument."

Tyrone bolted to his feet at the insult. Nigel seized his arm. "Save your breath, he is not worth the trouble." Not until Nigel tugged on his arm, did Tyrone sit. Nigel leaned forward, a focus of contempt on Gareth. "Mercy was extended to you in the past. Not this time. The headsman is waiting. Captain!" He waved and Chad removed Gareth.

"I think we need to cool our tempers. Especially with Braden being next and eyes watching," said Angus. He carefully motioned to the crowd where Valery stood. Ellis and Cody appeared beside her. Ellis spoke a few words. She shook her head and remained.

Chad's announcement of Braden turned their attention to the court.

"Lord Braden," began Nigel. "You are accused of sedition, treason and raising armed rebellion. How do you plead, guilty or not guilty?"

Braden caught sight of Valery when she drew closer and the flicking light caught her red hair. Ellis stopped her further approach.

The others also noticed, so Nigel divert attention back by asking again, "How do plead, my lord?"

Braden squared his shoulders and said, "Not guilty."

"Are you prepared to present evidence to support your plea?"

"Who is there to bear witness against me? I was captured unarmed. What proof do you have of the accusation except being in the wrong place at the wrong time?" He turned from Nigel to look at Valery.

"Your own actions bear witness to supporting sedition and armed conflict! And you will look at the court when you speak."

"I can give testimony, Sire." Valery stepped forward.

"Valery, don't," said Ellis. "Sire, don't let her."

Nigel spoke with compassion. "You don't have to do this. We know he meant to goad you, and there is evidence enough against him."

"No, Sire. I want to. I need to." She faced her father and spoke in a clear voice. "I observed Lord Braden meet with Sir Gareth, Lord Zebulon, Queen Ellan and the Guardian Hueil to plot a coup to seize the throne. He threatened to kill me if I told what I discovered. My mother was killed when he learned she helped me escape so I could warn of the plot." Her voice cracked and tears flowed. Ellis held her shoulder in support, as she continued. "Lord Ellis captured him and prevented him from killing me in battle, as he threatened to do."

"Please, Sire, let that suffice," said Ellis.

"Ay. You have given testimony and we are satisfied. Lord Ellis, take Lady Valery back to her tent."

This time she went with him when he steered her away.

Nigel's compassion vanished toward Braden. "You were saying about a witness?"

"I advise you to change your plea," said Tyrone.

"What does it matter? The sentence will be the same."

"Indeed, you will follow Sir Gareth's fate," said Nigel. "Captain."

Chad ordered soldiers to escort Braden away then addressed Nigel. "He was the last prisoner, Sire."

"Then court is adjourned."

"I'm going to sit with Tristine. She may not wake until morning, but I want to be there when she does," said Tyrone.

"You?" Angus asked Nigel.

"Not everything is done for me." He headed for his tent.

"You're not an invincible Guardian who can go days without sleep. And I know you haven't slept in at least two days."

Nigel paused in step. "I didn't want to say anything in front of Tristine or Tyrone and get their hopes up. Before the battle, I sent Kendrick to find Fraser and I've not heard from him."

"Fraser was on the battlefield."

"What? I told Kendrick to keep him away."

"I didn't see Kendrick. Fraser passed me to help Tyrone. Unfortunately when all was done we couldn't find him."

"Merciful heaven, I pray the worse hasn't happened. I hate to think our last words were spoken in anger."

"So do I. For all his faults, he is just a naive boy whom they duped. However, he isn't among the dead or wounded. Kendrick may have succeeded. Now get some rest." He escorted Nigel to the tent.

Mirit emerged to meet them. She was cleaned and wearing a dressing gown with her hair loose. "It's late and you need to get some sleep."

"I brought him back with the same thought." Angus handed Nigel to Mirit. "If he gives you trouble, send for me."

"He won't, he knows better." She and Nigel went inside the tent.

Mahon approached. "All is secure for the night, Your Grace."

"Good. I'm going to get some sleep."

Kell, Avatar, Vidar and Wren intercepted Mahon, but allowed Angus to continue, unaware of any problem.

"You owe me an explanation, Mahon," said Kell firmly.

"And one we'd like to hear," said Avatar of himself and the others.

"Mannix," said Mahon with a twinge of regret. "Well, my mercy was short-lived as a stygian arrow struck him down."

"Divine justice doesn't explain why you let him go," said Kell.

"I just defeated four Shadow Warriors when someone approached from behind. I turned, prepared for engagement. He appeared surprised to see me. When our eyes met, I couldn't strike as I suddenly remembered everything. Locan poured the potion down my throat while Hueil held my head and mouth open. Mannix just stood by, at least at first."

"Did he do something later?" asked Wren.

"Ay. Hueil rammed the device behind my ear. I hadn't felt such intense pain since my imprisonment, and I fainted. Upon coming to, Mannix was speaking to me. At first I didn't understand him, then he reached down and I felt the device move but not removed. Next time he spoke, I began to hear him, only I couldn't respond."

"Are you saying Mannix loosened the device? Why?" asked Vidar.

"He said something about wanting to help me. Although I could hear his words nothing made sense due to the effects of the device and potion. He kept urging me not to resist and by yielding I could save myself pain."

"So you pretended to yield?" asked Kell.

"It didn't seem like pretense when he attacked Avatar," said Wren.

"No!" began Mahon adamantly. "The device was only loosened so whereas it did affect me, I don't believe it fully turned me. Otherwise how could I resist killing Avatar, or recognizing you when you shot me?"

"I didn't want to!"

"I know, I'm just saying." Mahon turned to Kell to continue his argument. "Captain, how many Guardians do you know, who were turned yet resisted the mind device?" Kell grew thoughtful, so Mahon proceeded. "I don't believe I could have responded to Avatar's command to remember if Mannix hadn't loosened it."

"So you spared Mannix because of his actions?" asked Kell.

"Ay, for I believe it kept me from doing the unthinkable!"

"That's possible. Mannix was a fellow prisoner and understood the device," said Vidar.

"Not to mention Mahon survived the trial by fire. There should be no question to his motive, Captain," said Avatar.

Kell returned his focus to Mahon. "No question, and I understand your actions, but divine justice happened when he fell in battle."

"I'm glad to say, not by me. Any word of Locan?"

"No, nor Fitch. No Shadow Warriors survived, so I doubt they did."

"Be nice to knew for sure. They caused too much trouble to be left alive," groused Vidar.

"I'd have no hesitation about dealing with Locan," said Mahon.

"Or Kendrick with Fitch," said Avatar.

"We can only deal with what we know." Kell clapped Mahon's shoulder. "Think no more of it, as the matter is done. In the morning, the army returns to Waldron."

Tyrone watched Tristine sleep. Every event and conversation replayed itself across his mind. Ellan's threat, being told by Uriah her claim was legitimate, yielding the throne to Nigel, sealing the ruins, battle, and even dealing with Fraser's foolishness. None of those troubles compared to seeing Tristine wounded and the thought of losing her. Eldric reassured him of her recovery and Armus added his confirmation. Still, he wanted her to wake and see for himself. Telling her of the outcome also weighed on his mind. How would she take Ellan's death? Or should he wait to tell her until she was stronger? On the various scenarios he vacillated until around midnight when she stirred and finally woke.

He smiled and stroking her head. "How are you feeling?"

"I've been better. What happened? And where am I?"

"You were struck by a stygian arrow and Armus brought you to the field hospital."

She squirmed to get comfortable and grunted in pain of doing so. "I know about the arrow. I meant the battle."

"It's over, but don't be concerned about it. Concentrate on recovering."

"Then we won?"

He smiled. "Ay."

She flashed a weak smile. "Nigel, Mirit, Titus and the others?"

"All are well and unharmed."

She sighed with relief. "I'm glad. Fraser?"

"No word yet. When all is settled, I will search for him."

"Ellan and Hueil?" He hesitated and didn't reply. She gasped in alarm. "They escaped!"

"No! You just don't need to get upset right now."

She turned to Armus. "Tell me."

"Dead. Hueil killed Ellan while Avatar dispatched Hueil."

A sob caught in her throat and she screwed her eyes shut.

Tyrone try to calm her. "Please, my love, don't get upset."

"No, I'm relieved. It's finally over! Not that I wished her dead, just gone from my life forever."

"Now she is, so rest, my little one." Armus placed a hand on her forehead. *"Cadal an fois."* She flashed a weary smile and closed her eyes.

Armus drew Tyrone from the bed. "I realize you were reluctant because you didn't want to cause her any more pain. After everything she's been through with Ellan, for her own peace of mind and heart, she needed to know."

"I understand that now. Thank you."

Armus grinned. "Now, you go get some real sleep. She'll be fine."

Chapter 25

ALTHOUGH THE ARMY RETURNED TRIUMPHANT TO WALDRON, a personal bitter sweetness accompanied the victory for Nigel. One sister killed and another serious injured. He was glad the trip didn't aggravate Tristine's condition, and she would complete her recovery in her own chamber. Bosley dying while protecting him, served as a grim reminder of past danger they shared and Bosley's true loyalty. His personal feelings notwithstanding, now was a time to rejoice. Besides, he had several announcements to make.

The Great Hall filled with people, delightful aromas, music, laughter and a genuine atmosphere of celebration. At high table, Angus and Necie laughed. Tyrone enjoyed himself with good-natured ribbing of Titus' preoccupation with Jillian, who sat in Tristine's seat for the night.

Ellis and Valery sat next to high table. For this night, Valery was properly attired, adorned in an emerald green and gold gown with her hair pampered. What a stunning difference from the battlefield and Ellis gave her prompt attention. In fact, as Mirit predicted, Valery drew much attention and admiration. She only had eyes for Ellis. Even Cody was permitted to be in the Great Hall. The wolf gnawed on his own plate of meat and bones near Ellis and Valery.

"You did well, my dear," said Nigel to Mirit concerning Valery and Ellis. "I must say I was surprised by her change in appearance."

"They make a striking a couple."

"One to which I have something to say." He signaled the herald.

The man pounded his golden staff on the floor to get attention. The musicians ceased playing and soon all conversation ceased. "Give heed to the king!" the herald shouted.

"My lords and ladies, gentle folk, this is an evening of celebration for more than one reason. Is that not so, Lord Ellis?"

The address caught Ellis by surprise. "Indeed, Sire."

Nigel made his way to the front of the high table, speaking as he went. "You would agree that the title *lord* is inadequate for the future spouse of a royal ward, would you not?"

"If you say so, Sire," he answered with some trepidation.

"I do. Come forth, Lord Ellis."

Ellis tossed an uncertain glance to Valery, who encouraged him to comply. The platform stood several steps above the main floor, which made Ellis look up when he stopped in front of Nigel. "Sire?"

"Kneel."

Ellis did so.

Kell held the sheathed Sword of Allon and stepped forward when beckoned. Nigel took the hilt and withdrew the sword from the scabbard, the familiar singing sound made upon drawing.

"As a reward for your bravery in combat and your gallant service to members of the royal family, I hereby grant you the title, *Count* Ellis, Lord of the Meadowlands, Member of the Council of Twelve." He tapped Ellis on each shoulder with the flat of the blade. He pulled the signet ring from his doublet pocket. "Rise, Count Ellis."

Stunned, Ellis didn't move. Nigel tugged on Ellis' shoulder to get him to stand. Nigel gave him the ring and whispered, "It goes on your right ring finger." He smiled when Ellis fumbled to put it on. Nigel again spoke aloud. "As soon as it can be arranged there will a wedding. Now, return to your future countess."

"Ay, Sire." Ellis smiled and went back to the table.

Titus and Tyrone began the applause. Nigel put his hand up for silence and the crowd complied.

"There is more." Nigel looked to Chad, who sat at the table to the right of high table with Magan. "Captain Chad. Come forth."

He showed more decorum than Ellis in his military approach. "Sire."

Nigel fought keeping a smile from his face. "Kneel, Captain."

Although Chad's gaze grew inquisitive, he knelt.

Nigel couldn't help an impulsive glance to Mirit. She wore a pleased and proud expression. Avatar moved beside her chair, also grinning. Chad followed the glance, so Nigel cleared his throat to bring Chad's attention back to him.

"For years of dedicated service to the crown, bravery in combat, and personal loyalty to members of the royal family, I hereby and most happily, dub you *Sir* Chad, Jor'ellian Knight."

Chad bowed his head to accept the knighting on his left shoulder.

Nigel continued speaking and moved the sword to the right shoulder. "Lord of the North Plains, and Member of the Council of Twelve."

Chad's head came up in surprise.

Nigel proudly smiled. "Rise, *Sir* Chad." He gave Chad the ring. "You deserved it, my dear friend," he said in a private exchange.

Visibly touched, Chad put the ring on.

"Now return to *Lady* Magan."

"Sire." He caught Mirit's smiling gaze and Avatar's approving nod before returning to his wife.

Nigel took the scabbard from Kell and sheathed the blade. For a moment he gazed at the Sword of Allon. "Like my father, this sword deserves to be worn and wielded by the rightful king. I am first born and heir of the Son of Tristan, but all know I was not chosen to be king, save for this task." He faced Tyrone. "When my sister is recovered, the Court will travel to the Temple where I will abdicate in favor of Jor'el's chosen and return the Sword to whom it rightfully belongs."

Tyrone stood and used his cup in salute. "Long live the Son of Ellis!"

"Long live the Son of Ellis!" echoed Angus and the rest followed.

Nigel gave the Sword to Kell. The captain held his arm, met his gaze and said, "For your sake, Jor'el has granted Tristine full recovery by morning, and Uriah will be well enough to preside over the ceremony."

Touched, Nigel's voice was barely a whisper. "Then later make the arrangements, Captain." Kell released him to he returned to his seat.

The Temple once again displayed the pageantry and pomp of a royal ceremony with crowds inside and out. In a private room off the nave, Tyrone and Nigel met with Wess and Dylan. Although dressed appropriately for the occasion, Wess appeared somber. Six days passed since Bosley's funeral at Presley Manor. Dylan also appeared sober in attitude.

"Is there a reason you sent for us, Sire?" asked Wess.

Nigel grinned. "I won't have that title for much longer. There is a reason, and one we," he motioned between himself and Tyrone, "wish to speak to you about." He grew most sincere in speech. "Wess, you know I hold you, Bosley and your family in the highest affection. Words can't adequately express my sorrow or gratitude, so I hope what we present, you will accept."

Tyrone handed a sealed document to Wess. In silence, Wess opened it and read. His thoughtful expression, shifted between reading, to Nigel, then Tyrone and back to the document.

"What is it, Uncle?" asked Dylan.

"Read it aloud," said Nigel.

"To General Wess, Supreme Commander of the Allonian Army is granted the title Count, Lord of the South Plains and Member of the Council of Twelve and all the holdings, thereof, etcetera, etcetera." When he looked up from reading, Nigel held the signet ring.

"Please, Wess."

"I said I would retire the moment you abdicated."

"From service as general. You are too valuable a friend and advisor to see retire to raise horses while in the prime of life."

"Uncle," began Dylan. "I agree. Although we understand your feelings, to retire would be a shame because of all you still have to offer. I welcome your voice and advice on the Council."

"Then again," began Tyrone in feinted consideration. "The South Plains will require a firm, steady hand after enduring Gareth's administration for decades. He may well prefer breaking horses to taming insubordinate servants and discontented provincials."

Wess snorted an ironic laugh. "A well-placed shot at the ego."

Tyrone's tone changed to sober with a hint of disappointment. "I prefer to think that, than believe after all we have been through you would not swear fidelity to me again."

"To both of us," said Tristine. She entered unseen.

That stung, and Wess winced. When she stepped before him, Wess' gaze lingered on her a moment before speaking. "Your brother plays upon my sympathy and your husband upon my loyalty." He shook his head with an expression of fondness. "One look at you, and I can no more refuse you than I could your mother, despite looking like Ellis." He took the ring from Nigel and put it on. A small smile of relief crossed his face. "Life probably would have grown boring after a while."

Tristine gripped his hand between her hands. "Thank you, Wess."

He grinned and kissed her hand.

A priest arrived. "Sire, the Vicar is ready to start the ceremony."

Nigel waved and acknowledgment. "To our places."

***

At mid-day, Fraser waited with nervous anticipation in the shadow of the trees just off the road leading to Waldron. Kendrick went to the castle to inquire about a private meeting with Nigel. Several times Fraser felt the impulse to run away, only he kept recalling the story about Nigel. If they could forgive Nigel after so long, maybe there was hope.

Who am I fooling? People died because of me. No one died because of Nigel.

Fraser jumped when he heard something and reached for his sword.

"Be easy," said Kendrick. "I made noise so you wouldn't be startled."

"Well? What did you learn?"

"They've gone to the Temple where Nigel plans to abdicate and your parents once again crowned king and queen."

"Really?" He sounded relieved then became concerned. "I don't know if I can convince Father. With Uncle sending you, I had a chance."

"You won't know unless you go to the Temple for the coronation."

"What if Father sees me before I can talk to Uncle?"

"In such a crowd it is easy to get lost." Kendrick's grip made Fraser look up at him. "Isn't it worth the risk to find out?"

"Ay. Sleeping outdoors for a hunt is one thing. Spending a life aimlessly wandering the wilderness … I don't know how Nigel managed all those years. A cold lonely existence I don't care to experience past what I have. Maybe I can convince Father to let me serve as a page."

Kendrick softly smiled and drew Fraser to his side. "Hold on."

"Wait. Arc you fully healed to dimension travel?"

"Ay. We Guardians heal fast."

<hr />

They reappeared near the Fortress, a short distance from the Temple. An enormous crowd milled about.

"I don't think we'll get inside," said Fraser.

"We will," said Kendrick with a confident grin. "*Cead fofaic,*" he spoke the Ancient. They moved unnoticed through the crowd and into the Temple. People filled the pews. They stood near the back in such way that Kendrick placed Fraser in front of him for a better view.

Nigel and Mirit stepped down from the altar where the crowns were placed and resumed their places on the front row. That meant the abdication ceremony was complete. Uriah spoke to Tyrone and Tristine. They mounted the steps to the altar.

Fraser felt nervous and proud watching his parents follow Uriah's instructions and being crowned by Kell and Armus. His eyes swelled with tears at the guilt he felt for disappointing them. He looked down to wipe his eyes clear. When he looked up, his father stared at him. Rather than anger, Tyrone appeared surprised and seized Tristine's arm. She too saw him. Fraser went to back away, but Kendrick wouldn't let him. His father rushed down the altar steps and the aisle, coming towards him. He wanted to flee, but Kendrick held fast.

"Father—" he protested.

Tyrone threw his arms about him in a hearty embrace. "Thank Jor'el, you're alive!" He noticed Fraser's head wound. "You're hurt."

"A scratch."

"Sire?" called Uriah.

Tyrone's arm circled Fraser's shoulder to draw him from the crowd and toward the altar. "This a blessed day, Vicar! My son has returned!"

"Fraser!" Mikaela squirmed passed Titus and ran down the aisle.

Fraser scooped her up in his arms and held her close. He tried not to cry, but couldn't help himself. "You're all right."

"Where have you been? You didn't visit see me when I was sick."

"Some place I never want to be again. Away from you or anyone." He held her close again and kissed her cheek.

Tyrone escorted Fraser toward the altar. He held his sister. At the bottom step, Tristine greeted her son with tender kisses. Tyrone encouraged Fraser to put Mikaela down. Titus came to take her back to her place on the front row. He smiled at Fraser. Eli also smiled and Fraser flashed a brotherly grin.

Tyrone held Fraser's arm as they mounted the steps to the altar. He addressed the crowd. "Jor'el has shown his mercy by restoring that which was lost. From this day forward let no one question my son in any matter relating to the past. Today we celebrate a new beginning." He widely smiled. "When we assemble next year for the wedding of Prince Titus to Lady Jillian, the cornerstone for Jor'el's Palace shall be laid."

Kell's surprise at the announcement mirrored the stunned and happy reaction from the mortals.

Tyrone continued. "With Hueil's defeat, the last remaining rebel from the Great Battle is gone! The way is clear for the rebuilding to begin."

Kell lowered his head in an effort to resist being overcome with joy at hearing of victory. He always maintained decorum, but this almost proved too much. A hand clapped his shoulder. Armus' smile and tear-filled eyes matched Kell's jubilation at hearing victory declared.

Uriah spoke a prayer of praise and thanksgiving. "Let this be a day of celebration!" He signed his name to the document and placed the Jor'ellian seal in wax beside his name.

All members of the Council of Twelve came forward to place their seal on the document recognizing Tyrone once more as king. Uriah was the first representing the Region of Sanctuary. Next came Angus, Duke of Allon and Lord of the Southern Forest; Baron Ned of the Northern Forest; Lord Fagan of the Highlands; Sir Chad of the North Plains; Count Wess of the South Plains; Sir Hayden of the Lowlands; Lord Dylan of Midessex; Count Ellis of the Meadowlands; Lord Kasey of the East Coast; Baron Mathias of the West Coast; and Lord Eric of the Delta.

Fraser remained with Tyrone to watch the lords. A smile stretched from ear-to-ear, his eyes moist with joyful relief. Several times Tyrone squeezed his shoulder and they exchanged warm, proud glances. At that moment he couldn't imagine being anyplace else. When the lords finished, they stepped down from the altar and into the arms of family.

Nigel approached. Fraser wanted to embrace him yet hesitated to say, "My separation was brief compared to yours. I will gratefully learn whatever it is you want to teach me as your squire, Champion."

Nigel smiled. "Call me uncle. In public or private." They embraced.

Explore the Kingdom of Allon

www.allonbooks.com

Featuring:

- Read excerpts of Allon books
- Original Character Art
- Interactive Map of Allon
- News and Events
- Photo and Video Gallery
- Links to:
  - o Facebook - The Kingdom of Allon Page
  - o Contact Shawn Lamb

www.ingramcontent.com/pod-product-compliance
Lightning Source LLC
Chambersburg PA
CBHW071045250626
47159CB00002B/366